THE SCORE

Howard Marks

ISIS
LARGE PRINT
Oxford

First published in Great Britain 2013
by
Harvill Secker, one of the publishers in
The Random House Group Ltd.

Published in Large Print 2013 by ISIS Publishing Ltd.,
7 Centremead, Osney Mead, Oxford OX2 0ES
by arrangement with
Harville Secker, one of the publishers in
The Random House Group Ltd.

CIP data is available for this title from the British Library

ISBN 978–0–7531–9202–3 (hb)
ISBN 978–0–7531–9203–0 (pb)

Printed and bound in Great Britain by
T. J. International Ltd., Padstow, Cornwall

She feels dead inside. She is sixteen years old.

It is Saturday evening. She looks at her family as they watch the TV talent show.

Do they know it's a sham?

Real talent is fragile, marginal, would melt beneath the gaudy studio spotlights. She doesn't say this to her family — what is the point? — just burns a stare towards them, retreats to her room. Here she finds her books, her music, her kindred spirits.

She sits at her flatpack desk, boots her laptop. She has two friends. Neither are online.

She navigates to YouTube, watches the film of herself posted there. The film of her singing late at night at the bus stop, half drunk on cider. The sound and picture quality are not good, but she knows that she meant it when she sang it. She knows she is better than everyone on that TV talent show, because she is the real thing. She has the immodesty of the wildly insecure.

She boots over to Twitter. Her mother doesn't know she has an account. Her Twitter name is the same as her performance name on YouTube.

She had two followers earlier today. Still only two now.

A stab of disappointment, but it passes. It always does. She's an artist. A talent. Authentic. This feeling of deadness?

It goes with the temperament. You can't sing well if you don't have soul. And she does. What's that saying? "No matter. Fail again. Fail better."

She starts singing scales, warming up her voice. She is ready for anything.

CHAPTER
ONE

DS Catrin Price stared at her phone. She didn't want to listen to her messages. She already knew what was waiting for her.

She pushed the phone under a stack of bills on the table. It was no longer visible, but she still stared in a daze at the papers under which it lay. The phone had a new number, a new SIM card, but already he was calling again.

She forced herself to move away, peered through the curtains. Beyond the huts on the pier, the estuary sparkled. In the haze of the horizon a ferry lay motionless. She pulled the curtains tight. She had hung some blackout drapes over the velvet. That way no light entered and no one could see if she had the lights on inside.

Padding over to the small windowless bathroom, she sat on the edge of the bath as the water flowed. Her afternoon routine of Shen Chuan and Krav Maga hadn't calmed her. The calls were getting to her. That and everything else.

She turned off the tap and listened for a moment. Around her, the other flats were silent. It was too early for people to have come back from work. She could hear only the crying of the gulls. She caught a glimpse of herself in the mirror, her brown eyes, their ink-dark surrounds, her small breasts, the black swoops of her tattoos whose meaning only she could decipher. Lowering herself into the warmth of the water, she closed her eyes, shutting out everything except the sound of her own breathing.

Maybe she could deal with the withdrawal if it wasn't for the calls. Maybe. But she'd never know, because the calls kept coming. He was probably calling right now, filling up her voicemail, even as she sought peace in water. She could hear his voice in her ear, a voice she could almost place. Almost, but not quite.

The water may have been cold for all the comfort it was offering. She gave in. She had to know. Uncertainty was worse than having her fears confirmed. She got out, huddling a towel around herself, pulled her phone out and switched it on. She put in the code to access her voicemail.

The automated voice told her there was only one message. She knew it would be the same as before. But still she listened.

"Cat," the voice said, "it's Martin."

The message usually urged Catrin to call back as soon as she could. But today, the pattern was broken, a new detail was added.

"Meet me in Tregaron," the voice continued. "I'll tell you everything at the house."

Although there were more words this time, still there was no discernible accent. The voice sounded taut, the speaker betrayed no signs of fear or hesitation. At first

4

she'd thought they were all the same message, recorded. But now, with this new detail, she knew they were not.

Cat looked at the map of Wales Blu-tacked on the wall; put there to help plan her biking routes. She stared at it. Tregaron: a small town in the middle of nowhere. It was bordered in the south by the wilderness of the Brecon Beacons, and to the north by the Cambrians. On all sides was a sea of green, empty pasture and hills.

Cat had never been to Tregaron. She knew of no one who lived there except her old colleague DI Jack Thomas. She doubted the calls were linked to Thomas. He had told her he didn't want to keep in touch with the old-timers. He had moved more than a year ago, and she had not heard anything from him since. Maybe he'd talked about her to some nutter who could follow her changes of number on the force intranet? It was just about possible.

She snatched up her phone but then hesitated, feeling the need to dress before she called Thomas. She slipped on some old joggers and a battered "Death to the Pixies" T-shirt, then flipped to Thomas's number. He answered on the second ring.

"Well, well. Catrin Price." He gave what sounded like a morose chuckle. "I move out to the sticks and still you hound me. Do I need a restraining order?"

Others might have said that as a joke — made it sound affectionate, even — but with Thomas there was always an edge.

"Things quiet enough for you out there, Thomas? Any missing cats need chasing down?"

He half-chuckled. "Not calling to pass the time of day, are you, Price?"

She told Thomas about the calls from Martin in Tregaron.

"Never mentioned you to anyone. Think I'm always yapping on about you? Can't get you out of my head?"

Again, the edge in his voice.

"No, I don't think that. Not at all."

He paused. Cat heard him exhale. "Sorry, Cat. There was no need for that. Sorry."

It was only the second time he'd ever apologised as far as she could recall. Once before he'd said sorry about his behaviour on a certain night out. After a certain number of drinks. In a certain car. He'd said sorry about that when she'd explained how he'd made her feel. Thomas was crude, but he did know that other people had feelings, when you reminded him.

"I can't help you with the calls. I don't know anything about them." His voice was softer now.

She could tell he might have liked to talk more, but didn't want it to show. She wondered if he was lonely; of course, he would never admit to that.

"Jack," she used his first name, "can I ask you something?"

"As long as it's not on geography," he said. "I'm crap at geography."

"Why did you leave the city?"

The derisive snort told Cat he thought her naive for asking.

6

She ended the call, having learned nothing. She groped for her pouch of Drum, made a roll-up and heeled up to the headboard, pressing her back to it. Cat looked at the magnolia walls she'd never got round to repainting. She thought about Thomas's response to her question. She did know why he'd left the city, why he'd bailed out to the sticks. It was the same reason she'd gone on the tranks.

Cat's eyes lingered on the magnolia. She took a long drag. She'd always smoked rather than cried. She had the sense that the past was approaching her from below, winding its tendrils around her ankles and pulling her down.

She frisked her iPod out of her jacket. She span to Nick Drake, jammed it in the sound dock, and stuck on *Five Leaves Left*. The melancholia of the album would not help her state of mind, but she needed to think and sadness helped her do that. She lay back down and made another roll-up, sprinkling this one with canna.

If it had been a wrong number, the calls would have stopped when she changed the SIM card. But they hadn't stopped and the caller had used her name. The rate of calls was increasing, now up to six a day. When she called back, the phone was always switched off. She'd run a check on the caller's number, but it was a pay-as-you-go bought for cash in a backstreet store in Swansea a year back. The phone had no previous call history. Her next move was to check on mast signals for a fix on the phone's whereabouts. But now Tregaron had been named.

She moved over to the edge of her unmade bed. The sheets were tangled from another sleepless night. The mattress showed through the thin sheets a livid orange, the cover had come loose from the duvet. As she pulled, it tore. Fierce, sudden anger shot through her.

The online research she had done told her there would be times like this, that anger and fear were two sides of the same coin. She should expect a period when she felt little else, that it was part of the healing. She should have seen a doctor about coming off the tranks, of course, but trusting anyone with her head was as alien to her as putting a hole in it.

She peeled the cover off the duvet then threw it into the basket. She pulled the basket into the kitchen and jammed its contents into the washing machine. There was a stool there and she sat, watching the chamber filling with foam. Just put your mind and body in neutral, this had been her sensei's mantra. Let nature reassert itself. But the Klonopin and sleepers had taken their toll. Now she was paying the price: insomnia, anxiety, almost constant headaches and an apprehensiveness that never seemed to leave her.

She wrinkled her nose at the stuffiness of the flat, and walked to the window, grabbing at a breath of outside air. The only Martin she knew had been a boy in her class at school. She had not seen him for seventeen years. But they had been close enough that she could imagine him feeling he could depend on her.

She let her mind drift back. Martin Tilkian had been the least popular boy in the year, a loner and an outcast. She had been the least popular girl, though for very different reasons. They had formed a brief alliance. Hard case and the geek. Despairing at his unpopularity, and not approving of her influence over him — because that was how they wrongly saw the friendship — his parents had sent him away to a private school and they had lost touch.

She went to the wardrobe and rooted through the classic biker mags and old monitors and keyboards. She found what she wanted and brought it out into the light. It was the only photograph she had of him. It wasn't a good one. He looked like an Armenian Andy Warhol, dark glasses and his hair grown in bangs to hide as much of his face as possible. His skin had been the main reason for his unpopularity: dry, scaly patches often covered his cheeks and forehead. Sometimes he had come to school with his face in plasters, only his big brown eyes peeping out.

If this Martin was her caller he was unlikely to be a threat to her. They had shared that uniquely intimate bond of adolescent friendship. Tough little Cat had saved him from the bullies who had stolen his money and covered his head with bags, tying him to the railings like a scarecrow. He had been grateful for her protection, and had sworn undying allegiance to her in a blood oath. She had done the same. She smiled at this, gently mocking the theatrics; their friendship had been so melodramatic. She wondered if her name in the press over the Dinas case had brought her back to his attention.

Over at the desk she booted her Mac, running his name on Google. Not much came up. A Wikipedia stub written a few years before described Tilkian as a "games designer" and referred to some US games companies she had never heard of. It mentioned a wife who had died, and a daughter, Esyllt. There were a few entries from websites specialising in historic gaming, name-checking him in relation to a series of antiquated fantasy games with titles like "Gorgon's Revenge VII" and "Infiltrator versus Atilla". After 2003, the year his wife had died, his involvement in that industry seemed to have ceased. She could find no further references to him. He seemed to have switched profession. Maybe gone to live the quiet life with his daughter in Tregaron.

She clicked over to the police portal, and went into the National Police Intelligence Service. Tilkian had no form, and no current address was listed. Next, she tried searches on the names of the wife and daughter, but nothing came up. No Facebook or other social networking sites for the daughter, nor any reference to where she was at school. Cat tried the villages around Tregaron, but drew a blank. Why the fuck would you ask someone to come, but give no address and refuse to answer the phone? It made no sense.

She was getting nowhere. Frustration was rising, her muscles tightening around her neck and forehead. She needed to get out of the flat. Pulling on some old trainers, Cat locked the door and went down to the yard. Her flat came with a garage and a store room as large as the living space above, and this was the reason she had rented it.

Without switching on the lights, letting the daylight filter in, she pulled the deadbolt behind her. On one side was where she kept her small collection of motorcycles. The rest was taken up with punchbags hanging from the ceiling, a rack of free weights and a beaten-up sofa.

She gazed into the gloom. Ahead was her giant poster of Brando in *The Wild One*. Next to it, pictures of the Welsh Formula One cars from the Fifties. They had been left by the previous occupier. It had been a doomed team. On the day the cars were to compete in their first Grand Prix, the driver of the transporter had raced against the German transporter through the Portuguese mountains. He had careered down into a valley, destroying the cars. The team had never raced again. She had first heard the story as a girl, but it had always held a certain bleak fascination for her.

In the damp, some of the pictures had dropped from the wall and she knelt to pick them up. Outside it was quiet. In the dimness the chrome of the bikes glimmered. There was the Laverda she used for everyday, and next to it her Triton. It had the elongated tank and narrow handlebars of the classic café racer. The tank was matt and the rest polished to a shine. In the obscurity it seemed to hover above the ground.

As she flicked the light, she noticed something. In the dust under the Triton there were takeaway flyers and beneath them, an envelope. Most of the post came to the main entrance, but sometimes items would get pushed under the doors of the garage.

The envelope had her name handwritten on it. She held it under the one bare bulb. Inside was a single sheet, thick and expensive by the feel of it. There was an address in Tregaron at the top. Then two lines written in a sloping, old-fashioned hand.

Cat — I need some help. Can you come to see me? I'd prefer not to discuss this on the phone. Martin Tilkian.

So, her guess was right. She knew now who the caller was. Better still, she knew where to find him.

She felt calmer. Cat looked at the junk mail. Most of it was undated, but there were one or two advertising special offers relating to specific events. Assuming that the strata of junk mail were still lying in approximate order of delivery, it looked as if Tilkian had first tried to get in touch about a week ago.

The discovery made more sense of the messages. He had first called in person. Rather than leave a note in the communal box and risk her not getting it, he had left it in her garage. Then, when she'd not responded, he'd begun calling. The only reason he hadn't been leaving his name on those messages was because he assumed she already had it. He hadn't responded to her calls because, presumably, he wasn't responding to anyone. That didn't explain how he'd got her number, but already she felt herself relaxing. Most likely he just wanted her help in her capacity as police. An oddball like that, he probably had few friends to turn to. She had protected him once before. Now he was turning to her again. She nudged together a roll-up, lit it, and blew the smoke into Brando's face.

A song. It could be anything. Anything, that is, that reached out from the singer to the listener and changed them both.

She remembered the first time she had that experience. She'd been only four — so family tradition reported it anyway — and she'd heard the Beatles singing "Let It Be". She couldn't really remember much of the incident except the music itself. The astonishing sound. The sense that here was something removed from ordinary life, something better than it.

The sound had been magical, alluring — and inaccessible. The story was that the radio had been up on a high chest of drawers. She'd been too small to reach it, so she pulled the drawers out and started to climb. The adventure had ended the only way it could: with the whole thing falling down on top of her, a broken radio, a trip to casualty and three stitches just above her eye, the pale shadow of that scar still just visible through her eyebrow.

Her family liked to recount it as a tale of childish misadventure. She went along with that for the sake of peace, but she'd never thought of it that way.

Music called to her. She answered it. So what, if there had been a crash? So what, if there had been blood?

Music had called. She had answered.

That was all that mattered.

CHAPTER
TWO

Really, there was no decision to make. Although it was pledged more than half a lifetime ago, and although she now found their intense behaviour almost ludicrous, still, they had made a blood bond. They had meant it at the time, and once meant, well, one couldn't take that lightly. She noticed how good it felt to be needed again.

An unusual optimism seized her. She would take the Laverda on a run up to Tregaron, she would open up the bike, feel the wildness of old Wales that still clung on up in the hills. It would be a drive back into a better past. Suddenly everything felt up for grabs again.

Cat turned fluidly, delivering a roundhouse kick to a hanging punchbag. So this was what feeling good felt like? She had forgotten. She palmed her phone from her joggers and called her new boss, DCI Gwen Kyle, hoping to get the answerphone. Requesting permission for the trip was just a formality. Cat was on flexi-time, doing desk work while she dealt with her withdrawal. Out of the loop on the Drug Proactive Unit's current operations as she was, notifying Kyle was just a courtesy.

A secretary answered, a new girl, nervous and clearly a jobsworth, because she covered herself by telling Cat to talk in person with Kyle about it. The girl said Kyle was on the set of a docudrama about the drugs bust at Penarth Marina. She would be back in the office in about an hour.

Cat decided to go and talk to Kyle in person rather then risk missing her again. Kyle was a prickly sort, she would be easier to handle having just visited the site of the bust, her greatest triumph, where her ego would have been getting a stroking.

Some old scaffolding resting between the breeze blocks had become her clothes rail, and Cat flipped a hanger off the pole. On it was her battered all-in-one leather suit. She had bought it second hand and because it lacked logo or graphic design, and was scuffed up on the arse and back and knees, it was her favourite. She pushed legs and arms in, then eased up the chunky zipper to snug herself in.

Cat found gloves and helmet then swung the door open. She started the Laverda and nosed it out. The journey wasn't far. Although some po-faced Penarth burghers might dispute the fact, Penarth was now just another suburb in the sprawl of Cardiff. She could have ridden into town with her eyes closed — in fact, she might have been tempted to try had there been no other traffic on the roads.

On the far side of the water the familiar streets and shapes of the city gave abruptly into the Bay development. Up-scale regeneration had bulldozed the old streets, sooty terraces become proud civic structures and landmark hotels, cocktail bars and pizzerias. Even after all these years it still felt wrong.

Cat took the flyover into the centre of Cardiff, rat-running from the Bay to the DPU building in Cathays Park. The unit had oversight of drugs policing for all Wales but from the outside it looked like a tax office, which was essentially what it was.

Her office was at basement level next to the parking. There was damp on the walls and the window overlooked a toilet block. It was one of the spaces allocated to officers on flexi-time, far from the operations hub on the upper floors. But she didn't mind the solitude.

Cat quickly checked her work emails. There had been over twenty minor seizures since she had last checked in, mostly skunk and Es. Her task was to upload details of busts in Wales onto the National Criminal Intelligence database for use nationally. This allowed officers to track supply networks and vectors of transmission for each drug type. The uploading was usually given to civilians or officers on disciplinaries. But it could be important work. The charts might predict where moody gear would turn up next. Pills with one gang's press showing in another's territory could signal the start of a messy turf war. Classic brands were often bootlegged by the challenger's labs. D&Gs, Calvin Kleins, M25s, Mitsubishis, once a sign of purity and quality, were stepped on with adulterants and cheap amphetamines: small differences in the press could distinguish real product from knock-offs and potentially save lives.

Cat called Kyle's secretary again: Kyle was delayed on the film set, she wasn't sure how long for but thought at least another hour. Cat scanned the room quickly to check no new files had been dumped on her. They hadn't. Mostly, she guessed, because nobody from the plusher upstairs above could be bothered to carry them down so far. She sighed, looking at the two personal items she had added to the decrepit office: a photo of Giacomo Agostini taken at the Isle of Man TT, his sunburnt features incongruous in the damp half-light, and beside it, an origami raven which she had owned since she was sixteen years old. She nipped the raven between two fingertips and stared at it. The past weighed so much, while the future she had glimpsed earlier that afternoon, the image of her hooning deep into old Wales to help an old friend, still weighed almost nothing in her mind.

She thought she heard footsteps, glanced outside. But no one was there. On the wall the same graffiti had been up for months and no one had cleaned it off. "Narc Dog". This was the term used of undercover drug officers, and she had been one once, but the letters had long preceded her period in the office. She didn't know who had put it there, or who it had been directed at, but she left it. She shut down the computer, put down the raven and headed to the marina.

By the time she reached the road above it, dusk had fallen. Ropes clacked against masts, along the quays the small weekender cruisers bobbed next to unmoving ocean-goers. The marina was another regeneration project, older than the Bay. She had mucked about there as a child, sploshing its crumbling pieces down into the bay water, feasting on the bilberries that grew

18

up around its concrete. She saw the part of the marina where the bust had gone down was starkly lit by the film crew's arc lights. The near side was blocked by two film trucks, and glowing behind them were the cigarettes of the crew, hunkered down out of the stiffening wind.

Some gulls flapped slowly back towards the shore, seeking discarded chips and KFC. Further out, a large black bird she didn't know the name of glided at an even height, hardly moving its wings, above the glistening foam.

Cat toed the Laverda into neutral. She let the heavy bike glide down the ramp to where a line of rubberneckers were being kept back by the uniforms. A crowd was pressing around a large black car, but she couldn't see who was in it. Most of them looked young, student-types. One of the PCs recognised her and waved her through.

Inside the filming cordon, Cat spotted Kyle on the far side of the lights. She was talking to another tall blonde — the actress playing Kyle, Cat guessed. The actress looked healthy and attractive. Kyle would be happy about that. The omens were good, Cat thought, for her trip to Tregaron.

Despite all the people on set, there was a respectful hush. No one was speaking above a whisper. Cat walked forward and stared at Kyle, trying to catch her attention. Kyle flicked out a glance but then quickly turned her attention back to the actress. Cat had the sense she was ignoring her.

She leaned back against one of the crew's trucks. In front of her, a man in a puffer jacket — the director maybe — was studying some grainy footage on a monitor. She recognised it immediately. This was the famous security footage of the bust, now presumably being used to choreograph the reconstruction.

On the screen, four gang members could just be made out, their heads covered by hoodies, walking slowly along the quay towards the shore. The four men then disappeared out of shot, off the marina's walkways and into the shadows of the shoreline's buildings. Cat looked up from the footage towards the arc lights of the marina — four actors, dressed identically to the men on the screen, clustered, their heads down.

The man in the puffer jacket raised his hand, and the silence deepened. The quay was still except for the gently shifting shadows of boats and gulls.

Then, from the right-hand corner of the quay, the four actors walked out. They were heading back towards their boat, heads still covered. They carried on their shoulders an object that looked like a large coffin. Their burden was heavy as the four men moved slowly, in swinging, syncopated steps.

On the screen the men were a few steps ahead now, moving closer to the boat. Cat knew the footage well, knew what was coming. It had become something of a cliché. Every week one of the news channels would find a reason to drop it into a package, and it was a favourite on YouTube. Like the shots of Diana on the fateful night, or those of the 7/7 bombers walking through the station, the film seemed to hold a fascination for the public. It had become iconic, as had the leader of the busted gang, Griff Morgan. It had been the largest synthetic drug haul in recent memory, and Morgan had risen to a cross between Dillinger and Moriarty in the popular imagination, a pin-up in squats and student houses all over the land.

It took a while before she could make out the shape the actors were shouldering. As they passed under a light it became clear that it was a four-man canoe. A sea-going kayak, a serious piece of kit.

The men lowered the canoe carefully onto the deck of a large motor cruiser, visible just on the edge of the shot. Then the taller man — the one playing Morgan — covered the canoe with a tarp and the men climbed back onto the quay.

The shot cut and the men walked hastily back to their marks. A bulky arm shot across the screen as the man in the puffer jacket reached forward and sped up the original security footage. It just showed the same moves being repeated many times: four men leaving the motor cruiser then returning to it with a canoe held between them. After ten canoes had been placed on the deck and tarped over, the four men stayed on the boat and the large cruiser — now visible on the grainy night footage as a receding blur of white — purred out of shot towards the sea lock.

The sequence was still running in fast forward. Cat didn't need to watch to know what happened next. The men would return to collect more canoes and would be ambushed by Kyle.

The director had stood up. Over by the canteen van, he was talking with the actors who had been joined by others dressed as armed officers. Cat's attention was caught again by the crowd around the black car. Whatever was inside was apparently more interesting than the filming. Some looked like students, and were wearing T-shirts with Griff Morgan's face in iconic Warhol style. Others looked like press and passers-by who had got drawn in out of curiosity. At the edge, a woman in strappy heels and a sharply cut trouser suit was trying to peer through the car's back window. Despite the heels, she was pushing and shoving like the best of them. Cat recognised Della Davies, former police press officer and her one-time love rival, her suit creasing as she scrummed in deeper. People were pressing in around the car from all sides now, but whoever was inside seemed invisible behind the heavily tinted glass.

Out on the quay the final scene was taking shape. The arc lights had dimmed, and the concrete pathways lay in near darkness. On the cruiser deck, the actor playing Morgan was pulling the tarpaulin over a canoe. For a moment he glanced upwards, face still hidden, his eyes a momentary flash of light. At his side was his lieutenant, Mike Tulle. The third gang member, Huw Tulle, Mike's baby brother, was walking down the gangplank, ready to move back to the warehouse. The fourth man had his back to the scene and was staring out towards the open sea.

Tulle junior was the first to notice something was wrong. He stepped back towards the boat, his hand reaching instinctively into his hoody's front pocket. Looking at the original on the screen, she thought he was over-acting it a touch. The first shot caught Tulle in the shoulder. He staggered backwards like a drunk. On the second impact, he fell on the gangplank and lay still. Tubes of light flashed, the torches of the black-clad Armed Response, their faces masked, closing in around him. Quickly they were on him, and he was secured with plastic cuffs and left in place for the medics.

Then the actress playing Kyle appeared. Colleagues had levelled many accusations at DCI Gwen Kyle but nobody could ever call her a coward. Because although the ARs had taken out one gang member, there were still three more, and judging by the actions of the first, they were all armed. The woman stood now in full view of the gang, in full view also of the cameras. She was shouting at Morgan to surrender. In front of her, the ARs had fanned out in a semicircle, their Heckler lights trained on the men on the deck. Everything seemed to slow down. Kyle stood on the edge of the water. In the darkness there was a spark above her, rising into a long flame.

Later it had come out that Morgan had threatened to blow the boat and everything with it, but somehow in those desperate seconds Kyle had persuaded him to surrender. He had come quietly along with his lieutenant, Mike Tulle. Only the fourth man, one of Morgan's soldiers known as Diamond Evans, had swum for it. On cue, there was a splash. The AR actors immediately tramped the gangplanks, swinging torches across each bobbing inch of water and peering down the sides of the marina's every boat. The Kyle actress loudly called for back-up and for the entire marina to be locked down and searched. But to no avail. Somehow, in the darkness and the confusion, lucky Diamond Evans had got away.

Cat remembered how the press briefings had played down the escape of the fourth man, a minor player who had only recently joined Morgan's crew. The main prize had been the capture of Morgan himself, a fugitive who'd been on the run for ten years. He was that rare thing, a major criminal with no previous record, a figure so elusive that some, encouraged by the internet's conspiracy centrifuge, had even begun to doubt his very existence. But there he was, banged-up courtesy of the smart reactions and operational nous of DCI Gwen Kyle.

The criminal spook had human form after all.

Of the canoes recovered at the marina, nine were found to be loaded with MDMA, and the tenth with almost a million Mandrax pills. These were a niche product, but highly profitable. The street value of the total haul had been estimated at an eye-watering fifty million. A lot of money, Cat thought, and maybe twice that if the first ten canoes had not been lost. In all the hoo-ha over trapping the elusive Morgan, this point was also conveniently glossed over. Neither that first load nor the men that handled it had ever been found.

"Price."

Cat looked up to see that the real Kyle was standing next to her.

24

Cat realised it was the first time they had been one-on-one. Since being transferred to Kyle's unit, Cat had been working down in the basement, and when they had passed each other in corridors Kyle was always hurrying along with a secretary or task-force officers and merely levelled a stiff, silent glare.

"Ma'am," she replied.

Kyle said nothing, just looked away across the set. Kyle's face appeared so often in the press that it was like looking at someone Cat had known all her life. The short, fair hair, cut close to the scalp Joan of Arc style, the strong, classical nose and small, decisive chin. But closer, there was a dusky pallor to the skin, the long work hours showing in black circles beneath her eyes, a fragility uncaught by the camera's gaze.

"The thing is," Kyle's cut-glass voice broke in. She turned to face Cat then, scrutinising her and making no attempt to hide it. She was taking in Cat's scuffed leathers and witchy hair. "Everyone's telling me you're a screw-up, Price."

Cat looked down to her hands and finished making her roll-up.

"Want one?" Cat asked.

Kyle looked at the roll-up as though it were dog shit.

"I think you probably *are* up a screw-up." It was the kind of forthright remark Kyle had a reputation for, then momentarily her face seemed to soften. "But I keep an open mind."

Kyle was clearly in a hurry to leave. She was raising her hand towards a man parked in a Range Rover up on the marina's ramp. He was keeping his distance.

25

Through the driver's window, Cat could make out the broad chest and bull neck of a body-builder, Kyle's driver presumably.

"I know why you're here." Kyle sounded irritated. "Jill at the office told me."

"Ma'am." Cat could feel a throbbing over her left temple, one of the more persistent symptoms of her withdrawal. The timbre of Kyle's voice was making it worse.

"Don't leave town, not on my time," Kyle said.

"No, ma'am."

Their conversation was interrupted by movement beyond the cordon. The black car at the centre of the crowd was pulling out at speed. Following were a couple of other cars, one of them a convertible driven by Della Davies. Kyle silently watched her pass, her feelings expressed by a pair of pursed lips and an extra frown line.

"Who's in the Volvo?" asked Cat, curious.

Kyle shot a palely amused look at Cat. "The Volvo? Griff Morgan. Who else would it be? It's his film."

Cat couldn't really see much through the tinted back windows, but as the car turned the angle and the light shifted she got a brief view through the windscreen, beyond the driver into the back of the car. In the rear passenger seat, she saw the bunched-up shape of a man in a dark coat. He seemed thin. His pose somehow exhibited anxiety or something fragile, rather than anything commanding or curious. The man had long hair, fashionably unkempt — not unlike Griff Morgan's hair in the iconic poster shot — but it was grey and pitifully thinning.

Cat knew, of course, that the figure couldn't be Morgan. He was down for thirty years, and he would never get out of prison alive. They don't let prisoners out to watch a movie being made, even if it is about them. She would have asked again, only Kyle was already gone, striding away past the film trucks, face set against the wind. She looked fierce and pure, like a heroine from an older, simpler world. One of the rubberneckers from behind the cordon was following Kyle, asking for an autograph perhaps. She waved him away and got into the front of the Range Rover. Cat thought she saw Kyle reach across towards the driver, then the car sped away, merging with the lights of the passing traffic and into the night.

The black car had moved down the dock, beyond the film trucks, apparently with carte blanche to go where it pleased. Della Davies's convertible prowled after it, a terrier at the heels of a deer. Cat watched the show for another few minutes, wondering about the figure in the back of the Volvo. Then she'd had enough, and she left.

What is talent? It's not being able to hold a tune. There are thousands of people who can do that. Thousands of girls, plenty of them pretty, or pretty enough if they make the effort.

Writing? Yes, that is a talent, of course. Being able to find the melody, find the words, bring it all together. Not so many who can do that. That's true.

But that isn't *her* talent. She respects the writers, but thinks of herself only as a performer. The vessel for the song.

The first time she heard that phrase, she wrote it down. *Vessel.* It made sense. When the song is bigger than you, when it possesses you. You're not the singer any more. You're the channel, the vessel.

Of course, the music game needs other things, too. The promoters. The agents. The talent scouts. She doesn't understand that world, but knows she doesn't need to. You just have to nurture your talent, look after yourself, take care of your voice, your vocal chords, and trust that the rest will come.

And of course it will. That's important too. Important enough that she writes it down, writing the word on a sheet of paper, surrounded by an ever-widening net of doodles. *Trust.* That's what you need.

And when she checks her Twitter account, she's gone from two followers to three. She clicks through to see who's following her. She hopes it's someone exciting.

CHAPTER
THREE

So much for the tourist season.

Cat had only passed three people in the last five miles as the road curved between the barren, moor-like hills towards Tregaron. So much for her road trip. It was drizzling, fine soggy curtains of it drifting in from the hills. There was little oil on the road to slick, and as she gunned the Laverda the way narrowed. Hedgerows pushed in and tented over. Closer they came, and darker, forming bleak tunnels around her. She felt claustrophobic, but then her bike crested an incline and suddenly she was gazing down onto a hill-ringed view. The town was spread out like a piece of embroidery between wooded inclines.

Cat crunched to a stop in a layer of gravel off a bend. She flipped up her rain-smeared visor and pulled a pouch of Drum out of the pocket of her leathers. Drizzle persisted down in the valley, but here and there the clouds were pierced by brash arms of sun, so that although the place was mottled light and dark, she could see Tregaron well.

The west side looked genteel enough, the odd gingham tea place and café, and hopeful knick-knack shops trying to lure in the slender tourist trade. An architect's eye might have noted the stout neo-Gothic of the town hall, but Cat's cop's eye rested on the trouble spots: the dishevelled housing stock on the town's east side, and the pubs and slender alleys. That, she knew from a glance, was where the police work was done in this town: the minor domestics and post-pub tiffs, the small-time dealers hawking weed to bored mates.

The police station was just visible at the northernmost point. Even from this distance it didn't look much of a place, a small, boxy structure jockeying for room amongst the terraces. Except for the patrol car in front, it could have been a corner shop that had seen better days.

Cat flipped her visor back down. She could imagine why a bereaved husband might seek the safety of a town like this to bring up his precious only daughter. But that didn't explain the messages, the desperation. Perhaps Tregaron was not as innocuous as it seemed at first glance. She would need to be careful. The straightforward thing would be to drive straight to Tilkian's house, using the address he'd given her, but as a rule Cat distrusted the straightforward. Gather all the facts you can, then act. That's what Kyle had done down on the marina that night. That's what every cop worth their salt would always do. She clicked the Laverda into gear and coasted down into the valley.

She parked around the back of the police station and walked in by the holding cells to the rear. Magnolia paint was peeling off the walls. She flashed her warrant card at the baby-faced custody sergeant. The sergeant betrayed no interest. He nodded to her, motioning towards the swing doors before returning his attention to the *Western Mail* crossword.

The corridor on the other side was no more than a few metres long, with two doors on either side. Windows on the left side of the corridor peered into a small internal yard. Three uniforms stood in the wet outside, two with steaming plastic cups, the third, somewhat younger, brandishing a cigarette while providing the punchline to a tall tale.

"So I said, 'I can fart Calon bloody Lân but that don't make me Pavarotti!'"

All three laughed, the teller of the tale more loudly than his small audience.

Inside, there didn't seem to be anyone around. One of the doors on the side of the passage was ajar. Cat pushed her hand against it and it swung open.

In one corner, a mound of paperwork was balanced on the edge of a desk, an avalanche in waiting. Above it a wastepaper basket had been attached halfway up the wall. She knew immediately it was Thomas's office; he liked to keep his aim sharp.

Beside it hung half a dozen framed photographs of police rugby teams that Thomas had joined over the years. These were only team photos in the very loosest sense; each shot featured a group of sweaty revellers gathered round a bar, hands grasping pint glasses. Some of them looked so unfit it was surprising that they had made it out onto the pitch unaided. Thomas was at the centre of each. Compared to his teammates he looked like a serious prospect for national selection.

Behind the desk, a window offered a view of the yard. The young joker in his shirtsleeves was drawing on a cigarette so hard his concave cheeks seemed to meet somewhere between his teeth. Inside the office, a half-gone Embassy smouldered illegally in a brewery ashtray. Cat made her way over to a low metal chair that seemed designed to look uncomfortable. The door creaked open and she turned, seeing Thomas's barrel-chest enter the room before the rest of him. He looked the same, a little more salt around the temples, a few more crows had walked around the eyes, but he was ageing well.

"Thomas."

He didn't reply, just moved around to the far side of the desk, to establish control of the room. He plonked his mug down on the desk and picked up a pen. He assumed his usual pose, chair swivelled to the side, pen vibrating in the air as he flicked it between his index and second finger.

"Come in, sit down." She was already sitting, but his sarcasm was gentle. By his standards.

"Looking well, Jack."

"Country air, Price." The pronunciation of her surname was not gentle. "Cathays Park told me to let them know if you dropped in."

His smile told her he wouldn't be doing that just yet. Not until he'd found out what he wanted to know. She said nothing. He moved his desk diary from the right of the desk to the left. "So, what brings a girl like you down here to Nowheresville?"

If it was a line from a film it wasn't one she knew. He paused for a laugh that didn't come.

"It's those calls I told you about."

"And?"

Cat looked at Thomas, wondering what to tell him. Whatever she said, she knew he'd remember it. Thomas had the demeanour of a laid-back rugby lad, but beneath lurked a shrewd and logical brain. She paused, took too long for his taste. He chivvied her along.

"They came from a friend. Martin Tilkian — if that rings any bells."

"No."

"Moved here a few years ago. Daughter, no wife. Daughter's name is Esyllt."

"How old? The daughter, I mean."

"Teenage."

"Specifically?"

Cat raised her head with interest at the precision of Thomas's question. She took her mind back to the Wikipedia stub. "Sixteen," she calculated. "Why?"

Thomas ducked the question. "Tilkian. Tell me what you know about him," he said.

An order, not a request. Cat felt herself prickle with refusal but her operational brain was also telling her that Thomas was only behaving like this because he had something for her. She felt trapped and gazed beyond Thomas, weighing up her options. Through the window, she could see one of the PCs hunch his shoulders in the rain. He pulled a packet of cheapies from his pocket, looked hard at it, as if deciding whether to light another cigarette from the dying stub.

If she wanted Thomas onside, she'd have to give him something. "The calls I was getting are from an old schoolfriend — Martin Tilkian. Haven't seen him for the best part of seventeen years. Then, out of nowhere, he starts leaving messages."

"How did you figure it was him?"

"He left a message. A proper one. But I didn't get it until later."

"And?"

"And nothing. I went to school with the guy for a while. Nothing on our systems. Google tells me he used to be a games designer. That's it. Google's also where I got his daughter's age."

"From here, is he?"

"No. Whitchurch, Cardiff. Father worked for the council. I think his mum used to be a receptionist for the local doctor. Very respectable."

Thomas looked up at the wall. There was a picture of the Preseli Hills. Low green moorland, a standing stone circle, captioned *Bedd Arthur*. Arthur's Grave. The picture was faded from too much sunlight.

"Tilkian, Tilkian, Tilkian . . ." he muttered, as though something danced tantalisingly out of his reach.

"Come on, don't play games with me."

"I don't know shit about him."

The PC outside had been joined by a young female colleague. Her blonde hair had been fashioned into an elaborate French knot. She was hatless, in shirtsleeves despite the wet. She stood close to the PC, so close it would have been difficult to slide a piece of paper between them. Then she must have felt Cat's gaze on

36

her. She looked round, through the window into Thomas's office, moved away quickly.

"Must be difficult to keep anything private in a place like this," Cat said.

Thomas lowered his head, gave her a knowing look, held it a while. For a moment she wondered if there was something specific he expected her to recall.

"Like I said, I don't know anything about him." He leaned forward, opened one of his drawers, pulled out a newspaper, slapped it onto the desk. "But I think I know why this Martin's called you over."

Apart from the masthead and a few small adverts for local businesses, the front page had been entirely dedicated to the disappearance of a local seventeen-year-old called Nia Hopkins. The picture showed a girl with dyed black hair and a black T-shirt; her face was powdered white.

Despite all the social networking media that had come the way of teenagers since Cat had grown up, some of the kids still looked more or less the same. They called themselves emos now, whereas Cat and Martin had called themselves goths, but the look had the same feel to it, and seemed to say the same thing: I am dark and in earnest and I reject your shallow, trivial world.

She looked more carefully at the girl. Dark eyes, darker surrounds, the classic dusky Welsh look. Not a hundred miles from herself. The hole left inside her by the absence of the tranks seemed suddenly to expand. She sweated although she wasn't hot, and her head throbbed.

"You want some water, Price? You're looking a bit peaky."

"No . . . Thank you."

"Something stronger, maybe?" Thomas slid his bottom desk drawer open and there was the chinking of a bottle rolling against glasses.

She wanted some, of course, but she shook her head. What was the point coming off tranks only to fall again? It was a classic error.

"No." She forced herself to concentrate. Looking back at the paper, she noticed that it was dated two days earlier and that the girl had been missing over a week. She scanned the report. "You've got a list of friends, I assume?"

"Friends? Shit, Price, I never thought of that. You think I should ask Nia Hopkins's relatives for a list of her friends, in order that I could conduct interviews with the aim of identifying information that might point to the cause and circumstances of her disappearance?"

Cat rolled her eyes. Thomas's act was getting tiresome. "Well?" she persisted.

"Apparently Nia Hopkins didn't have any friends. She might well have known Tilkian's kid — small town like this, same age — but I've got nothing to suggest a close connection."

Cat nodded. Thomas's phrasing was telling. Having no information about something was not the same as being sure that something did not exist. A connection, or a friendship, or some link of cause and effect.

The silence in the room continued for a few moments.

"You weren't planning on coming here when we spoke," he said softly.

"I didn't know who the calls were from when we spoke."

"So why me first? Why not just go and see your friend?"

Thomas's eyes narrowed in the way that she remembered. She recalled how Thomas was a great weapon to have on your team, a bloody nightmare to hide anything from. Cat met his look, steeled herself not to react, not to fall headlong into his silence.

Then, abruptly he unsprung his body, the hands now on the desk, clasped in front of him, his posture upright. He looked more than five feet eight, which was all that he was. Only, like many men who were neither tall nor truly short, he made himself seem larger with the force of his personality, something wild and dark that promised a decent fight should anyone rile him sufficiently. Here I am, world, come and have a go — if you think you're hard enough.

"You'd better start to spill, Price, or I'm on the phone to Cathays."

"You got phones out here, have you?"

"Yes, Price, and computers too."

"I saw Kyle yesterday. She was down on the docks reliving her moment of glory."

"Bet she loved that."

"She told me I couldn't leave town on her time. I interpreted that as meaning she'd be fine with me coming up here if I took it as holiday. If you want to call her?" Cat gave him a don't-give-a-damn shrug. She let the shrug fade. "Something like this, you don't just rush in. You'd be the same."

Thomas considered this and seemed to accept it. He resumed his casual pose, hands folded behind his head, and gave her a smile. "You sure you didn't come to see me? I mean, nobody would blame you."

Cat dropped the paper onto the desk. "Wouldn't want to break the hearts of the milkmaids of Tregaron, would I, Thomas?"

As the paper hit the desk the outer page became slightly detached, and she caught sight of a familiar scene. It was the quay from the previous evening, lit with arc lights. There was the crowd of students in their Griff Morgan T-shirts around the black Volvo. Next to it was another shot of a painfully thin man going into a large house in Hampstead. The piece below had been syndicated from Della Davies's column. It was only a couple of paragraphs, and Cat didn't need to read it all to get the gist. Morgan had been released the previous day on compassionate grounds. His melanoma had spread and he had no more than a few weeks left to live. The visit to the set had likely been his final public appearance.

She turned her back, made her way towards the door.

"No goodbye kiss, Price?"

She smiled, making sure he didn't see her doing it. She didn't reply, just raised a hand of farewell.

She walked on out of the station and back to the car park. Martin's address was on the note in her back pocket. It already looked like something that had lain forgotten for too long. Martin could have called her from South Island, New Zealand, she wouldn't have cared, she'd have dropped everything and come. It didn't matter that they hadn't seen each other for nigh on seventeen years. What Martin had done for her all those years ago needed to be paid back.

One thing was certain — Thomas being on hand made no difference. His importance rested only on how easy or hard he made it for her to do this job for Martin. She fastened the strap on her helmet. As she pumped the throttle a PC came out to see what the noise was and she swung out onto the road.

Cat rode up and down the street three times before she found the place. The council houses were identical two-up-two-down structures divided by pathways choked with weeds. Italicised plastic numbers were fixed next to the front doors. Martin's note gave his address as number twenty-two. Cat found number twenty then, next door, number twenty-one. After that, there was a bank that obscured sodden fields beyond.

She checked her satnav, punched in the postcode again. Yes, the marker was pointing at the exact spot where she had stopped. She was about to turn back when through a gap between two overfull wheelie bins she noticed a lane, just wide enough for a car. She followed the track as it wound around the side of the houses. Immediately past the narrow back gardens it dipped, then rose slightly into a clump of mature beech trees. Through the rain the lights of windows glowed.

The property was a three-storey Edwardian villa, which looked as if it had been a vicarage or small local manor. It now appeared down at heel. The smells of dampness, rotting wood and compost hit her as she removed her helmet. Most of the front garden bloomed extravagantly, the path edged by flower beds overflowing with salvia and lobelias. Like the house, the garden had once been loved, but now ran amok.

She imagined that the land that had once belonged to the house had been sold to build the council estate. Surrounded by newcomers, the old house seemed to have turned in on itself. Cat climbed off her bike. Her throat was dry and her head buzzed. But this was not withdrawal. It was nerves. From taking one long step into the past to try to free up her present. She stood still, uncertain, undecided.

At the front of the house was a porch crammed with ferns that partially obscured the doorway. The glass of the door was veined with elaborate patterns and clouded over from the heat inside. She could still turn back. Cat stood motionless for a moment. The decision was taken out of her hands, as the door opened.

Cat struggled to trace her old friend in the man stood in front of her. He looked smaller than she remembered, his sad brown eyes circled by black: shadowed water in a well. The black linen suit and white shirt looked crumpled, as if he had just pulled them on. He wasn't wearing any shoes.

He took Cat's hand, guided her into the porch where he embraced her fiercely. Unsure at first, she reciprocated. He held her for a few seconds, then

42

pulled back, holding both her hands. She looked past him to a wide staircase with an impressive carved banister, which gave the entrance a feeling of grandeur. Beneath it framed posters for computer games were propped against the wall.

He mumbled greetings, and something about a cup of whatever she wanted, but she held up her hand to show she was all right.

"She's gone. My daughter's gone."

His voice now was choked, desperate.

She was going to make some answer, but he turned abruptly and went off down a short corridor that led to a family room. Cat followed. On the floor, a home cinema system rested on a rough stone rostrum. The few pieces of art on the walls had clearly been chosen with care. One looked like a Kyffin Williams original. On the left side several muted abstracts hung in an unevenly spaced line.

The room's modernist theme was contrasted by four mahogany tables, each of which held framed photographs. These scenes had been arranged in chronological order from left to right. Martin in a hospital gown, smiling broadly, presenting a wrinkled, snub-nosed baby wrapped in a towel to the camera. Next to him was a girl with a flushed and beaming face. Martin, in a dark winter coat, pushing a beaming toddler on a swing. Martin in the background, hands in pockets, looking apprehensive as a blurred pre-teen girl on a bicycle rode past him. The final photo of Martin's missing daughter was a head-and-shoulders photo of her as a teenager. She wore a grey sweatshirt bearing the logo of the Welsh College of Music and Drama, her hair swept back into a complicated chignon, at odds with her casual clothes, and her face was set in a firm smile.

Next to this portrait stood another framed photograph. Cat recognised the scene immediately. It would be a cold day in hell before she forgot her seventeenth birthday. Her mother had insisted that she go out with "some friends". Her only friend from school was Martin. There they were, the odd couple. She looked like a kick boxer after a bout, head hung under her hoodie. His face was covered with his shades and bushy hair. The two of them were standing outside Screamers, a club with a justified reputation for admitting the underage, and one that had long since closed. Captured on the edge of the photo that a passer-by had taken at Martin's insistence, were some girls from school in pelmet skirts and lurex tops, who had just run past, shouting abuse at them.

The night is freezing. They join the queue, the bouncer at the door playing the usual power game of "who's hot, who's not". Downstairs the walls sweat a mixture of body odour, smoke and alcohol. They push into the scrum at the bar, three deep, every punter for himself. They buy their drinks — a pint of Felinfoel for Cat, a weak-as-water screwdriver for Martin, the classic choice of the reluctant drinker.

Then leaning her back against a pillar to watch the action on the dancefloor, she turns around to see one of the boys from school. He is a year older, had a reputation for trouble. She doesn't need him to speak to her to know the evening is ruined. He goes to find his friends. She goes to find Martin. The pack of boys are following her around the club, making the sign of the cross and hissing like cats.

"Witch's bitch. Witch's bitch."

Outside the club, the boys follow them back to the station. She had seen farm dogs working sheep in the same way. They board the train while the boys press their noses against the windows, running their fingers over their throats to tell them they are both dead meat.

Cat glanced at the picture and then grimaced at Martin. He grimaced back, as far as his grief-stricken face allowed. She tried to recall the last time she'd seen her own copy of the picture. Tried and failed. Martin's determination to cling on to their shared history acted as a gentle rebuke. Was this memento usually on display or had it been put there specifically for her visit?

Martin led her through to a conservatory. This was a shadowy space, the large panes of glass covered by blinds that further muted the dullness of the day. There was a small iron table, a folded paper lying in the centre, two matching chairs pulled up close. Martin gestured to the chairs and Cat took a seat.

"Cat." He tried to be polite. "How have you been?"

He nodded, acknowledging the futility of his question.

"I still don't travel on trains too much, Martin."

He smiled at that, and so did she. She didn't ask Martin how he had been. He pushed the newspaper on the table towards her. "You've probably seen this already."

His voice faltered. He put a hand in front of his mouth as if about to vomit. The front page of the *Echo* was again dominated by the story of Nia Hopkins's disappearance. The girl was the same, but the picture was different; a close-up shot, but still with the same black eyes, white skin and straggly black hair. Again Cat thought that it could almost have been herself. She pushed the paper back to Martin.

"I've seen it."

Martin swallowed, removed his hand from his mouth. "I just thought. Esyllt . . ."

"Facts, Martin. I need facts."

His face had turned in on itself, a man in the grip of deep emotion. "I'd hoped you'd come straight away."

"You shoved a bit of paper under my garage door. Lost under about two hundred flyers for pizza delivery. You didn't even use my letterbox. Didn't leave your name on your messages. Didn't pick up your phone. How the fuck was I to know it was you? Or where to find you, if it comes to that?"

Cat was angry because those phone calls had scared her. Angry because the withdrawal was playing devil with her emotions. Because of the headache that never fully left. But most of all, because her friend had allowed a whole week of investigation to get lost. The first week. The most precious week.

"Sorry, I didn't know. I assumed you'd got the note."

"Why not call the police? I've just spoken to the station. DI Thomas. He knew fuck all about your daughter. You shove a note under my garage door and you don't even call the local police."

"I know. But I was in a panic, Cat."

She felt her anger fading. There was nothing phoney about Tilkian's reactions. He was a man overwhelmed by his own loss. Or, more accurately, his fears about a possible loss.

"Facts, Martin. Start with the facts." Cat's voice was gentle. She had a notebook and pen stowed on her bike, but there'd be time for all that later. She'd start this as a friend. See how to take it later. Tilkian nodded, gathering himself.

"Esyllt's been away at college in Cardiff, but her college room is only for term times. She broke up weeks ago, she's been here most of the time since."

He was about to rush forward in the story, but Cat raised a hand to stop him.

"She sees her friends when she's here, presumably? Everything seemed normal?"

"She doesn't really have friends here. She thinks the locals are, well, a bit rough and ready."

"She leaves here when?"

He named a date. Cat counted backwards. It was two days before he'd shoved the note under her garage door.

"Leaves for Cardiff?"

"Yes. I drove her. Left her at her college dorm block. Apparently, she'd sorted out a way to get access to her room. She was fed up here. You know. Teenage girls. You can't fence them in too much. The way to lose them."

Cat nodded. It must be hard being a single dad. Maybe it was a bad move of his coming out here to

Tregaron. You keep them safe for a while, but they feel the safety and want to fly from it. Cat knew the feeling.

"OK. So you drop her in Cardiff. By car?"

A nod.

"Everything fine? No hint of a problem?"

"No, it all seemed, well, fine."

"And?"

"It *was* fine. For a while. She was texting, calling. Just like normal. We spoke every day. Always do."

Cat frowned. This wasn't heading the way she'd been expecting. She asked the key question. "When was the last time you spoke to her by phone?"

"Four days ago." His voice a whisper. "Her phone has been switched off ever since."

"And before then, everything was normal?"

A nod.

"But you wrote to me a week ago. You left a note under my garage door. Started calling not long after that. That was *before* she went missing."

"I had this awful feeling. I was worried." He shrugged. "Dad's intuition, call it."

Cat stared at him. The silence pooled in the room for a second or two.

"There was a guy."

"A guy?"

"Weird-looking. White streak in his hair."

"Approximate age?"

"I don't know. Forty, maybe."

"Description? Fuck, Martin, work with me. I'm on your side."

48

He seemed to pull himself together. "White guy. Pale. Jeans, I think. Dark jacket. Nothing so unusual. Black hair, or dark anyway."

"And you saw him where?"

"He was around here. I saw him twice in Tregaron."

"So? What made you suspicious?"

"Nothing really. Not then. He was in town, just glancing at her from a distance. I noticed him — because that white streak in his hair made him look like a badger."

"So then you take Esyllt into Cardiff, drop her back there. Everything's OK."

"Yes. Then she tells me she saw that guy again. The badger. She didn't think it was a big deal. Just a coincidence."

"And that's when you get scared. When you start trying to contact me."

"Right."

"Why me, not the police?"

"You are the police."

Cat looked hard at Martin's face. He looked resigned to the worst but part of him was still praying for a reprieve. It was a reaction she had seen before. Denial, fear, hope. She knew she didn't have the full story yet, but you often didn't. Not straight-away, not ever.

"What about her friends? You've contacted them?"

Martin nodded, sort of. "Nothing. They're all abroad on holiday, know nothing."

"She knew the other Tregaron girl who's gone? Nia Hopkins?"

"I don't think so. But it's a small town."

Cat knew that most teenage runaways came home of their own accord after a few days. She imagined the two girls up in London somewhere, staying with a friend, talking about how adults didn't understand them. She'd been there, done that.

Martin nodded, to himself as much as anything. He looked down into his lap trying to compose himself. "She wouldn't go missing of her own accord; she was going to appear on that talent show on S4C." He glanced towards the home cinema next door.

"Talent show?"

"It was a big deal for her. What she lived for, really."

"Maybe she changed her mind. Didn't want the pressure."

"It was all her idea. She's been rehearsing all her audition pieces with her tutors at the college. You must have seen her on TV?"

Cat shook her head. Martin rose, moved next door. He motioned for her to sit, picked up the remote from the coffee table. Esyllt appeared on the screen, a younger version of her teenage self in the photo on the table.

"It's from the Urdd Eisteddfod a few years ago. She came first in her category."

Esyllt's voice had a depth and a richness that singers of that age rarely possessed. Cat could detect a slight nervous tremor in the first few bars, but Esyllt soon settled down. Although "Ar Lân y Mor" had been a regular feature of Cat's own days in the Urdd, this was as good as hearing it for the first time. Throughout, the girl's eyes were bright and wide, as if watching the sounds descending to her from somewhere above. Martin was holding his hand over his face as if he could barely watch. On the screen, Esyllt stopped singing, stood back from the microphone, accepted the applause with a small bow of her head. Her face was closed, showing nothing.

Martin concentrated on wiping his eyes. Cat noticed that the set of his mouth looked just like Esyllt's when she had finished her performance.

"Don't you think that she might have been friends with this Nia? Maybe they met up and went off somewhere together?"

Martin shook his head again, more vigorously this time. She noticed the skin on his neck was raw and scaly, just as it was as a teenager. As if aware of her eyes on him, he tugged his shirt at the collar.

"No, that copper's right. She might have known her to say hi to, but they weren't friends. I'd have known."

Cat was about to ask something further, when she felt a vibration against her leg, pulled her iPhone out. The screen flashed Thomas's private number.

"Thomas?"

"Price, we've found something and it's not pretty."

From Thomas's end came a dry, hacking sound. Cat wondered whether he'd been sick.

"You got a name?"

"We're trying to ID her right now."

Cat glanced sideways at Martin. His face looked calm. His hands were so tightly interlinked that fingernails were digging into flesh. He was trying to follow the gist of the call. Cat turned her head slightly to the right, spoke quietly into the phone. "Get me a picture now. Take one on your mobile and send it to me."

"You know that's against the rules."

"Get me photographic. Just pretend you're looking for a number and press capture."

"You know any magic words, Price?"

"Please."

There was silence for several seconds, finally a theatrical sigh from Thomas. "You owe me one, Price. This time I'll be calling in my marker."

She ended the call. Martin's mouth was so tight with tension the words had to fight their way out of him.

"What is it?"

"Probably nothing that you need to worry about."

Cat's phone beeped, alerting her to a new message. She hesitated, brought up the picture. She spied Martin from the corner of her eye. Be strong for him. Her feelings were not the most important in this. She forced herself to look at the phone. Thomas was no photographer and the body seemed to lie quite far off, in some kind of pit, but she could see enough to know that the face on her screen wasn't Esyllt Tilkian's.

"It's not her," she whispered to Martin. As he released the breath he had held for too long, he slumped down, his eyes obscured by the palm of his hand.

Cat pulled the newspaper towards her, glanced again at the picture of Nia Hopkins. It looked as though she had dyed her hair again before her death. Apart from that, the facial features looked the same. Her head was tilted to the side, pushed out of position by whatever force had struck it. The rest was blurred by the poor quality of the camera on Thomas's phone.

Cat looked up at her friend. "We need to make this official. Report Esyllt as a Misper case. Do it right."

Martin was bent over in his chair, index and second finger of his right hand now pressed to his eyes as though expecting a migraine. He nodded. Good enough.

"I'd like to see Esyllt's room," Cat said.

Martin sat up, got hold of himself. He stood and walked out of the conservatory. Cat followed him up the staircase. Esyllt's room was at the start of a corridor leading to the back. Martin pushed open the door, stood aside. Tidiness was the room's most obvious feature. It looked the opposite of teenage. Either Martin made sure that it was clean and clear at all times or his daughter had developed a housework mania.

A single bed was pushed up against the left wall. The duvet was cream and grown-up, no patterns or girlie frills. Esyllt had arranged her work area along the back wall, a long desk containing a line of reference books and classic novels.

"Nothing like your old room," said Cat, trying for levity, regretting it as the words left her mouth.

"No," Martin managed in reply.

The wall behind the work space was taken up with an enormous poster of the Stereophonics, Kelly Jones swamped by a Welsh flag, the other band members slouching around him. The only personal touch was a framed picture of Esyllt herself, posing at a party with an enormous cocktail glass containing an orange liquid, decorated with a miniature umbrella and pieces of fruit. She wore a Hawaiian-style outfit, a tissue paper lei around her neck, and was smiling broadly.

"No computer?"

"She had a laptop. Took it with her."

Cat edged to the wardrobe and opened it. The clothes inside looked plain, serious, like the room itself. She felt she had no real sense of the girl from the place nor from the TV appearance. The room was anodyne, Vulcan almost. It was puzzling.

"Did you clean this room after she left, Martin?"

"No. It's how she was. Spic and span."

Cat stood back, tried to take in the room as a whole.

"That picture — it was Nia Hopkins, wasn't it?" Martin said.

The identification wasn't official. She shouldn't let him know yet, but the personal outweighed the professional on this one, had done since she had disobeyed Kyle.

"I think so," Cat confirmed.

"Someone did her?"

"I can't say, Martin."

"Someone did her."

"Honestly, I don't know."

Martin shuddered but he did not speak. If Nia Hopkins had been murdered, he knew that Esyllt's chances had just got slimmer. They walked down the stairs without speaking. Martin went straight back to the front door. He wanted Cat to go, it was clear; he needed to be alone. Was that wise? Grief and anxiety multiplied in solitude.

"I can stay for a while," she offered.

"No," he said simply.

Their catch-up would have to wait. If it ever came at all. He opened the front door and Cat began to step out. Martin looked at her then looked away. He made a choking noise, raised his hand to his mouth, holding back something that was half-scream, half-sob. For a moment, it looked like he would speak. Cat put her arm out to him, but he twisted, pulling free so violently that Cat almost fell out of the porch. She steadied herself, called his name, but Martin had already shut the door.

The new follower has no photo up on their account, merely uses the ovoid avatar provided. Their user name is a jumble of letters and numbers that might be a product description of a circuit-board for all she knows. It tells her nothing.

Is the new follower someone from school? Is she about to be bullied again?

She feels nervous as she looks at her Mentions. She has a new one. A Tweet from the latest follower. She feels elated as she reads it, vindicated.

@purevoice94: Saw your YouTube film. You have REAL talent.

From the TV downstairs she can hear the sound of studio applause. As her hands move across the keyboard, she begins to feel revived.

CHAPTER
FOUR

There were no police lights, but Cat could tell that this was the place by the occasional flash of torchlight that appeared between the trees around the abandoned pithead as the SOCO team battled the rain and the dusk.

The ground was too muddy to use the Laverda's stand so she leaned the heavy bike against a tree. Ducking under the police tape, she flipped her warrant card open in the face of the PC who had been smoking outside the station. She was waved through.

The path petered out into bushes. Cat pushed her way through them, drawing in her breath sharply as she turned her foot on the uneven ground. There was a bust-up old wooden door across the entrance to the pithead tunnel. She swung it open. The air inside was still, stifling. She took a deep breath as she entered, saw the blue and white of the police tent erected inside the tunnel which led on to the mine shaft. A few police lights were placed on the floor here and there. Thomas's familiar outline was a few yards further down.

"It's Nia Hopkins, isn't it?"

Thomas straightened up, winced as he flattened a hand along the small of his back and rubbed at his spine. He could only just stand up straight beneath the low, bowed roof.

"Yes. Just now got positive ID from the friend who found the body."

"Martin Tilkian's daughter's gone. Four days ago."

Cat looked around, saw something beyond Thomas on the floor. A luminous glow, growing brighter as her eyes adapted to the dark. She stepped forward, bent closer. The glow lit up some areas of glitter that formed a rough oval. It was a helium balloon, somewhat deflated. Next to the balloon was a bright mauve sleeping bag, glistening with damp, and a row of empty superstore vodka bottles lined up against the wall. A pair of black pumps were splayed next to a plastic bag half-filled with socks, a Griff Morgan T-shirt, a heavy black jumper.

Thomas stooped over to Cat, stood next to her by the balloon. "There." He pointed further along the tunnel. "Down the shaft."

"She fell?"

"Looks that way."

If she'd fallen, then that meant that there was no killer; if Nia had fallen then Esyllt was safer. Thomas nudged the sleeping bag with the toe of his shoe. "Looks like she'd been here alone for a while. The friend said she'd been depressed, agitated."

"How do you know she'd been here alone?"

Thomas pointed at the busted door Cat had just come in through. "Locked from the inside."

60

"So how did her friend find her?"

Thomas moved a little deeper into the tunnel, pointed to an opening close to the roof. A crude gap formed a skylight. It had been plugged with industrial glass, cobwebs restricting the light still further. "The friend looked down, saw the sleeping bag, recognised it as Nia's."

Cat walked further into the tunnel. Thomas pointed upwards. He'd clearly asked himself the same thing that she was. "You seen those cobwebs, Price? Thick as a bloody curtain. Nobody's been down that way in years."

"Are there other entrances?"

She could just about make out Thomas shaking his head. "Been closed up for years. It's a huge system, stretches for miles underground. They've been mining here since Roman times, so there's bound to be another way in somewhere, but this one's been nobbled by Health and Safety. Too close to civilisation for comfort, apparently."

Further down the tunnel, almost disappearing into the darkness, an old piece of plastic sheeting had been fashioned into a tent, to keep off drips from the rough rock ceiling above. A few dry branches did the job of tent poles, sheltering a mound of polystyrene containers, two Domino's Pizza boxes and a mountain of empty cans. It was away from Nia's things, and Cat guessed that the girl had neither made nor used it.

She looked over at Thomas. "What's this stuff here?"

"Kids used to use the place as a drinking hole. Council found out eventually, closed it up."

Cat pointed back towards Nia's sleeping bag. "Did her friend ID all that stuff as belonging to Nia? Nothing here of Esyllt's?"

Thomas shook his head. "No, it's all Nia's. I called around when you left the office. Can't find any connection between the two girls. But," he shrugged, "early days."

Along the tunnel, yards beyond the drinkers' den, Cat felt Thomas reach for her, felt his burly hand. He was shepherding her. A darker area appeared on the floor.

They stopped and peered down the sudden drop. Thomas aimed a torch beam into the hole. The figure below looked like a crumpled white doll, a gash on her throat the only colour. Around her something was glimmering, shallow pools of water. Cat wanted to climb down and hold her and lay her arms along her sides, set her head straight so she looked at peace. But her training held her back.

"The gash caused by the fall?"

"There's sharp ledges all the way down, she could've caught one, but we'll have to wait for confirmation on that."

"Any drugs on the scene?"

"Nothing found so far. We'll know for sure when the tox report comes back."

Cat motioned back towards the mouth of the tunnel. "All that stuff. Looks like she was here for a while. If she came to do herself in, she thought about it plenty."

"We'll probably never know what made her do it. These teen cases are a nightmare. Nine times out of ten there's no clear answer."

"Her friend say anything? Boyfriend trouble? Exams?"

Thomas shook his head. "Nothing like that. Just that she hadn't been herself, wanted to be alone."

The last phrase was accompanied by a vampish Garbo accent. Cat looked hard at Thomas until his mouth twisted in a wry apology.

"Well, you know how girls are at that age. They keep a lot to themselves. The slightest thing goes wrong and . . ."

Thomas made a plosive sound with his lips.

Cat closes her eyes. She is back in the train on the night that she and Martin celebrated her birthday. They are on their way home. She leaves her seat ten minutes out of the station. She makes her way to the space between their carriage and the next, pulls the window down, feels the icy air blowing her hair back, sucking the breath from her lungs. It is one of the old carriages, the door opening from inside. The next few seconds bring together clarity and confusion, her hand on the door handle followed by a bang as the momentum of the train pulls it out of her grip. She stands outside, between carriages, the train lights flashing past. Then looking down at the tracks, she wants to jump, into the alluring blur of the metal lines, into the irresistible feeling that she could keep on falling for ever and never hit the ground.

Then "Cat! Cat!" the shock as she is pulled back, Martin's horrified voice shouting her name. She collapses onto the floor, her head on Martin's shoulder. For what seemed hours she couldn't look up, only stare at the ground. That was all she trusted herself to look at. Martin was kneeling on a discarded flyer, a second-hand furniture store advertising repossessed dining tables and chairs. She remembered that still. Then glancing up, the pallor of Martin's face.

Looking back, she wasn't really sure why she had done it, tried to do it. She'd been picked on and abused before. It was nothing new. Why was that night different? Maybe she'd had an intimation in those moments that her life was only going to get more isolated, harder in every way, and there was nothing she could do to stop it. And so she'd gone for the nearest exit. If people knew what lay ahead for them she wondered how many would do the same.

Thomas was staring at her. She caught him studying her face and he shifted his gaze away. In the darkness of the tunnel he looked different, not the cocky hardcase of the day but the vulnerable animal everyone is at night. Cat pulled out her phone, moved to the mouth of the tunnel where there was a weak signal. Punched in Martin's number. As usual there was no reply, it was switched off. This time she left a short message, confirming that there did not appear to be any connection between Nia's death and Esyllt's disappearance.

Suddenly Martin's voice broke in, ragged with anxiety. "It was an accident then, the other girl?"

"We think so but we're still not sure."

On the other end of the line there was a stifled sob. Martin breathed out noisily and deliberately. Cat waited for him to finish.

"Martin?" she prompted, but all she got was that sound again. Half-sob, half-choke. Then silence. She prompted a second time: "Martin?" But the line was dead.

Cat shouted back into the tunnel, telling Thomas that she was going. She neither saw nor heard any reaction.

The bike was parked just the other side of the trees. She edged it onto a flat piece of ground carved out of the verge to allow vehicles to pass each other. The route to Martin's house was almost deserted as she sped through quickening rain. Darkness was slowly falling, the light limited, but it wasn't yet dark enough for headlights. Cat checked her speed, aware that this was the time most accidents happened.

The driveway to the house was lit by a single lamp. The porch was dark, all the curtains closed. Cat ran her hand down the porch door, noticed for the first time how many locks had been fitted. Two Yales had been added to a mortice. Martin would have to be well organised to avoid shutting himself out of the house.

She rang the bell, waited for a minute, rang again. Then she knocked on the porch door with her fists and called out. Still no answer. She made so much noise she expected someone from the council houses to come down. But no one did. She tried Martin's phone again, but this time he did not break in when she spoke.

She punched in Thomas's number.

"Bloody hell, Price, you come and you go, and then you call. You need to settle down, girl."

She ignored the sally. "Any troublemakers moved to the area recently?"

"Why do you ask?" Thomas sounded distracted.

"Martin Tilkian said something about a guy with a white streak in his hair. Might've been following his daughter. Seen here and in Cardiff. I don't think Tilkian is giving me the full story."

Thomas made one of his noises, a dismissive puffing.

"Highly strung that Martin, by the sounds of it. Everyone's bloody paranoid these days."

Cat could hear harsh, raised voices in the background, Thomas talking to someone, his voice far away from the mouthpiece of his phone. Then more rustling as he moved it back to his face. His tone was different when next he spoke; strained, tired.

"You'd better get back here. They've found something else."

Cat ended the call and looked up at the big, old house. Grand but overgrown, like the garden. Neglected. The games industry must have made cash for Tilkian, but there was no sign of an income stream still coming in. There was something weird about the place, but maybe that's just what you got in cases like this: seeing old friends when you've both moved on. Or maybe it was just the tranks.

She jumped onto the Laverda, heart thudding — and that *was* the tranks. This time she did not check her speed. She gunned over to the pithead. Cat parked the bike well off the road again, among the trees. The lights were circling a different area now, several hundred metres west of the first discovery. She ran through the long grass. It was some time before she reached the scene. Someone had hitched a floodlight on an abandoned JCB, a yellow hulk being claimed by rust. To the left an ancient Portakabin had sunk into the ground. Mud sucked at Cat's boots.

As she neared the Portakabin she could see the dark circle of another mine shaft. At the side of the opening, several lengths of chain lay coiled around each other. To the left, a uniformed figure was bent double, expelling his lunch onto the grass. Thomas stood next to the PC, patting his back but looking distracted. Seeing Cat, he headed her way.

"One of the search dogs found her." Thomas was shaken but was trying to be matter-of-fact.

"Is it Esyllt?"

Thomas shrugged, wrinkled his nose. "Difficult to tell yet."

She ran over to the hole. This opening was less a tunnel, more a sheer drop that ended in a pool of water about five metres down. Cat peered in. The body looked like a half-finished three-D jigsaw. What remained of it lay bloated under torn rags that had once been clothes. Cat stifled a retch. She could not tell who this was. But still she stared, trying to make out what she knew she could not. Behind Cat a figure in white coveralls, one of the SOCO team, was whispering to Thomas. Her temples throbbed with the absence of tranks, her belly with anxiety. She tried to calm down, waited for Thomas to join her.

"Easy, Price: it's not Esyllt."

"How can you be sure?"

"This one's been there a couple of weeks at least, they reckon."

Cat glanced again at the body in the pit. Thomas flicked his hand against hers, directing her back from the edge. He breathed out. "One of our boys thinks he recognises her. Though God knows how."

Thomas's face was pale. Cat noticed that he looked middle-aged. "Delyth Moses. A waitress from the Owain Glyndwr café, went missing a month or so back. He says he used to see her walking up here." He gestured vaguely back to the road.

"Any connection to Esyllt?"

Thomas shook his head. "Doubt it. Wasn't a local, as such. Hadn't been here long, either. Just came down to pick up a bit of seasonal work."

He grimaced and rubbed his face. Cat knew what that meant: the case had been booked as a Misper according to the rules, but no one had really done anything because it was assumed the waitress had just upped and left for reasons of her own. Ninety-nine times out of a hundred, that's the right decision to make. One time in a hundred, and the stuff hits the fan.

"Oh well," said Cat, with a shrug, "if she wasn't a local."

Thomas looked at her, made a face, then grinned weakly.

They heard the dog team before they saw them. The gentle soughing of the grass punctuated by panting and the occasional excited bark. Torches switched on, they fanned out, the furthest handlers disappearing along the width of the area, stopping only when the ground dipped, moving in formation.

Following them, a tall, lean figure with a receding hairline made his way through the long grass. With red hair turning grey and a face so gaunt his nose looked like a beak, he was the physical opposite of a typical Welshman. In his left hand he carried a plastic evidence bag. As he reached Cat and Thomas he raised his hand in greeting.

"*Noswaith dda*, Price. Long way from home."

Cat eyed the pathologist, Dr Matthews. She knew him from his occasional visits to Cathays Park. He'd already been attending the previous scene, so he would have been among the first to see the body. If there was any indication of time and cause of death at the scene, and often there weren't, he would have seen them.

"Any idea what happened to the Hopkins girl?"

"No, but from rigidity and eye condition she's been dead more than two days."

"And this one?"

"Body's in too bad a state to tell."

Tell me something I don't know, Cat thought. She looked over to a tarpaulin about fifty metres to the left of the pit, stretched over a mound, the bottom layer of which was partly visible. Smaller, freshly dug pits ringed the pithead and continued down to the JCB. She could just about make out signs on the fences, scarlet danger notices. They looked new. The pathologist caught her glance.

"Another couple of days we wouldn't have found either of them. This whole place is due to be levelled. The MoD want it as a firing range, apparently."

A volley of barks rang out not far from the pit. There were shouts from the other dog handlers. Some of them were still making their way across into the wood beyond.

Cat followed the line of handlers with her eyes. A narrow track of bare earth wound through the long grass. The land was sloping steadily upwards. A building stood perched at the top of a drop, back towards the road where Cat had parked her bike. Its shape was barn-like, but it had several windows, all on the upper storey. It looked as if it had once been associated with the pit in some way, possibly a foreman's cottage.

From up close, the place seemed to have been designed back to front, the house facing into the woods. It sat snugly on the edge of the drop, a small gated garden claimed from the wildness. The gate was padlocked. The windows were covered by iron grilles despite their height, and the curtains were all drawn.

Cat jumped the gate. The top had been rimmed with broken glass to deter trespassers. A concrete path led round the back of the house. There were some arrow-slit windows, not visible from the other side. The glass was opaque, revealing the outline of a bottle of toilet cleaner on a shelf inside.

She stepped off the path, picked up one of the large stones that lay on the grass verge. She spun round to see a figure looming behind her. Thomas. He had followed through the trees. He could move pretty fast still.

She threw the stone through the window, clearing the glass away with the sleeve of her jacket before clambering up. The sound of the search dogs was closer now as they headed to the house.

She knocked the toilet duck to the floor, stepped over the cistern onto the seat and then to the floor. She opened the bathroom door and saw a short passageway leading to the front entrance. The door had been fitted with several heavy dead-locks.

The first room was entirely empty, the other contained a three-seater sofa and two battered armchairs. The arms of the sofa leaked stuffing. A coffee table bore the marks of countless mugs, a thin covering of dust mingled with cigarette ash.

Cat left the room and walked to the far end of the passageway, glancing through an open door into the kitchen. She flipped on the harsh strip light. The worktops were piled with pizza cartons; an empty vodka bottle, the same brand as the empties at the tunnel, lay on its side on the lino floor. A plastic ashtray from the Owain Glyndwr overflowed with butts.

Cat heard Thomas behind her, his breathing ragged after the climb through the window. She looked round at him.

"What is this place? There seems a lot of security."

"Holiday cottage. Owner died. It's been locked up since." He sniffed the stale air. "The lad who ID'd the Moses girl said she came up here sometimes when she wasn't working. Looks like it was another teen drinking hole."

Cat pointed to a small pile of clothes in the corner of the kitchen, woollies and socks topped by a hairbrush, some Dove moisturiser, and a pink make-up bag embossed with a cartoon image: Betty Boop.

"Same socks as with Nia's stuff, and the same cheap vodka."

They moved over towards the shelf. Thomas stared at the objects intently. Cat rifled through the pile of clothes, pulled out a grey T-shirt, the logo of the College of Music and Drama on the front. Beneath the logo, just above the T-shirt's ribbed bottom, was a rusty stain the size of a clenched fist.

She put it to her nose, thought she caught the metallic whiff of blood.

"Anyone else in town a student at that college?"

Thomas shook his head. "Not that I know of."

"Looks like Esyllt was here too," she said. "All three of them, seems like."

"This will all need going over by the SOCOs," Thomas said, looking out of the window beyond the garden. The dogs were standing on the edge, shuffling, their breath clouding the air.

On the table, there was an A3 sheet of paper. Cat picked it up by the corner. Under it were several "Free Morgan" T-shirts. The face was instantly familiar from the YouTube footage at the marina. Familiar from newspaper photographs. Familiar from student posters and cartoons.

The portrait showed Griff Morgan as he was that day of the bust. Simultaneously dangerous and alluring. It had all the glamour of sin.

The image was predictable enough in the setting. Morgan was a popular icon, especially so with the counter-cultural young. But then as she moved away, she felt Thomas tap her shoulder and saw he was pointing to the inner wall. The whole central section had been covered with scarlet graffiti. It looked as if it had been done hastily, with no interest in its artistic merit. There was a Kilroy figure staring morosely over a wall, with the typical droopy nose and wide peeping eyes. The words underneath read: *Griff Morgan was here and he did the girls. Chwith.*

Thomas stared at it wide-eyed.

"Fuck you make of that?" she said.

Thomas's face twisted, though his expression was hard to read. "Looks like someone's trying to yank our chain. Matthews said Nia has been dead over two days, and the other girl definitely has. That rules out Morgan. Morgan was still in a maximum-security prison at the time these girls died. Probably the second most guarded man in Britain after the Yorkshire Ripper. Not the most likely murder suspect, is he?"

"No, not exactly."

Cat palmed her phone and waited for a signal. The online version of the *Echo* article about Morgan's release flickered over her small screen. His movements were described hour by hour and fully accounted for.

Morgan had been released the previous day at noon, a pack of journalists had been waiting for him and followed him down in convoy to the film set, then back to his house to Hampstead. It was inconceivable that he had made the five-hour round trip to Tregaron, and even if he had, it would have been after the girls had died.

Thomas was right, of course. A celebrated prisoner in a maximum-security prison was not a likely murder suspect. But the house they stood in looked as if it had been used by the dead girls, Nia and Delyth. If the grey T-shirt matched back to Esyllt, then the house had been used by two dead girls and one missing one. And someone in the house had named Morgan as the killer. It made no sense, but Cat knew that life often didn't.

One of the things you learn early: music is never only about music.

That's what they don't tell you when you start. You think it's about the purity of your voice. The ability to hit a note and hold it. The ability to find the heart of the song and let yourself dissolve into the song, let the song merge with you.

And then, slowly, you figure out that music is about more than that. It's an industry. Men in suits who want things from you. Men in suits who smile at you with their teeth just as they're still doing sums in their head.

You don't have to be a genius to do the maths on that particular combination. But she's no fool. You don't get anywhere by hiding. You just have to keep your wits about you, know what you want.

She looks back at that Twitter message.

@purevoice94: Saw your YouTube film. You have REAL talent.

How do these things start? Answer: you never know. It could start any way at all. A song in a nightclub. A YouTube video. A message on Twitter.

It could start right now.

CHAPTER
FIVE

Cat woke. The room was narrow, one wall taken up by a window with a view between thin curtains onto an empty square. In the corner was a wardrobe made out of plywood and a dressing table with a pink plush seat. This was the only furniture as far as she could see; the place smelt of beer and industrial detergent.

Then it came back to her. She had refused Thomas's loaded offer to stay over and buzzed up to The Lion, a pub in town with rooms. The light outside told her it was already dawn and she had overslept.

Cat cursed and clicked into her messages. There was only one, from Thomas, telling her the dog search of the vicinity of the mine had been completed and nothing else had been turned up. He added that all the items found in the tunnel and the cottage had been bagged for prints and DNA. Some items had been confirmed by her employer at the café as belonging to Delyth Moses, others as Nia's. He had been unable to get hold of Martin Tilkian, but one of the DCs had seen Esyllt wearing a similar T-shirt around town; as no other locals were students in Cardiff it was a fair bet that the T-shirt was hers. His voice sounded bored, as if he would rather have stayed in bed. Although he'd been shaken the night before on finding the bodies, it seemed that his compassion had passed.

She tried Martin's number but his phone was still switched off. She left a quick message telling him to call. He had probably not slept, she thought, maybe he'd knocked himself out with pills. She went looking for a bathroom, found one and showered quickly. Downstairs no one was up. She made herself a quick breakfast in the kitchen. She felt shaky, her balance slightly out of kilter, but she knew it was the withdrawal from the tranks and tried to ignore it. She made herself a roll-up and sprinkled it with canna, already feeling she'd find it hard to keep it level through the day ahead. When standing in the kitchen, she kept one hand on the counter for balance.

At the police station she found the street silent, the two-storey terrace with its Chinese takeaway under morning mist. The station looked as quiet as the neighbourhood. The entrance to the holding cells at the back was locked behind a pull-down metal flap.

She tried the front door: locked, a small glass panel revealing only a faint light that appeared to be coming from somewhere deep inside. She knocked but there was no reply. She couldn't see a bell. Finally, feeling along the chipped paintwork of the doorjamb she found a small bump. She pressed it without any particular hope.

The door was solid, so the buzzer was barely audible, but there was the sound of the door swinging open. Ahead she could see the reception desk. Behind it slouched the PC she had seen the previous night, the one who had yakked his lunch into the grass at the sight of the dead waitress. He seemed to have recovered his appetite by now, though: a small piece of escaped breakfast dangled from a frond of his moustache. He looked half-asleep still.

In front of him was an old magazine, the pages yellowed, the spine broken; some true-crime publication, one that had already done the rounds, by the look of it. She noticed how his hair was tousled at the back. He suppressed a yawn as he turned to face her.

"DI Thomas?"

His face contorted as he lost the battle with a second, more powerful yawn, glanced down at the magazine, his attention focused on a black-and-white image of a woman sprawled on a grassy bank. She was young and attractive, wearing only underpants and bra.

He flapped his hand in the direction of the door she had just entered. "He's at the Hopkins place."

His posture relaxed, now he knew that Cat wasn't looking for him, and he turned his attention back to the magazine. She pulled her phone from her jacket, clicked through to a map of the area. Thrust it across the desk. "Where is it?"

He took it from her, screwed up his eyes. First he held the phone right up to his face, then he extended his hand as far as it would stretch. Seconds passed.

Tapping the screen he pointed to an area roughly in the centre. It looked like a farm, not a large place. The satnav's map showed it to be surrounded by wooded areas and a couple of miles from the mine.

It didn't take her more than ten minutes to get there. There was little traffic. She had to stop only once as a herdsman helped his Friesians across the road from their field. The size of their udders suggested that they were off to be milked; their legs bowed under the weight, their teats like the fingers of huge latex gloves.

The farm was signposted, a warped hardboard with the name roughly painted in black. A sharp sweep left off the road took her into a yard piled with manure and feed bags.

She kicked out the Laverda's stand, took off her helmet and gloves. To the right a shed contained an old tractor, its paintwork flaked and peeling. To the left there was a cavernous barn with milking equipment in it. She took a muddy path up an incline at the side.

Thomas was standing by a pile of wood stamping his feet, hand cupped around a cigarette. In the other he held a stick. He was staring down at something in the mud at his feet. Beyond him, the ragged line of the police search team was moving slowly over the land. Mostly it was open pasture, there was little ground cover. The cottage they had visited the night before was just visible, maybe a mile or so further over to the right. Arranged on top of the hill opposite were some small, free-standing barriers which the army used for target practice.

Thomas had disturbed a blackbird, which showed its disapproval with a loud rattle. She walked over. The mud at Thomas's feet was covered in a series of wavy lines. Some were already losing definition in the ooze, but she saw he had been trying his hand at Kilroy cartoons. They had the same droopy nose and peeping eyes as the figure on the wall. They were the sort of eyes that seemed to follow you as you passed.

He acknowledged her presence with a wry nod. He looked as if he'd been up most of the night, the skin around his eyes dark and drawn.

"Someone's trying to mess with our heads, Price."

He pointed down at the figures, and passed her some crumpled sheets from his jacket. They were printouts from the internet, short histories of the Kilroy image. Some of it was already familiar from her own reading the previous night. It seemed the original Kilroy of *Kilroy was here* fame had been an American rivet inspector. He'd marked work he passed with the famous line, which had then appeared in inaccessible parts of the ships carrying the troops over during the Second World War, high up on hulls, on chimney stacks and down in the bowels of the ships in crevices no person could reach. The idea caught on and a graffiti craze spread. The cartoon of the figure with the eyes had originally been British, its origin was obscure, but when British soldiers took up the craze they had yoked the two traditions together. The man with the eyes had become the ubiquitous Kilroy.

"These little fellows don't mean much in themselves," he said. He was giving her a knowing, apprehensive look. "But do you remember Operation Plato?"

It was a rhetorical question. Any Wales copper who had anything to do with drugs had come to hear of the operation. It had been perhaps the most embarrassing in a long string of failed attempts to capture Griff

Morgan prior to the marina bust. Cat had not been in Drugs then but she knew the basics: reliable intelligence had placed Morgan alone in a remote cave on the Pembrokeshire coast. A rival drug lord had got the details through a leak from Morgan's gang, and passed them on. Morgan was said to be waiting in the cave while the Tulle brothers and minor soldiers unloaded cargo somewhere further up the coast. The intelligence had been precise on the location of the cave, and that Morgan would be there alone. It was a particularly inaccessible spot, halfway up a cliff. The escape routes had been cut by land, air and sea, and the area tightly encircled: it looked like they had finally snagged him.

But the operation had proved a damp squib. The AR squad found the cave empty, except for some recently smoked cigarettes and a half-eaten snack. An exhaustive search of the area failed to find him. After the marina bust, during a long grilling Morgan had finally admitted being in the cave alone that day. It turned out they had missed him by only half an hour.

At the time of the op, Cat remembered, Della Davies had still been press officer at Cathays. As the affair had been a costly failure, she had run a press blackout afterwards, and no details of the operation had ever reached the public.

Thomas was staring at Cat intently. She had a horrible feeling she already knew where this was going. Tentatively, he passed her a faxed photograph. She recognised the old evidence sheet numbers from five years back. She was looking at a photo from the

Operation Plato evidence file. It wasn't that well defined, but the basics were clear enough.

"Last night, when I saw the wall," he made a clicking sound, "it reminded me of something, then I remembered this." He hesitated. "At the time no one really made much of it. Everyone was too pissed-off at having missed Morgan."

The focus of forensics at the time had been the objects recovered at the cave and not the place, so the picture was not a close-up. It showed the narrow base of the cave, about six feet across. Among black pools was a dry patch with some cigarettes stubbed out on the rocks, some sandwich wrappers and a couple of empty water bottles. On the wall above was a solitary Kilroy, smaller than the one on the wall, but visibly in the same style.

"I've scoured online," Thomas said. "All the true-crime sites, but there's no sign any member of the public has ever seen this picture. Difficult to imagine how they could since it's locked away in the evidence vaults under Cathays. No one has looked at this file for years."

Cat remembered vague rumours going around at the time about how Morgan had someone on the inside. This had been floated as the reason that he was always one step ahead of all the attempts to snatch him. The Kilroy looked like Morgan was taking the piss out of the officers he knew were coming for him. Could it mean something else? She wasn't sure. Despite exhaustive investigations, no inside man in the force had ever been identified as having assisted Morgan, and under questioning he had never admitted to having one. The inside man was likely a myth, the paranoid reflex of a provincial force that had repeatedly failed to catch their man. But over years the rumours of one had created an ever tighter information loop around any Morgan-related operations. The day of Operation Plato, only Kyle and a few trusted officers close to her would have known who the target was. These were the same officers in on the marina bust, and Morgan had not got away that day.

She glanced back at the picture. The eyes seemed to stare back at her, mocking. If someone wanted to fuck with their heads, they had found a good way to do it. The graffiti, she reckoned, had been phrased to be understood as a plain statement of fact. The Kilroy figure had been offered as proof of its bona fides. Whatever its original private significance to Morgan may have been — if it had any — it came over as a crudely territorial gesture, like a piss on a lamppost, or a notch on a tree.

They were being taunted.

"The only person we can safely say at this stage did not kill these girls is Morgan," Thomas said. He paused. He looked visibly shaken. "I checked in with the governor at Belmarsh. He thought I was short of a deck for even asking. He assured me Morgan had been in the secure unit and had no day releases. The last few months he's been so unwell he could barely walk more than a few paces unaided."

Cat took this in. None of it was any great surprise. She knew all security protocols in Category A prisons were rigorously monitored and enforced. It had been over two decades since there had been a break-out by an A'er, and this had been from a transfer van; as for a break-out followed by a break-in, and by a sick man, it was fairyland stuff.

Thomas shuffled. "He could even show us video of every minute Morgan has been in there if we want." He sniggered. "Made a big song and dance about his communications being monitored too, chance of him organising anything on the outside less than nil."

"Well, he's the g'vnor, he's going to say that."

"No, but I checked in with Sol Bowles, remember Sol in Prisons?"

This was another rhetorical. He might as well have been asking if she remembered her own name. There was also a reproach here, Thomas had been keeping up with Sol, and probably knew she had not. A fellow Drugs man, Sol had switched into prisons inspection after a bad burn-out, going down to booze and painkillers before cleaning up big time. "Had a cosy with Sol," he continued, "says Belmarsh is being given its annual inspection currently and there were no surprises. Security around Morgan has been tight as a mouse's arse."

Cat shrugged. "All right, I get the picture." She bent down and tapped out a text to Sol. She would check in with him later.

She took the stick and had a go at drawing the cartoon. The ledge over which the eyes peeped came out wobbly, and she hadn't got the eyes right. She passed the stick back, took out a biro and had a go on the back of the printout Thomas had passed her.

She broke it down. Tried each line separately. One wavy line did the nose and the eyes, two straight for the ledge. Then two half-circles the pupils. Five strokes in all, with some shading in the eyes. Even after six more goes, it still had not come out quite right. It was something that needed practice, but once you'd got it you'd always be able to do it, she reckoned. Like writing your own signature.

She had another go, but still it wasn't right. She felt the frustration building inside herself and put the paper aside.

"Enjoy your lie-in?" he asked.

"Breakfast was the full spread."

"Really?" He looked surprised.

She gestured up towards the pit. "So what do you reckon, then?"

Thomas made a sour face. "There's another angle we'll have to eliminate." He rolled his eyes. "A couple of recent teen suicides down in Bridgend spoke of having imaginary friends. People who they thought would be waiting for them on the other side. Cobain, that sort of thing, just predictable teen barminess. Bridgend isn't too far away. Maybe these girls saw Morgan as something similar, he had a symbolic role of some sort for them?"

He smiled at Cat's drawings.

"Psychopomps."

"Steady on, Price."

"They're mythological figures who guide souls from one world to the next."

"Right, it's shite obviously but the sort of shite that young girls believe in."

"And Morgan is still alive."

"Just about."

Cat thought about this. Her searches the previous night had turned up no Free Morgan campaign, not even an informal one. The T-shirts were just fashion items, prisoner cool, like the *Charlie was a surfer* T-shirts from a few years back. It seemed a big leap from a few T-shirts and some nonsensical graffiti to a suicide ring. And until the forensics were in, she knew Thomas was just pissing in the dark.

The places where Nia and Delyth had been hiding out had felt like typical teen dens but also like refuges, safe-houses of a sort. Judging from the T-shirt, Esyllt had been one of them, though Cat would have to wait for the reports to come back to be sure. Her best bet, she reckoned, was to shadow Thomas for the routine inquiries at the homes of the two dead girls, see what they turned up, then tackle Martin again when she had more information.

"No sign of Esyllt, then?"

She had raised her voice and Thomas waved his hand to the area behind him where a woman stood, gazing into the fields. It was a warning. The woman looked briefly towards them, then away again into the trees.

Kyle. She was wearing a townie's version of country gear: a padded jacket and sensible boots. She looked like she was off to a corporate clay pigeon shoot somewhere. Had she spotted Cat? Hard to tell. There had been no obvious reaction.

Cat stepped back behind the stack of logs so she wasn't so visible. "Why didn't you tell me?" she asked Thomas, wondering if it was his revenge for the night before.

"Because you'd have gone back to town like a good girl, would you?" His voice was sneering, but also held some admiration for her tenacity.

Kyle moved away from them, skirting the edge of the hill.

"Why is she here, Thomas?"

"Spends a lot of time in the area. Renovating her weekend cottage."

"But why's she at the scene? One of the families call her in to help?"

A light shake of the head came from Thomas. He took another drag on his cigarette, looked around. He could have been a man at a bus stop, mildly irritated by a late bus.

"No. She expressed an interest in the other two girls when they were filed as Mispers."

"Bit small-time for Kyle, isn't it?"

Thomas snorted quietly. "It's not a professional interest, it's personal."

"Personal?"

Like most other members of the force, Cat found it hard to imagine Kyle having a personal life. Cat peeked out, seeing Kyle stood under one of the trees, peering at the bottom of the field. There was nothing down there, just the bare banks and a shallow, freely flowing stream.

"She lost her foster-daughter five years back. Suicide."

Christ. "She blames herself?"

Thomas shrugged. "The girl just did it, right out of the blue. Standing alone at the station, jumped out in front of a train. No sign she was unhappy. There was nothing Kyle could do."

Poor cow, thought Cat. Having to carry that around with you. That might be a reason Kyle was so fierce and cold at work, pushing everyone away. Thomas stubbed the cigarette out under his shoe, turned back towards the farmhouse. Cat looked briefly over at the trees, and at Kyle staring at the field. Kyle had moved further away, was looking down towards the stream, then back towards the trees. She seemed lost, unable to focus.

The front door to the farm was open. Thomas stood aside, ushered Cat in before him. Not from chivalry, she thought.

At the end of a passage she could see a farmhouse kitchen, the threadbare arm of a settee, an old sink packed with washing-up, a corrugated draining board. To the right a female Family Liaison Officer stood beside a chintz sofa. A woman was lying on the sofa, stretched out flat, one arm bent above her head, clearly sedated. Nia Hopkins's mother. Every so often the FLO softly patted her arm, as if she were a pet dog.

Cat became aware of another presence near her in the hallway, turned back to where a tall, dishevelled youth stood, swaying gently, at the foot of the stairs. He wore a khaki T-shirt, sweat stains under the armpits, decorated with an image of a cannabis leaf. His jeans were mud-spattered, although his trainers were a brilliant white, and looked as if they'd just come out of the box. His face was pale, his mouth partly open. He caught Cat's eye, then Thomas's. They turned back to face the kitchen. Seconds later the sound of his feet dragging up the stairs filtered down to them.

"That's the half-brother. Calls himself Moose."

Thomas went up after him and Cat followed. Thomas gently pushed open the door of the room at the top of the stairs, revealing a modern bathroom. Judging by the smell of bleach it had recently been cleaned. The room to its left was a large double bedroom, clearly the master. The next door but one was shut. Thomas rapped it with his knuckles, pushed it open before there was any response. Cat and Thomas stepped inside.

The room was narrow, the curtains drawn. Moose was sitting on the bed, wiping his nose with his hand. He was putting something away, his long thin hands skipping over some debris on the bedside chest of drawers, shoving it into a bag. It looked like grass and tobacco. Thomas cleared his throat. Moose turned, the sleepy half-closed eyes that Cat had seen downstairs were gone, replaced with a feral unease.

"Nia been unhappy recently, then?"

Moose leered unconvincingly at Cat. "No."

Thomas moved closer to the bed, gently kicked his foot against it. "She been going up the mine a lot, has she?"

Moose opened his hands, pushed his palms together, slid them between his knees. He met Thomas's gaze and shrugged slowly.

A lot of teenagers were turning into go-getting MBA fodder, with no rough edges, Cat thought, or else they were inexplicably tidy, like Esyllt. It seemed Moose was the original moody shrugger. Cat moved to the next door on the landing. It was shut, but she swung it open, noted the hiss as the wood caught on the carpet that still had the smell of newness about it. Thomas followed her in and Moose came behind them, hanging back in the doorway.

Nia's room resembled Esyllt's in its lack of obvious feminine touches. She had been no fan of frills or lace. Her bed was covered with a plain duvet, her chest of drawers a flatpack job. A desk, too small to be a comfortable workplace for a secondary school pupil, sat in the corner behind an equally small chair. An iPod dock with speakers sat on some flatpack drawers on the room's opposite wall. The screen showed a recent playlist, mostly emo and goth artists and a few childhood favourites: *The Jungle Book, Beauty and the Beast*. On the wall behind the bed a poster advertised a My Chemical Romance gig at Brixton Academy. Her dark taste in bands seemed to contradict the banal neatness of the room; as if she hadn't fully committed to the teenage give-a-shit attitude.

Cat stared straight into Moose's eyes. "No computer?"

Moose looked blank.

"Nia was tight with the waitress at the Owain Glyndwr?"

Moose still looked blank. "Never been in there, far as I know," he managed.

"Knew Esyllt Tilkian, didn't she, Nia?"

Moose shook his head. "Doubt it."

Cat lowered her voice slightly. "Esyllt's dad seemed well upset about some lad. Esyllt have boyfriend trouble?"

Moose flapped his hand in the air dismissively. "Doubt it. Esyllt's right stuck-up. I've never seen her with any local lads."

"What lads, then?"

"None. Never see her much at all, like."

There was a built-in wardrobe behind the door. Cat glanced in without touching anything. There were black jeans, T-shirts and dresses, all the goth basics. At the end were some long coats and frocks that looked as if they had been bought secondhand.

Cat closed her eyes then slowly opened them, took in the rest of the room. Nia's chest of drawers was bare for a teenager but there were a couple of keepsakes on it. A small ornament of a witch with a black cat, back arched, ceramic fur spiked into tight peaks stood next to an Indian box covered with fake jewels with a painting of an elephant on the lid.

She flipped the lid open: cheap earrings and necklaces. Peeking out from the jewellery box there was a scrap of card. Cat picked it up by its corner, not touching the surface. It had Nia's full name printed, no address or number, but a link to an address on

YouTube. It looked like a young person's idea of a business card, the type made at an automated machine. Cat reached in her pocket for her phone, keyed in the address.

The performer was listed simply as Nia, and there was only one track, an acoustic version of Radiohead's "Street Spirit (Fade Out)". She clicked play on the YouTube clip. As she waited for it to boot, her mind went back to the rainy streets of Cardiff, back to the bay, before it was the Bay Development. It was early in 1996. She was sat in an unmarked car with her first love, Rhys. He let her do that when they first got together, before she was a copper even, before she was old enough to get into pubs she had seen things many people never see.

He had made her a compilation. It might have been a cheesy thing to do, but because Rhys had done it, the songs were profound to her; each one a message about life. Rain rivuleted the car windows. She was safe. She was with him. A song ended — the Velvet's "Venus in Furs" — and another started, "Street Spirit", which had not long been released. He began to talk, music was the only thing that got him talking. Love, his past, their future: on these subjects Rhys was mute. But music was always his best friend, even later, when he was married to the skag. He spoke like a teacher, which was what he was to her then.

"The KLF said that vocalists confuse their roles as singers in bands with being world leaders. Thom Yorke is Bono, without the shades or the hotline to Mandela."

She laughed. But Rhys never laughed at his own jokes, never saw them as funny. Could she even remember the sound of his laughter?

"Radiohead are so worthy, so dull," he continued, "normally. But this song is pure, so despairing that it can only be true."

"What do you mean?" she asked.

"Listen to it. This song could have been written by the devil. Or by God about the devil."

She had never understood what Rhys had meant by that. But a sound from Nia's room pulled Cat from her memory. It was the YouTube clip on her phone. It had started, not with music, but with a demure cough from a teenage girl on an empty stage. Cat looked up to see Moose and Thomas close to her, staring at the screen on her phone.

Either the stage had been arranged to look like a traditional theatre with a proscenium arch or it really was one. In its centre stood Nia, gently lit to reveal nothing more than a small performance area and the edge of a plush red drape. She was dressed simply in a long, white, shroud-like dress. Her dark eyes were heavily lined with kohl, her lips the crimson of a Hammer Horror starlet. The low light was bleached out as a spotlight seemed to come out of nowhere, lending an added layer of strangeness to her appearance.

As Nia sang to the backing track of "Street Spirit", she swayed, her voice swooping and dipping. Occasionally she closed her eyes, clasping her hands in front of her as if undergoing some religious transformation. She seemed powered by something greater than self-confidence; a sense that she was completely in the moment, driven along by the song. Cat knew it well, and Nia's performance had retained the essence of the original, but she had added another layer. It was as if she was pleading with some unseen person or deity, asking them for help.

Cat shivered involuntarily. It was an impressive performance, and it had already attracted a few followers. On the message board beneath the video Stevie21 had written, "Awesome!" while Rockettothestars had noted, "I love this song — Nia, you rock!"

Cat searched YouTube for all Nia's postings, there were three or four others, but the last one had been almost a year previously, another Radiohead track. She looked up at Moose, who betrayed no obvious feelings at watching the film of his recently deceased sister. "Nia hasn't been doing any music recently?"

"No, gave it up, I think."

"Did she ever mention a man called Griff Morgan? The drug smuggler?"

"I know who he is."

"That's not what I asked. Did your sister ever mention him? Have a thing for him? Anything like that."

Moose shook his head. He'd relapsed into sulky teenage silence, tapping his foot, eye fixed on the door. Cat and Thomas took the hint, followed him out of the room. Downstairs, the mother was still out for the count. Cat went over to her, tried to make eye contact, but the woman just lay there, staring at the ceiling, a moan rising from her lips. It sounded like all the pain in the world turned down low.

They left the farmhouse. Out of earshot of the building, Cat turned to Thomas, "Boy got form?"

"Nah. He's a stoner, smokes spliff but that's it."

"And Nia?"

"Nothing."

"They were close?"

"What do you think? As far as I know, he has his own friends but she didn't mix much."

They walked over to Cat's Laverda. She picked up her helmet. "They're locals?"

"Not originally, they came in from Cardiff a few years back."

The rasp of the catching four stroke engine broke the stillness. "The father?"

"Died. They came into a bit of money, his insurance probably, bought that farm."

She followed Thomas back into town until he pulled over at a roadside café.

The Owain Glyndwr had a mock-Tudor facade, which lent the establishment what limited charm it possessed. The windows needed a clean and the paintwork was chipped. The menu outside was faded and most of the dishes looked like frozen microwave jobs.

Inside, any pretence of gentility had all but been abandoned. The tables were covered with plastic sheets, little better than oilcloths. Glass bottles of salt, pepper and vinegar stood on each table with sticky, half-empty bottles of ketchup and brown sauce.

96

A small, middle-aged woman was using a mop; judging by the dirt on the floor she hadn't bothered to sweep it first. She had tied back her greying hair, dyed auburn but growing out at the roots. Hastily applied make-up failed to conceal the age spots on her cheeks. She wore a striped pinafore over a pair of jeans, a fraying rugby shirt poking out over the top. Thomas took out his warrant card. "Delyth Moses worked here, right?"

The woman glanced up briefly at Thomas's warrant card, unwilling to meet his eyes, and continued to mop the floor. This was the reaction of people with experience of the police. No piece of information would be offered freely. Anything Cat and Thomas learned here would be down to their own powers of observation, and by reading between the lines.

"She did the late-morning to early-evening shift."

Cat stepped forward. "Where was she rooming?"

The woman sighed, motioned at Cat and Thomas to follow her up the stairs. On the way up, the doors were all closed. At the top there was a landing into a low attic space. A bedroom and adjoining bathroom took up the whole of this upper floor.

Most of it was empty, of both furniture and personal effects. In one corner under a dusty dormer window there was a three-quarter bed, then a chest of drawers underneath a tiny window that offered Cat only a view of the roof. Standing on her toes she was just able to see the drive at the side of the property, the street, some playing fields beyond.

She stepped back, opened the wardrobe. It was barely a quarter full. Jeans, sweatshirts and tops, two skirts, one a tweed pattern, another black and decorated with patches of sequins. One white blouse that would be suitable for formal wear. It didn't look as if Delyth had had much interest in clothes or fashion.

The only homely touches were provided by a CD player painted pink and, in the far corner opposite the bed, a Spanish guitar with a red ribbon tied around the neck. Cat looked over at the café owner, who was standing by the door, preparing to usher them out.

"Where do Delyth's family live?"

"Doesn't have any. She worked at farms in Pembrokeshire over the winter, came here for the summer. Never any trouble."

Cat picked up the CD on the top of a pile, a copy of Cerys Matthews's *Awyren=Aeroplane*, looked over at the woman. "Anything unusual in the last few weeks?"

The woman began to shake her head before Cat had even finished the question.

"Any sign she was unhappy?"

She bent and picked a roll of fluff from the carpet. "Used to play her music a bit loud, but then she got an iPod. Just went to her room after her shifts. Never heard a peep from her."

Cat put the CD back on the pile. "She didn't go out with friends?"

"Not often. Never saw her with anyone. Weekends she was away usually."

"Know where?"

The woman shrugged. Cat stood on her toes, looked out at the drive. "Anyone pick her up? Any vehicles you saw?"

The owner shook her head emphatically. "Never heard any."

"She didn't mention any names you remember?" Behind her, Cat caught Thomas's *sotto voce*, "Oh God, here we go", but she ignored him and ploughed on. "Did she ever mention Griff Morgan."

"Morgan? The drugs man? Threw away the key, didn't they?"

"Spoke about him, did she?"

The woman looked blank. The name Morgan didn't seem to catch any fish. Cat moved towards the guitar. "You hear her playing this?"

The woman's face softened. "Occasionally she'd play simple songs: country, I think." Her eyes moistened. "Nice voice she had, I never complained."

"Remember any of the songs?"

The woman shook her head again. Thomas was standing by the door, his expression suggesting this was a waste of their time. They thanked the woman, made their way out through the café, where the two customers were making their cups of tea last.

Thomas led the way down the road towards The Lion, where Cat had stayed the night before. Not that she had seen the inside of the bar, having accessed her room via what was termed the guest entrance, aka the back stairs. The bar had seen better days. Its red flock wallpaper was faded and the carpet worn bald. The half-dozen figures around the bar were male, most of them casually dressed in tracksuits or denim jackets, and they had the air of the long-term unemployed.

Thomas and Cat approached them, Thomas waving at the barman to attract his attention. He passed Cat her bottled water, eyes raised in mock disapproval as he did so. They moved away from the ears at the bar towards a snug table in the corner, beneath a handsome etched window. Thomas stared at his pint for what seemed an age.

"All bets are off till the path's reports come in." He took a swallow. "But I'm still feeling suicide ring."

"And the Kilroy?"

"Wind-up of some sort, or it had some private significance for the girls. Either way it can't literally mean what it says — we know that, at least."

Cat needed his help. She would be gentle. "Esyllt and Delyth were musical like Nia. It's what brought all three girls together maybe."

"Ok, but how come no one ever saw the girls together?"

Cat had already thought about this. If the girls had been online friends this might explain it. But then why had they used the cottage and the tunnel? They felt more like hiding places than hangouts, though at that age the line between the two was blurred. But why two places? Why not just use the more comfortable cottage, why also the tunnel? She didn't have an answer, though she knew there might be several innocent ones.

Thomas looked down at her glass of water as if he'd only just noticed it. "What's with that?" he said.

She didn't want to go there. Bad enough having to live each day as a cold raw birth without having to share it. He wanted her to be vulnerable to him and she wasn't playing. Alcohol worked on the same receptors as the benzos, and one drink would set recovery back months, maybe irreparably — would be like pulling open her heart then fastening it with a stapler. Maybe she'd have said something like that, if he'd asked her right, but then again, probably not.

He could be all right, Thomas, but he could be a boorish prick as well. That was the thing with other people, you couldn't pin them down, they were riven with competing traits. Just like she was. Because to everyone else in the world, Cat was one of the other people too. She looked away.

At another table two youths were having an animated conversation about rugby. And then Cat caught a glimpse of a familiar figure sitting at a table in the back room. She shifted behind Thomas but she knew Kyle had already spotted her.

Kyle was with an officer Cat had seen from a distance around Cathays Park. He was bulked up like a bodybuilder and wore the off-duty uniform of rugby shirt and chinos. She recognised him as Kyle's driver at the marina, waiting in the shadows of her car. When he turned towards her, his eyes were narrowed and blinking as he took her in.

Thomas followed her gaze. "That's Mo Probert. Armed Response Unit. He was the marksman at the bust."

She remembered the actor playing Huw Tulle on the gangplank at the marina. The first shot catching him. Tulle staggering back like a drunk. On the second impact the lights flickering as the black-clad ARs, their faces masked, closed in around him.

"The inquest cleared Probert, said he'd had probable cause for shooting. Tulle reached into his pocket. Though later it turned out he wasn't armed."

She glanced at Probert. "He's Kyle's bit of rough?"

Thomas chuckled. "Talk is when they come to her cottage they don't go out for days. So it's a fair bet."

"Right, the trigger man."

Thomas chuckled again. "Pill man, more like. Think you get built like that from oat bars."

"Roids gave him the itchy finger?"

Kyle was walking towards them now. Her tan jodhpurs were spattered with mud from the search. Probert was a couple of paces behind. There was no pretending she hadn't been seen now so Cat just smiled at her. She expected Kyle to rip into her, but Kyle didn't address her at all, just looked coolly at Thomas.

"The third girl," she said, "any sign?"

"No, ma'am," Thomas said.

Cat thought of the T-shirt at the cottage, the stain at the waist, the metallic smell of it. Thomas had already pulled the medical records of all three girls. Some depression in Nia's file, but nothing in the other two. If Esyllt was a cutter she had hidden it well. But as Thomas had said, all bets were off until the path's reports came in. Until then they were all walking blind.

"The father's a friend of yours, Price?" Kyle wasn't looking at Cat as she spoke. Her voice was cold, final, as though after their conversation at the marina, when Kyle said she was keeping an open mind, that mind had now been closed by Cat's disobedience.

"Yes, ma'am. An old friend."

Cat tried to remember if she had given Martin's name when she'd rung Kyle's secretary. She couldn't imagine she had, but the withdrawal symptoms were playing with her memory. Maybe Kyle had spoken to Martin. But it wasn't her case, that would be out of line even for Kyle. Cat felt hot suddenly in her biker's gear, sweat was gathering under her collar and her head throbbed.

Kyle exchanged a look with Thomas that said she expected to be kept informed. Then she strode ahead of Probert to the door. As she opened it her profile was caught for a moment against the stained glass. She looked somehow medieval, Cat thought. Like an effigy in an ancient church, one of those who had been away on the crusades out of zeal rather than to plunder. Kyle headed out to her Subaru and got into the driver's seat, not waiting for Probert to close his door before firing the engine. It sounded modded, rally-tuned. She disappeared up the lane into the quickening rain.

"That's a pity," said Thomas, finishing his drink.

Cat refused to rise to his bait directly, but threw a look at him.

"I was looking forward to hearing one of Kyle's bollockings. Maybe she's saving it up."

Cat ignored him, said nothing. Kyle's exact words to her down at the marina had been: "Don't leave town, not on my time." Cat had interpreted that as meaning she could go, but only if she took the time as unpaid leave. At the time she'd presumed that Kyle had meant exactly that, which was why it hadn't been a hard decision to leave. But now she felt something else. Maybe Kyle had *wanted* her to go, had chosen her words in such a way to nudge Cat into going. Maybe or maybe not, but this was for sure: there was something weird about Kyle being here so quickly. Coincidences happen, but this one was already stretched beyond the snapping point.

Thomas shoved his glass away from him, and headed out for the street. Cat looked down at her water, finished it, then followed Thomas out into the rain.

@tt33w67h: Thanks. Who are u?

@purevoice94: A friend. Your voice is perfect. Are you a pro?

@tt33w67h: LOL! I wish!!

Then, annoyed with herself, she clarifies.

@tt33w67h: Do want to sing professionally. Practise all the time. No band though.

@purevoice94: You don't need one. Not with my help.

@tt33w67h: Help me? Why?

@purevoice94: I believe in you. Know talent when I see it.

@tt33w67h: But who are u?

@purevoice94: I'm in the business. I'll help you.

CHAPTER
SIX

Cat parked in the half-flooded yard at the back of The Lion and had a smoke while she was at it. She needed to call on Martin but couldn't face it yet. She went upstairs, closed the flimsy curtains in the bedroom and put in earplugs. She lay in the semi-darkness. She shut out everything except the sound of her breathing and waited for the throbbing in her head to stop.

It didn't, but gradually it became manageable. She sat up, cracked the window and smoked another. The first three months of benzo withdrawal were the worst. Most people stayed in bed resting but she didn't have that choice. She just had to roll with the punches and keep her eyes on the light.

She booted her Mac. There was an unsecured wireless connection, probably the pub's, and she piggybacked on that.

While she was waiting for the connection, she made a call to Sol Bowles at Her Majesty's Inspectorate of Prisons. It was a pay-for line. After getting through several recorded messages, a receptionist came on and told her Bowles was busy. She asked to be put through to his secretary and after a wait was told he would not be free. Then abruptly he came on the line.

She didn't offer any excuses for not having been in touch. She didn't want to sound fake. She apologised for troubling him, and asked him to go through with her the conditions Morgan had been held in.

She could tell right off from his tone that he thought they were both wasting their time.

"Go on. Talk me through it," she said.

"What, the strip search? The multiple visual confirmations? The thirty-foot walls with anti-grip paint? The security lighting and CCTV? The pressure sensors? And that's just the prison as a whole. The maximum security units are even tighter, cameras everywhere. Prisoners spend most of their time locked in their rooms, with repeated visual inspections through the day. Cell checks are frequent. Morgan has been on communication blackout for several years. They have detectors that can pick up mobiles or any electronic devices. Unless he's psychic he's not talked to anyone they don't know about." He was gathering steam. "If I put my prison inspector's hat on, I'd say there were issues with the way Belmarsh is run — a propensity to use excessive force when it comes to prisoner restraint, overcrowding obviously, inadequate recreational and educational facilities — but if you want to ask me whether a dying man could get out of that place, then no fucking way. It's impossible. Forget about it."

"Mouse's arse," she said.

"Sorry."

"Something Thomas said." She thanked Sol and they chatted for a bit about the old days until the talk ran

108

out on them, then after an embarrassed silence, they said their goodbyes and hung up.

Cat felt relieved that she would not have to bother her mind any longer with Houdini-like scenarios. Morgan, in person at least, was out of the frame. She clicked through to her personal emails. In among the spam and follow-ups from letting agents, one item pleased her. It was from "Rob Benzo". On the top margin was his forum avatar. It showed a cartoon Jack Nicholson from *One Flew Over the Cuckoo's Nest*. Next to it, some children's verse. They had started chatting on a site for trank survivors. He was meant to be cyber-buddying her through the withdrawal process. But things had quickly gone the other way. Rob had wanted to unburden himself and confide. It was his way of making her feel better about what she was going through, because what he'd gone through was so much worse. He was someone who'd had everything — a loving family, an involving job, true friends. But the tranks had sneaked in and pilfered the lot.

He had encouraged her to talk to him in ways she hadn't talked to anyone for years. Gratitude tumbled with affection, tumbled with reliance, tumbled with need.

Cat sensed he was shy with women. She'd asked to meet him, to make him smile, to buy him coffee, anything to give back a small portion of what she had taken from him. But he always refused. When she finally coaxed him onto a webcam, he had reminded her in appearance of a young priest. She had expected someone tough and streetwise, but his eyes were soft still, and tender. His face had the pallor of a scholar. He sat in such a way that she couldn't see his hair. From what she could make out it had thinned at the top, and looked unwashed. He had the air of a man with no pride or illusions left, except in his respect for the truth. That was the only condition he'd set on their friendship, that she never lie to him. She wasn't sure what drew her to these unworldly types, or them to her; Martin had been the first of them.

For a moment she caught her reflection in the screen. She didn't like what she saw and looked away. It was time to do some proper work. When her Mac came to life, she ran searches on the names of Delyth Moses and Nia Hopkins. She found that beyond Nia's YouTube clip, neither had any presence online. Same with Esyllt. The girls all seemed uncharacteristically antisocial for their age. She clicked onto Nia's YouTube site. There were no links to other sites the girl had used.

There was a screech of brakes outside. Cat raised her head. It was a local in a souped-up Mini. She watched the boy racer hunched now over his wheel, talking to a friend. Cat looked beyond the kids at the row of shops opposite. Two had been boarded over. The door of a travel agency displayed stickers for holiday companies, but the window had been whitened with cleaning fluid. A To Let sign hung there. Behind the shops stretched an area of public land, partly visible over the roofs. A group of youths slouched on a bench looking bored.

Cat went back to her Mac. She began running searches on Gwen Kyle, looking for more about the suicide of her foster-daughter. It had no obvious connection with what was happening, yet Kyle was involved in this, or felt she was.

Only one article from the right period came up, a page scanned from a local paper. The details of what had happened seemed as simple as they were sad. The piece reported that the girl had broken into a country train station about five miles from Kyle's cottage where she'd been living for two years, having moved there from a previous foster-family in Llanelli. It had been early morning. CCTV footage showed how she'd waited alone on the platform for half an hour, not moving. At ten to five a night train had entered the station at speed. Tilly had walked fast to the edge of the platform, then thrown herself in front of it. Cat winced. The article went on to say that it had taken three days to recover all the body parts. Kyle had returned immediately from the flat in Cardiff she used when working but had refused to answer any questions put to her by the reporter. The writer described her as "visibly upset" and mentioned that Kyle was known to have been a "devoted and caring foster-mother".

Clicking over to the newspaper's own website, Cat searched on "Gwen Kyle". Several pages were suggested. The first was the report of her foster-daughter's death, then a brief account of the funeral. The girl had been a promising singer and had won several local competitions. After the "tragedy", as the episode was described, Kyle had involved herself in a campaign to keep the local youth club open. A photograph showed her standing in front of an ugly grey concrete building, talking to a local councillor.

Kyle's involvement seemed to Cat like a classic displacement activity; she was sublimating and displaying her grief at the same time.

Cat bookmarked the page about the funeral, then called up the missing persons files on the PNC. Apart from a few teens that had disappeared, run away to Cardiff or London before resurfacing, there were no local cases that still remained open in the five years between Kyle's foster-daughter's suicide and the three current cases: Esyllt Tilkian, Nia Hopkins and Delyth Moses.

Cat sighed, fingers hesitating over the keyboard. Her history screamed at her not to do what she was about to do, but the case demanded otherwise. She made a canna roll-up, started to smoke, then began the next phase of her searches. She was looking for websites aimed at teenage depressives and potential suicides. There were a lot of them out there.

At the top of the Google list were responsible websites specifically aimed at parents and teachers. Young Minds, all pastel shades and informally blocky lettering, ran a service dedicated to counselling and advising children, teens, parents and professionals. There were links through to cosy public information notices issued by the NHS or semi-official bodies like EXIT. Concerned adults could sign up for a newsletter and an outreach programme. Another site, Battlefront, featured the subtitle, "You're already involved". Its "Teenage Suicide" page contained videos and messages of support, mostly from teens who had lost friends, family members. There were links to Bebo, Facebook,

Twitter, Myspace. It was earnest, dull, well-intentioned stuff.

Cat surveyed it then ignored it. She dug down through more sites, more pastel positivity, and soon started to get where she needed to be, the sites she knew would tell her the most, the ones she felt least prepared for. She would do it for Martin. Do it for her own past self.

These were created by the suicidal kids themselves. They had a more basic design layout, hinting at an underworld of suggestible teenagers reaching out to others from the privacy of their black-painted bedrooms, a network of emo kids. The format was always roughly the same: a black background with gothic lettering and morbid symbols — skulls, guttering candles, barbed-wire crowns. There was little sophistication here, no acknowledgement of advances in web design. This was like a trip along the internet's memory lane. She scrolled down — through all the advice about seeking help, through all the tributes to famous victims like Kurt Cobain and Lee McQueen — looking for links to the sites that offered practical information. "How to" pages for wannabe suicides.

These were more clinical, lacking the goth references of the previous webpages, but still basic, functional. They had no cosy public information notices issued by the NHS, no encouraging pastel colours, no chirpy think-positive crap. No names or contact info either. Cat guessed the sites had been set up on anonymous servers and wouldn't be easily traced back to individuals. On one page, teen suicide was referred to as "going to the happy place". The same unnamed author called it "catching a balloon". Cat flicked to another site. Again, the reference to suicide as catching a balloon.

She recalled the glittery shape in the pithead tunnel, near the shaft where Nia Hopkins's body was found, the glittery shape that had composed itself into a balloon as she had got closer. The balloon had jarred at the time, not fitting with the rest of the belongings. Maybe its being there was a sign of suicide, and so perhaps Thomas's theory was correct. Maybe they were dealing with a suicide ring in Tregaron, whether inspired by Bridgend or not.

She pushed on with her research. There were lists of drugs recommended as painless for suicide, techniques for obtaining them, links to online pharmacies that wouldn't ask questions. Most of the traditional techniques — hanging, drowning, jumping, weedkiller and bleach — were dismissed as uncertain and potentially agonising. The focus was on a completely painless death. For those sold on cutting "for that unbeatable look", it was suggested that blood-thinners like warfarin be taken and a bath of water used to assist flow. From the same site came "Click here for our top ten list of celebrity cutters".

Cat felt herself pulled back to that birthday night on the train, felt the icy air between the carriages blowing her hair back, sucking the breath from her lungs. Outside, the train lights flashing past, the blur of the tracks, that feeling that she could keep on falling for ever and never hit the ground. If she'd had access to the information on these sites, would she have tried again? Refined her methods? Did they simply help destined suicides to kill themselves more efficiently? Or did they push borderline cases over the edge?

Her synapses flinched with the trank need. Her mind was back on the train again. Back to the tranks. Back to the train. Christ, she was sick of it, sick of herself. She closed her eyes, then slowly opened them. She needed help. She picked up the phone to call Thomas, hesitated, put it down again. She wasn't ready to open up to Thomas. Would she ever be?

So instead she messaged Rob. Benzo Rob, rocksteady Rob.

He got back to her within seconds, inviting a call, and she Skyped him.

As before when she'd done this, she felt simultaneously shy but eager. Wanting to reveal herself, but to hide herself too. She canted the screen so the camera captured a side section of her face, like a teenager might drape a self-conscious fringe to cover some hated feature. She did not say anything at first. She knew he could tell by just looking at her what she was going through.

"That bad, eh?" There was that familiar hint of the confessor in his voice.

She nodded slowly.

"Headaches?"

"Yeah. All the time, pretty much."

"Insomnia?"

"No," she said, before correcting herself. "At least, not too bad."

"APOTS," he said. "All APOTS."

APOTS: trank speak for All Part Of The Syndrome.

"Yeah. Only there's my job. Investigating some suicides. Maybe suicides. We're not sure yet."

There was a break on the line before he spoke again, "You're a — what, social worker?"

She hadn't told him. "Nope. Cop."

"Fuck, that's heavy. They shouldn't get you doing that stuff. Not the way you are at the moment."

They chatted for a few minutes. Professional benzo-users comparing notes. After a while, Cat forgot some of her nerves. The headache was still there, but some of the blackness was going.

"Hey, you want to meet up?" Rob said. He'd never asked before.

She did a double-take, then said, "I can't." As far as she could remember, mentoring was meant to be a phone-only thing. The website where they'd met had a code of conduct governing mentoring and meetings were supposedly prohibited.

"It's your call. I don't want to weird you out. Just — I don't know, sometimes phone calls aren't enough. I know that's not what the rules say."

She thought about that. She did need more than a voice from a laptop. "It's not that," she deflected, "it's because I'm miles away. In the sticks."

"OK. Well, when you get back, and if you want, come over and see me, yeah? It's your call, no pressure."

"OK."

Things had moved on with Rob. He was the one pushing things forward now. Was it sympathy because

116

she looked — felt — so bad? Or did he want to see her for other reasons? Futures with Rob flitted stupidly around her mind: a big dark room with a big white bed that they shared; hooning trips up into the hills, gigs maybe. Kids maybe. So they could grow up and catch a balloon. Stop it, she told herself, you're thinking like a mad bitch. Witch's bitch.

She talked briefly then cut the call.

Again, she was alone.

She put on some Drake, smoked with the window open. The room had grown darker. She looked out, a mass of clouds were scudding slowly in from the hills. On the patch of public land the youths had disappeared. Cat's attention was drawn back to the street as the door of the craft shop was opened by a woman wearing a beige anorak. Just before the door swung shut behind her, the woman glanced quickly down the street, then did so again. Cat wondered what had caught her attention.

She swept her eyes in the same direction, caught a flicker of light. Between the row of shops and a freestanding post box, a figure was backing away. Cat watched him carefully now. He was about Thomas's height — maybe an inch taller — and was slipping something — a small object — inside his jacket. Had he been watching her as she smoked at the window? She felt unsettled. Was he watching her last night too, when she undressed? Anger came now, anger mixed with fear. She stared right at him. As he turned his head she saw a hatchet face, unnaturally pale. A stripe of white hair streaked the front of his head. She shivered.

Martin's unease now made sense. On the face of it, there hadn't been anything so odd about a man from Tregaron being seen in Cardiff. Wales wasn't so huge a place that coincidences like that couldn't happen. But now everything had changed. A voice inside screamed at her to go after him. To do it now.

She snatched up her keys and helmet, ran downstairs and to the door. In the yard, she dodged the bins, squeezed past a delivery lorry, scanned for him. A few yards down the road, the man was sliding into a battered black Rover. It was stretched and looked like the type of vehicle used in funeral cortèges several decades back. She jammed her bike keys into the ignition and fired up. Out on the street, she tucked behind a Saab that had moved out after the Rover. She drove carefully, staying out of sight, knowing that her damped engine wouldn't give her away.

The car headed for the edge of town. The road narrowed after a mile or so and wound through half-flooded fields. The Saab pulled into a farm cottage just before the stretch of council houses near to Martin's place. She slowed to avoid the Saab's back end, then accelerated again on the approach to the council houses. The black Rover was nowhere. Where the hell had it gone? Beyond the council houses, there was a small estate and she drove inside, checking the parked cars. Nothing. Damn. She made another circuit the other way, peering down the short driveways into the yards where some vehicles were parked in long grass and on bricks. Still no sign of the Rover. She had lost him.

118

Frustrated, she turned around, gunning the engine. Her fault for being too clever. Rule two when you're following someone is: Don't be seen. Rule one is: Don't lose the bastard.

She reached the short panhandle leading up to Martin's house, drove down it, looked for signs of life. An old Audi was parked outside — Martin's, she presumed. She squinted as a shape appeared, then disappeared just as quickly in a window upstairs. Cat edged the bike along the track, parked behind the Audi, stowed her helmet on the back of the bike. Her boots crunched on the wet gravel as she made her way to the porch door.

She rang the bell and waited.

Martin peered through the glass before opening. He looked as if he'd been lying down. His hair was sticking up and his shirt was buttoned at the top though not further down. He pulled it to. His mouth was set in a firm line.

Silently he led Cat through to the sitting room. The TV was on the news channel, a makeshift bed on the sofa in front. He stood still with his back to her, as if transfixed by something in the conservatory beyond. He seemed to be struggling to retain his composure.

"Do you want anything to drink?"

Cat smiled, shook her head. He shook his head, echoing her, a gesture that Cat remembered from their school days. On a Thursday afternoon all pupils were expected to participate in at least one extra-curricular activity. She and Martin had chosen the Debating Society. The topic was, "This House believes that the death penalty is a suitable punishment for murder". Martin had taken on one Young Tory, a rope-'em-high type, and ripped him to pieces, using that characteristic headshake of his as a way to patronise, to undermine. He had easily won the debate, perhaps his only success at that school, by playing on the innate compassion of the young. Cat wondered if he'd take to the theme with such fierce idealism now, if his own daughter turned up murdered. Would Martin still oppose the death penalty then? How little she knew of him. He was just a stranger with an old friend's name and mannerisms.

"You're sure you don't want a drink?"

It seemed important to him. "OK. Thanks. Water."

He went to the kitchen and she moved towards the golden afternoon light that just then burst through the rain clouds and flooded the window. He returned and motioned to Cat to sit down, then followed. Sat looking at his hands.

"You've heard about the second girl?" Cat asked softly.

Martin swallowed hard, as if to combat nausea. Cat watched him closely, waited for him to level out. "But Esyllt had nothing to do with the waitress. Or with Nia Hopkins."

"Maybe not. But there was a T-shirt of her college at the scene."

He flinched. "I heard."

"Obviously until it's tested we can't be sure it's hers, but likely it was."

120

He looked forlorn. "If she knew those girls, why hide it from me? They were loners, depressives, what would she be doing with girls like that?"

She said nothing. She didn't want to give Martin false hope, nor did she want to speculate until she was on firmer ground. She knew if this was suicide the fact that the girls might not really have known each other made no difference. Each would have had different, private reasons for doing what they did. Reasons that wouldn't make sense to anyone else. Reasons that might never be known with any certainty. One girl's death gave permission to the next to take her own life and so a cluster had formed.

But those thoughts were too harsh to look at directly. Too harsh to say out loud. She obfuscated, gesturing to the coffee table's spotless surface. "You're keeping it tidy in here. I'm rubbish at getting the housework done."

"Looking for things to do. Dusting is about my limit these days."

"This house believes in dusting."

He smiled, weakly. He had got the reference. This was her Martin still.

"Martin, you need to come clean with me. If you hold out on me, I'm going back to Cardiff."

He looked at her with those watery eyes. He was thinking of blanking her again, but after a moment, decided not to.

"OK," he said. "Whatever you want to know."

"Griff Morgan. Did Esyllt ever mention him?"

"The smuggler?"

She held his gaze. "Was she involved in a campaign to free him, anything like that?"

"No, definitely not. She never mentioned him. All her interests were musical."

"How did you get my number? It was an unlisted mobile."

"From someone who knows you, I wouldn't want to get them in trouble."

She let this go for the moment. She had half an idea who he had got the number from. She nodded noncommittally. "OK. So who the hell is white-stripe man? She cocked her head to the window. "I've just seen someone who fits his description in town. Give me everything you know about him."

"Well, it's what I said." He paused and Cat shifted her bodyweight, ready to get up and leave, but he stopped her with a hand. "It's what I said, plus Esyllt met him a few times."

"Here or in Cardiff?"

"Here. Tregaron."

"She met him. *And?*"

"And — I don't know. She wouldn't tell me anything. She met him, as far as I know, maybe two, three times, and that was it. But she changed after that. Became more private. Seemed as though she'd entered her own world. She wasn't as open with me."

"So you think he influenced her in some way, unhinged her?"

Martin put his hand to his mouth, eyes shut, nodded.

"And he had a very pale face? Sharp? Streak of white in his hair?"

"Yes."

"And Esyllt told you that she'd seen him in Cardiff? That's how you knew?"

"Yes. She seemed upset and I felt worried. That's when I contacted you."

"Do you know of anything at all that connects this man to the other girls?"

"No."

"Do you know anything else about him at all? Martin, if you hold back from me . . ."

"No, no. I don't know anything." He stopped abruptly, correcting himself. Showing he was on best behaviour. "His car is black — an old model, I think. I only saw him twice."

"OK. Thanks."

Cat sat upright. This man was perhaps more relevant than she'd realised. If Esyllt had been close to him, he would need speaking to and before he got too far away. "I've got to go." She rushed across the room, whipping out her bike keys at the same time. "I'll call you."

"Cat! What do you know?"

"Later," she said over her shoulder as she left the front door.

She was on her bike, down the drive, back onto the estate. She had to check again, be certain. She made another circuit of the estate, looking for the black Rover. In the rain the streets were almost empty. Up ahead of her a grey-haired man in an anorak emerged from the corner shop. One of his hands was gripping a carrier bag, the other extended to count his change. As he did so his lips moved, his head shaking. About fifty yards further on a black car pulled out into the road ahead of her. The same long shape as the Rover, funereal.

She slowed down, wiped her visor free of rain. Yes, definitely. *Christ. We're on*, she thought. Let's catch this bastard, bring him in, be home before nightfall. She smiled beneath her visor, at her luck in picking up the tail when she thought it had gone cold. She allowed the car to pull well ahead, then followed. He wouldn't slip her this time. He didn't even know she was there.

The Rover stayed on the street that ran through the centre of Tregaron, slowing down rather than stopping as it turned left at the T-junction onto the road to Lampeter. She let her quarry gain some distance on her before pulling out. About two miles from town the car's brake lights flared, brilliant red in the now grey light. She dropped back, feeding the driver more slack. Two miles beyond, the car slowed again, turning left onto a minor road, then almost immediately right.

Cat rode past, slowed down about a hundred yards beyond the turn-off. Parked her bike as close to the hedge as she could, running back just in time to see the car parking in front of a modern bungalow. She waited for her man to emerge. He didn't. The driver's door opened, and a short, overweight woman gradually climbed out. Her movements were slow, ponderous. She put both hands against her lower back, grimacing as she stretched.

"All right, all right!" the woman said.

She opened the Rover's back door. Two small, blonde girls emerged, both wearing navy blue sweaters over powder blue polo shirts and navy skirts. Each held a pink Hello Kitty rucksack, dragging them on the tarmac of the drive as they rushed to the front door.

"Wait! Mamgu has to get her keys out first!"

The woman spoke with the subtle hesitancy of someone for whom English was a second language. Cat walked up and asked in Welsh if she could speak to the woman's husband. She looked blank. Her husband was an oil-rig worker, she said, away for six weeks.

"A streak of white hair?" asked Cat, gesturing.

The woman shook her head, getting suspicious.

Cat jogged back to the bike, fishing her phone out of her pocket. Should she call Martin? Or prowl Tregaron again? The light was failing and any chance of success was vanishing with it. As she was hesitating over whether to call, her phone vibrated against her palm. Text message. She opened it: Kyle's name noted as the sender, an address and postcode, and an order: *Come over now.*

She'd wondered when she'd hear from Kyle. The dragon was in Tregaron. It was about time she felt its fire.

Gunning the bike into life, Cat headed back towards town, asking herself how she'd lost the Rover. Was it the withdrawal, dulling her instincts? She used to be good at this. But maybe the driver was good himself. She wasn't thinking properly, not concentrating.

The road back to Tregaron offered little interest, just the usual high banks that hid the fields and the occasional glimpses of cud-chewing cows peering curiously through gates. In the background hung the shadowy outline of the mountains. As she blinked, she caught a flickering of light. A bar of sunlight breaking through between the clouds perhaps, but as she looked up the clouds looked as implacable as ever.

The road narrowed. There was a flash of darkness in the top right-hand side of her visor. A shape. Moving fast.

She was on the thing before she could react. There was a double impact. A hard one, painful, across her chest. A second, an instant later across her helmet. Something possibly on her arm too, though maybe she only felt that later.

Her head spun under the blow. Her arm jerked involuntarily. The bike swerved. She attempted to correct, but it was too late. The wheels hit mud on the side of the road and lost grip. She hit the verge, ramped up it, fell. She smacked back hard onto the ground, helmet crunking onto the edge of the road. The bike plunged on into the hedgerow, revved a moment longer, then the engine cut.

Cat found herself lying on her side, arm twisted, feeling concussed despite the helmet. Her boot had somehow got tangled in the bike wheel and her foot had been pulled on into the hedge, so that she was lying head downwards into the road.

To get her helmet off, she had to sit up. Which meant freeing her foot. Which meant getting enough of a view to see what was caught. Which meant sitting up.

She was just noticing the smell of crushed nettle and long grass, when she heard an engine bark to life somewhere close. The sound neared, increased in volume. She looked towards it, saw a long black car moving fast towards her. Too fast to stop.

She was snared by her foot, trapped between the hedge and the road. Her face met the hedge wall. Sticks of elder and hazel blocked her movement. She flailed at the blank green wall, groped for a hold, found nothing. She could feel herself falling back, headfirst into the road. The Rover closed on her. Air and gravel rushed her head. She closed her eyes.

The car swerved aside into the mud and came to a stop. It idled a moment, then glided off down the road.

Basic biker know-how kicked in. Check limbs, check breaks. She started flexing her joints one by one. Everything hurt but nothing too intensely. Her foot was still caught, but that could wait. Next step, visuals. Check for wounds. She twisted round, trying to view herself. No blood that she could see. Her suit seemed to have held. Next step, remove the helmet, check for any blood injuries. She didn't think there was anything, but still.

She swore again, continuously, but quietly. Ran through her checks. Bones, joints, blood, head. Found a way to release her trapped leg. Everything hurt and her thigh hurt like hell, but nothing seemed broken. The worse thing was her nerves. She knew she'd been a second away from having her neck snapped on the lonely road.

She forced herself back through the hedgerow, and tugged her bike out onto the road. There was no question of trying to follow the Rover now. She looked at the bike. A few scratches, as with herself, but no real damage.

Had something been thrown from the car into her path? She looked but couldn't see anything, though there were fallen twigs and bits of branch dislodged by the wind lying everywhere. It would be next to impossible to prove what had happened had been deliberate, if indeed it had been.

She flipped up her visor, lit a cigarette, felt tender towards her scarred bike. The drizzle turned into light rain and her mind turned to Kyle. She woke the bike and rode slowly on. Everything inside her was trembling from shock.

As part of your trank withdrawals regime, very definitely not APOTS.

The road curved gently to the right. A café was tucked in off the road about two hundred yards after it straightened out again. She let the lorry in front pull away, and steered the bike off the road. She pulled up outside the café, a prefabricated hut grey as the sky. It would barely have registered on the radar of anyone who didn't know the area well and wasn't looking for it. Cat parked as close as she could to the entrance, making use of the roof's overhang to cover herself and the bike. She climbed off, walked in.

Inside, the air was a humid fug that steamed the windows and filled the lungs. The place held eight small tables but was empty, except for the frail-looking middle-aged couple behind the counter. She ordered a burger with fried onions, a cup of builder's tea, went to sit at one of the Formica-topped tables. Sitting hurt. When she stripped off that night, she knew she would have huge, livid bruises.

Large windows reached almost halfway down the front wall of the café, allowing her a clear view. All the time she watched the road outside. Few vehicles passed. No black Rovers. She kept an eye on the road as she ate her gristly burger, drank the harsh tea.

With every chew, every gulp, she tried to calm. She texted Rob: *Tell me I'm not mad.* A reply came back within a minute: *You're lovely, Cat. What's mad anyway?*

She grinned and felt better, calming down.

She had the Rover's registration plate and phoned it through to Cathays. They'd place it on the national Automatic Number Plate Recognition database and every ANPR-equipped camera and every police car would automatically flash through any sighting. If the Rover driver was an idiot, he'd be caught within an hour or two. If he wasn't an idiot, he'd have ditched his car.

Cat dropped her phone on the table and sat staring out at the road a while, monitoring the flow of traffic. After half an hour of no traffic except two tractors and no lethally inclined Rovers, she got back on her bike, and checked Kyle's postcode in the satnav. She felt all right about seeing Kyle. Cat knew she was in for a hard time of some sort, but she also felt they understood each other. And not because they were both tough women in a man's game. No, it ran deeper than that. Something ran deeper anyway, though Cat didn't know what, or quite how she knew it. But she planned to find out.

What do you do when fortune knocks?

No. That's not the question. You don't know who or what it is on the other side of that door, that Twitter handle. All you hear is the knock, the call, the invitation.

After all, it wasn't her who chose her voice, chose to make herself open to song in this way. That came from outside, from somewhere else.

She doesn't make a decision straight away, but he's asking to meet her, loves her voice, believes they can go places. And why wouldn't she believe that? Why wouldn't she say yes? If you don't open the door when you hear the knock, you'll never know who it was came a-knocking.

She gives herself time to make her decision, but the truth is her mind was made up from the first minute.

Her answer is: Yes.

CHAPTER
SEVEN

The turn-off to Kyle's place was just before the first sign that gave the town's name, black letters on a white background, the type that identified small towns and villages all over Wales. The lane snaked for minutes, hedgerows thickening, looming higher, closer. The place was well out of the town. The entrance, much narrower even than the lane, led up a small incline, a rough path mostly overgrown with long grasses. A strip of crushed vegetation tattooed by tyre marks was the only sign that anybody ever visited.

Cat followed the marks along the track. It seemed to wind around on itself. Anyone not absolutely sure that this was the right way would be tempted to give up on it long before they reached the end. On the left of the track a stone wall blocked any sight of what was on the other side; on the right, branches from a line of rowan trees reached out onto the path. She heard the scrape of branches on her helmet, flattened her body on the tank to avoid them. A quarter of a mile later the trees came to an end, a low stone wall taking over from the rowans.

She stopped the bike at the entrance, climbed off, feeling her muscles ache. She was stiffening up. She swung the heavy wooden five-bar gate inwards. A large barn was set well back from the gate. In its day it must have been for farm machinery but now, like so many old barns in Dyfed, it had been turned into a home. A sign of a depressed county being revived with out-of-town money? Depended on how you looked at it. Depended mostly, she guessed, on whether you liked the look of who came in.

A generous area around the barn had been stripped of grass, laid with tiny brown and cream stones. She could see no car anywhere. She parked the bike in the carport, pulled off her helmet, left it with the bike.

She crunched her way over to the front door. In the cold, grey afternoon the carriage lamp above already cast a patch of yellowish light over the gravel. She knocked on the dark wood, then, when that provoked no response, with the knocker, a brass hand that connected with a satisfying rap. She counted to twenty, knocked again. The door, when she pushed her shoulder against it, was firmly closed. There was no handle, just a smooth knob that slipped beneath her hand when she grasped it. She slapped her hand against the solid wood, pushed her foot against the bottom, more in irritation than with any belief that it would yield.

Was this Kyle's idea of a joke? Ordering her to come round even though Kyle herself was out, just to mess her about. Or maybe Kyle wanted her here because she didn't want her somewhere else?

She stepped back. The gravel crunched. Simultaneously there was another sound, like the crackling of paper, but louder. Cat turned quickly, expecting to see something. But the driveway was as deserted as it had been when she arrived. She followed the noise along the line of the house. The gravel was a feature all the way around, although at the back it tapered to a narrow strip. To the right, on the lawn, near the wall, a rotary clothes drier was empty but for a peg bag designed to look like a tuxedo. It swung on its own orbit in the wet breeze. Cat thought she must have heard the sound of the drier, spinning on its axis.

Beyond it stood a small stable block, its doors secured with rusted padlocks. It looked as if it was long out of use. Next to this a paddock, empty apart from tall weeds and grasses gently shifting in the damp breeze. Unlike the rest of the property this area appeared semi-derelict. On the near side stood a large shed bleeding light onto the grass. It looked like a DIY store unit, but about twice as big. A home office maybe. Cat moved towards the shed's light, came in close, knocked.

"Hello?"

She edged the door open, flooding the yard with the brightness of several spotlights. The shed seemed abnormally bright. She paused at the threshold, blinking.

Her eyes adjusted. The outhouse had been fitted, on both sides of the room, with long shelves at hip height. Neatly stacked on the right-hand side of the door were a dozen mottled grey box files, labelled from one to twelve. The desk on the left was less orderly, untidy stacks of cardboard folders spilling their loads onto its top. Two enormous cork noticeboards had been fitted to the walls, one each side of the door. Both were plastered with photos and newspaper clippings. Cat stepped closer. She took it in.

This seemed a themed space, like a shrine or trophy room. The story that ran through it was the hunt for Griff Morgan. Of course Kyle had been in on the bust that finally collared him at the marina. She had made damn sure of that. But now, looking at all the clippings going back many years, Cat saw that Kyle's interest in Morgan had long predated the bust.

The Morgan material on the cork boards was arranged roughly chronologically, starting with the sketchy details of his childhood. A journalist from *Bild* had managed to get hold of an alleged photograph of Morgan as a toddler, smiling shyly at the camera. The wealth of cuttings from around the world that covered the two noticeboards showed that Kyle's obsession had been shared by many others.

The one theme that leaped from the chaos of the material was that Morgan had been a businessman first to last, seeking the biggest margins and biggest market share. He had specialised in only those sectors that yielded the greatest profit: synthetics, crack cocaine, and heroin if margins were right. Almost every major seizure on the British mainland for the ten-year period prior to the bust had been ascribed to product being imported by his network, but until the bust itself no gang members had been apprehended.

She reached up, unpinned one bulky item that had been folded, smoothed it out. Taken from the News Review section of *The Sunday Times* it tied Morgan to

136

a number of North African Islamic organisations. The suggestion was that as violence had consumed his earlier hosts in South America, Morgan had built labs and airstrips in the Northern Sahara, closer to his home market. The cocaine had been landed at remote beaches in West Africa, then flown to bases to be processed, the precursor chemicals for the synthetics also flown up from small, failed African states; a cut of the end profits diverted back to the Islamic radicals. Yet the body of the text was merely a fine web of speculation and supposition with little fact to support its central thrust.

The stories went on, mutated. A later clump of cuttings hinted at Morgan, the criminal without political portfolio. This was a man who robbed security vans, high-end jewellers, banks. Increasingly Morgan seemed to have become a scapegoat for any serious criminal episode that remained unsolved. She noted that some of the crimes he had been accused of would have required him to be on different sides of the globe simultaneously. He had even been suspected for a time of being the Dusseldorf Ripper. A profile in the *Guardian* ridiculed the idea. It offered that Morgan was a man who had always acted for significant financial gain, something that he was unlikely to achieve raping teenage prostitutes.

Cat sighed, rubbed her hand over her eyes. Her concussion was still there, but not too bad. More a background buzziness than anything else, a buzziness that blurred into her withdrawal headache and merged with it. The bruising was worse. Her limbs felt too heavy, stiff.

Partially hidden by the box files, the edge of a porcelain picture frame poked out. Cat picked it up. The photo showed Kyle leading Morgan in cuffs to a police van, her face dourly professional. Probert, his black AR mask partly lifted, walked at Morgan's other elbow. Who knows how much willpower Kyle must have drawn on to keep the triumphant smile from her face? This was an original, not a press clipping. Some photographer must have been paid or leaned on to provide her with this memento of the collar of her career.

Under the photograph, a plastic folder contained two pages photocopied from *The Times*. The report started with a short reminder of the bust, a small photograph of Kyle with Morgan, similar to the one in the frame but taken from a slightly different perspective.

Cat remembered those days well. The London press pack had rolled into Wales en masse, stunned that Morgan had finally been arrested.

Some of the more patronising comments by the press had infuriated the local force. This *Times* report was less noxious than many, but a sense of amazement that a regional police force should have been instrumental in the arrest of an international criminal bubbled just under the surface. The main focus here, though, was the incineration of the haul from Penarth Marina.

Cat took the two pieces of paper, laid them out side by side, as they would have originally appeared in *The Times*. Down the far-right column of the right-hand page and the extreme left of the left-hand page a series of photos recorded the event. South Wales Police had invited the press to be present when Morgan's stash was destroyed. The first photos showed a large institutional building and a warehouse. She recognised it as part of the Queen Elizabeth Building near Heathrow. It was where most large drug hauls were incinerated.

Interior shots showed the sheer scale of the confiscated goods, the ten hollow kayaks, package after package wrapped tightly in transparent plastic, the cream-coloured tablets and powder showing through. At the far end of the room the incinerator was being tended by a figure in a silver, heat-resistant suit. Kyle and some of the coppers who had been present at Morgan's arrest stood by, watching as the parcels were piled up by the incinerator, an industrial oven with a reinforced glass door, behind which the flames bulged.

The last pictures showed the line-up of Kyle and the policemen, faces hidden by protective goggles and masks, watching as the packages were fed to the fire.

The next page showed operational details of the bust, with black-and-white diagrams of the sequence of events. After the first ten canoes had been placed on the deck and tarped over, the four men stayed on the boat and the cruiser had disappeared for three hours. The men had then returned to collect the ten remaining canoes and an ambush by Kyle.

The bust had been the result of quick planning on Kyle's part. A security guard at Penarth Marina had noticed it was taking four men to carry canoes that would normally be light enough work for two. And though there was nothing strange about canoes in a marina, it was weird to see ten of them carried onto the deck of a motor cruiser. And at night. Suspicious, the security guard had called the operations room at Cathays Park, and then Kyle had taken control.

Kyle had got the security guard to lead her to the lock-up from where the first ten canoes had been removed. Inside, Kyle found the second ten. Opening one she had found it loaded with MDMA powder, the raw material used to make ecstasy pills.

Re-sealing the canoe, and knowing the men would be back to pick up the second half of their cargo, Kyle had summoned an Armed Response Unit — and lain in wait on the quay. She couldn't afford to delay anything further, because the first load of drugs had already been shipped and she couldn't yet risk sending teams out to search for it, in case those search teams inadvertently let Morgan's gang know the police were on to them, in which case they'd just disappear into the night.

So Kyle had laid her trap and kept to her plan. Cat could only imagine the tension there must have been in Kyle's team that night. Silent, watching, as wired as hell.

Cat put the article back, moved to return the picture frame. The frame tottered, fell on its back as she put it down. The noise it made wasn't loud, but in the emptiness of the shed it rang out. Cat swore under her breath, set it upright again, then froze. Alongside the rhythmical creak of the rotary drier, she could hear the crunch of gravel. Footsteps. Nothing was visible in her sight-line. As she listened she heard something else too. A human cry? A cry of pain? Or just a bird howling somewhere in the low woods beyond the house?

Cat stepped out, closing the door of the shed behind her. If she bumped into Kyle, she'd pretend not to have seen her little shrine. She'd say she'd been knocking on the back door.

She walked to the back of the house and called out. There was no sign of anyone, but the back door was ajar. She pushed against it with the flat of her hand, felt a slight resistance as it caught on the mat. She stepped inside. The scale of the converted barn was impressive. Kyle had left the living space open to the roof. At the end of the room a mezzanine had been added, a screen made from clouded glass partitioning it from the lounge.

That room was sparsely furnished. Rugs occupied small sections of the varnished oak floor, leather sofas and matching armchairs were arranged around a low table, a glass top resting on struts leading off a single spine, like the carcass of some extinct creature. Four enormous windows topped off with stained glass stretched along the length of the room, making the space look as though it might once have been a church, rather than a barn.

Cat called again. Still nobody around. No sounds. She walked through the living room, bearing left under the mezzanine floor. There were three closed doors along the wall.

She hesitated a moment. Why was she here? She'd been ordered to come, yes, but if that was the limit of it, she'd have done what any cop would have done: called for instructions. She wouldn't have entered the shed, wouldn't have entered the house. Truth was, she wanted to know more about Kyle, more about why Kyle had let her fly off to Tregaron, then turned up there so speedily herself.

Out in the middle of the room, she called out, "Hello? Ma'am?"

The noise bounced a few times round the room, then lost itself in silence. So much the better. She'd come to where she was summoned, she'd entered, called out, got no response. All that was, give or take, acceptable behaviour.

Which meant it was time for a little initiative. She went to the little row of three doors, opened the first, took one step inside.

A bedroom. The beige curtains had been pulled over the window, leaving just a small strip where some murky daylight still struggled through from outside. Was this Tilly's old bedroom? It might be a guest room, it seemed so neutral. The beige curtains and cream walls seemed to suck any character from the room. Against the wall stood a matching wardrobe and desk, next to that a shelf containing a collection of silver ornaments. A dressing table with a triptych mirror had been placed at the far end, a stool in front of it. Some photos had been stuck into the mirror's frame.

Cat moved away from the door and took a closer look. Teen idols of a few years ago, official signed prints from the record companies. They gave the game way. This had once been Kyle's foster-daughter's room. Cat touched the surface of one. There was no irregularity in the texture of the card, meaning that it had probably been signed by computer. Cat had heard of the singer. He had started his own band, was trying to shed his manufactured, teen-idol image, replace it with a new indie sound, something less clean-cut.

The dressing table itself held little of interest, just a small set of brushes and a comb on a china tray. Cat stood, moved over towards the desk. Again, it was tidy. The room lacked the claustrophobic clutter, the yelpingly chaotic identity of normal teenage rooms, just as Nia Hopkins's and Esyllt Tilkian's rooms had done.

Perhaps Kyle had blitzed the room after Tilly's death, denuding it of the girls's things, so that it could function as a guest room, at the same time as a keep-house for some of Tilly's more precious things. Who could say? Only Kyle, and Cat certainly wasn't going to ask her.

From the desk, Cat picked up a stylised musical quaver on a pale wood base. A small plaque revealed that the prize for 2005 South-West Wales Schools Best Soprano (15–18 category) had been won by Tilly Booth. The metal quaver held no tarnish. Kyle still polished her foster-daughter's prizes, or more likely instructed a house-keeper to do so. Cat put the trophy back down, positioning it carefully so that it was in exactly the same place.

Cat thought about Nia's YouTube performance, Delyth's guitar, Esyllt's Urdd Eisteddfod victory, now Tilly's soprano award. There was too much music here. Too much music and too much dying.

Cat moved quietly out into the passage. Further down, a half-open door revealed a refectory table long enough to seat ten. She doubted Kyle had ever filled the table, she did not come across as the most gregarious type, the barn was her hideaway, not a drop-in pad. At the end of the room, high windows led onto a patio area. The cry came again, coming from that direction. This time she was sure: not a bird, not an animal of any sort. The cry was human and getting stronger.

The doors were closed. Cat pushed the lock in the handle down and slid the door open.

The patio covered an area separated from the garden by high fencing. An annexe — a small bungalow — had been built on the opposite side. A holiday let, most likely. This was where the sound had come from — was coming from. She could still hear it.

The annexe's back door faced the patio. The door was shut, but not locked. Inside it was darker, much darker than the main house, and damp, as if the place had been shut up for too long. On the right a door opened onto a small room containing two worn armchairs and a three-seater. A bulky TV sat on the floor, its plug resting in a coil to the side.

Ahead there was a corridor with a light flickering faintly. The door at the end was ajar. She pushed it further open. Different colours washed over the walls, magenta, a deep blue, then flesh tones, accompanied by low moans. She stepped hesitantly forward, expecting to see somebody in the room, her shoulder bumping against a storage unit that jutted out into the entrance.

There was nobody in the room. Six shelves stretched to the back, packed with reels of film in canisters. A matching unit stood on the right, though this held mostly film equipment, old cine projectors, a couple of rolled-up screens, a battered slide projector. Another stack of canisters poked out over the rim above the top shelf. A screen hung from a heavy-duty eye hook in the ceiling, stretched out tight with the help of a crude wooden batten that was partially visible through it.

On screen, a woman was being pinned down on a bed by two men, one gripping her shoulders while the other seized her flailing legs. The decor was sumptuous, the king-sized bed laid with exotic materials in intense colours so bright they hurt the eyes. The two men wore some semblance of historical Arabian dress. The woman was wearing a costume that evoked the seraglio, auburn hair escaping from an elaborate headdress. Her skin was so white under the lights that it was almost translucent.

Still holding her legs with one hand, the man standing at the foot of the bed took out a scimitar, cut through her jewelled top. The tip of the knife scratched her skin, creating a tiny bead of blood that slid slowly down her stomach. The two men shook with laughter. The woman struggled more vigorously. Her nipples stood out, deep pink against the pallor of her skin. Her captors looked across her body at each other. The pair twisted their arms, flipping the woman onto her stomach, the dominant male, the one who had cut off her top, ripped off her elaborate harem pants. He slapped her backside hard, a deep pink imprint appearing almost immediately. Her cries seemed authentic, the struggles now stripped of their previous theatricality.

Straddling her on the bed, the man was roughly parting her buttocks. Although it was becoming edgy, Cat knew this wasn't a filmed rape, because while the woman was struggling, there was something excessively dramatic in her resistance that signified she was an actress. But where was its audience? The film was playing to an empty room.

She found the power button for the projector and turned it off. The film died in a flicker of yellow light and warm celluloid. The room suddenly seemed quiet.

Too quiet. She spun around, but still started when she saw the figure standing behind her in the doorway. Probert. Kyle's muscle man. The expression on his face matched the man on the screen's: dispassionate, as if he was choosing a joint of beef at the butcher's.

He was barefoot, naked except for a pair of worn jeans. What had attracted Kyle to him was also quite obvious to Cat. He wasn't a bad height for a Welshman, maybe five ten, five eleven, and well proportioned, something she hadn't been quite so aware of when she had seen him in the pub with Kyle. He held her gaze, his expression giving nothing away.

"I got a text, telling me to come."

He didn't say anything, just stood there, the face as immovably sculpted as the body.

"I looked around, couldn't see anyone. Came out here."

"Heard you used to train at Walter's dojo," he finally said, dropping into a fighter's crouch. "In Shen Chuan."

"Not now, for fuck's sake," said Cat, thinking of her headache, her multiple bruises.

But Probert ignored her. He grinned, then lunged forward, knees bent, right arm shooting out straight, large hand like a spade, the left arm pulled back parallel with the right. He was squaring up, challenging her.

Cat groaned inwardly. She didn't want to play his game, didn't want to fight, didn't want to do anything other than get her shocked and battered muscles into a warm bath. Still, his behaviour was a threat. Instinctively, Cat stepped backwards to give herself room, to plant her stance, but pain seared through her leg. Some bruise she hadn't yet found out about.

Her right shoulder knocked against the metal shelving. Reels fell over, their metal canisters clattering loudly, startling her further.

She looked back at Probert. He was smiling now, getting off on her discomfort. Cat leaned away from the storage area, keeping her centre of balance, moving closer to him. She was ready to pounce. His arm darted out. God, he was quick. He grabbed her. And he was strong too, stronger even than he looked. He pulled her into him backwards, one arm tight around her neck, the other gripping her body, a hand finding her breast. She hated him for that, almost as much as she hated him for being quicker than her. He laughed quietly, puffs of air tickling her neck. He pulled in closer, rubbing his crotch against her. Cat twisted violently, ramming her elbow into his stomach. He gasped, released her.

Probert noticed Kyle before Cat did. He pulled away from Cat panting heavily. She straightened her clothes, trying to morph quickly into good subordinate officer. She waited for Kyle to fly off the handle — with her, with Probert, she didn't know. But Kyle said nothing. It was hard to read anything in her impassive face.

Cat coughed, rubbed her neck. "Ma'am," she said, as normally as she was able. "You asked for me."

"*Asked?*" said Probert loadedly, emphasising that an order was an order.

Kyle flicked her head sideways in Probert's direction, telling him to leave. He reacted immediately, showing Cat that rank marked their relationship, even at their holiday home. Probert sidled out of the room, careful not to brush against Kyle. Probert raised a hand to Cat, smiled boyishly, made his way down the passage.

Cat looked again at Kyle and Kyle implacably returned her gaze. Then the poker face cracked. It was a smile of sorts that came next to Kyle's face. "Pick your battles, Price."

It could have sounded like a warning, but to Cat it sounded like advice, sounded affectionate almost. It seemed that Kyle knew what Probert was and accepted it.

"I wasn't expecting that one," Cat said, with a half-grin.

Kyle nodded, but her expression had changed. She didn't look invincible, impenetrable any more. She nodded at the room around them.

148

"This used to be her den, you know. Tilly's. Now Mo uses it for his film archive." Those last two words were swaddled in invisible inverted commas, disapproving but — just about — accepting.

"Tilly's den."

"Yes."

"I'm sorry." Cat glanced, without meaning to, back in the direction of the room with its polished trophy and photographs. Then she stopped, forcing herself to look at something else, anything else, at the cabinet on the right. On one of the low shelves two film canisters were propped against the wall, both labelled: *Salo*. Cat wasn't a connoisseur of porn, but she knew about this: an Italian art house porn movie, which used scenes of extreme sado-masochism as a way of commenting about Italian fascism. Either that, or as a way to create nasty fantasies for the middle-aged male mind.

"Why do you put up with it?" Cat said gently.

Kyle moved her jaw, but said only, "Let's get coffee."

They walked back out across the patio into the main house. Cat sat in the kitchen while Kyle made coffee, bending over one of those complex Italian devices, all polished chrome and hissing steam.

They hardly spoke. Cat didn't nudge, just waited. Finally, the coffee was made and served. Cat didn't particularly want any, but took it anyway.

"I hear Esyllt Tilkian's father spoke to you," said Kyle at last. "He mentioned to Thomas there was a boyfriend he was worried about," she added.

"Not a boyfriend necessarily. Wrong sort of age, in theory. I'd guess he was someone she hung out with. Sex may not have been involved."

Kyle raised her eyebrows and Cat went on to explain what she had: the information from Tilkian, the sighting in Tregaron, the search for the Rover, her own experience in the lanes outside town.

"He tried to run you down?"

"I can't be sure, but it felt that way."

"You got the reg?"

"It's on the ANPR list. Bet he dumps the car though."

"You OK?"

Typical Kyle. Check the case first, then check the officer.

"Would have been more OK if your boyfriend hadn't decided he needed a workout."

Kyle grimaced at the word "boyfriend". Cat wondered about what kind of relationship they had, then decided she probably didn't want to know. But she didn't need to worry that Kyle would unburden herself.

"You checked Esyllt Tilkian's room?"

"Yes. Exceptionally tidy. Musical interests. No computer. We haven't found a computer for the Moses girl either. And — sorry, ma'am, but —"

"I know. The music thing. It's a connection, isn't it?"

Cat nodded. Kyle's grief was still present. You could feel it in the room, in the house. Maybe that's what Probert was: a coping strategy.

"Also," said Cat softly, "this is going to sound stupid, but did you hear about the graffiti found down in the cottage by the mine?" Kyle nodded slowly. "The reference to Morgan as the killer. I know it doesn't make any sense."

"No. No, it doesn't." Kyle's response, though, was thoughtful, not dismissive. "Some big-time prisoners find ways to get messages out. A lot of them still control networks from inside jail, so in principle he could still be paying someone to do his dirty work. But my understanding is that he was too closely monitored to communicate."

Cat said nothing. Her fears and suspicions still felt too confused and half-formed to share.

Then Kyle again: "How well do you know Tilkian?"

"Now? Hardly at all. Back when we were at school together, we were best mates." Cat stopped. Outside, the light was grey heading into dusk. It had stopped raining, but the wind was up and Cat could see the rowan trees on the drive thrash and bend under its force.

Kyle raised an eyebrow. "But he got in touch with you after all this time?"

"I know." Cat hesitated, then added softly, "We were close once. Not boyfriend-girlfriend close, but — well, as a teen I once tried to harm myself. Was about to do it. He stopped me. Physically held me back. I'm sorry, Gwen." Cat let herself use Kyle's first name. Anything else seemed inappropriate, given the context. For a moment, the two women just sat in the darkening room, remembering the past — what they might have done, and what had been done.

"Are you going to be OK on the bike? I can get a lift for you."

"I'll be fine."

"I want you back in Cardiff. We'll handle this the right way. By the book, using local officers."

Cat opened her mouth to object. Kyle herself wasn't local, after all — not local in an official capacity, at any rate, and had seemed happy to get involved. But technically she knew Kyle was right. Cathays was part of the South Wales Police. Tregaron was deep inside Dyfed-Powys, where South Wales had no reach. Still she was Kyle's subordinate, even off their territory, and so she would have to return.

"Yes, ma'am. But I'll stay in touch with DI Thomas. He's an old . . ." What? Friend? Colleague? He was more than the latter, but their relationship was too prickly to be the former. She opted for "colleague"; she didn't need to explain herself here.

She got up to go. Outside, with Kyle standing at the door watching, Cat made a roll-up and lit it. Smoking, she zipped her jacket up all the way to her neck, pulled her gloves on, held the cigarette clumsily between gloved fingers. Kyle still watching, Cat finished and stubbed it.

"Have a good trip back."

"Thanks."

"And sorry about —" Kyle jerked her thumb towards Probert's annex. "He can be an idiot."

Cat shrugged. "He's hardly the first."

"And at least you hit him back."

It was hard to tell, out there in the dark and the wind, but Cat was pretty sure she saw it, something few people in Cathays ever saw: Kyle smiling.

She works the letter up herself. It isn't hard for a smart kid with a laptop. She pastes on the school logo copied from the website, makes up an itinerary, prints it off. She fakes the head's signature.

Downstairs, her mother barely glances at it, just sighs, "Can't afford to send you on that."

If you stopped drinking, you could, she thinks. "Won't cost you nothing."

"It's 'anything'."

"School's paying. From the gifted and talented budget."

Of course her new fan had sent her the money, but her mother buys the line, seems pleased, in fact. Not pleased because her daughter is seen as gifted, but because she won't have to fork out for the trip. Plus the little precious will be out of the house for the weekend and she can stay in bed all day with her new man.

But she doesn't mind. She is going to see her new follower, and he believes in her.

He says he has a song in mind for her, that they can record it together.

He says he has his own studio.

She runs all the way to the train station, then dodges into the Ladies as soon as she arrives.

In the toilet cubicle she pulls out the long white dress he has sent her.

She follows his instructions. She paints her nails the colour he says, puts on purple eyeshadow, black mascara. She pulls the silver rings from her bag, slides them on her pale fingers, drops the outsized crucifix necklace over her head. She comes out of the cubicle, looks at herself in the mirror.

She looks, she thinks, like the most powerful witch in some secret coven. She isn't like the other lot at school. They are so shallow, such children.

The dress gives her maturity. Gives her something deep, something stately.

Her train isn't due yet, so she stays in the Ladies, adjusting her nails, checking her eyeshadow, but mostly gazing at herself in the greenish light of the overhead bulbs.

A graffiti behind her says, Vikki WLF Mikey ♥ ♥.

Such children.

She looks back at her reflection. The long hair. The flowing white dress. The red nails and dramatic eyes. She's not just a pretty face. She's in control. She's in this to win.

Even so, under the greenish light, she shudders.

CHAPTER
EIGHT

Cat kicked her bike into life. She was still weary as a dog, everything felt sore from the previous day, and she didn't fancy the long trek back to the coast, in foul winds and on wet roads. In her mind, like something half-glimpsed, hung the shadows of a theory about what was happening. Parts were clicking into logical patterns, but some stubbornly were not. Plus, there was something strange and new in her relationship with Kyle. There was something floating there, something not yet fixed down.

Cat pointed the bike towards the A48 and Swansea. She drove slowly, took it easy, watched the bends and watched the winds.

When she reached town the rain was getting heavier and the traffic was at a crawl. Going around two roads blocked by roadworks she closed on the pathologist's. It was housed in a former residential building with no parking for visitors without appointments, but she tucked her bike in among the vans at the back and walked around to the entrance.

A wooden desk separated visitors from the pathologist's secretary who, owing to recent cutbacks, doubled as a receptionist. The woman looked closer to sixty than fifty, close-cropped hair, overweight body tented by a dress with a brown leaf pattern. Her bespectacled eyes were focused on her computer screen, not looking up as Cat entered.

Cat flashed her warrant card, and asked for the report on the two dead bodies from the mine.

The secretary carried on typing then leaned on the desk, tapping her fingers on the wood as if she had no idea what Cat was talking about.

Cat wasn't in the mood for bullshit. "I'm working for DCI Kyle. Are there prelims on the cuts yet?"

The secretary called up a PDF, a form topped with the pathologist's letterhead. "They weren't done here, that's why I hadn't heard about them," she said.

"Cardiff?"

"Yes. They got passed up the chain."

"Any reason?"

"They don't need to file a reason." For the first time she looked directly at Cat, her face closed, not welcoming further questions. Behind the square, gold-rimmed frames, her eyes were bloodshot, weepy.

OK, fine. Cat would hoon back over to Cardiff. But first she had to make a call. Stepping out of earshot, she speed-dialled Thomas. He came on after a single ring and spoke before she did, anticipating what she wanted.

"Nada. I had the uniforms take the photofit of pale face round town. Nothing."

"Your guys are sure, are they?" Cat didn't ask if the uniforms had spent all the time they were supposed to be door-to-dooring in the pubs of Tregaron, but the implication was clear from her question.

"People do work up here, you know. If they didn't I'd fuck them off the force. They're sure. According to you, the bloke's got a whacking great white stripe in his hair. A few people have seen him around — enough that we can confirm he's been in town — but no one knows him. We don't have a name, which means he won't be local. The people we spoke to think he's probably English."

It was Thomas's turn to leave an implication hanging and Cat knew what it was. Tregaron was so deeply Welsh that locals there probably thought Cardiff was another country, Birmingham as far away as the moon. An "English accent" might just mean a boy from South Wales or the eastern side of Powys. In any case, Cat knew the CCTV was the more crucial avenue. You didn't need to bang on its door to ask it questions, and there was nothing it ever forgot. "And the Rover?"

"We're running back on the footage now. Car was definitely there when you say it was there. We're trying to build up a list of other dates."

"Check garages, yes?"

"I'm not thick, you know, Price." Thomas sounded bored now. The kind of bored that lived next door to angry.

"Yeah, I know. But Kyle may ask me. If you hold out on me, she'll think I'm doing the same to her."

"I told her this was a Dyfed-Powys matter and she could fuck right off."

"Fair enough."

"And as it was on my pitch, you should have come to me, not her, about the hit-and-run." He didn't say anything more, and Cat supposed that from his point of view, you could see it two ways. Maybe the guy with the white streak had tried to kill her. Maybe it was just one of those stupid motorbike things. More fool anyone who trusts themselves to two wheels on Tregaron mud. She didn't push it.

She sensed something more was coming, and waited.

"I had another chat with Nia Hopkins's brother Moose," he said.

"Oh, so you don't trust our interviewing now?"

"Not that. More I was curious to see what he'd say man to man."

"And?"

"He said Nia went to the mine to meet someone. He visited her there occasionally when she was on her own. An older person. That was all he said."

"That it?"

No answer. Just breathing down the phone. Then Thomas spoke into the silence. "He clammed up, wouldn't say any more. He had never met the person himself. It was just something he heard from Nia, so maybe she didn't tell him anything more." He paused. "I got the sense he's genuinely upset. He wanted to help, to know where we'd got to. He was giving it the full water works at the end."

"He's her brother. That's natural."

On the coffee table in the reception area lay a copy of that morning's *Echo*, which led with the story under the caption, *Death at Tregaron. The young of Wales mourn their dead.* It didn't take long for these journos to get stuck in.

Cat read on. The piece confirmed the identities of the two suspected suicides as Nia Hopkins and the "seasonal worker" Delyth Moses; no further details were given apart from their ages and educational accomplishments: decent in Nia's case, almost non-existent in Delyth's.

"You still there, Cat? Just like to breathe at me, do you?"

"I was reading."

"Very cultured. You off the case now? Kyle sent you home."

Cat thought about that. She hadn't exactly been on the case and hadn't exactly been pulled off. "Yes and no. She sent me home. But when I mentioned I might continue to liaise with you, she didn't actually object."

"Ha. You'll be lucky," said Thomas and signed off.

Again: not quite a no. She could get used to this way of working, maybe.

The journey east to Cardiff was slow, the traffic snarling up around Port Talbot. The rain was not letting up. Her withdrawal headache was back, drumming insistently. Around her the jammed drivers crouched over their dashboards, seemingly oblivious to each other. Five miles beyond the skeletal profile of the steelworks she turned off where she knew there was a transport café of the old school. To reach it she followed the A48 for a few minutes. The wording painted on the window read, *We're not posh — but we're cheap.*

A waitress goth with a nose ring brought her a plate heaped with sausages, baked beans and chips. At least

Cat still had an appetite. Almost every table was full, truck drivers mostly, but a couple of teenagers sat by the window happily feeding each other chips dipped in ketchup. She felt she was being watched. She looked around. Nothing. Probably just an old trucker letching her.

She considered what the pathologist's secretary had told her. She knew that there were many reasons why autopsies got passed up to Cardiff, ranging from staffing levels to resource management. But unnatural death cases — still a comparatively rare occurrence in Wales — were often handed direct to Cathays Park. She swilled the dregs of her tea in the mug. Leaving, she felt eyes on her again, and she hoped it was just an old road warrior imagining her topless in his cab.

She cruised for ten miles then pulled up at another hold-up, cars filtering into a single lane around a line of cones that snaked along the M4 for a while then disappeared, leaving no hint of their possible function. Once the traffic was in three lanes again she picked up speed, looked in her mirror, spotted a hulky blackness dart back into the lane she was in. She couldn't see it now, covered as it was by the lorry behind her. Reason told her the car couldn't really be white-streak's Rover. The ANPR database would have picked the vehicle up by now, if it was on the move.

She took the exit onto the A470 then merged onto the ramp for Cardiff and followed the traffic along the North Road, turning left onto College Road. Again a flash of black in her rear-view.

She pulled into one of the spaces that led vertically off the pavement. She looked around, checking, seeing nothing. The rain pelted down and showed no sign of stopping. There was something consistent, almost unnatural about the rate it fell, as if someone had left a shower running.

Cat walked to the end of College Road, turned into Museum Avenue. She glanced back again. No cars were following. On either side were the elegant pale stone neo-Classical buildings, the largest of which was City Hall. Less than a hundred yards along was the building that housed the pathologist.

Its entrance was at street level, lacking the imposing sweep of steps that gave the larger buildings a sense of grandeur. Inside it was as if a campaign of determined uglification had taken place, from the chipped melamine and chipboard table in the cramped waiting area to the scuffed plastic chairs. There was no sign of the receptionist. Cat heard the slam of a drawer, then Pugh's thin, ginger hair appeared as he rose up from behind the desk, puce bow tie slightly askew.

"Cat."

He came round and put a paternal hand on her shoulder. A soft, lopsided smile crept onto his face. He looked genuinely pleased to see her. It wasn't a reaction she was used to, particularly among colleagues.

She felt guilty now for not responding to his emails asking after her. She hoped he hadn't taken it badly. Cardiff was still a village socially, if geographically it was now a sprawl, and she'd known Emyr Pugh since she was a kid — he was an old boyfriend of her

163

mother's — and he seemed still to give her the latitude that emotionally developed adults give to children.

She followed him into a large, high-ceilinged room, tall windows offering a view of a flooded patch of garden. Most of the room was occupied at hip-height by glass cabinets that contained textbooks and bound periodicals. Displayed along the length of the polished surfaces there were objects made from twisted chicken wire. Some kind of sculpture collection. Two of the sculptures had been made into the shape of rudimentary vehicles, complete with a handle also made from wire. The others were human torsos, lacking heads or limbs, their stretched, elongated shapes reminiscent of Giacometti.

Pugh motioned at Cat to sit in one of the visitors' chairs. She turned her head to look at the wire sculptures. Pugh made a low, amused-sounding noise that seemed to come from his throat.

"My new hobby. I bought the two cars at a street market in Johannesburg on holiday. Thought, I can do that. Started me off. The rest I made myself."

"It's nice." Cat realised that she sounded as though she was questioning his taste. She wasn't. She was happy that Pugh was getting into something. After the death of his wife, he had gone into himself, picked up the drink again, which made Cat feel all the more guilty for having neglected him.

"Do you sculpt people you know?" She was trying too hard to be nice now. Pugh noticed the false note, and ignored the remark.

"So what can I do for you, Cat?"

164

"The bodies from the mine."

Pugh sat up straight in his chair. "It's not your case." His posture remained rigid. He held Cat's gaze, raised an eyebrow.

She paused, gave him a look that she knew he would understand. He still didn't move. Then slowly, "There's interest in this from high up, from Kyle?"

Cat nodded. She wasn't sure what Pugh really knew. In her head she counted the seconds. Ten passed before Pugh cocked a wry eyebrow, smiled and rose. Pugh motioned at her to follow. Behind his office, towards the back of the building, a door led off to the right. This was a more modest space, made smaller by the piles of folders that covered every surface. He locked the door behind them.

In the centre of the room there was a plain wooden table, on which a computer stood, a memory tower stored away underneath. He positioned the two chairs in front so that they could both see the screen, motioned to Cat to sit.

He waited for the computer to boot up then, with a few clicks, dragged three folders onto the desktop. He turned in his chair, looked hard at her, searched out her eyes.

"I'm going to make some tea. I'm going to be five minutes. Not fifteen. Not ten. Five. And you are not allowed to look inside those three folders. Is that perfectly clear?"

"Clearer than springwater."

"Milk, sugar?"

"Milk no sugar."

165

Pugh left the room, and Cat turned to the screen, clicking through to the folder with the first set of images of Nia Hopkins. One glance at the top photograph and she was back at the mine, the damp grass tearing under her feet, then inside, the clammy pull of the tunnel. A feeling she would happily never experience again. The first few shots were standard scene-of-crime pics of the body *in situ*, white markers pointing out the objects around it, the bottles, the deflated balloon.

Then, following these, came the pathology shots, close-ups of the body during the autopsy. She felt Pugh's consoling hand on her arm. Pictured on her back, Nia was pale against the stainless steel. Small discoloured patches showed up clearly, broken skin exposing pink flesh beneath. Cat looked closely at these marks, forced herself to take time before turning to the next shot. Worse than the one before. Nia's small breasts were damaged. Cat saw the variety of bruises; some were the bluish-purple of recent injuries, the others yellowish, older. Her flesh was also torn, small serrations defining the area around the nipples.

Cat made herself push on. She flicked through the list of jpegs until she came to the close-ups of Nia's hands. Most of her nails were long, square cut, French varnished, the tips polished to a gleaming white. Cat looked closely at the right hand. Two of the nails, her middle and ring fingernails, had been removed. A close-up of the index finger showed the nail broken neatly in half, framing raw flesh beneath.

166

She minimised Nia's folder, clicked on the file that contained the pictures of the second girl's body. Delyth Moses, the loner. Cat winced as she looked. This body was in a much worse state. The skin had darkened, it was difficult to see the exact nature of the injuries, even under the light of the autopsy table, which normally bleached all it illuminated. Cat zoomed in on a picture of the girl's back, stopping when she gained the clearest view. She could see multiple abrasions, patches of discoloured skin.

The next photos showed the frontal sections of the girl's body, exposing the damage done to her breasts. Cat noted the same serrations that she had seen on Nia's body, the remains of bruises giving the flesh a jaundiced appearance. The left nipple had been almost entirely severed. Cat looked away, exhaled heavily.

She turned back to the screen, opened the photographs of Delyth's hands. She noticed the same damage to the fingernails and that several were missing. At some point, Pugh had returned to the room. He put a cup of tea softly down by Cat. His face was closed, revealing nothing.

"Not pretty, is it?" he said.

She thought of the pictures published in the local papers, Nia Hopkins in school uniform. The shy smile to the camera. She shut that thought out, carried on. She used the mouse to flick through the autopsy shots again, ending on the final shot of the fingers stained with dried blood.

"Did you do rape kits?"

"Of course. Nothing. It looks like torture, pure and simple."

He took hold of the radio mouse, paged back to the close-ups of both girls' breasts. Pointed at the serrated scratches. "These are marks left by jump leads, so it seems the perpetrator used electricity on them. Look at the marks on the backs."

He clicked the mouse again, dragged the pictures so they appeared side by side. He pointed his finger at the discoloured, broken patches of skin. "Those are burns, electrical."

Cat met Pugh's gaze. "A pathological sadist?"

He pulled his mouth to one side.

"No?"

He shook his head. "This is not recreational torture. More likely someone was trying to extract information from the girls. With a sadist there is hysterical escalation in how the pain is applied, but this seems methodical. Whoever did this may have wanted to know something."

There was the sound of someone trying the door handle. Cat looked at Pugh. Knuckles tapped gently on the door. Cat minimised the files, stood up from the desk, found an empty coffee cup on one of the tables, clutched it. If anybody came in she was dropping in on an old friend for a brew. Nothing wrong with that. There was silence, then more knocking. They waited until they heard footsteps retreating. Cat hadn't been keeping an eye on the time, but she was already past her five minutes.

He clicked back to the first folder. "Toxicology prelims mostly showed nothing unusual internally. Except for this." He tapped the screen. "Methaqualone."

Methaqualone — ludes or Mandrax, the commonest street names — was a pharmaceutical sedative and muscle relaxant. Recreational use often took users to total blackout, with no recollection of events. Cat took in the information on screen. The lab's logo and contact details were at the top of the page. She looked carefully at the lists of blood, urine and hair tests. None of the more usual drug categories showed strongly positive. Some cannabinoids found in hair samples — the same would be true of countless young people — but the traces were not present in large quantities.

Cat was ready to pull back, having seen all the material she expected to, but Pugh had put a third folder on the desktop at the beginning. It sat ominously at the end of the row.

"This is?"

"You're the copper, Cat, you tell me."

She clicked the file and saw autopsy notes on the body of an unidentified girl found at a landfill site in Stratford, East London, a year previously. The body was in an advanced state of decomposition, but she could see why the trauma cross-referencing search had flagged it up. The pattern matched the mine bodies, even down to the serrations of the jump leads used on the breasts.

"That case was caught last year by one of the Met's North London Murder Squads," Pugh said, "and it remains open."

Cat checked the notes. The Met's investigation hadn't got far. The body had been found naked, but a tongue stud had led to a tattoo parlour in Tower Hamlets. The owner remembered fitting the item to a girl living nearby. A search of her room had turned up no real leads on her identity. She had paid her landlord in cash, had never given a real name. The flat had been thoroughly cleaned out, presumably by her assailants. Some cash and Mandrax were found under the floorboards, leading the team to suspect she was part of a drug gang. After that the trail had gone dead.

As Pugh shuffled uneasily, Cat clicked into the NCIS and the drug-related killings database. The information uploaded was the same but there were photographs of the drugs found. One of a transparent baggie with nine Mandrax in it, another a close-up of one of the pills.

She pulled the second image up to maximum size and stared at it silently. To Emyr she knew it looked just a plain white pill with a linear score in the centre where it could be broken. But Cat was trained to see more than that.

"Can I get a print of this?"

"Come on now, Cat."

"OK."

She stared hard, memorising the image, then closed everything up on the screen. She acted the zipping of her mouth. Pugh double-checked that the desktop was clear, shut the computer down then moved their chairs back into their previous positions. He exited first, making sure the coast was clear,

170

ushered Cat along the short passage to the waiting area. Behind her eyes, her mind felt tight and throbbing. They said goodbye.

The train comes.

She gets on, attracting glances. They don't even know what she's going to London for. They don't know the dream that is just beginning to tip over into reality.

She finds her seat. Headphones on. Listening to the song she's going to cover.

But today, unusually, she can't find focus. Can't get into it or anything else on her iPod. So she leaves the headphones on but stops the music. Wet fields slide past the window. Dripping trees, slow moving rivers, incurious cows.

Why can't she feel these things? The greatest day of her life. The start of everything.

The fields make way for industrial sheds and those new brick housing developments that look as though they've been clipped together from prefabricated parts.

She's been to London before, but not often. At the station, she looks for the cab rank and climbs into a taxi.

She tells the driver the address.

"You sure, love?" says the driver. "There's nothing down there." She's sure, yes. She says as much. His eyes catch her in his rear-view mirror. Friendly eyes.

As they get closer to their destination, she sees what he means. This isn't Soho. It isn't Notting Hill. It's not some cool backstreet full of indie film production companies and graphic designers. She falls silent.

Then the cab stops. She has clutched her money in her hand the whole way and the notes are sweaty. She peels one off. Gives him just a little more than the fare on the meter and says, in what she hopes is a jaunty way, "Keep the change."

CHAPTER
NINE

Cat saw Thomas before he saw her. He was standing in the drizzle by her bike, kicking his foot at the back wheel and smoking. As she got closer she smelt the booze on him and noticed how tired he looked and the sweat stains on his collar. She knew then he had already seen the pictures of the girls and they had got to him. She guessed he'd probably been in Cardiff when they'd spoken earlier, checking up on the pathology.

Thomas acknowledged her with a nod, but didn't seem to want to talk at first. He led the way back along Museum Avenue, making for Plas Sant Andreas and, beyond that, the strip of pubs on Salisbury Road. He went into the first they came to. Inside it had been modernised to attract a young crowd. The ceiling was high and some tables were arranged in front of long benches.

Thomas gave the place a disdainful look then headed straight to the bar. A sign over the bar offered "All-day Happy Hour" specials of cocktails and Bacardi Breezers. He motioned at Cat to get a seat. She ignored him, stood at his shoulder as he waited behind the line of punters that stretched along the bar.

Cat looked around. The modernising conversion had been a bodge and the place still looked tatty, with cracked plaster overhead and the mean, stained bar itself, retained to cut costs. And the new look had not been sufficient to see off the old crowd, the strip of all-day drinkers at the bar were young townie hard cases while silent older drinkers killed time alone in what nooks remained.

She carried the drinks over to a long table and Thomas flopped down beside her, pushing the change into his pocket. He picked up a beer mat, leaned it against another. "I'm thinking whatever bastard did this was not expecting us to find the bodies." She'd had the same thought herself. "A couple more days," Thomas continued, "and that whole place was due for inclusion in the army's target range. You saw the signs, it was getting blasted. We'd never have found them."

There was a scuffle and a bit of finger-pointing at the bar. A couple of lads got off their stools. Thomas turned abruptly, "Bloody lowlifes!"

A few faces scowled angrily at him from the bar.

Cat was surprised. Thomas was aggressive, but he usually managed to keep a lid on it. Their strange relationship meant she somehow enjoyed this. It made her feel more in control and it calmed her down. She picked up her bottled water and took a long sip, shook her head at him.

The drinking at the bar grew fiercer. Three youths in jeans and Cardiff City football tops were downing shots. They roared and slammed their glasses down, congratulating themselves and ordering another round.

Cat put her bottle back on the table. Thomas had shuffled along the padded bench until his thigh was squeezed against hers. This was a development; he had been relatively respectful in Tregaron, even though she had been on his patch. Cat thought his interest might have cooled. The pressure on her leg meant he'd just been hiding it better.

She ignored him. A shadow fell across them. Cat noticed that Thomas was already looking up at one of the football boys who had been taking shots at the bar.

"Pigs, aren't you?" said the kid.

Thomas stood up. He wasn't quite as tall, but the expression on his face made up for the imbalance.

"Your sort aren't welcome. There's no grasses here," the boy continued.

Thomas gave a short, sharp bark of laughter. "Do us a favour."

Thomas sidestepped the younger man's charge but left his foot in. The lad stumbled over it, fell against the table sending the drinks onto the floor. Thomas reached down, hauled the boy up by his scruff. The lad shot out a fist. Thomas pulled his head back, avoiding the blow. Anger and drink made his opponent's movements wild, uncontrolled, but Thomas was losing his cool too. He smacked the lad like he meant it. Cat glanced over to his friends, raised her eyebrows in caution.

She got between Thomas and the kid, gave him a chance to stop without losing face. He took it, knowing she'd saved him a kicking, but still puffing out his chest. He moved off with a theatrical show of reluctance.

"Idiot," she snapped at Thomas, steering him away from their table towards the door.

Out into the fresh air she waited until his breathing returned to something like normal. Then while he stood outside, she went back in and got water. He drank it without dispute. He knew he'd been out of order.

He said nothing, just looked at her with "oh yes?" eyes.

"Come on," she said, "I want you to see something."

She walked him round to the Drug Proactive Unit. Using her swipe card she went in at basement level. The car park was almost empty. There was no sign of Kyle's Subaru. That was good. Cat didn't feel like handling the strange dynamics of that particular relationship right at this moment.

She took the stairs up to the presentation room on the first floor, Thomas tramping heavily behind. As she had expected, the room was empty. She drew the blinds and flicked the lamp over the lectern. Next she stood over the terminal until the screen was projected on the wall.

She used the screen divide function. First she went into the NCIS file, and called up the data relating to the girl found on the landfill site. She found a photograph of one of the Mandrax pills recovered at the girl's flat and dragged it onto the screen, so it filled the left side of the wall. It loomed over the room like the image of a distant planet surface. Thomas, she could tell, was studying the image carefully.

178

"You want a quick Mandrax refresher?" she asked.

Thomas nodded. "Better had. Not really a big thing in Tregaron."

Cat went into the NCIS file on Mandrax and pulled up the video introduction they used in police drug training. The package was given by an academic from Berkeley. Period flavour was provided by a backdrop of West Coast discotheques and buggy cars. The basics were as she remembered. Mandrax — street name mandies or ludes — had been a popular prescription tranquilliser. Through the 1970s illegal use had been at epidemic proportions. Comprised of four parts Methaqualone, one part diphanhydramine, it had been a potent aphrodisiac and was highly addictive when smoked. Then in the early 1980s a number of deaths had triggered an international clamp-down. After Roche and the other manufacturers had agreed to cease production, supplies of the drug had dried up almost overnight.

The package ended with a picture of a grinning Roman Polanski. Before it had been banned, the drug had achieved notoriety when the director used it on a thirteen-year-old model he had sex with at a private Hollywood party.

"It's a street drug with a kind of retro feel, if that makes sense. It's got a sort of Beach Boys era California vibe, if you like. Most people, if they've heard of it at all, connect it with Roman Polanski."

"Right," Thomas said, his voice still slurred. "I remember all the jokes. What goes into thirteen twice and so on."

Cat clicked on the chart for Mandrax seizures in the last ten years. Each was shown on the map as a pill icon. In the margin were links to photographs of the drugs seized and persons charged.

"Notice anything?" Cat said.

"It's been creeping back."

"But not in any great volume."

She moved the arrow by date over each of the seizures. For the first five years the screen was blank. No seizures in the UK at all. Then the first seizure had been the million pills in the canoes at the marina bust of Morgan's gang. Six months later, twenty pills had been recovered after a rave raid in North London. There had been several small seizures the next month at club busts in Greenwich and the Manchester area. No one had been charged. After that the nine pills found at the dead girl's Tower Hamlets flat were logged. Several small seizures in single figures had followed, mainly at raves and festivals. Again, no one had been charged or cautioned.

She clicked over to the European chart. It was almost blank. There were a couple of isolated incidents at free parties, one in Hamburg, the other in Northern Italy. The police had only realised later what they had seized and no one had been arrested.

She went back to the UK map. "Notice anything about the timeline here?"

"Everything post-dates the Morgan bust."

"Yeah, but there's more."

She filled the screen with close-ups of all the pills seized. On the left side of the wall still hung the giant image of the Tower Hamlets pill. Part of Cat's job at the Drugs Proactive Unit was inputting this data. Her employers had reckoned that a cop fighting trank withdrawal shouldn't be given any task more taxing than computer bashing. They were right enough to think so but, though the work had been as boring as crap, she'd come to know her subject in a new way.

"Look at this," she commented.

"I'm not getting it," said Thomas.

"Look hard. They're all the same batch as Morgan's. Press, grain and scoring all match." She pulled up image after image, showing the tiny indications suggestive of identical manufacture. "The only difference is that the Tower Hamlets pills were wholes, the rest are halves."

Thomas sat forward, looking puzzled now. Cat did a quick search, and pulled up the press photos of the incineration of the drugs from the Morgan bust. They were the same pictures she had seen at Kyle's. She kept a link open to the footage of the bust itself.

"I know," she said, "it doesn't make sense. All the lab equipment that made Morgan's stash was destroyed after the bust. How can they be the same? We know the canoes were loaded at the lab then taken directly to the marina. No leakage. The million pills from the marina were destroyed following strictest protocols. They were counted and photographed by independent observers before being incinerated. None went sideways."

Thomas said nothing as he took in the implications of this.

To make her point, Cat magnified the shots of the incineration. They showed tests being done by independents on each package as it went into the incinerator. The drugs that had been seized were the same drugs that had been destroyed. Further interior shots showed the confiscated goods, all the packages clearly visible in transparent plastic. The cream-coloured tablets and powder showed through. Kyle and some of the coppers who had been present at Morgan's arrest stood by, watching as the parcels were counted, weighed then fed into the reinforced glass door of the incinerator.

"There is one other possible explanation," Cat said. "Remember that Kyle's marina bust only recovered half the drugs involved. The first ten canoes were never found, the drugs never located. Now, everyone assumed, and Morgan among others confirmed it, that the whole thing was basically about ecstasy, or MDMA to give it its proper name. There were well-attested reports of large amounts of MDMA coming onto the market at around that time, and no reports of any increase in Mandrax. So all the evidence pointed to the missing drugs — the stuff in the first ten canoes, in other words — as involving ecstasy and nothing else. We assumed that the Mandrax was just a side-show, an experiment — to test the market. If it had worked, they'd have made more. To be profitable they needed economy of scale, a real market out there for it and there wasn't one."

"But you're thinking maybe all that is wrong. Maybe some of those ten lost canoes were also Mandrax."

Cat brought the UK chart back, the pill icons showing the seizures.

"This pattern suggests small samples, freebies. Someone trying to build a market, but build a market on a *national* scale. They wouldn't be bothering to do that unless they had a lot to sell. Maybe there was Mandrax in the other canoes."

She knew Mandrax could not be wholesaled like Ecstasy. It was a less liquid asset. But the E market had been softening for a while. The Vietnamese gangs had been knocking out adulterated product at bargain-basement prices. Suppliers were looking for alternative product with better margins. Even if only half the canoes had been Mandrax and the sale price conservative, there was a potential net profit there of about twenty-five million.

She told Thomas the figure, and he did a double-take. He came alongside her and stared at the chart. Since the marina bust all the seizures had indeed been small and at raves, clubs and festivals. Whenever the police arrived everyone had dumped their drugs so at each incident there had been hundreds of different pills recovered and no arrests made. It was a pattern he was familiar with. Such events provided an environment where drugs could be tested while the larger suppliers stayed out of sight.

But none of this was necessarily helpful from a police perspective. There were thousands of people who had been at the clubs and raves where the seizures had taken place and many had given false IDs. Most were untraceable and there was no guarantee, even if they could locate suppliers, that they would know anything about the Tower Hamlets pills, the ones that connected to the three dead girls.

The same logic applied to the man who had escaped the bust, Morgan's soldier, Diamond Evans. He was the potential controller of distribution if not the distributor. He knew where the ten canoes had been hidden. Maybe he was the only person to know. But that didn't directly tie him to the Tower Hamlets pills or to the girls. Most likely he had lain low for six months then used proxies to handle the roll-out in the raves and clubs.

Cat pulled the NCIS file on Evans. It was another disappointment. There had been no confirmed sightings of Evans since the bust. There had been no reported sightings by informants. He had disappeared, probably overseas.

The database on Evans's known associates looked equally unpromising. Most were in prison, awaiting trial under strict conditions, or they were dead. Only one still seemed active, a middle-level wholesaler operating in London, a former associate of Morgan's called Hywel Small. One current address was given in Brentford. Unlike Evans, who had no prior convictions, Small had over twenty, all drug-related though none exactly major-league.

Thomas sighed. "We don't know Small and Evans have recent history. They're on the same tree but their branches may not cross."

Her head ached. "Small's all we've got."

She closed down the projectors and the screen went dark.

She went through it all once more in her mind. The only Mandrax seized in the last five years had been identical to Morgan's pills from the bust. The dead girl from Tower Hamlets had some in her flat. The two dead girls in the mine had a tox report heavy with Mandrax, most likely the same pills, as no other recent type was known. And then there was graffiti at the cottage near the mine identifying Morgan as the killer. It made no sense, but sometimes, Cat knew, the truth didn't.

The taxi drives off.

At first, she thinks there's nothing there. Nothing and no one. Just a former industrial street in a forgotten part of town.

Then she sees that someone is watching her. The gate that looks locked actually isn't. The patch of ragged ground beyond isn't empty. In front of what is — surely? — a derelict building, a man is standing. He looks smaller than she expected. Shy almost. Is that the right word? Or curious? Expectant?

She's not sure, but she knows what to do.

She smiles back. Tries to seem confident. She needs not to look like yet another teeny-bopper girl with delusions. So her smile is slow, considered, grave.

Her movements are the same. Slow. Authoritative.

The dress has a swing to it now. A purpose.

There's a little plop of understanding. About the song. The dress. The make-up. Even about this whole set-up, this choice of place.

There are depths to the song she hadn't understood. As though love always has to talk about its opposite: death. As though the two things go together, hand in hand, like lovers walking through a garden.

The man greets her with old-fashioned courtesy. She replies as well as she can, given how strange she's feeling. But

what's this? He lifts her hand and kisses it. Says, "Welcome."
And then again, "Welcome."

They walk inside. Ahead, in the dimness, she sees the halo of a spotlight.

CHAPTER
TEN

Outside, Thomas led the way through the wet down Fitzalan Place, Windsor Road. "My turn to show you something," he said. He walked almost wordlessly, grim-faced, over the railway line, left into the heart of Splott, and down Inchmarnock Street.

"There it is," he growled. His face was stretched, tense. She could see he was still itching for the fight he'd almost had. He was pointing to a house in the run-down terrace.

She noticed the tell-tale signs — the semi-jammed door, the furtive glance and quick steps past of a nervous potential visitor. outside were a couple of unshaven lookouts with sunken eyes, scarcely capable of seeing a double-decker bus, should one ever pull up.

It was a well-known crack house. The front door swung slowly open, and an attractive black lady wearing grey clothes and flowers walked out laughing. "Wake up, Bra. Mi soon come back wi' me VIP frens," she called to one of the lookouts, in the Tiger Bay Jamaican accent.

Cat held back, intrigued, watched Thomas approach the woman who smiled at him. She clearly knew him and Cat feared for a moment that Thomas had got himself a habit. But she dismissed the thought, Thomas was a drink man, through and through. He talked to the black woman, who nodded, beckoned Cat towards them. The woman turned around and began walking back into the house.

"Irene will get us in," he said.

"What have you told her?" she whispered.

"You've been locked out by your boyfriend and need somewhere to get your head together."

"Jesus! Couldn't you have done better than that?"

He smiled. "Fits perfect."

"Fuck off," she said.

The lookouts stood aside so they could pass. Cat knew in Splott, Grangetown and Ely, a crack house was not merely a marketplace: it was a home. Cocaine was invariably used, but not always sold by the occupiers, typically an ex-cocaine dealer and his girlfriend who had progressed from occasional use to heavy abuse. The fashionable sniffing culture that had first made a home for itself in after-hours clubs was dying out, and cocaine addiction had moved from the glamour professions to the lives of the mentally ill, the undomiciled and other cast-offs from the over-ground economy. It was the same old story.

Once inside, Cat recognised the familiar stench. Human odours mixed with garbage, crack freebase and unwashed floors. The empty entry hall retained signs of its former elegance: the marble floors were braided with yellow and red designs woven down the long passage. From the ceiling, gargoyles looked down with their mouths wide open. Only two sculpted faces remained;

190

the others had been replaced by cheap lightshades. In the corner were old appliances, partially stripped and shedding peels of lead paint. Remnants of alpine wallpaper hung from the walls.

To the right was a front room. A big colour TV auto-surfed its way through channels picked up by a coat-hanger antenna. Latex gloves, an empty container of cornstrarch, water bottles, a half-full Pepto Bismol and tourniquets covered the floor. A lost-looking girl smiled up at them.

To the left of the hall was another room. Mattresses and a ramshackle armchair sat on the bare linoleum. An old heating grate, removed from the wall, was waiting for someone to have the energy and motivation to sell it for scrap. A poster and broken clock adorned one wall, gazing Dali-like over a slough of candles, lighters, tin foil and empty Stella cans. A couple of wooden crates served as extra chairs.

"All right?" Thomas addressed a smartly dressed, balding, middle-aged man lounging on the armchair. White pills, some powdered, lay beside him in an ashtray

"Fine. I've seen you around, haven't I? Please."

He gestured at the mattresses. His accent was an unnerving mix of Manhattan and South Africa.

The man was jamming a blunt pencil against the base of copper gauze at the bottom of a glass tube. Satisfied, he took a smattering of the crack cocaine in his pocket, some ground powder from the ashtray and evenly distributed the mixture against the top part of gauze wire. Then, he methodically brought a lighter to it before once again commencing his approach to heaven and hell. A wild look took root in his eyes, as he delayed the exhalation of white smoke. The stench momentarily hung in the air.

Cat glanced at the window. For a moment she thought she'd seen a sharp, pale face peering in through the rain-spattered pane. It was gone now. All was dark. She shivered, looked back to the user in the armchair. He slouched catatonically backwards.

"This has to be the best smoke on God's earth — crack and good old-fashioned ludes."

"You selling?" asked Thomas.

The man looked at them blankly.

"Anyone selling ludes?" Thomas asked more softly. "We're gagging, man."

Thomas shot Cat a fierce, concealed glance. Her turn.

"They get you going," she added, pushing back her shoulders.

"These come from London," the man said.

"Is the bloke here now?" Thomas asked, leering.

The guy looked up, heavy-lidded, from Thomas to Cat, imagining things, no doubt. He loosened his mouth. "Nah. He only drops them once a week. Just a few."

"You've got a number?" asked Thomas, pushing it.

The man shook his head, went back to banging out the copper gauze. Thomas tried again. He clicked his fingers and murmured as if he knew the dealer in question and his name was on the tip of his tongue.

"He's a biker." The man glanced at Cat. He ran a hand down his face. She understood. It was a gesture common among bikers. The delivery man had kept his visor down.

They thanked the man, left him to his stupor, picked their way back through the detritus onto the rainy street. Cat glanced around, half-expecting to see the black Rover, the white face. There was nothing. She was tired, couldn't tell if they were getting closer or further away. She felt agitated, began to hurry down the dark street. Thomas caught up with her, put an arm on hers, showing her she was going too quickly, drawing attention. He was right, she'd forgotten herself. She slowed up, turned to look at Thomas. "Well?"

"Guy from Swansea I busted a few weeks ago had a Mandrax pill, said he'd got it here."

"But we don't have time to wait another week and begin tracing the distribution chain. That could take weeks, months even."

Thomas's phone was flashing. He looked at it, then passed it over so she could read the reports from the screen. A second search of the mine had turned up no signs of Esyllt. Nothing else of hers had been found at the abandoned pit house the girls had used as a den. But the lab test had confirmed the blood type on the T-shirt as matching Esyllt's.

Checks of phone records for Esyllt and Nia had turned up nothing useful. Neither phone had been switched on again since the girls had originally gone missing.

Cat clapped a wet palm to her aching head, thought of Martin, of the sort of wound that might never heal. She felt so old suddenly, like Methuselah.

"There's more," said Thomas gently.

Cat looked back at the screen, forced herself to focus on the next page. Matches had been run on their own initiative by the techies between the Mandrax traces on the two girls' bodies, traces at the cottage and those found at the dead girl's flat in Tower Hamlets. They had no other types to run against except the marina Mandrax, so it had been a one-stop cross-reference job. All were chemically identical to those from the marina bust.

Cat looked at Thomas. Her anguish must have been visible. "I know," he said softly. "I know."

With all the recent developments, the case had blurred and complicated. Cat's legs jellied, wanted to fold. She'd had enough. Nearly. Before she gave in, though, she raised herself for one more task. She called Martin, mercifully he did not answer. She left a message, hoping her voice did not sound as ragged as her hope felt.

"They've searched again and not found her body," she said. "We won't give up Martin, we won't. This house believes that." She omitted the details she had learned. Martin didn't need to know. He was probably getting no sleep as it was.

Cat hung up and she went with Thomas back to her Penarth flat. They ordered a take-away, which Cat only picked at. She watched Thomas glug the best part of two bottles of wine as she smoked canna in silence,

John Martyn trying to soothe from the iPod dock. Thomas talked about the case. The pictures of the girls were there when she closed her eyes. She felt weak, felt she might give in to anything. It was the sort of mood that made people throw themselves off trains.

This wasn't how she assumed it would be.

She's seen clips of studios. Abbey Road, that kind of place. Mixing consoles. Microphones. The live room for the vocalists. She always laughed about that. The "live" room. What are the other rooms called, then? Dead rooms? Dying ones?

So she said something. "This is it? I thought there'd be more . . . stuff?"

That got a laugh.

"Stuff? The stuff comes later. The first thing is to get the song right. No point in recording any old crap, is there?"

A friendly voice. Warm, in some ways. But controlling. You felt the power. Not someone you'd want to disobey or anger.

Is the room cold? It must be, though it's not particularly cold outside. Or perhaps it's nerves. The lights. The single spot and the empty stage. The moment. Anyhow, whatever the reason, she feels shaky. The whole place is ABFW. That was code she had with a couple of her friends at school. One of the ways they rated boys, parents, teachers. Lots of things were ABFW, but she's never felt anything quite like this.

"It's OK, is it?" she says, approaching the microphone. "It's all OK?"

She doesn't know what she means by that, but she's reassured by the answer.

"Yes, it's all OK. Just sing. That's all you have to do. Just sing."

ABFW: a bit fucking weird.

But singing is what she's here to do. She approaches the mic, starts to sing.

CHAPTER
ELEVEN

Just after dawn, Cat looked at Thomas's sleeping face: soft and almost childish without the bolshy carapace of the day.

She thought back to the night before. He had asked her and she had reached out, almost touched his hand. Loneliness and its antidote had clung to her but the thought of Rob had given her strength, she would stay clean of men for a while now. Certainly of this one.

She had got some bedding out, chucked it down on the sofa for Thomas then retreated to her bedroom. Now, this morning, she looked at him asleep on the sofa that was too short for him. Before she woke him, she decided to contact Rob.

Cat went to the kitchen and booted her Mac. She messaged Rob, knowing he was an early riser. He got straight back, and they opened up a Skype connection. Rob looked sleep-creased and wan. Next to him on the desk was a pot of tea. Cat didn't think about how to position herself for the camera, did not think about how she looked. She felt close enough to Rob that morning to show herself as she was.

"Thank you," said Cat.

"For what?" asked Rob, smiling anyway at the praise.

"You saved my arse last night."

"Huh? I was asleep."

"I was going to do something, then I thought of you and didn't do it."

"Benzies?"

"No, another type of drug." She guessed Rob would understand. "Just as bad, when taken at the wrong time."

"Want to tell me 'bout it?"

"Maybe. I'm coming to London. I'll look you up."

It was her turn to move the relationship forward. But before Rob could reply, she heard a grunt from the lounge, a morning belch. "Got to go, Rob," Cat said, ending the connection.

"Fuck's sake," she heard Thomas say from the sofa. "My back's killing me. Price? You there?"

"Coffee and aspirin?" she asked from the kitchen.

"That'll do."

They chatted. Thomas didn't seem annoyed about the rejection of the night before, probably expected it, or else couldn't remember. He was affable, in his way, seemed keen to get going.

As he pieced himself together, Cat ate and moved through an edited kata, some jabs and kicks, then they drove through the terraced streets parallel to the river. It was the route she had taken as a girl on her bicycle. After a while the terraces gave way to warehouses and out-of-town shops. She followed a road between disused lots to a house with blackened windows.

Cat told Thomas to wait in the car. Thomas's police-issue Mondeo would attract the wrong sort of attention where they were going, as would any of the unmarked cars she could have taken from the Cathays pound. A hire car was easily traceable. They needed something more discreet.

The lower part of the house was taken up with a workshop. She stepped inside. The close air was filled with the scents of oil and old leather. Along the walls were the carcasses of many bikes. In one corner she recognised Norton featherbed frames and Triumph engines waiting to be frankensteined into collectables. In the other there were trail bikes, Montessas and Puchs, their forks bent out where they had fallen hard from jumps.

She passed through the workshop and up the stairs into a small martial arts dojo, with an office in the corner. The man she had come to see, sensei Walter, was middle-aged with a gut on him, but he was taking on two hard-case teenage boys simultaneously. He wore the striped belt of a sandan, the colours faded. She suspected he could have reached the level of sayhun, but lack of outward ambition prevented him acquiring tokens that would mean nothing in his current surroundings. Walter saw her and his bearish face ignited with a smile. There were no words of greeting because one of his pupils flew at Walter then with a leg outstretched, and Walter stepped aside so the boy's own force flung him against the padded wall. When the second boy came forward with a chopping action, Walter grasped his wrist and flicked him down onto the mat. Cat walked around the edge of the dojo's matting towards the office. Walter shot Cat an "in a minute" smile.

Cat waited in the office. On the walls were pictures taken in the city of Kyoto, with Walter as a younger man in a dojo. Others were of the Sony plant in Bridgend and Walter as part of the cultural exchange programme which had traded rugby skills for martial arts. She sat on the desk and leafed through the local *Echo*. The lead story was still the release of Morgan on compassionate grounds. The picture showed a painfully thin man struggling up the steps of a large North London house. The docudrama at the marina would no doubt be released to coincide with his imminent death.

Walter had now dismissed his pupils and he entered, a towel around his neck and another as a turban. He was clearly pleased to see Cat. As a girl, the dojo had been her refuge and for a while he had tried to play a paternal role with her. He had taught her everything he knew.

"I can't stay long," she said, and she explained what she needed on the vehicle front.

Walter looked a little deflated. Maybe he was hoping it was a social visit. But his expression told her what she was asking would not be a problem. For a few minutes they talked about the past until the talk ran out on them.

Then Cat asked a question. "Remember Martin who came with me in the old days." Walter nodded. "He kept up at all?"

"He came in now and again, like you all do, when you want something, or when you're in trouble."

202

Cat nodded and smiled. Half of the screw-up kids in Cardiff had passed through Walter's dojo at one time or another. Walter could remember them all, their habits, bad and good, their birthdays even. "He was some big-shot games designer. Then his wife died. He came here to tell me that."

"He wanted your sympathy."

"Course. He was worrying about his daughter, he got all precious about her when his wife died. Said he was taking her out of the city, out to the sticks where she'd be safer."

"He lost it then, after his wife died?"

"A bit, maybe. Got stuck in his gloom," said Walter.

She couldn't picture someone as delicate as Martin looking after a young girl alone. She imagined it must have been a strain for him.

"Then he called a few days ago," Walter said. "He sounded in a right state. Said he needed your numbers. Something about his daughter going missing."

"You gave them to him?"

"Yes." He paused. "Knew you two used to be close."

She had told him never to give them out, but she wasn't going to call him on it. He had done the right thing. Cat said nothing, waited.

"She used to come by here when they lived in Cardiff, so he was just checking for her. I phoned around. Nobody had seen her." He paused. "Fancy a pot?"

Walter eyed his antique stoneware tea service, sitting delicately among the filth of his office like a nun in a flea market.

"Genmaicha. Always was your favourite," he said.

She told him she didn't have time, and left with keys to a Passat on EU plates. He told her it was on dealer's insurance, everything kosher, and the papers were in the glovebox. She'd take him for sushi as a thank-you when she got back.

"You must know him quite well, then," said Thomas as she pointed over the road at the Passat.

"Yes." Cat didn't answer further. What was Walter to her? A martial arts instructor, for sure. He had been that once, and still was in some way. But he was more than that. Had been from the first. A wise presence whenever her life seemed most certain to go off the rails. He had been that once too. The obvious thing would be to call him a father figure, only paternal relationships are messier than that.

They left the Mondeo at Walter's and she drove the first leg to Swindon fast while Thomas slept some more of it off beside her. She tracked Chill FM then slotted quiet tracks from Koop and Ghostland.

"What the fuck is this?" was the first thing Thomas said when he woke.

She didn't bother telling him. "Prefer MOR AOR, would you?"

"What?"

"Middle of the road, adult-orientated rock. Huey Lewis. REO Speedwagon. Nickleback. Classic *Top Gear* sounds."

"Better than this shit," he said, wafting a hand towards the stereo. "Sounds like a load of depressed aliens."

"That's not a bad description," Cat said, smiling.

When Thomas took his turn at the wheel he rifled her bag and put in Neil Young. That was probably the only thing she had that they both could handle. "Needle and the Damage Done".

At the end of the motorway they hit the tail of the rushhour, and at the Chiswick roundabout Cat took the wheel again. She had been biting her nails. She was going into the past again, this time not her friendship with Martin, but back to London, where she had run when Rhys, her first big love, had left her. She had not been so different to a lot of people who flee there to dissolve and remake themselves in its carnival of chances. And she *had* remade herself in London, enough to keep living, enough so that her heart had only walked with a limp.

She took the exit before Brentford. They had reached the mixed area of suburban streets and warehousing where the only connection to Evans and the Mandrax they had, Hywel Small, had his last known address. She knew they were pissing up a dark alley, but it was the only alley they had.

They pulled up a street short of Small's close. Thomas's anti-perspirant and the smell of his service-station coffee were getting to her, so she walked down to an open car park below the houses and did some breathing exercises from the Hatha. Thomas watched her from the car, wound down the window, called out, "Fucking Gandhi."

The breathing exercise helped a bit, but the air felt metallic and stale. What did she expect, it was London air. She waved Thomas out of the car, and he walked, chest first, straight over. She'd noticed that the end of the car park gave a clearer view up to Small's house. Thomas came alongside her, pointed at the two stone dragons either side of the entrance to Small's driveway. "At least he's still a patriot," he said.

Cat made no comment, looked at the two late-model SUVs outside the garage. "The door's been reinforced, Thomas."

"And the windows."

A delivery moped with a square carry box behind the seat was pulling in to Small's drive as another moped was just leaving.

"Busy, busy," said Thomas.

The arriving rider pushed a temperature-controlled pack through the letterbox then hurriedly rode off. Cat saw a dart of light as an upper window opened, probably a bedroom, saw a man lean out, survey the driveway as he smoked a large joint. He was in boxers and his hair was dishevelled, as if he had just got up. Behind him Cat glimpsed a poster of a Welsh dragon puffing smoke.

The whole set-up looked two-bit and this pissed Cat off. She knew the mopeds were not a good sign. They were suitable for local drops within a radius of a few miles. A dealer running a national Mandrax roll-out wouldn't use them. Cat felt a wave of depression trying to push its way through her headache.

Thomas moved back towards the car and Cat followed. They snugged in, watched another moped followed by a larger Parcelforce bike arrive in convoy.

Both riders waited by the letterbox, their intercoms crackling. They waited with their hands by the aperture of the letter box. Someone inside was pushing packets out to them without opening the door.

"Doubt he's our man," Thomas said, grimacing.

Cat pursed her lips, frowned. She knew this amount of traffic spelled a slack approach. Small probably wouldn't be taking these kinds of risks if he was holding real inventory.

"You can never tell with dealers, though, Thomas, some are born fuckwits. He could be sitting on a hundred kilos in there and still dealing like a child."

"*Could* be, Price, but I doubt it."

Heavy reggae leaked from the front of the house as the bikes pulled away. She could see from Thomas's expression that he regretted coming. Small might as well have stuck an ad in the Yellow Pages saying he was a dealer the way he was carrying on. Thomas was checking the other houses in the close for signs of a Met stake-out. He was sweating, his collar crumpled and stain-ringed. A few minutes later a larger Parcelforce bike returned and the courier went through the same routine at the letter box.

The previous packets had all been about A3 size and bulky, grass she reckoned. But this time, it looked smaller. That didn't mean much but she knew they were wasting their time staring at the door. Likely the same routine would continue all day and night. If they wanted any kind of progress they had to see where the packets were going.

She woke the car, followed the Parcelforce bike, staying a couple of cars behind. "The size of the pack he took," she said, "it's smaller. Samples maybe."

Thomas didn't look convinced. The bike continued along the North Circular and took the Golders Green exit. As they took the hill up to Hampstead, Cat glimpsed a chunky darkness in her rear-view, glanced again to see it was gone. Just another car on a busy road, she told herself, but this did not lessen the sense she had of being followed. Her head muzzed up to an ache. "Make me a roll-up," she asked Thomas, but he ignored her. His rapid blinking said he thought they were on a fool's errand.

At the top of Hampstead Hill, the Parcelforce bike made a circuit of the ponds. The biker was either lost or checking for tails. Cat carried on over to upper Heath Street. She listened for the drone of the bike and lost it momentarily, then it was back. She cut down the side of the heath after it. The bike drone began to falter. She saw it right-hook into a pleasant chestnut-tree-lined lane. She followed. The bike was moving slowly, then it stopped. Cat pulled up five cars short, tucked in out of sight.

For the first time they got a clear look at the man. The box on the back of his bike bore the characteristic red and white logo of Parcelforce. It looked genuine. His helmet with its air-filter gave him the appearance of an insect. He moved quickly across the road, bounced on the balls of his feet like an athlete preparing for the starting block.

Cat leaned across to take a closer look, shading her eyes and covering her face at the same time. "That bike looks a bit tasty for Parcelforce?"

Thomas sat back in his seat, looked across at her, said nothing.

"One of their guys moonlighting, you reckon? Or Small and co parasiting their system?"

Thomas flexed his lips non-committally and Cat took out her phone, called up Google, found Parcelforce's website. It offered information listing the courier company's services, coverage and prices. She typed "database of couriers" into the search box. The results page showed: "There are no matches for your search".

The redelivery section of the site featured a shot of a courier with a package standing next to a van, smiling as if he loved his job. He wore a high-vis orange tabard — he loved his tabard too — but his uniform underneath was similar to that of the biker.

Zoning in on the logo on the van on her phone, Cat then stared at the logo on the delivery box of the bike in front of her. She looked back at the screen. She pulled her head back, blinked. The curve of the stylised white globe on the Parcelforce website was clear, the lines of longitude and latitude sharp. The lines on the bike's logo seemed indistinguishable. The Parcelforce wording on the website's logo also had firm, clean lines. The letters on the logo on the bike's delivery box had been arranged identically, but the outline was not quite as clear. It lacked the straight edges seen on the website. She narrowed her eyes, it probably meant nothing.

She passed the phone to Thomas, pointed at the screen. "Have a look at the lettering."

Thomas looked, then across the road to the bike. It was beginning to rain again.

"The official logo is sharp. The lettering on the bike is a little fuzzier. Most people wouldn't notice the difference."

Thomas still didn't look convinced.

Cat took the phone back, logged into the DVLA database, keyed in the bike's registration number. There were two recorded keepers for the vehicle, Parcelforce originally and now a company called All Solutions Ltd. She saved the page, called up Company House's open-source database. All Solutions Ltd was newly formed, hadn't yet filed accounts. She scanned the names and addresses of the director and company secretary. The addresses were in Bayswater, an area that she knew for its rooming houses and residential hotels. The names — Mike Martin, Paul Johnson — looked generic. Fake. None of these details would get them anywhere.

Cat tapped the screen. "That reg is one of a fleet sold at auction last year."

"You'd think Parcelforce would have taken the liveries off before they pass them through?"

"My guess is whoever bought it copied in the logo again. Probably scanned it off the web and copied it. Maybe the scanning is why the focus isn't quite all there."

Cat scoped the street through the quickening rain. The houses were imposing Georgian and Victorian piles, most of which had been redeveloped from flats into houses, or had never been divided. Each property opened directly onto the street, although one or two were partially concealed behind hedges. They looked much like houses in any other inner-London suburb. But she knew that in this postcode they cost many times what an average person earned in their lifetime. The rich stuck together, paid over the odds to exclude the others. The street was quiet. Most of the owners would work long hours in the City, or else they'd be musicians and actors, still sleeping off a night in the clubs.

The biker was on the move. He'd climbed off his seat carrying a package. As he made his way across the street they could see the package was wrapped in midnight blue paper with silver stars. It looked innocuous, could be any birthday or wedding present, bought online, company-wrapped and couriered to cover up the embarrassment of a forgetful giver. The rider was heading for a white-painted house, a Meccano of scaffolding covering most of its front, raw stone walls visible on each side.

Behind the scaffolding, the rooms either side of the door appeared to jut forward, framing a Cape Dutch pediment. It was a seven-figure house maybe, and had just changed hands if the scaffolding and skip sat outside it told the usual story.

Cat watched the delivery rider make his way round the front. He went down a passageway along the side, disappeared. Cat and Thomas waited, neither spoke. After a couple of minutes the driver reappeared. Strangely, he was still clutching the parcel, its dark wrapping and silver stars clearly visible despite the now-sheeting rain. In fact, the parcel was all too visible. The rider was not even trying to shield it from the rain, holding it in plain sight.

Cat turned to Thomas. "Looks like he's been unable to make the delivery, but my guess is he's made a switch."

Thomas did not look surprised. "It's a nice spot for a drop. Nobody around in the day. Local residents loaded, a lot of courier deliveries from their online shopping. He fits right in."

They watched the driver reach his bike, begin to do his paperwork. They looked at the house: all was quiet. The view into the front room was limited, obscured by scaffolding. Little furniture was visible. Cat found the land registry site to check on the owners, keyed in the street address. She paid the small access fee with her debit card. The house was owned by a company registered in Panama. Cat punched the name into Google. It was mentioned on several sites with names like Overseas Property Dreams and seemed to be an international investment shell.

She showed the reference to Thomas. "These places get bought and sold as tax vehicles. My bet is whoever owns this place doesn't know what it's being used for."

He nodded. "They're hardly going to use an address traceable back to themselves."

212

The courier kicked his bike into life, made a U-turn then headed away. Cat slid out of her seat, winced slightly as she straightened up on the pavement. She had been so intent on the chase she'd forgotten her withdrawal. But now she noticed that all her limbs ached, the stress had brought the symptoms on again with a vengeance.

She stepped back into the cover of a spreading beech tree, glanced up and down the road. But there was nothing; the street was quiet still. About five houses down a silver Merc reversed onto the road, drove right past. Its driver, a middle-aged woman, studiously ignored them.

Cat leaned into the car and patted Thomas's arm. "Buzz me if anyone enters. I'm going in."

She made her way across the road to the house. With the withdrawal aches came thoughts of Martin. Images of their old friendship, the blood-stained T-shirt. Every step she took across the Hampstead street was guided by that blood. Suddenly everything felt clear and stark. The gusting wet brought with it the smell of damp foliage from the Heath, the sound of a large dog barking. Underlying everything was the habitual London understone of traffic, a sound that she guessed wouldn't be audible to a local, but that was agitating her now as though her head was stuck inside a hive.

She pushed on, entered the passageway that the delivery rider had taken. The high house wall cut out much of the light. The looming scaffolding gave it a weird, mechanical appearance. The plastic tarpaulins snapped and cracked in the wind, making her head hurt.

A slatted gate stopped her progress. She looked closely. There was a slight gap between gate and post. Cat teased a key into the gap, ran it up and down, found a catch and lifted it, pushed the gate open.

Beyond it was a small yard, empty apart from a green garden refuse bin. More scaffolding on the back of the house. Always the same with big London houses: you pay ten million and get a prison yard for a garden. She glanced around. There was no obvious drop-off. Cat lifted the lid of the bin, the smell of decaying vegetation filling the air. She sneezed, then looked again. At the back of the bin was a rectangular box, built into the container. It held only a pair of rusted secateurs. Nothing for it, she'd have to go fishing. She dipped her hand into the decaying grass beneath, could feel only slime and grit. She pushed down deeper, felt a hard object. She moved more of the grass aside and saw a package, lifted it out.

The pristine wrapping paper was now splattered with decaying compost. She opened it carefully without tearing the paper. Inside was a box, filled with used notes. She didn't count, but there looked to be about thirty thousand, mostly in twenties. She put everything back as she had found it, made her way out through the gate.

Just outside the house she stopped, had the sense of someone watching her. She glanced around, expecting to see a face. But there was nothing. The windows around her were now empty, if they hadn't been before.

214

Several streets away a child screamed, broke off into laughter. There was the faint buzz of a motorbike, a distant grinding on a gear change. She listened to its progress until she could hear it no more. She glanced up the street, saw a corner shop. Outside the shop were the usual hoardings advertising the lottery and that day's *Evening Standard*. Beyond that another street rose steeply, towering above the neighbourhood. She recognised the incline of its house fronts. Had she staked it out when she was in London? Or attended a private party there working undercover? She'd definitely seen the street before.

She struggled for clarity — and then it came. The front page of the *Echo* with that photo of a thin man struggling up the steps of a large Hampstead house. That was where she'd seen the street before.

Bloody hell. Her disenchantment with the Hywel Small trail evaporated. She bolted back across the road towards the car and jumped into the driver's seat. "You know where we are?"

Thomas raised a finger at the street sign that stood just ten yards from them. His way of saying, *Stupid question*.

She didn't care. The street name wasn't the point. "We're only a block from Morgan's house." She pointed.

For a moment, it all felt clear in her head. The murderer who couldn't have killed anyone. The victims who were nevertheless perfectly dead. A line of light bulbs shone: the graffiti in the cottage — the Mandrax traces there — the dead girl in the landfill and the

Mandrax found in her flat — the link to Diamond Evans and Hywel Small. And now to Morgan. For half a second, it was as though everything was there, as though the logic was all in place, just needing to be teased out.

Then the bulbs disappeared abruptly. She was plunged back into darkness as completely as if she had been in the mine tunnel. Nothing made sense any more except their immediate reality. She saw Thomas's forehead was corrugated in a frown. "He's not going to shit where he eats."

The stage is dark, but then a second spot clears a circle for her. A circle of light. A microphone.

An invitation.

She doesn't need to be asked. She finds herself stepping forward. In the long dress, the scarlet nails.

Again, from nowhere, that shudder.

What is there to be nervous of? In any case, she's practised this. She plays it cool.

"I'll sing some scales first, if you don't mind. Can you give me a middle C?"

The man has a tuning fork, a good one. The note sounds out, totally pure. It steadies her.

She warms her voice. Tripping up and down those scales. A few bars of simple songs. Stretching her voice. Loosening her vocal cords.

And then, all of a sudden it seems, she's ready.

She launches into the song. No, that's not right. She becomes the song. Sinks into it, and the song becomes her. One music, one light, one circle, one song.

She sings until the last note is completely finished. The sounds roll away down into the last recesses of this strange old building.

She notices for the first time that there are holes in the roof. Pigeons roosting above her.

She smiles. Pigeons! It's funny.

She asks, "How was it?"

But she already knows the answer. So does the man. His smile says what his words only later confirm.

"It was perfect!" he says. "Perfect."

CHAPTER
TWELVE

She pulled the seatbelt around her. "The drop's cash. My guess is he wants an eyeball."

Thomas smiled impassively. She started the car, following the satnav around the one-way system, down Well Road to the end, then left onto East Heath Street. The houses looked even bigger, most of them set back from the street. They might even have enough garden for a kick-about. They followed Heath Street until they reached the hill that formed Morgan's street.

They got out of the car, spotted a loose group of people hanging about in front of the house. Journalists, she realised, the remainder of the scrum that would have been camped out for Morgan's release on compassionate grounds, trying to get the last shot of Morgan before he died.

She looked down the hill towards the house where they had just found the cash. The way the roads were positioned meant she had a clear view to the back of the drop house, the one with the scaffolding. She glanced up at the edifice of the Morgan house; somebody in the upper storeys of that mansion would have a good view of the back yard, of the seemingly everyday garden-waste bin.

Things were coming together, pointing in the same direction. But this clear view from Morgan's house also meant she could have been spotted herself poking around in the bin. She wondered if this was the reason she had felt watched. Not from the house she was investigating maybe, but from up on the hill.

She felt angry with herself. She had moved too fast. She leaned back into the car, told Thomas to hop into the driver's seat, park it, and walk back towards her.

"Ma'am," he came back with, but he did it anyway.

She studied the Morgan house. It stood above the street and all the curtains were closed. In the stillness, with its black front door and black railings, the place seemed already in mourning for its owner. To the side, a gate gave onto a private parking area where three black saloons stood like a cortège in waiting.

She looked again at the journalists. They seemed dispirited, had the air of having given up on seeing Morgan. A couple were kicking a ball through the puddles. Another was huddled over his BlackBerry. Others were sitting on the terrace of the street's gastro pub, smoking as the sun peeked out hesitantly between the clouds.

Cat scrutinised the journalists outside the pub, her attention caught by a women sitting on a heavy wooden pub bench, sheltering beneath a large, designer umbrella. Beneath the curve of the umbrella, Cat gained a partial sight of her face: a taut profile, a mane of immaculately maintained black hair. The woman yawned, and stretched her arms up as she did so, the umbrella moving up in the same motion, showing Cat

220

the woman's whole face, sleek as a racehorse: a face that seemed accustomed to soak up glances.

Della Davies — Cat had last seen her following Morgan at the marina. In a former life Davies had been a press officer at Cathays Park. But then she had begun walking both sides of the street, making spare cash by running her own press agency on the side, handling stories with a Welsh connection. When the agency had taken off, Della had left the force, got herself a column in the paper, equipped herself with a Merc, a town house in Llandaff and a weekender in the Mumbles. Become a proper rich tart and a handful to deal with.

Cat dipped back close to the walls of the houses opposite Morgan's, out of the sight line of Davies. Her limbs ached again, the tick started up in her left temple. She tried to get a better look at who Davies was with.

Up close one noticed the twitching lines of determination around her pillowy lips, the loneliness behind the eyes. She was talking to a stocky mixed-race girl with a buzz cut. Perhaps a photographer. It made sense that Davies was here. Morgan was a national figure, but he was also a Welshman. Many of the press stories — the human interest ones, "Griff Morgan: the person I knew" — would link back to Wales. Davies's agency would be the first and easiest line of enquiry for most of the nationals. This was her chance to cash in.

Cat didn't like Della's life choices, but she couldn't hate her. After the Dinas case, Cat had gone up to Della's country house a few times, had even gone there with Thomas; the three of them tied together by a case that had screwed them all up. But then Della had stopped being so fragile, had got better; returned to her press agency, dredging up the misfortunes of others to make her own fortune. Della had returned to her venal game-playing and Cat had let things slip. She had not spoken to Della in three years.

Thomas hadn't yet noticed her, and was walking over to the pub, chest swaying as he crossed the road. Cat beckoned him to stand back, out of sight, nodding towards Davies beneath her umbrella.

"Fucking Davies," was Thomas's comment. "What now, Sherlock?"

In answer, Cat pointed almost directly upwards, to an open window in the building just to their left. The glass in the window was flickering, some of the meagre London light bouncing off something placed just inside, she guessed. The building was a large redbrick structure, a hostel or a student hall of residence maybe, and it was virtually opposite Morgan's. Thomas followed Cat's gesture, followed her logic, and grunted assent.

"Let's go," he said.

They took the few steps towards the entrance, palmed the hefty wooden door open, stepped into a hallway. On the stairs a couple of paparazzi types were loitering. They went past the boys, up the stairs.

The landings were all empty. They carried on until they came to the floor where Cat thought she had seen the lens flicker. They didn't need to speak now. Thomas gave the knock and pushed the door. By the window was a sallow boy in a Band of Horses T-shirt, his camera on a stand. Cat flashed him her card from the door so he wouldn't see the details.

"Out," she said, "there's been complaints."

Thomas stood over the boy as he picked up his camera, and when he'd gone, Thomas locked the latch. Cat looked for signs as to when the room's real occupant might be back. On one side a desk with built-in shelves reached to the window. The desk was a mess, papers and files piled in no apparent order on top of a scuffed laptop. Cat rifled the pile, found a nurse's timetable from the Royal Free Hospital. Parts were highlighted with marker. It looked like they had a few hours before the occupant returned.

It was a small space. The floor was covered in a cream carpet that had seen better days. On the fridge were a few basics: a kettle, teabags, a milk carton, a half-eaten packet of biscuits. The window gave a view down over the front of Morgan's house but with the curtains closed there wasn't much to see, beyond marvelling at its scale.

Cat scanned each window carefully. On the upper storey three of the curtains had been left with a small gap between them. She guessed this was deliberate. It allowed Morgan, or whoever was with him, to peer out without any movement that would attract the attentions of those outside. In the rooms where the curtains were parted the lights were out and nothing was visible.

"We need the binocs, Price. They're in the car."

She smiled. "Go and get them then, Thomas."

"You go," he said. "You're fitter than me."

"Let's toss."

Thomas agreed. Thomas lost. In the minutes he was away Cat studied the three windows but nothing moved.

With the binoculars only a little more was visible. A patch of wallpaper and something that might have been shelving in the first room. In the second there was more of the same wallpaper. In the third, a table was covered with dusty antiques magazines.

Cat tried to seem calm and on the level, but she was nothing of the sort. They might just be wasting their time, watching empty windows. Her temples pulsed and twitched, as though some epileptic fly was caught under her skin. Her limbs felt lactic and cold. She couldn't bear it, and if she was like this, how was Martin? Worse, no doubt, exponentially worse, pacing his lonely house, sleep a stranger to him.

"Where are you at with Kyle?" asked Thomas.

"Honestly? I'm not really sure. She told me to get back to Cardiff, but somehow I don't think she wants me in that basement inputting data. Don't know why, but I get the feeling she's not going to kill me for this."

"No, I don't think she is."

There was something in Thomas's face which signalled that he was withholding. "What?" said Cat and then, when he showed no sign of answering, she gave him a swift chop to the upper arm, and said again, "What?"

"Fuck off." He rubbed his arm. "She called while I was back at the car — said something about how she knew you were with me. But she didn't sound pissed-off, not by her standards. She said it was all right as long as I had no objections. Of course, I *may* have objections."

Cat decided that he was telling the truth about Kyle's call, which meant that Kyle did want her involved. And that meant it had to be for personal reasons — because of her foster-daughter. But why pick Cat? Kyle had always indicated that she thought Cat a waste of space; now here she was making the opposite moves. Strange. Cat noted the issue and filed it for future thought.

Meanwhile, she took out her phone to call and reassure Martin. But she had no reassurance to give. They were out on a limb and she knew it. She went through to the answer machine, said what she could, knowing that Martin would hear the lack of hope in her voice. She had managed to fake a message the night before, but she felt worse now.

Thomas sat in a chair by the desk, picked at his fingernails. Cat steeled herself, re-focused on the watch. Another hour and she felt she had been staring at the three windows all her life. Letting Thomas take over she palmed out her phone and checked her mail. There were three messages from Rob — Benzo Rob, her mentor — asking if she was coming to see him, as she'd said she might. He asked her to give him notice if she did come over, so he could clean the flat, which just confirmed to her his shyness around women. Rob had left her an address in Battersea: "Brand Wharf". Must be one of those new blocks by the river, she thought. It was a fancier address than she'd expected for him.

As Thomas glassed the Morgan house, Cat stepped towards the window, peered down at the street, watched the movements of the journalists below. Some were already giving up for the day; others were milling about looking disconsolate. Cat knew it was a waiting game that could go on for weeks.

She saw Della had left the terrace of the pub. She was on the steps of the hostel now, smoking with the mixed-race girl. The girl was probably also using a room somewhere in the building. Cat had a better view of her now. She was wearing cut-off jeans and a khaki top and had the air of someone who'd knocked around on the streets. The girl followed Della to a waiting Jaguar, and Della turned and patted the girl's shoulder before getting in. Then the car moved off and the girl sauntered back towards the hostel. Cat saw her take the entrance stairs below and disappear from view, in through the front door, no doubt.

Moments later Cat heard the girl's boots on the stairs as she approached the room she was in. The steps neared, seemed to move away again. She guessed that the girl had climbed to the next floor. Then they heard footsteps in the corridor above them and a door opening. They waited, listened. A minute more and there was the sound of the same door locking, steps in the corridor above and on the stairway, then the girl surfaced on the entrance steps below, walked down to the pub. She was checking something in her hand, it didn't look like a phone.

Cat knew it was common practice for paparazzi to set up several cameras on a stationary target.

Sometimes they could be movement-triggered, but it looked as if the girl was keeping control from a handheld device.

Cat asked Thomas to keep an eye on the girl. Then she went upstairs and stood in the corridor. She couldn't hear anyone in the other rooms. The lock on the door was a basic Yale latch. After a short struggle with a credit card and Vaseline from her bag, she opened it. Not exactly a procedure taken straight from the manuals of acceptable police practice, but you couldn't have everything.

She locked the door from inside and leaned with her back against it until her breathing returned to something like normal.

The room had the same layout as theirs but didn't look as if it had been occupied. There was nothing on the shelves and the mattress was bare. By the window there were cameras on tripods, each focused on one of the three gaps in the curtains. Cat checked their memories but no pictures had been taken except some test shots to get the light and focus right.

She looked around to see if the girl had left anything else behind, but apart from some back-copies of the *Echo* and plastic cups the room was empty. It seemed a fair assumption that, if the girl had got nothing through the windows, then neither had the other paps. Apart from that picture of Morgan on the steps, there was no evidence he was even still in the house. Cat sat on the bed and tried to think clearly. She felt the sweat gathering under her collar and a mounting sense of futility. An image came to her mind of herself standing, feverish, outside a series of locked doors, and nothing behind them.

Quickly she leafed through the three back-copies of the *Echo* to see what angle Della had on the story. On each day Della had devoted her whole column to Morgan, but the contents seemed thin. Della was trying to build human interest around Morgan, but so little was known about his life that this had not proved easy.

The first column quoted interviews with unnamed inmates at Belmarsh. It seemed Morgan had been aloof with the staff and other prisoners, hardly talking to them. The second column was titled "Morgan's Lost Love": it claimed that early in Morgan's career there had been a fire on a yacht Morgan had been using as a drugs lab. Morgan's first girlfriend had perished in the blaze and he had never forgiven himself. Over the years the guilt had eaten away at him and he had ceased to care whether he lived or died. No sources or names were given. The story had the feel of a rumour rather than an account by credible witnesses. It was sloppy journalism.

In the third column there was a picture of an urban fox that Morgan had apparently fed from his bed in the hospital wing. This story was a joke, the journalistic equivalent of desperation. Della clearly had no real information on Morgan. She was waiting for the money shot like the rest of the pack.

Cat folded the papers, put them back as they had been, went over to the door. She stepped into the hallway outside the flat, heard footsteps coming towards her up the stairs, then laughter, two female voices talking. Shit. It sounded like Della and her snapper. Why hadn't Thomas called her when he'd seen them coming? She checked her pocket. No phone. She must have left it downstairs. Nerves and fatigue making her careless. Think quick, she told herself.

The flat was at the end of the corridor. Nowhere to go but forward. She mussed up her hair, coaxing it to hide some of her face, bowed her head and walked briskly forward.

The steps sounded close now. She looked down the dim, long hostel corridor, saw the mixed-race girl and behind her, clacking in her heels, Della carried some delicatessen bags from Hampstead High Street. Inside bottles clinked. Her car journey had clearly been a local one. Cat hardened herself, walked towards them, head bowed. They drew level, passed by each other. Cat exhaled. She'd made it.

Then, "Price." A throaty voice came from behind her. "Saw you outside the pub."

Cat turned, faced her head on.

Della was standing still, staring at her, the other girl by her side.

"Looking good, Cat," Della added. She passed the deli bags to the girl then tapped her hand against the girl's thigh, signalling she should go. The girl scowled but took her key out, walked by towards the room Cat had just left. Cat looked at Della, she was dressed more for cocktails than a stake-out. Her tight suede dress left little to the imagination. The corridor was filling with Della's scent, Rive Gauche mixed with menthols.

"Nice to see you getting out," Della said, her bared teeth gleaming like porcelain.

Cat was calm. Now she'd been caught, she didn't care, wondered why she'd been so furtive about her little break-in in the first place. It was nerves, that's all. The worst that Della could do was to try to milk the situation, use it on her later when she needed a favour. It was something she would have to live with. She'd lived with much worse.

The girl had entered the room, checked her gear. "It's all here, Del," she called back. Della smiled.

"All right, Del?" Cat asked, breaking her silence.

"Interested, are you? In my welfare, I mean? Thought you'd dropped me."

For a moment Della fixed Cat with her stare. But behind its confidence something like fear seemed to linger. Cat wondered what its source was. "Thought you'd be out in the Mumbles with Zeta-Jones, Della. Not like you to do the dog work yourself these days." Della declined to answer. Still the apprehension in her eyes. Cat pushed again: "So why are you here?"

Della regained her composure, smiled. "Maybe it's love," she said.

Della walked on, and Cat turned away, heard the door close and the women laughing. The sound of Della kicking off her heels. Back downstairs Cat found Thomas still crouching at the window looking bored. He didn't look up when she entered.

"She came back, the girl. With Davies," Thomas said.

"I know. I saw her."

"Your phone was here, though. Stupid ring tone you've got."

She was tired, couldn't even be bothered to bicker with Thomas.

"Davies caught you, then?"

"Yes," was all she said.

Cat felt time was running out. She uncovered the nurse's scuffed laptop from beneath the pile of papers on the desk, booted it. In the wireless section there was a list of a dozen networks within range. She suggested Thomas call his support and get addresses for each, see if any matched Morgan's.

When she brought back food from the pub, an all-day for Thomas and a tuna melt, she found he had got one address that matched. It was protected by a standard BT single-password, and using NetStumbler she sniffed out the internal IP. With a little further ingenuity — finding a working webmail address, calling for a password hint, making some guesses — she was in. She flicked through the web pages: no email accounts or messaging were being actively used. It seemed the only sites being accessed were wildlife and cancer charities. Morgan hadn't been long out of jail, but whoever else had had access to the network had been as cautious as he would have been. It had been said that, during his years on the run, Morgan had refused to own a mobile or a laptop, and had never used a phone.

The only bookmarked webpage she found was devoted to the urban fox. She smiled and wondered if Morgan had left it there as a taunt to the journalists, either suggesting that Morgan himself was as uncatchably sly as that animal or else as a joke aimed directly at Davies regarding the flimsiness of her recent column.

She lay back on the bed while Thomas continued to watch the window. Despite being alone together in a bedroom he wasn't trying any banter. He was sober after all. After her knockbacks she guessed he needed the buffer of drink before he tried again. Plus he was professional, in his way. She could think of plenty of coppers who'd be whining by now, blaming others for the wildness of the goose chase they were on. But not Thomas. He was bored, yes, and he was sullen, but he kept his eyes uncomplainingly on the Morgan house while she rested.

Taking three aspirins she half-closed her eyes, looked out of the window. The rooftops snaked up the hill. Some shimmered in the weak sunlight. Others were covered in plastic sheeting which billowed in the breeze. There was something hypnotic in the light and movement. Was this a dead end? Or were they one inch from a breakthrough?

Cat didn't know. She slept.

She comes round.

She feels awful, like after that night on the vodka with her friend. But worse. Much worse. What can she remember? She had done the song, sung it exactly as asked, looked right into the camera too. Then what?

She opens her eyes, looks down, thinks for a moment that she is falling as she sees some old flagstones directly beneath her. No, not falling, just facing downwards. She cannot move her head, it is held in some kind of hole.

Her arms won't move, nor her legs. She is strapped down onto some bench, her face looking down through a hole cut into it.

And what is that sound? She begins to hear a voice, singing the song that is her song, the song that brought her here. But it is not her voice. The same song but a different girl's voice. Because she is strapped down she cannot see that behind her, on a large screen, plays an image of the singer.

The girl on the screen is young, about the age of the girl strapped to the table. They have the same coloured hair. They sing the same song in the same way. They both wear the same white dresses, the same crucifix, the same ghostly make-up.

She cannot see it, but from behind her a figure approaches,

dressed in black. She smells rubber. There's a leap in her brain, which is like memory, but not quite.

There is a canister by the table she is strapped to. There is a mask attached to the canister. She does not know about the canister, cannot see it, but she feels the mask as it is fastened over her face.

She remembers now. This has happened before. It feels cold, a death mask. As before the bitter smoke fills her lungs.

She coughs. The convulsions start and she kicks uselessly against her straps. She might as well not bother. She hears laughter now. Soft laughter, like the sound of broken promises.

CHAPTER
THIRTEEN

Cat didn't know how long she'd slept when Thomas woke her.

She blinked herself awake, following his gaze out of the window. The scene was the same. Wet slates glistened. The plastic sheeting crackled in the breeze. But there was something else, too. He pointed, directing her still-tired eyes: a man was descending the scaffolding at the house where the cash-drop had been made by the courier. Cat began to blunder up, ready for the chase, but Thomas, grim-faced, passed her the binoculars first. She pointed and focused. She caught the man just as he was disappearing from her sightline. Pale, thin face. A streak of white hair.

They rushed out of the room, downstairs and outside, down the hill back to the scaffolded house. No sign of the man. He hadn't time to get away. Cat indicated the side passage and started to pant out something about her sliding-key trick, but Thomas was ahead of her. Ahead, and altogether more basic. A crashing blow from his boot burst the side-gate open.

The garden was empty, the same as before. Cat peered into the window. She couldn't see much, but what she saw wasn't promising. Thomas was ahead of her again. There was an iron gate at the back of the garden leading out into a little alley that serviced the backs of the gardens. The gate was unlatched, slightly open.

They ran through. No one there, but they could hear footsteps now, tracking away from them.

They hammered down the length of the slender passageway, came out into a building site. Still no one visible. Her breath was pounding in her ears. The area had been levelled and cleared, some old building demolished by speculators, no doubt, to fling up another seven-figure house. The reconstruction had not got far. Piles of breeze blocks and planks lay on one side and two cement mixers stood idle, one at either end next to bags of cement. They waited a moment and listened. Nothing.

Thomas started to explore one side of the site. She took the other. She wondered if Thomas believed her now, about the attempted hit-and-run. Perhaps he always had.

They moved more slowly, picked their way forwards, making for the far end of the demolished space. Thomas slipped on the edge of a pile of sand, hit his knee on a pile of timber. He let out a hiss of pain, but quietly. Cat didn't look round. A lane matching the one she had just run down headed off the far side of the building site. She peered down it, saw a man's coat just disappearing round the corner. She ran, but quietly.

"Fuck's sake," she heard Thomas say, but she couldn't hear him follow.

She grazed her hand on a wall as she raced down the passage, back onto the road much further down now, out of sight of the Morgan house and the waiting journos. The street started to get busy here. A small high street, filled with traffic and shoppers.

She saw the man — running, but running in a gentler way. The run of someone who thought he'd evaded any pursuit. Perhaps he didn't even know he had chasers. They'd been reasonably discreet.

Cat clocked his direction, his clothes, his appearance, then ducked down out of sight as she saw him turn. She guessed he was checking his trail. She gave him twenty seconds, keeping out of sight.

Then she rose carefully. He was walking forwards, calmly, up the high street. She followed. Next to a shop front, someone had put out the rubbish. Some cardboard boxing and a long roll of bubble wrap. She tore off the bubble wrap and jammed it up her coat. She was aiming to look pregnant, not fat. She took a hat out of her pocket and bundled her hair up into it, changing the shape of her face. Pale Face probably didn't have a clear fix on what she looked like and was hardly expecting to be pursued by a mother-to-be, apparently just a month or two from her due date.

She got close enough to the man to make pursuit easy, then settled into his slow walking rhythm. He stopped at a bus stop. She nipped into a Boots just beside it. She bought a lipstick — bright red, not her colour — a diet sandwich and a magazine on mothering. She applied the lipstick, keeping an eye outside all the time, checking that Pale Face was still waiting.

She checked her look in the mirror. She hardly recognised herself: scarlet lips, hair out of sight, bulging tummy. Even flushed cheeks — a combination of exertion and trank withdrawal but which looked every bit like the bloom of pregnancy.

She took her sandwich and her magazine and waited at the bus stop. Pale Face barely clocked her, just moved up so she could lean on the sloping bum-rests provided. She ate her sandwich, cradled her bubble-wrap tummy, read her mag.

When a bus came, Pale Face got on and so did she. She bought a ticket to the end of the line, took a seat on the bus as far from him as possible.

After a minute or so, she got a call. Thomas.

"Sorry, I fucking knackered my knee in there."

"No worries. You in the car?"

"Yep, you still on him?"

Cat gave the number of the bus and their direction and current location.

"You want to hand this over?"

He meant to the Metropolitan Police. Who would, to put it mildly, expect two Welsh coppers to hand over news of a major drugs deal taking place on their patch.

"No. Do you?"

"No."

"Then you better catch up as fast as you bloody can."

A minute went by. Not much conversation, just the odd bit of swearing from Thomas.

Then: "I'm flashing now. Is that you?"

She looked out of the back window of the bus. Thomas was two cars back, headlights flashing. She spoke quietly into the phone, confirming he was in position. She told him that she'd call and ring off as soon as Pale Face was off the bus.

Three stops later and he got up. She buried her nose in her magazine, staying put. He glanced down the bus, maybe checking on her, probably not. He got off. The bus closed its doors. Cat rang Thomas. Two rings, then cut the line. Thomas flashed again. He was onto the target now. No way Pale Face could guess Thomas was on him. Cat let the bus travel up the road for twenty seconds, then walked up to the driver, showed her warrant, told him to stop to let her off.

From there, it was simple. Thomas by car, her on foot. She ditched her bubble wrap and her mag, and, in constant phone contact, they tracked Pale Face to the opposite end of the heath from where they had started. The houses here were set back from the road behind high walls and hedges. The man entered the courtyard of a small mansion block that appeared more down at heel than its neighbours. Some tiles and brickwork had fallen from the facade, giving it a dilapidated air. Two rusting tricycles stood among weeds at the door like forgotten museum exhibits. Higher up some windows were broken. A tattered Anarchy flag fluttered from one. The building was likely a squat.

Thomas was outside, idling his engine, when Cat arrived.

"Candy from a fucking baby," he said, pleased with himself.

"You fell over," she reminded him. "He just walked away from you. Just *walked* away."

They argued mildly as they watched the building. A light flickered on the second-floor landing. Just as quickly it flickered off. No lights showed on the other floors. Cat made a quick three-quarters circuit of the building and could see no alternative entrances. Parked at the back there was an untaxed combi up on blocks but no Rover. She was sure he'd ditched it. But the Rover didn't matter. She juddered with adrenalin. They were closer. The London lead was not a dead end after all. There was a true line from Tregaron to where she stood, and the bastard was in his house. Suddenly she felt hopeful, imagined it possible she might be calling Martin with news other than of death. Her body did not ache, her temple did not tick. She made another roll-up to steady her for the next bit.

"He the guy that tried to run you down?" said Thomas, as she rolled.

"Yes."

"How do you want to play it?" Thomas meant: by the book or with a little more imagination.

"I think he's likely to resist arrest," said Cat coolly.

Thomas grinned: what he wanted to hear.

They stood under a tree. It started to rain. Cat smoked her roll-up, then made two more: one for her, one for Thomas. They didn't talk much, just smoked. Then there was a blur of movement behind the frosted glass in the front door. They chucked their roll-ups and went to the door. Cat bent over, pretending to fumble for a key as the door opened and one of the residents came out. A bearded Asian man. Thomas said, "Ta, mate," and held the door open. The guy looked at them, but said nothing, walked on towards the street.

Inside, the lifts didn't work so they took the stairs. On the second floor where she had seen the curtains moving there were only two doors. One had clearly not been opened for some time. Mail spewed out over the doormat. She gestured behind her at Thomas to be quiet. They both moved to the opposite door, leaned in close to listen, trying to pick up any noises from inside. Nothing. Just the distant sound of a dog barking.

"What's your plan?" said Thomas.

She shrugged. "Your boot, then a little Krav Maga?"

"Oh, I do like the sound of that, Price," he said, then stepped back, sighted himself, and delivered a smashing blow to the door about six inches in from the lock. The door frame was cheap pine, cut too thin. The lock was fine but the frame just collapsed. The door belted open, and rebounded hard back again, but they were in already.

The darkness slowed them up. The hall itself was normally lit — the movement they'd spotted from below must have come from here. But the flat beyond was totally dark. Blackout dark, not ordinary dark.

There was music somewhere, playing at very low volume. Cat had to strain her ears to make out what it was. "Karma Police" by Radiohead. The music was so subdued it might have been from headphones or another flat, but she sensed the source was close.

Thomas was about to yell again, but Cat raised a hand to shush him. As they moved into the flat proper, she felt the walls. They seemed thickened somehow, as if covered by some stiff material. She ran her fingers over it and felt the cones used to absorb echoes and block out sound in a recording studio. She whispered as much to Thomas.

"Why whisper? He must have heard us."

Cat mimed headphones. It was possible Pale Face really hadn't heard anything. The whole place was built against noise intrusion.

They felt their way on through the gloom. Cat put her phone into torch mode. It was poor light, but enough to navigate by. They found a door, soundproofed and heavy, but not locked. She moved it open, as softly as she could.

The new room that opened up was bigger, not as dark as the one before. A human figure loomed out of the darkness. Cat started, assumed her fighting stance, drew back her hand to strike. The figure did not move and she saw it was a statue. She peered closer, saw a papier mâché figure of Michael Jackson, a promotional item discarded from a tour. There were other statues ranged down the wall. The floor felt padded, multi-layered. More soundproofing. Cat wondered if it was cork for insulation.

They started to move forwards cautiously, when a door opened and the blue light of computer screens leaked out.

The man emerged from his booth — a recording room? A listening room? — but Thomas and Cat were on him straight away.

"You're under arrest, hands on your head, turn to your left, kneel down. Oops, too fucking slow."

Thomas spoke the first part deliberately fast and incomprehensible. There was nothing incomprehensible about the big Welsh fist that caught Pale Face on the ear and dropped him to the ground. Thomas's boot followed and Cat got in a blow of her own, before stopping it all. Violence sometimes felt good in prospect. It never did in practice. Already she wanted to rewind.

They dragged Pale Face into a chair. Found a light switch, snapped it on. The room was as she'd thought: a soundproofed recording studio, some tacky statues, a few signed posters.

Pale Face looked as Cat had been picturing him in memory, only smaller. Lesser. Cat was struck by how much older the man appeared close up. He wasn't yet middle-aged but his face already showed deep crow's feet and lines around his mouth. His wrists and neck were scrawnily thin. He sat there silent, un-moving, unnervingly calm. But they had him. She'd get it out of him, what he'd done to Esyllt.

Thomas stood by her side.

"Stay with him. I'll check the flat."

She did so. The windows had been taped with blackout blinds. The first room they'd walked through was set up like a police operations room, the walls covered with wipe boards, cork tiles containing photographs studded with brightly coloured map pins. She looked at the cork board over his shoulder, catching sight of a photograph she recognised: Nia Hopkins in her long white shift dress, arms lifted as though in the throes of some religious ecstasy.

Next to the photo of Nia was a photo of another teenage girl dressed entirely in black — black skirt, black jumper, black lipstick, black nails, clutching a guitar, head thrown back, no longer trying to communicate the meaning of the song to an audience, but lost in some private world. More photos of girls. How many were there?

Cat went back to Thomas and Pale Face.

"Take a look," she said and listened to Thomas stomping around the ops room. Pale Face wasn't doing much of anything except holding his head where Thomas had hit him.

Thomas came back, silently angry, barrelled forward and picked the man up by the neck of his jacket. The man stood passively; stayed passive as Thomas back-handed him hard across the face. Then again. The man took his punishment wordlessly, allowing Thomas complete control of the situation. His face said this was what he had been expecting.

Cat's own anger had long cooled. What mattered now was the case. She moved over to the desk. Except for the area nearest the window which contained a computer, its top was entirely covered with papers. Some of the papers were covered with spidery handwriting, although most were printouts from music websites. A stack of business cards — the logo: stylised crimson guitars dripping blood — announced Pale Face as "Paul Riley — Web Music Journalist". Two phone numbers and an email address followed.

"Riley?" said Thomas.

Riley nodded.

"Who the fuck are you? Where is Esyllt Tilkian?"

"Hey, aren't you forgetting something?" said Cat plaintively.

"Oh yes, and why the fuck did you try to kill my colleague here? That's my job."

Thomas gave him another slap.

"Sorry. I thought . . . It was a stupid thing to do. Sorry." The bruises were already rising fast on Riley's face, not that Cat was too upset about that, but his apology sounded almost genuine.

She wanted Thomas to stop hitting him, though, so she took control.

"Your name is Paul Riley?"

He nodded calmly.

"You are a music journalist?"

"I am."

"You write for — who exactly?"

"Freelance. Web-zines. Music mags. Whatever gigs I can get."

"OK. And you were in Tregaron recently?"

"You know I was."

"Don't get fucking lippy," said Cat. "Thomas here would like any excuse to rip your head off. Any excuse at all."

Riley nodded. His words were slurred because of the blows he'd taken to the mouth. "Sorry."

"Why were you in Tregaron? What was your fucking interest in Esyllt Tilkian? Or in me, if it comes to that?"

"Can I show you? Next door?"

Cat nodded. Shadowed closely by a brooding Thomas, they went to the ops room. Riley used a remote to turn on a ceiling projector. Jiggled a mouse to un-hibernate a PC.

"OK. The ultimate picture show," he said.

He clicked first to a YouTube page and let the video play. It was difficult to pinpoint exactly how old the woman in the video was, but she was several years older than Nia. Cat estimated early to mid twenties. She wore tight-fitting black jeans and a T-shirt embossed with the image of a vampire. She was standing on a small stage of which only a limited section was lit. She looked nervous, was massaging her left fist in her right hand.

"Lisa Marr," Riley said, his voice softer and more cultured than Cat had expected. "From Glasgow. She disappeared fourteen months ago."

Lisa Marr started to sing along to a backing track. Cat felt the jolt of recognition. She was performing Radiohead's "Street Spirit", just as Nia Hopkins had done. But Lisa was not enjoying the song, her hands were clenched with anxiety, her eyes fixed on the ceiling, a place, presumably, where she felt some salvation lay.

She was transported with the same intensity that Cat had noted in Nia Hopkins's performance. Her voice was heavily influenced by folk, Joni Mitchell maybe, a dash of Emmylou Harris. The performance area was cropped into a small circle by a spotlight, darkness at the margins.

Riley clicked on another link, another video, another performance of the same song, this time by a hippy chick with hair dyed magenta. She sang in an accent that sounded Eastern European. "Katie Tana," Riley said tonelessly. "From Croatia. Another wannabe. Lived around the East End. Disappeared a year ago."

The last girl was British and closer to Nia's age. Also, apparently, missing. The girl, Riley told them, was seventeen but she was tiny, looked tired, fragile. Her voice was thin and reedy, not pleasant to listen to. Her accent sounded Mancunian. Riley gave her name as Sara Armitage.

Thomas took the names they hadn't been aware of and called them through to the police database. He listened and, holding his hand over the mouthpiece, he said to Cat, "They check out."

She said, "The Croat girl, lived around the East End, she could be the body from the Stratford landfill. Do you want to order dental checks? DNA if we can sort it?"

Thomas followed her reasoning and nodded. He spent another few minutes on the phone. Riley sat dabbing at his face, trying to measure his injuries. Then Thomas was done.

"Now," said Riley, "Esyllt Tilkian, like the others, covered the track online." He took in the effect of his words. "She didn't use her own name," he explained. "*EasyT*, her handle."

Cat realised her mistake. She'd searched for Martin's daughter's web presence under her real name, had not thought to ask Martin if she had a nickname; not thought either to search for the song itself, to cross check her information that way. Stupid. A few years ago she'd have thought to do that, a few months ago maybe, but the trank withdrawal had dulled her brain. "What about Delyth Moses?" Cat asked before Riley had even booted Esyllt's online video clip.

"Delyth: *DeMo*. Her username."

"Fuck," said Cat, and Thomas glared at her, not, she guessed because he thought she'd failed, but because she was showing Riley her exasperation.

Thomas waded in, tried to put Riley on the back foot. "So, some girls sing the same bloody song. What cobblers have you made out of that?"

In answer, Riley stopped Esyllt's booting clip, called up a page captured from an online music encyclopaedia, the page's title "Street Spirit (Fade Out)". He slapped his hand against the wall, his eyes wide and staring as if his point was obvious. He was jubilant. Riley was taking control now and they were letting him.

No matter, Cat and Thomas still stood between him and the door.

"Thom Yorke, Radiohead's singer, has been quoted extensively about 'Street Spirit'," Riley went on, his voice challenging, insolent, a believer revealing sacred knowledge to the uninitiated. "He says that the song is about how no matter which way you play it, the devil always wins."

248

"How did you make these connections?" Cat's question.

"I knew one of the girls a little — Sara Armitage, the Manchester girl. Saw her at an open-mic night, kept in touch. Then she went missing. I happened to see the other YouTube videos. I think the site itself suggested the links. Then I pissed around seeing if there was any connection there."

"Then you thought, Let me see, what should I do with this information?" said Thomas. "Shall I go to the police and maybe save some lives? Or shall I fuck around trying to sell a story?"

"I don't make a lot. It was a big deal for me."

Thomas gave Riley another crunching open-handed slap then put his mouth up close to the man's ear. "I'm not going to hit you any more because Price here doesn't like it. But we don't like fucking journalists who leave girls to be killed because they're chasing a story."

Riley nodded. His earlier passive acceptance was starting to look worn now. He was hurting.

"What's your theory?" Cat's question. Quiet. Not aggressive because there was no need for aggression here. There had already been too much.

"OK. Have you ever heard of the Tartini Devil's Trill myth?"

Riley wasn't expecting an answer. He pulled up an image, a picture of the devil wearing a frockcoat and playing the violin. "Giuseppe Tartini. Eighteenth-century composer. Composed a piece for violin called the 'Devil's Trill Sonata'. Story is that Tartini had a dream in which the devil dictated the sonata to him. When it was first performed it was so ahead of its time, so technically demanding, that the story gained currency."

Thomas's scepticism was etched on his face. "And you think that 'Street Spirit' is like this 'Devil's Trill' thing. Like a curse."

"Yes."

"So the devil's killing girls, is he, for singing his song?" snarled Thomas.

"Not the devil, no," Riley answered. "One of his followers perhaps."

"What, someone like you?"

Riley looked at Thomas. "I was going after a story, yes. I should have talked to the police, yes. But in truth, I also thought you'd tell me to get lost. I mean: the Devil's Song, some missing girls, some YouTube clips? What would you have done with that?"

It was a fair point. Neither Thomas nor Cat felt like answering.

"I *did* speak to Esyllt. I told her about the disappearances. I told her to watch out. I gave her my mobile number and told her she could reach me at any time. She *was* more important than the story. I thought I could do both: help her, get the story."

Thomas and Cat exchanged looks.

"And running me over?"

"I panicked. I saw your bike following me around, thought *you* must have been *them*. Whoever *they* are. I'm sorry."

He seemed stupid, but genuine. Scared of another thumping from Thomas, but even he was losing the appetite.

"You're *sorry?*" Cat was incredulous. "You tried to kill me." She felt her feelings rising despite herself. Some late-release afterburn of shock.

"No! No, it wasn't that." Riley's face was working. Real anxiety now, nothing fake.

"Yes?" Cat felt herself hard-wound for action. She could see her next moves, feel them. The blow to the face, hard. Knocking the head back for a clean chop at the throat. She almost felt the actual shock of each impact. But she didn't move. Just said it again. "Yes?"

"When I saw you were trying to follow me, I assumed you were after the girl. Her or me. When I threw the branch, I meant to give you a shock. Same thing when I came back. I thought I'd zoom past your head, scare you off."

Riley didn't finish, but Cat remembered the mud on the side of the road. She'd lost control on it. He probably hadn't been in control when he came by. A bloody stupid manoeuvre, and it could easily have killed her, but she believed him.

She breathed out, releasing.

Final questions then. "And what were you doing an hour ago? And why? We know half the story already. If you lie about one single tiny detail, I swear to God we will arrest you right now. Conspiracy to murder."

Riley dabbed his swollen lips with his hand, playing for time, maybe, but also being careful.

"OK. There's another angle into all this: Griff Morgan. He's just been released from prison. He's holed up at home, terminal cancer, waiting to die."

Thomas and Cat exchanged glances. *That* name again. Cat experienced her light bulb moment, or a pallid echo of it anyway. The killer behind bars. The impossible murders. It was strange how often his name threaded its way into this whole thing.

"Go on." Thomas's command this time.

"There are photographers camped outside his house, trying to get a view of him. I was over there too. There's an empty building — big renovation job — scaffolding up the side. I thought I could get a view of it all from there."

"Why?"

"Because." Riley clicked on another file then hesitated. "A few years back there were rumours that Morgan had a girlfriend who also sang the song. Not long afterwards she died in some fire on a boat. Apparently Morgan was never the same after that." Cat remembered Della Davies's story from the papers she'd looked at in their stake-out.

Thomas groaned as if he'd already heard enough, but Riley continued.

"In the chatrooms there were rumours that after the girl's death some worker in a hotel Morgan was staying at heard the song playing over and over from his room. He went in the room, and there were all the girl's things out, as if she had just walked out of the room. But the room was empty, just the song playing over and over."

He caught their eyes.

"And the names? A version of that story's been in the press, but no names."

"No names. This was on chatrooms a good few years back. But when I looked — and I looked for hours — I couldn't find anything there any more." Riley shrugged.

Thomas raised his eyebrows and laughed. "So, what, that was really the devil in Morgan's room was it? Playing his song. That's just urban myth bullshit." He stared hard at Riley.

Cat tried to laugh, but felt a shiver pass through her body despite herself. She wasn't quite sure why, the story was nonsense, just a camp-fire tale.

Riley's laptop had returned to his screen saver, a still from an old horror film. On the ground a pentangle made of candles flickered. A Hammer House starlet stood on a stage, her mouth open in a frozen scream. Across the stage fell a shadow from a large, horned shape off-screen. Thomas made a snorting noise. "Stay here," he commanded. Riley wasn't looking like a man about to go anywhere fast.

Cat and Thomas moved out of earshot.

"Spirited off by bloody devil worshippers," said Thomas. "And I've got a fucking pixie up my arse." He reminded Cat that Riley's story hadn't mentioned any drugs yet there *was* almost certainly a deal going down in the scaffolded house. Then again, the scaffolding had been as good a place as any to watch Morgan's from.

Cat thought it through. "We give the drugs lead to the Met. I think we have to do that. Get them to do forensics on this place — she waved round Riley's apartment — in case he's lying about the drugs. But we take him to Cathays and interview him under caution. Get a proper statement about his relationship to Esyllt and everything else."

"There's an ABH charge there, if you want it."

Thomas meant the assault outside Tregaron. Riley had already admitted enough to make a charge of Actual Bodily Harm stick. Possibly even attempted manslaughter, though with a skidding in the mud defence, that would be hard to prove. Cat shook her head. What was the point? And ABH was a minor offence anyway.

"OK. But it'll be Camarthen not Cathays, Price." This would remain a Dyfed-Powys case, not a South Wales one.

She nodded, shrugged, like she didn't care.

Cat's shrug was good enough for Thomas. He pulled out his phone, came over all official. Rang the drugs info into the Met, called for a stake-out at the scaffolding house, forensics on Riley's place. Phoned Camarthen, brought his commander up to date. They'd love that there. Bloody love it. Small town on the fag end of Wales and all of a sudden a case of national magnitude. The two dead Tregaron girls, Delyth and Nia, plus Esyllt, the missing one. Plus Lisa Marr, the Glaswegian; Sara Armitage, the skinny Mancunian; and Katie Tana, the Croat, quite possibly last seen dead in a landfill. All that, plus another link, albeit a tenuous one, to Morgan.

Cat went back through to Riley. Told him what was happening. They'd be willing to drop any talk of arrest, but in exchange they'd demand maximum cooperation.

A full statement. All notes from his enquiry to be handed over. His computers and phone records to be taken. And he would confirm that a scuffle had taken place when he'd encountered her and Thomas.

His broken face grinned a bit at that. "Resisting arrest, eh? You still use that one?"

"You did try to kill me, you little fuck," Cat said gently.

Riley shrugged. "It's OK. I'll call it quits if you do."

They shook hands.

Cat took a spare memory stick from Riley's desk and downloaded what he told her were the relevant directories. The computer itself was heading off to Camarthen, but Cat wanted the opportunity to explore further herself. She picked up his phone, copied the caller records to her own, then passed it to Thomas.

A moment later, there were sirens outside. White forensic vans and uniformed officers. Showtime.

You wanted to be a vessel. You wanted to be authentic. You've spent your whole life wanting not to be one of those others. You want to be you. You want to express passion. You want to find the right song and let it speak through you.

And then you discover the cruel truth. There are no short cuts. You can't choose when you opt in. You can't just flip the telly over and listen. True passion does not allow short cuts.

The darkness cannot be faked.

There are only two paths to authenticity and you have to walk them both. Pain. And fear. They have you by the hand, and you are theirs now.

You know already, you will never see your family again.

CHAPTER
FOURTEEN

The dojo was on the east side of Bethnal Green. Seen from the outside it was a fight centre from central casting. Reinforced door. Laminated noticeboard advertising an upcoming fight. Graffiti. Just twenty yards away, a dimly lit alley bursting with rubbish.

Inside, it was different. A dojo is not a boxing ring. The spiritual aspect is as important as the martial one. More important, in fact. The original dojos were adjuncts to monasteries, cared for and used by the novice monks as part of their spiritual practice.

The sensei here was older than Walter but, to judge from his accent, a much more recent arrival. His face was very lined, very smiley.

Cat bowed her head. It had felt strange doing that to begin with, with Walter, but now it seemed respectful. Ordinary. She'd called Walter an hour ago, looking for support really, but he'd been in the middle of a class and just told her to go to this address. "He's a friend of mine. A very good teacher, a good soul. He'll be good for you, Catrin." Cat had accepted his order at face value. She'd learned to do that.

The sensei took her to a small windowless room, spotlessly clean, with a single bed, white sheets, white duvet, one pillow. A small basin in the corner. A tatami mat. "We have shower room downstair." The older man made a gesture, as though uncertain that she would understand his accent.

She smiled and thanked him.

"Please. You sit."

He indicated that she should sit on the bed, and she did so. He sat beside her, took her wrist and began to feel her pulses. The six pulses of Chinese medicine. Three shallow, three deep. He muttered to himself as he read them.

"You are not so well."

If that was a question, the answer is "yes". Cat nodded and said, "I've had a rough few weeks."

"Heart meridian very weak. Heart, also heart protector. Very important for body." He felt the pulses again and said, "Body and soul. Is same thing. Please, come."

She followed him down to a tiny office off the dojo. The walls were crammed with glass storage jars filled with strange things. Herbs some of them, perhaps, but there was one jar with what looked like the rind of some dried fruit, some containing bark or twigs, one with what looked like dead locusts.

The sensei started throwing bits from some of the jars into a small saucepan. Cat saw bark go into the pan but not, she was relieved to see, any of the locusts. The sensei took the saucepan to a small kitchenette and put the pan on to boil.

"You go up. You wash. You relax twenty minute. Then come down. And I give you medicine."

Cat showered, feeling every bruise, every ache from the last weeks. The dull beating of the tranks in her system was like another ache. A pain she'd grown half-used to living with. She had brought clothes with her to London, unsure if she'd be staying, so she changed into some clean things. She still felt bad, but at least she felt clean and bad.

She went down. The sensei was typing an email one-fingered and with concentration.

"Computer, very difficult," he said, worked a bit longer, then stopped and gave Cat one of his full-beam smiles. There was a stink coming from the kitchen, as though some dead cats had been boiled up with a splash of ammonia.

He took her through. Drained the water from the saucepan into a mug, added some cold, and passed it over. He laughed at Cat's expression of dismay. "Taste very bad. Is very good."

The drink was worse even than it smelled. She gagged once, then drank it down.

"Good." The sensei checked her pulses again, and gave her a minute or two of acupressure on some points on her inner arm. The pressure was hard enough to hurt. Then he checked her pulses one final time, said "good" again and ordered her to bed. She fell asleep almost instantly and slept straight through for eleven hours, dreaming of nothing.

She woke up feeling refreshed. Stronger, clearer, sharper. It was as though she'd been looking at the world through some grimy glass and someone had come along to wipe away the grime.

She went looking for Walter's friend to thank him, but he wasn't there, just a couple of spotty teenagers practising kick-boxing moves. She left a thank-you note and left.

What to do next? Thomas was in Camarthen now, debriefing Riley, setting up a major inquiry. His technical team would be sweeping the computer and phone records for anything which might add to — or contradict — Riley's tale. Meanwhile, the Met's forensics people would be doing all they could to locate evidence of drugs in Riley's flat. She vaguely hoped they'd damage it along the way. They probably would.

Cat thought about calling Kyle, any copper's first move in her situation, but she desisted. Kyle somehow wanted her on the team, but not quite on it. Since that's how Cat liked working anyway, she wouldn't push the issue.

She found herself a café that served a full English breakfast and had wi-fi. Not an easy ask, but after half an hour tramping about she found somewhere. She ordered food and tea and booted up.

She started to sweep the net looking for anything to confirm or disconfirm Riley's theories. It wasn't long before the first disappointing news started to appear. She went through to the National Missing Persons Helpline. Its pages were more recent than the press reports Riley had relied on, and Cat saw that the first two of his girls — Lisa Marr and Sara Armitage — had been accounted for, or almost accounted for. They'd been in touch with their loved ones by phone and skype, saying that they were "on tour", working as "singer/songwriters", very "involved in the music scene". That alone might not be decisive, but Lisa Marr had twice been home for special occasions. Her family reported that she was behaving a bit strangely, but was OK. They told police they thought she might be on drugs. In the case of Sara Armitage, the local officers had a suspicion — nothing more than a hunch, really — that she had walked out on her long-term English boyfriend, because she was fed up with him. They thought she had probably returned to Poland, her mother's homeland, though they had not been able to verify that. But they had spoken to her by phone and she had seemed fine.

Cat started to feel hopeless again, but she remembered that she was here because of Martin Tilkian. He needed her now, and she had once needed him. Push on, Price, she told herself. Occasionally, she remembered, missing persons files were closed prematurely. Abductees were pressured to give misleading accounts of their well-being or make forced visits home. She went through the girls' closed files again, checking for some signs of this, but there did not seem to be any, aside from the comment about possible drugs from the Marr family.

She ordered more tea, worked hard for two hours, but still she had nothing useful.

She had already hit a wall. The freshness and clarity she had woken with were fading fast. For no real reason, beyond the desire to take a break and out of mild curiosity, she ran a search for the website Riley had shown them with the original reference to Tartini's "Devil's Trill". She hadn't expected anything much to come up — yet thousands of pages were indexed. Pages from intelligent sources, too. Finally she found what looked like the material Riley had been using. On the relevant page there was the same reproduced etching of the devil in a frockcoat playing the violin. It was a patchily maintained site from someone calling himself "Edgar Joseph, Musicologist". Below the image was Guiseppe Tartini's own account of the original episode:

One night, in the year 1713, I dreamed I had made a pact with the devil for my soul. Everything went as I wished: my new servant anticipated my every desire. Among other things, I gave him my violin to see if he could play. How great was my astonishment on hearing a sonata so wonderful and so beautiful, played with such great art and intelligence, as I had never even conceived in my boldest flights of fantasy. I felt enraptured, transported, enchanted: my breath failed me, and — I awoke. I immediately grasped my violin in order to retain, in part at least, the impression of my dream. In vain! The music which I at this time composed is indeed the best that I ever wrote, and I still call it the "Devil's Trill" . . .

Then, keeping the page open, she found Thom Yorke's bleak commentary on the "Street Spirit" song that Riley had referred to. "They don't realise," he said, "that 'Street Spirit' is about staring the fucking *devil* right in the eyes, and knowing, no matter what the hell you do, he'll get the last laugh." The words shook her somehow. Perhaps it was her withdrawal speaking, but she felt a certain darkness entering her. Though *she* didn't believe in the devil, others did.

She checked the details of the site. The "contact us" address was in the East End. She ran the map function on her phone. It was not far away. This was hardly a conventionally promising avenue of enquiry, but as she was in the area she would check it out. At least that way it would be eliminated. This time could be used to let all she had learned in the last twenty-four hours settle into patterns and routes forward.

She needed a break to clear her head anyway.

Her phone led her away from the high streets, the brash, universal shops and their cheaper, local cousins. She found herself instead in a part of town that felt much closer to its original nineteenth-century state. A place of bleakly terraced streets and large brick-built warehouses. Neither bombs nor regeneration had left their mark. She half expected to see a housewife leave her house in corset and bustle.

She kept her eye on her phone map, but the system hadn't fully penetrated these streets. Her phone led her confidently to a dead end. It was wired-off with scrub beyond. The old factory building ahead had three storeys, a dozen windows on each storey, and a dozen panes to each iron-paned window. She couldn't see a single piece of glass that wasn't missing, broken or cracked.

She pocketed her phone and beat a retreat. Turned instead to older methods of finding her way. She asked three girls hanging moodily on the corner for the address she wanted. To start with, none responded, then one of them pointed back down the alley.

"It's down there, where you've come from."

"It's a dead end."

The girl seemed to have turned mute but the shortest of the three said, "You can go through the wire. It's cut." As the youngster spoke, Cat realised it wasn't a girl but a boy. All three of them had the eyes that knew too much for their age.

Cat thanked them, went back to the alley and, sure enough, there was a strip of wire that could be pushed back, a path that wound its way across the scrub beyond. She forced her way through. Her police eye noted a scatter of hypodermics beneath the bushes.

She traversed a hundred yards of rough ground. There was a stink somewhere close by. An open drain? Some stagnant water? At the end of the path was a wire gate, the lock long since forced. Cat went through it and found herself on a short stubby street, the one she was looking for. There were more Victorian buildings, mostly boarded-up.

She found the right door. The buzzer was set next to a mirror behind thick, vandal-proof wire. She rang it, heard nothing.

The mirror was set at an angle and she wondered if it corresponded to another inside, so a person in the building could observe the porch. Peering in, she glimpsed a shape quickly moving out of view. She rang again and finally she heard the door click open.

There was no one behind it. She stepped through and closed the door.

The flooring was black and white tiles, the walls were panelled in dark mahogany. The only illumination was from a dim brass lamp and the play of light through a stained-glass window. There were doors to either side of her, a flight of stairs rising ahead.

She tried the first door: it was locked. Tried the second and it opened on to a huge room, crammed with dark oak furniture and the same mixture of dim lighting and coloured light through stained glass. The walls swirled with what looked like original Victorian wallpaper, all dark green foliage, heavy violet blooms and implausible, tropical birds. On the tables, the floor and mounted on the walls was a collection of musical instruments. A gilded Welsh harp. A group of round-bellied string instruments — lutes? A type of sitar? Some keyboard-percussion instruments. African drums.

There was no one there.

"Hello," Cat called softly, but as she did so she heard a board creaking above her. She realised that the arrangement of mirrors at the front door had flashed her image up not sideways. She had been inspected from above.

She looked up.

There was a man on the landing. He was dressed in a corduroy suit with rounded lapels that looked almost as ancient as the furnishings. His hair was purest white and disorderly. It did not look as if it had been cut for many months. He had a distracted air, like an academic disturbed in his studies.

"Really, I don't know why they need to send someone different each time," he complained.

"Sorry?"

"The last one didn't even know how to do it. I had to show her myself."

"Maybe I'm not who you think I am."

"I don't care, as long as you'll do what I pay them to do."

He pointed with a quivering finger at a long mahogany table. Some cleaning equipment was set out beside it.

"French polishing, huh?" said Cat, but she raised her warrant card as she spoke. "I'm Detective Sergeant Catrin Price and I have some questions to ask."

"Really!" The man — Edgar Joseph, presumably — was impatient and irritable, but not resistant. "Well, it can't take long, because I have someone coming."

"But first, my questions. I'm working on a case that has . . . that has raised some unusual questions. A possible relationship between certain music and Satanism." She paused, looked closely at him. "And someone involved in the case was using information from your site."

"Yes, yes." When she didn't immediately respond, he continued. "Well, of course there's a relationship. As old as music, I suppose. In medieval times almost any music was associated with the devil, unless it was church music. But even that, if it was too ornate or beautiful, could be considered suspect." He stopped. She sensed there was a lot more he could say on the subject, but he seemed hesitant to do so.

She tried to catch his eye in the dimness.

"I know, but in contemporary satanic practice, is there any way a certain song, for example, could have sacred associations, so that singing it could be considered blasphemy?" She hesitated. "Like it was a curse to anyone who sang it?"

"Naturally. These stories spring up always. Every age possesses them."

He started to tell her a story about an eleventh-century religious community in Denmark. His white head nodded in the dimness. Cat wondered whether the guy even knew what century he lived in.

She interrupted. Played "Street Spirit" through her phone. He tutted at the electronics, but listened.

"This song has been associated with a number of deaths and disappearances. Real ones, not fictitious ones. You mention it on your site."

The man looked bemused. "Well, I'm not very familiar with 'contemporary music'." His fingers formed inverted commas round the despised words. "But that song makes extensive use of the flatted fifth, the tritone. Quite successfully, in fact. I listed a few such songs."

"You've never heard that people covering the song have been dying or disappearing?"

The man shook his head.

"And this flatted fifth thing?"

"That chord was long banned, of course. Banned by the Church because it was associated with states of satanic possession. The Devil's Chord it was called. It was explicitly prohibited during the development of the hexachordal system. Named the *diabolus in musica*, some singers were excommunicated or otherwise punished by the Church for using it. Avoidance of the interval for musical reasons has a long history. You'll find it underlying modern works where a certain darkness is invoked. Wagner's "Gotterdammerung". Britten's "War Requiem". No doubt it occurs in much popular music also. I wouldn't know."

"And the chord. Does it, in your view, have any power to alter state?"

"Oh really! What an absurd question!" The man flung his hands in the air. His bony white fingers fluttered briefly, like moths. "Of *course* it does. Listen." He walked over to an old-fashioned record-player and selected a record from a large rack of vinyl beside it. He put something on — Cat couldn't see what — and placed the needle carefully on a track. Church music filled the room.

Godly, dignified tones. Elevated and solemn.

The man listened intently. As the music swelled, he raised a finger and said, "Now."

And she heard it. The flatted fifth. The devil's interval. Beckoning through the half-light like an unsatisfied hunger. The tone never left the music from that point on. The melody kept circling back to it. The earlier golden tones felt like an abandoned heaven, the rest like the death of hope.

"Can it alter state! Why would we listen to music if it couldn't? Why would every religion, every ritual, whether sacred or profane, require it?"

The man snorted in contempt. He was done with her, but not his music. He replayed the record but at full volume. Standing white-haired at the player, the unpolished mahogany table behind him. The house filled with the music, the darkness, an ancient and vengeful past.

Cat backed away. He didn't notice her go. He was doubtless still standing there, still listening to it, when Cat left the room, left the house, and found herself back out on the empty, sunny, expressionless street. Music still played from that upstairs room.

She made her way back through the scrubland and the wire.

The little posse of teenagers had thickened. Three more boys, dangerous looking. They looked at Cat but let her pass.

What had she been thinking of, going there? She reprimanded herself. She had wasted her time. She had real work to do. Real murders, real investigation. And already she knew where she needed to pick up her search. Music could have power: she knew that. You didn't have to believe in the Devil's Trill and the theories of medieval theologians to believe that. You could probably explain the whole thing with neurochemistry and alterations in the dopamine receptors. It didn't matter how you explained it. What mattered was that fantasies could sometimes have greater power than the truth.

The man. The man you trust. Or trusted? Or will trust?

You can't say. Those thoughts confuse you. They don't help.

So keep it simple. Watch his lips. Listen to his words. Assess the facts yourself and draw your own best conclusions.

In his left hand, your old life. In his right hand, your new one.

But do you want to go for it? To erase yourself?

That's not what you signed up for, you're well aware. Not something he told you when you first met. Nothing to do with the song, the singing, that talent which you still half-believe to be there.

Your choice.

Left or right. Old or new. Either way a death of sorts.

Your fingers move towards his right hand.

CHAPTER
FIFTEEN

She made her way back to the cafe, ordered more tea and proceeded to crunch the data she'd already collected. The answer lay here. Discipline, rigour and the odd flash of imagination might just be enough to find it.

She started work. She tabulated her evidence as much as she could, so any overlaps or cross-references would jump out at her.

More tea. Her fourth cup now. She hadn't yet re-watched Riley's videos, but she needed to do so. She found them on the memory stick. Each girl had her own video: Nia Hopkins, Delyth Moses, Esyllt, Lisa Marr, Katie Tana, Sara Armitage.

Nia first. Cat only watched the clip for a few seconds, trying to focus on the performance but all she could think of was the broken body in the pithead shaft, the autopsy shots. She shut it down, called up the *DeMo* clip, saw the waitress standing on the same stage as Nia, or one much like it. Delyth opened her mouth to sing and Cat saw her bloated corpse; Delyth hit an opening note and Cat saw her tortured body, her serrated nipples. She shut the clip down.

It was a bad gig. Would she have got onto tranks if she hadn't had to cope with stuff like this? There wasn't an answer.

Still wanting to retch, she tried Esyllt, got as far as the opening seconds of the *EasyT* clip — Esyllt with uncannily neat hairstyle marooned on an ocean of stage — before she shut that down too. She'd watch them later. See what they told her. She couldn't face it now. Her limbs and body felt heavy, as though they were subject to some new double gravity.

She closed the video player and, for relief more than anything else, went back to her web browser, clicked through to YouTube and entered "Radiohead Street Spirit" as her search term. Somehow, she'd expected only a few videos to show and Riley's names to pop out, but there were dozens of versions of the song. She checked the names of some of the YouTube singers against their Facebook accounts and found that, where she was able to correlate one against the other, the singers appeared to be living an ordinary, untroubled life. If this was the Devil's Song, he had a funny way of picking his victims.

Was this the final collapse of Riley's theory? For a moment Cat thought so, except that Griff Morgan's name still flashed over this whole case like a broken light. The drugs tied Morgan into the case, just as the graffiti in the Tregaron cottage had done. Somehow Kyle's interest did as well. That meant, Cat decided, that there might be *some* truth to Riley's conjectures, it's just that neither she nor Riley himself had yet discerned it.

In some desperation, after rooting around, she found a version of Riley's campfire tale. It was pasted in a metal music chatroom, apparently from an older chatroom that had closed many years previously. The original poster was anonymous, and all the elements were the same. Morgan's girlfriend singing the song and dying in a fire shortly afterwards. The hotel worker who had heard the song playing after the girl's death. His entering the suite and seeing all the girl's things, as if she had only just walked out of the room. It felt like the sort of story teens circulate to frighten each other. She wondered if Riley might have invented it himself, and posted it to give colour to his story.

Feeling more ready to watch the videos of the dead girls, Cat searched for them on YouTube. The three Welsh girls had their videos online, but there was nothing from Lisa Marr, Katie Tana or Sara Armitage. Weird.

Cat thought there was something off with the YouTube search function, then remembered that she'd first watched those videos from Riley's memory stick, not from the site itself. All the clips Riley had saved had now been withdrawn from their respective online homes. As far as Cat could tell, via some web-archive libraries and Google caches, the clips had been withdrawn at about the same date, about a week after the Croatian girl's disappearance.

Had Riley begun contacting the girls at this time with his theory? If so, the girls had apparently decided not to chance it. The performances of the three Welsh girls seemed also to have been withdrawn with the others, but then posted *again* a month before the mine bodies had been found. That was something, some type of pattern in the chaos. A further hint that Riley might have been onto something. But what did it mean? Maybe they had felt that whatever threat existed had passed and it was safe to go online again.

Cat tightened her grip on the mouse, ignored her feelings, dived in.

She called up the Moses girl, the YouTube original, not Riley's curt ID version. This time she watched the song properly. The performance began assuredly enough, with barely any hesitation. The girl's eyes were almost closed throughout. The words were slow and whispered like an incantation, until in the central section, a change of Delyth's vocal register was partially disguised by a sound that was part sob, part whoop. Cat dragged the cursor back, listened again. It was a curious noise to come from so accomplished a singer; an unholy marriage of grief and celebration.

Cat minimised the *DeMo* clip, exhaled heavily, called up Nia's YouTube window, moved the cursor to the mid-section, listened. She heard the same sound from Nia. Delyth and Nia seemed to have the same eccentric singing technique.

Faster now, because that was the only way Cat could face it, she called up Esyllt's performance, heard the same strange vocal tic in the mid-section of the song, noted the long shift she wore like the others. They looked like novitiates, transported by the power of the song. All held their hands clasped in front of them at waist height, like figures in some Pre-Raphaelite religious scene.

The girls had lived within a tight radius of each other. They hadn't been known to mix socially, yet there must have been a connection between them, a connection close enough to enable them to develop similar performance styles. Was that possible? She didn't believe that they were simply imitating each other. Why would they want to? More likely they would want to develop their own individual interpretations, yet the style was undoubtedly similar.

She clicked back to Nia's video, the earliest to be posted by almost six months. She watched more closely now.

From a close-up of Nia's face the camera pulled back to reveal the performance space, a proscenium arch partly visible beyond the small circle of light that encased her. Something about the scale of it made Cat stop the video momentarily. She had thought it had merely been mocked up to look like a theatre, but now she could see that it really was a theatre, albeit one that had an unused appearance.

She clicked on the play icon again, let the scene go on a little longer. Towards the end of the song the camera moved, an amateurish pan that momentarily confused Nia. For the briefest of moments the girl lost focus, then found the camera again, followed it round with her eyes. Just before her final notes died away Cat saw a rectangular shape, one corner of it caught by the follow-spot.

Cat pressed pause, moved her head closer to the screen. Squinted. It was a theatrical flat, a wooden frame upon which a sheet of canvas had been stretched. Primed with undercoat then painted, this would have formed part of a scenic backdrop. It wasn't clear exactly what was depicted, but it was an outdoor scene. The layers of *trompe l'œil* grey stone made her wonder whether it was supposed to be an old wall of some sort.

She called up the other two girls, found stills that showed as much background detail as possible, then clipped the images, and copied them over into Photoshop. She did what she could to enhance the images and set lighting and contrast settings similarly.

In the *DeMo* clip, the space had been lit so tightly that she could see nothing behind the circle of the follow-spot, yet in super-zoom mode, where you could see every pixel, you could see a clear similarity between the Nia clip and the *DeMo* one. The paintwork on the proscenium arch just visible on the right had a deliberately loose quality, so that you could almost see the brushstrokes. In the *EasyT* clip Cat could just make out, leaning against the back wall, another right-hand section of the theatrical flat. It was unmistakably the same as the Nia one. You could superimpose one image on the other and almost not notice the difference.

But what did this mean?

All the performances looked as though they'd been filmed in a similar place. Maybe even the same place. Some sort of theatre, a large formal stage. Not something that one would find in the heart of the country. A city, maybe. A town, at the very least. There was the Sherman Theatre in Cardiff. But not all theatres in Wales were in cities. There was the Torch Theatre in Milford Haven, the Theatr Hafren in Newtown and Theatr Clwyd. Where was that? Wrexham? Mold? Towns, then, but not right out in the country.

The girls would need to travel there. She seemed to remember something about Nia disappearing now and again. She called Thomas, who sounded busy.

"Price?"

"How are things going? Get any more from Riley?"

"*Nada*. Lots of details. Nothing new. We could find a charge that would stick, but it's probably not worth it."

"Any drugs in his flat?"

"Marijuana. Personal use quantities."

"His phone records?"

"Nothing useful."

"And the surveillance team? The guys staking out the back garden with the rather valuable compost bin?"

"Nothing from them either. That's probably fucked up."

"Maybe Morgan monitored all the activity that took place there yesterday and decided to cancel the deal."

"A lot of money to lose. Fuck, if no one else wants it . . ." said Thomas.

"Yeah, but I think there are quite a lot of Met officers watching that bin at the moment, Thomas."

"Yeah," he agreed sadly.

"Look, quick question: did Nia ever go away? Take weekends away from her family, that sort of thing?"

Thomas checked something by yelling the question out at a colleague and getting an answering yell back again. "Yeah, apparently. No big deal, though. Why?"

"I might have something. Not sure. I'll give you a call later, OK?"

Thomas put on his I'm-going-to-be-obnoxious voice. "Yes, Price, but not too much later, you know what I mean."

Cat ignored him and rang off.

She turned back to the screen, remembering now the owner of the Owain Glyndwr, how she had mentioned a few occasions when Delyth had asked for days off on the weekend. She knew from Martin that Esyllt used to head off too.

She thought she could see a basic pattern beginning to emerge, not much admittedly but something to work with. First Nia, then the other two girls had posted their clips. Perhaps all the clips had been recorded while the girls were away for the weekend. Of the girls, only Esyllt would have been able to afford a private music tutor — or Nia at a push — so it seemed unlikely that this was the shared link. In an age of talent shows, it wouldn't have been difficult to tempt girls into recording their big shot at stardom, clandestinely or otherwise.

Yet Cat couldn't shake off the feeling that whoever had coached all the girls to sing in that strange way, if that's what had happened, hadn't been a talent scout or a legit part of the music industry. There was nothing wrong with shooting a video, teenagers did it all the time and there wasn't anything indecent about the performances she had witnessed. Yet none of the girls had spoken of what they were doing when they went away for the weekend. Something about the process had persuaded them all to keep silent.

Cat leaned back in her chair, her right hand rifling around in the pile of papers until she found a biro. She twirled it between her fingers. Her thoughts led her back through the case.

Nia had already had a presence on YouTube prior to her performance of "Street Spirit", had even attracted a small following. So here was a theory: someone had spotted Nia from her earlier videos, then persuaded her — trained her? — to sing "Street Spirit" in *that* way and in *that* theatre. Maybe Nia was the first, the catalyst that had led to the other two girls being targeted.

But perhaps there had been something about Nia's reading of the song that hadn't satisfied the shadowy force in some way — so that person had persuaded Nia to recruit the others. The evidence from Tregaron was that the girls barely knew each other, but in a small community people always knew each other *enough*. She recalled her own youth, and how any upcoming talent was discussed throughout the whole town, and not just in school. This one was a real actor in the making, could be another Anthony Hopkins, even. That one was going to challenge Bonnie Tyler in a few years. So Nia would have known who the talent was, but who was the figure behind the videos? And what had he, or she, been looking for?

She returned to YouTube and entered "Street Spirit" in the search window, waiting as an alarmingly long column of amateur performers assembled. She scrolled down, clicked on one entitled "Street Spirit-Sian C", attracted by the Welsh name. This turned out to be the work of an art student. The music was just a soundtrack to an animation of a bleak landscape where the bare trees sprouted thorns and birds of prey arrived to perch on the branches. It was skilful enough, but Cat worried about Sian C's state of mind. The scenes quickly became too depressing to tolerate.

She called up a video further down the page uploaded by "Sharkskin", four boys in their late teens or early twenties who were singing in someone's garage. It was just another lousy YouTube video.

She clicked on to the next page, waited as another list of performers appeared. Cat felt deflated. Her head had started to pound again. Had that Chinese medicine worn off? Or was it just this case? It seemed like half the world had covered the Radiohead song. Which really was strange, because it wasn't exactly "My Way", was it? Seemed there were a lot of despondent people out there.

She pressed on, peered at the performers, searching for some intuitive connection to the murdered and missing girls. Nothing jumped out. Sighing, she booted over to another music site, scanned the long lists of covers, again found nothing. She went to another site, telling herself it was the last. More wannabe indy kids, an overweight male lounge lizard from Suffolk, some smiling sequinned triplets from Hull who hadn't got the message. She was giving up, was about to close the window when about halfway down one page a head-and-shoulders shot caught her eye.

A teenage girl, dressed in what appeared to be a type of choirboy's outfit, white and flowing, though with no ruff at the neck. The still captured from the upload gave little away, but the setting could, just *could*, have been the same as the one in the other girls' videos. The performer was named as *RhiP*. Rhi, short for Rhiannon? It seemed like a reasonable guess. Still, it didn't necessarily mean she was Welsh. Maybe her parents had been Fleetwood Mac fans.

She clicked on play.

The girl was captured in a tight spotlight, her voice cracking with nerves at first, but once she settled down her talent was obvious. She was a natural alto, a lower register than the other girls, had more trouble reaching the higher notes, hadn't yet learned how to sing across the break in her voice. The scenery in the background looked vaguely similar to the others. It was less clear, but there was a wash that could have been the same grey stone effect.

The waitress who had been patient with Cat that day came over, clearly wanting her to pay up and get out. Cat dropped money — too much money — on the table. Her mind was elsewhere.

She took a still of the girl, clipped it down to a headshot and loaded it to her phone.

She called Thomas. He was all ready to give her more of his bullshit, but she cut through it.

"I've got an IP address that I need tracing. There's a girl on YouTube who might fit the profile. I think I should go see her."

"*Might*. Sounds a bit vague. You'll have a warrant for that request, of course."

She said nothing.

"It's an offence to get that kind of thing without a warrant." He didn't say he *couldn't* do it, Cat noted, just that he wouldn't.

"Right, and yesterday you felt that Riley was resisting arrest for really quite a long time. Resisting arrest quite hard and repeatedly."

"That's different. Look, if you can work up an application for the warrant, I'll see if I can get it. But this is a big case now. It's like every fucker in Camarthen wants a piece of it. I've got to play it by the book."

"OK."

"Sorry."

Cat rang off. Sod it.

She was standing on the street outside the café. For a moment, she couldn't remember where she was. Just stuck out on a big London street, breathing exhaust fumes. A cycle courier drew up to some red traffic lights and, by twisting his front wheel, the courier managed to stay balanced until the lights changed, his foot not once touching the ground.

Cat retreated to a quieter side street and called Kyle. She explained what she needed and why. She didn't give full details, just said that an internet search had identified another possible woman at risk and she wanted to check on her.

"You need a warrant for that," said Kyle brusquely.

"I know. But all I've got is a hunch, not evidence."

Kyle paused a moment, long enough that Cat wasn't sure she was still there. Then: "OK. Hold."

Cat held. She could hear Kyle talking on another line in the background. It was true: you couldn't source an IP address from the provider via Command and Control without getting a warrant. But a tame SPOC dealt with the same liaison at the service providers every day. Inevitably things got matey. For a highly placed officer to source that kind of information on the quiet wasn't a big ask. Maybe Thomas just wasn't senior enough. Maybe Camarthen was too far out of the loop.

Kyle came back. "OK, I've got it." She gave Cat an address in Blackheath, South London. An address and a phone number. A surname too: Rhiannon Powell.

Cat noted the details.

"Got that?"

Cat said "yes" and would have said something else, but Kyle was already gone.

Cat made a roll-up and smoked it quickly. That full English breakfast was still making its presence felt. It was bad food for her. Her body needed vits and good quality proteins. She looked down at her forearm, the skin puckering to gooseflesh. Sweat was cooling on the small of her back. Her face was hot then covered with a creeping chill. It was partly the withdrawal symptoms, partly exhaustion.

Enough prevarication. She called the number Kyle had given her. It went straight through to voicemail.

Sometimes she still thinks of home.

Her mother, her father. The tinny sound from the TV downstairs as she was practising her singing upstairs.

Her room. The pictures she'd clipped out of magazines. Singers she liked, men she fancied.

All a world away.

She is frightened to let him see.

Sometimes she cries. Not for any specific reason, but the way exiles cry. For a country that was hers and will never be hers again. Sometimes the tears seem to go on for ever.

CHAPTER
SIXTEEN

The taxi driver drove fast, aggressively, in tune with Cat's mood. Rain gusted against the windscreen. There were only a few people out, huddled under umbrellas.

In three-quarters of an hour they made Blackheath. The street turned out to be a well-lit cul-de-sac, fringed by trees and houses whose frontages at least seemed as impressive as the Highgate properties. But the multiple doorbells suggested most had been divided into small flats and bedsits: dimmed lights flickered over galley kitchens and over living spaces just big enough for a couple of armchairs and a portable TV.

Cat paid off the driver at the head of the road, somehow not wanting him to know her final destination. He gave her a blank receipt, which she pocketed. She could argue with her conscience later about how to fill it out.

The girl's house was about fifty yards down. It was set back from the road, the hedges lacking any structure, growing out onto the pavement. The paint of the front door had faded to a dull brick and partly peeled away. The column of ill-assorted doorbells gave no hint as to the house's inhabitants. There was no list of flat numbers. On the ground, a crumpled KFC box spilled chips onto the concrete.

She started with the bottom doorbells, worked from left to right. The right-hand bell on the second row brought a response. A gruff voice, apparently not surprised at a visit from a stranger on a rainswept night. A buzzer sounded, releasing the door. Inside, the lighting was dim. She followed the stairs up to the next floor. Two doors led off the landing. She listened for signs of life. Silence at first, then the sound of a floorboard wincing behind the door on her left.

She slapped her palm against the door. And again. Another creak. The door opened, revealing a chain. Cat pulled her warrant card out of her pocket. Thrust it forwards. Reached back into her pocket, took out the image of the girl frozen on her screen, held it to the door with her other hand.

"Which flat?"

The door closed.

She shouted, "Hey!" Slapped her hands hard against the wood.

"If you want me to call my colleagues and have them break this door down, I'll do it."

From inside: "Give me a moment."

The man disappeared for just long enough to hide his drugs, then came back and unslid the chain. He backed away down his small hallway, seemingly caught between fear and politeness. She was police, but she wasn't behaving like police. Cat tried to take in the flat, but the lighting inside was only just brighter than it had been in the hall. The walls were covered in framed prints to an eccentric extent. There were so many that they acted as wallpaper, each only millimetres from its neighbour. She peered at them. They all seemed to depict ships in painstaking detail, but they were more like engineer's drawings than conventional art.

The flat-owner stood in the kitchen doorway, scratching his beard. He was wearing jeans and nothing else, backlit by a dying fluorescent strip which flickered on and off. The light lent him a corona that gave the scene an unearthly aura. She approached with her warrant card and her phone. He glanced at the girl's picture briefly, motioned with his hand.

"You want the top floor."

She backed out quickly, took the stairs at a run. At the top there was a door on its own. This was a converted attic room, the door much shorter than normal, the slope of the roof cutting the hinges on the diagonal. Unless the landlord had a habit of renting this room out to the seven dwarves, the tenants must have had to crouch to enter.

Cat knocked but there was no reply. She crouched, pushed at the door, pushed again. Back down to Mr Jeans downstairs. She asked him if he had a key, if anyone was a likely keyholder for the girl on the top floor.

He knew nothing.

Cat went back upstairs. There was no real choice here. Not after Nia and Delyth. Not after Esllyt.

She sprung out a straight kick at the door, so she met the wood with the sole of her foot. Stupid. A jolt of pain went through her ankle. The lock was tougher than she had expected. She changed feet, kicked again, using the walls to steady herself. It was only on her fifth attempt that she heard the reassuring crack of splintering wood as the door swung open.

"Rhiannon?" There was silence.

Cat called again as she shuffled into the flat, straightened up on the other side of the door. Light bled into the room from the landing, the far side partially illuminated by the street lamps outside. The curtains had been left open. The place smelled stale.

Ahead there was an attic living space. In the right corner a galley kitchen contained the basics: a two-ring hob and sink over a small cupboard and bar fridge, a microwave. In the opposite corner there was a single armchair, a table on which stood a mug, a partly eaten digestive biscuit on a coaster. The mug contained an almost full cup of tea.

At the end of the room a door led through to another space. This was darker than the first, but a gap in the thick curtain admitted a limited amount of light. The room was dominated by a small double bed. There wasn't room for anything else.

Some attempts had been made to make this space more homely. On the window ledge stood three large pebbles painted with psychedelic patterns, a couple of small plant pots holding cacti. Cat peered through the gap in the heavy curtains. Streetlights weakly illuminated the house's back garden. Close to the wall she could make out an assortment of objects — rusting bed frames, old paint cans. A path, partly overgrown with weeds, bisected the grass, the wind moving the grass softly. In a tree in the garden next door, multicoloured lanterns swayed homely light — orange, yellow, red — across the detritus of the back garden.

Something caught her eye, a movement amongst the rusting debris. A shadow from the lamps maybe, as they lolled in the breeze? She looked again, another movement. No, what she had seen did not configure with the lanterns. What was it then? She glanced back into the living space, saw Rhiannon's mug. She ran, cracked her head on the flat's low front door as she left, took the stairs two at a time. Below she found a corridor leading to a back door, the glass in its top half latticed with wire like in an institution. She flipped the Yale latch down, headed into the garden. Cat stumbled on her way across the grass, fell to her knees, stopped still for a moment, dazed.

Out of the corner of her eye she saw something, a lithe movement followed by complete stillness. Slowly and cautiously she moved her head, saw two shining beads ten feet away from her, suspended from the ground. She focused. The beads were two eyes, staring at her from above a fragile snout. A fox, quite a young one. That's what she had seen from the flat's window, an urban fox nosing through the rubbish.

She stared at the creature, it stared back, stock still. It seemed to tremble with fear of her. She felt tender, she relented, waved her hand quickly to scare and release it from their immobilising gazes. The fox flinched, darted on silent paws deeper into the darkness of the garden and was gone.

Cat rose up from her knees, pulled out her mobile to try to call Rhiannon again, peered across the garden as she dialled. The phone rang, and what was that? Some trilling like cicadas. She moved towards the sound, which now increased in volume. She closed the call to Rhiannon and abruptly there was silence.

Cat pelted deeper into the garden, towards the sound she now knew was Rhiannon's ring tone. She reached a patch where the long grass lay differently, wasn't moving in the wind. She glimpsed something light, a silver belt over white jeans. Cat fell to her knees, crawled along the grass, parting the tall stalks with her hands.

The girl was lying on her back, the body that used to be Rhiannon Powell. That used to be a singer. That used to choose a silver belt to go with her new white jeans.

Cat reached across, carefully pulled the jacket open. Dark crimson. The breasts of the girl were punctured and soaked with blood. Cat touched her. She was as cold as the garden.

Cat felt herself tremble. She made to retch, but nothing came. She looked up and the surrounding windows were dark. It was unlikely she had been seen by anybody. Some crazy part of her wanted to stay with the girl, offer her some respect, some consolation, but she knew she couldn't. The part of her that felt the most warred with the part of her that thought the most. The thinking side won, as it had been trained to.

She called Kyle, told her what had happened. This situation wasn't just Cat's problem, it was Kyle's too now. What story could Cat give for finding the body that didn't simply track back to the IP address, obtained without warrant?

Kyle thought briefly, then said, "Just call it in. I'll handle the IP address."

"And link it to Riley? What do I tell the Met?"

"This is Thomas's case. Tell the Met anything you like, but this is Thomas's case."

"OK."

Cat left the garden through the house and made the call. The police operator told her calmly a response team would be with her shortly.

Cat made a roll-up, hands shaking. She would call Thomas but not yet.

She would call Martin too, but she had only bad news for him. Her chances of finding Esyllt alive, already poor, had just diminished significantly. The night suddenly seemed very dark.

CHAPTER
SEVENTEEN

It took Cat four long hours to fight her way out of the Met's clutches. They were pissed off that she — some junior cop from a force that the Londoners regarded as half-assed — had beaten them to a murder scene. But twice as pissed off that she couldn't offer a plausible story about how she'd come to be there. She'd heard one of the detectives on the road outside the crime scene trying to explain it to a newly arrived colleague. "Something about a YouTube video. The girl was singing it wrong or something."

No one liked Cat's explanation. No one liked the little IP dodge, though no one wanted to do anything official about it — after all, it was a dodge that had led to a dead body. No cops were going to get their wrists smacked for that. But most of all, no one liked the way that when any question got too close to the nitty-gritty, Cat just clammed up and said primly, "I'm not sure I have authority to answer that. You should probably consult DI Thomas in Camarthen." The lovely people from the Met chose to interpret that as a big Welsh *fuck you*, which was precisely how Cat intended it. They tried to give her a hard time for a few hours, then got bored and let her go.

Walter had told her that she could stay at his friend's dojo for as long as she needed it, but that didn't feel right. It was too clean. What she had in her head didn't fit there. So she settled instead for a Travelodge, checked in with a girl at reception who looked like the job had already killed her brain.

Cat walked the nylon carpet under fluorescent bulbs to her room. She let herself in, then carefully relocked the door. She sat down on the regulation chair, its cheap upholstery pristine, still scented with the shrink-wrapping it had recently shed. Then she stood and moved to the window glowing with lights from the car park. Cat flicked the curtain, checked for any new vehicles outside, saw nothing. And what was she looking for anyway? She dropped the curtain back.

In her mind she ran chronologically through the roll of the missing and the dead. Lisa Marr. Katie Tana. Sara Armitage. Nia Hopkins. Delyth Moses. Esyllt Tilkian. Rhiannon Powell.

She realised in her mind she'd counted Esyllt as among the dead. Maybe she was right to do so. She went to the bathroom, took the hand-towel, stood on the chair to jam the towel into the room's smoke detector then sat on the bed and smoked some canna. Fleas held a carnival beneath her skin.

Before she thought about it too much and nerves jittered her out of it, she made another call. It was long overdue. She left a message for Martin saying there had been developments. She made sure there was nothing in her voice that would give him false hope. That wasn't difficult.

She felt too tired to even undress, just lay on the bed, staring at the ceiling as though it were the night sky. She dipped into sleep but after a few moments something yanked her back into half-consciousness, and she noticed she was sweating. Images from her past came back to her, unbidden. Sneaking out of the house to Martin's home. Jogging round the corner onto the long stretch of Bryant Road that led to Martin's. Number twenty Bedder Terrace — probably wearing her Death to the Pixies T-shirt, the same one she still had, and her favourite pair of trainers; black with black fraying laces. In better times they would have talked to each other and got through this.

Cat lay back on the bed. Although she was now a husk, a nothing with only the need to rest, sleep evaded her. Bad thoughts. She needed company. She only knew one person in London — or at least only one person she could face seeing. She asked reception to call her a minicab and got it to take her to Battersea. They drove slowly into Lombard Road. To the right were the towers and ziggurats of the riverside complexes. Oyster Wharf. Falcon Wharf. Candlemakers. The wedges of Battersea Reach, vague and placid presences.

They got to the address she had on her phone. Rob's address. Her benzo buddy. He could cope with her.

His apartment block was shaped like an L and covered in glass like a giant crystal. She wasn't sure what she was doing. He was almost certainly sleeping. Even if he wasn't, she knew she should have called first;

he had told her that, been very clear. His shyness demanded it.

In the brightly lit lobby a concierge was sitting. He looked half-asleep. She walked in through the open doors, and he didn't look up. She looked at the postbox to the flat number Rob had given her. There was no name on it.

Next to the lifts there were service stairs that went up the outside of the building. She took those. The steps were concrete, and on each landing were yellow safety lights. There was a view down to Putney. More darkness, more dim lights.

On the stairs she did not think, she was an automaton. At Rob's floor, she came out into the L-shaped passage. The air felt close and artificially freshened. She checked the flat numbers then counted round, breathing heavily now. She found the flat, wanted to walk away and so knocked hard and quickly. She waited, butterflies in her stomach. There was no answer. This was stupid: she turned to go. A sound behind the door, footsteps muffled by carpet, locks clicking open.

"You're late, you fuck. It better be good," an uneven voice came before the owner of that voice was visible. Was that Rob? If so, he sounded coarser than he did on Skype.

The door opened. A dim face in the entrance, clammed with night sweat. It was Rob. He frowned, scowled, recognised her and looked down.

"Rob, I . . ."

"Cat?" The word seemed hesitant.

"It's late, I can go. Sorry." She felt a fool.

She thought he wanted her to go, but, "God, no come in," he said. He was obviously middle class. He stepped aside, slumping against the door jamb as though he were dizzy, mussing his hair, bowing his head. She stepped inside over wooden floors.

"I was expecting someone else." His voice came from behind her as she walked timidly down the hallway. "Hours ago, though. In here," he said. "On the left."

His voice seemed slightly slurred. The effects of abrupt awakening maybe. They made the lounge, a deep cream sofa, a large plasma screen on the wall, turned off. She saw a rocking horse by the sofa, a small blue plastic feeding chair, a jumble of primary-coloured plastic figures on the floor by a walnut coffee table. Her heart shrank.

"You've got a kid," she said, turning around, catching the glassiness of his eyes before he averted his face, looked down at his bare feet splayed on the wooden floor.

"Two," he said. "Boys. I should have said."

"Why should you have?"

He ignored the question, told her now. "One by the wife who chucked me out. Another by, well, someone else."

"You're not with her now?" Cat was not being subtle, but then she had just come to his flat in the middle of the night. Such behaviour precluded subtlety.

"No, I'm not. The kids don't live with me. I see a lot of the youngest though, am trying to get visiting rights for the older. Ex-wife's not too keen." Still he would not look at her, he turned his back, sloped over to the open-plan kitchen off the back of the lounge. He fussed in the kitchen, accidentally knocked something over, swore.

"Are you OK?" Cat asked.

"I'm fine. Er, do you want some wine?"

"Wine?" It was the middle of the night, but still. Rob knew, if anyone knew, that Cat and wine would not be a good combination right now.

"Of course you don't, sorry. Coffee?"

Did he drink wine himself? He shouldn't with his history of Benzos. Still, it had been a long time since he'd kicked them. Maybe he was allowed.

"Sit down," he said, his back to her still as he filled up the kettle. "You surprised me."

"I surprised myself." Cat did not sit, she was wary of her worn clothes touching the cream sofa. She became self-conscious, remembered the sweat she had woken with, the coffees and roll-ups she had consumed. Her breath must stink; her body also.

"Can I use your loo?" she asked. Nerves had almost had her say, *Can I freshen up?* She was glad she hadn't.

She thought he hadn't heard her, but just as she was about to ask again, he reacted. Without turning, the arm inside his red dressing gown pointed towards a door that led from the far side of the lounge. "Help yourself."

"Thanks," Cat said, stepping towards the door.

She went in, turned the light on, surveyed the marble, stood in front of the mirror on the bathroom cabinet, looked away from it when she saw herself.

Again the exhaustion; she knew she wasn't the best judge, knew also she had shocked him in the night, but wasn't there something weird about how Rob was acting? It was making her uneasy. Her hand was on the bathroom cabinet door, opening it, then she was rifling through the creams and toothpaste. It didn't take long. She pulled it out, a half-used blister pack of 30mg Temazepam, another two full ones behind it. All trust fell away from her. Although she was stood on a firm floor in a steel building, it was not really there, and nothing was between her and the hard pavement, nothing stopping her soft flesh from falling down to smash against the kerbstones far below. She pocketed a blister pack and turned.

She grabbed the bathroom handle, yanked it open, marched across the lounge, glanced into the kitchen. Rob wasn't there, gone into the bedroom maybe to put some clothes on.

"You fucking liar," she shouted to the flat. "Moron."

She ran down the hallway and out of the front door. She made the stairwell, her heart seemed as big as an elephant's, knocking away insupportably inside her.

She made the foyer and the concierge stared at her as she ran towards the exit. Out on the street, she walked a bit before looking for a taxi. She didn't even make a roll-up, just cried. Who did you really know? Who could you really trust? Not Rob, obviously. Kyle? Thomas? They both had agendas of their own. Cat wasn't sure her welfare figured high up on their lists. Martin? He had been a friend once, but he had more pressing concerns right now. Walter, of course, could be trusted always. You could depend on him, the way you could depend on the rising sun. But like the sun, his rays couldn't always fight through to reach street level.

Cat found a cab and got back to the hotel. Back in her room, she sat on the edge of the bed, her knees parted, hands holding the pack of Benzos in front of her. Her fingers twisted painfully over the packaging. A vision of a train came to her mind, of herself as a teenager, opening the door that led between carriages, the shingle on the track blurring with speed below her, then Martin's hands pulling her back. Pulling her back so he could lose a daughter to murder, pain and evil? And so he could save her for this: betrayal, dependence and failure.

She pushed the pack and popped out a pill — half red, half blue — held it between finger and thumb. She was still sitting like that when she fell asleep.

He sees her as if in a dream. She is still singing on the stage.

That is how he remembers her.

He half-closes his eyes. Yes, he is there again. He can see her eyes gazing shyly back at him, as they used to. How much trust is in her face. She still believes that something wonderful lies ahead. She has not given up hope.

It is almost the end.

He tells her to stop. The room is empty, the lights down. It's not much of a place. Just a few tables, the candles in a circle.

"Here," he says. She tries it on and it fits. He guides her to the mirror and the old make-up there. Then to the bed. It is still the same, nothing has changed and nothing will.

She lets him at first. She does not seem frightened.

"Why do you keep your eyes closed when you touch me?" she asks.

She is no different from the others. They all ask. Of course he cannot tell her.

How weary he feels. How long it has all been going on — several lifetimes, it feels like.

He puts the mask over her, watches her inhale the white smoke.

How innocent they are, they do not know what he is.

He is a clock which only tells one hour of the night.

She lies still. She seems hardly conscious. Maybe he has given her too much this time. He slaps her to bring her round. Then he gets down to his work.

CHAPTER
EIGHTEEN

Cat woke in the half-light of dawn, fully dressed, stiff and cold. She had a piss, splashed water on her face, set her alarm clock, checked her phone. She'd had eight messages from Rob: five texts, three calls. She deleted them all, blocked his number, deleted his number from her phone, felt better for doing it. She was back to where she was before meeting him, trusting nobody. It was easier that way. She slept another two hours and woke before her alarm.

She was doing her best to deal with a Travelodge breakfast — rubber egg, flaccid bacon — when she got a call. It was Kyle.

"I'm in London. Victoria. When can you get here?"

"Where's here?"

"The SOCA building." Kyle gave an address. SOCA: Serious Organised Crime Agency. Cat thought about how long it would take to get to Victoria, added an hour and gave Kyle a time.

"OK. Ask for me at the desk."

That was that. Kyle was gone. Cat ordered more coffee, wished she could smoke, then went back to her room to pack.

She scrubbed her underwear in the basin and then put it under the blow-dryer. She got dressed, feeling rank, then she called Thomas.

"Found a corpse, I hear, Price."

"Another one."

"You pissed off the Met boys, all right. They sounded well furious."

"I aim to please."

They bantered a bit, then Cat asked if anything more had come up from Thomas's end. Not much, was the answer. The dentals had come back on the Croatian girl, Katie Tana, and, as they had predicted, they matched the landfill body, the dead girl from Tower Hamlets. Thomas had run Tana again through the PNC and NCIS and had turned up only minor form. In January the previous year she had been cautioned twice for smoking weed at bus stops in Deptford. Four weeks before she had been reported missing, she had been busted with Mandrax at a rave in Greenwich, only small, personal use quantities. This was not exactly a surprise as they already knew Mandrax had been recovered from Tana's flat.

"It doesn't get us anywhere we weren't already," Thomas said morosely before he rang off.

Cat did some Krav Maga, a few jabs and kicks. Not much of her routine, just enough to check she was in working order. The withdrawal symptoms still gnawed at her, but after last night she knew she was stronger than they were; knew that the only difference between her now and being clean was time. Rob had lied to her, offered his help to pull her from the edge of the cliff, then dragged his hand away at the last minute. Why had he done it? There were a thousand deviant reasons, and she would never know which one was his. Because the only important thing was that she hadn't fallen; had found that the cliff edge was solid, that she could step away from it. She felt relieved.

This was good news, even if it didn't feel that way.

Cat used the hotel room's Lilliputian kettle and a sachet of bad coffee to make herself a cup and got to work. It felt better to match a body against an existing Misper than have an unidentified corpse *and* an unresolved Misper case. She checked the Deptford bus stops Tana was busted at on lists of soliciting points on the NCIS and then on Punternet and other online punter guides. Neither were listed nor were the streets around them.

On her laptop, she reviewed the original missing persons report. Tana had lived alone, had no friends or family to miss her, but her absence was noticed after some weeks by the landlord. Her set-up in Deptford had been the same as at the room her body had been traced to a month later. She had paid in cash and not given the landlord her real name.

Next, Cat ran a search for Rhiannon Powell, the murdered Blackheath girl, to see if there might be anything that tied her to Tana. Rhiannon had no form at all, she did not even have a driving licence, but she was on the system from a DNA swabbing at a stop-and-search a couple of years back. Stopped in a speeding car with two males in their early twenties. The car had belonged to one of the males, and everything seemed legit. Cat ran the names. Roberts and Fuller. Both males had minor drugs form, the sort of thing anyone of their age might have, but there was no mention of Mandrax, no connection she could see with Tana, or anything else in the case for that matter.

The only thing she noted was a different address given for Rhiannon on the report. Chances were it was just an old address, and Rhiannon had since moved to the flat in Blackheath. But she would check it. With any luck the Met would not get round to it for a day or so.

Next Cat went back to the NCIS drug seizure chart to match it with Tana's form.

The Mandrax seizure in Greenwich was recorded along with several others that month in London and Manchester and the pills photographed, but there was no other mention of Tana. The original incident report just told the usual story. When the police had entered, dozens of pills had been dumped by those present. No one admitted anything. Body searches had revealed nothing significant. The quantity of the pills on Tana, five only, had been deemed consistent with personal use and she had been released with a verbal warning. Other items seized were mostly ecstasy and amphetamines. That there was no other Mandrax suggested that the rave had not been part of the roll-out. Tana had likely been there in a private capacity not as a supplier.

Cat sat for some moments in the room collecting herself. She had a feeling that they were close to something. But she had had that feeling before, and each time the case had seemed to pull away from her.

312

She checked out of the Travelodge, a better feeling than checking in.

It was still raining. The air felt humid and close. She made her way to Victoria by tube and reached the SOCA block in Victoria just half an hour late. She was shown to a waiting room on the first floor. On the opposite side a solid flank of imposing Georgian terraces blocked out the view.

The door of one of the offices opened, exposing a rain-spattered window. A woman called her in, a civilian, and left her alone, told her to help herself to coffee from a thermos. Cat had a queasy feeling in her stomach. The same sensation that she had known during her years at school when summoned to the headmistress's study for what always felt like it would be the last time. Cat gazed at the chairs with mock leather seats. On the wall opposite a peeling cupboard flanking a khaki filing cabinet. Rain washed the window. London traffic wound and groaned below.

Finally, Kyle arrived, dressed in a crumpled trouser suit and plain white blouse. She sat down in a large leather swivel chair, the only symbol of status in the room. She said nothing at first, letting her eyes pass around the room as if it was of more interest than Cat.

She saw Kyle differently now: she was not the careerist automaton everybody took her for, her composure was as fragile, and her private life as messy, as everybody else's. But being treated by Kyle like this, it was difficult to like her.

Finally Kyle stared at Cat. "Don't bother to get comfortable," she said, "this won't take long." She

313

spoke quietly, but her tone was icy. She reached into a drawer, took out a folded *Echo*, threw it across the desk. Nodded at Cat, a command to read its contents.

The paper was open on a half-page article. The photos of the three Tregaron girls that accompanied the story had been selected for their power to move. These were pictures of innocence, school portraits dating back to what must have been the girls' earliest high school days. The photos of Nia Hopkins, the middle-class abductee, and of Esyllt, the missing college girl, were more prominent than that of Moses. The prevailing impression was of bunches and braces. Cat scanned the story beneath.

The gist was clear enough; the article was suggesting a cyber-stalker. It argued that the girls had been groomed online by their killer, that they'd been hooked by the oldest trick in the book, the promise of stardom. Clips of the YouTube videos were shown as stills. Threaded through everything was Riley's crazy account of "Street Spirit" as the Devil's Song.

"The story is in one of the national tabloids too. Your friend Della Davies gets a byline."

Too much emphasis on the word "friend".

Cat said nothing. She hadn't been asked a question.

"Well?"

"Sorry, ma'am. I'm not sure what you want to know."

"Why the fuck you gave this to Davies? How much did that earn you?"

Cat felt herself flush with anger. "I'm not the source," was all she said.

"Right. You're not. Let me see, though. The only people on the inquiry team who knew this stuff are you, me, DI Thomas, and a very small and closely supervised group in Camarthen. I didn't give this to Davies. Thomas would hardly want to fuck up his own inquiry. Same goes for the officers around him who, by the way, are reporting directly to the Chief Constable on this. Which leaves you. A friend of Davies's. Who saw her the day before she writes this story. Who had access to all the facts. Who was not under any kind of supervision for the relevant period. And who, quite frankly, could probably use the money. Am I right?"

Kyle's delivery was nasty. Deliberately so. Intended to wound.

Cat checked back over the relevant day to see if she could provide anything like a sensible alibi, but what she had was the exact opposite. She'd spent most of the day researching the YouTube stuff online. A log of her computer would, if anything, provide further evidence for Kyle's misbegotten accusation.

"You are completely wrong. Is that all?" Cat stood up.

"Sit down."

Cat paused, then sat.

"Sometimes," Kyle said, her voice weary now, not intimadatory, "sometimes the thing that's obvious is also the truth. You. Davies. This." She gestured at the *Echo*.

"Why isn't Riley the most obvious source? He's a journo. He makes his living from this kind of thing."

"Because we took precautions. He's not technically under arrest, but he can't fart without one of Thomas's officers there."

"Thomas must have a big team. It only takes one."

"The Devil's Song? Come on. That's something you knew about and Thomas and Riley. And me, because I've spoken to Thomas. And no one else. Thomas didn't release that kind of rubbish to his team, they'd have laughed at him."

Cat nodded. "You know, if I'd really wanted to make some money, I'd have produced this."

She flipped open her laptop, and jiggled it out of hibernation. She showed Kyle the images which suggested that the girls had sung their songs in the same location. The proscenium arch, the flat leaning against the back wall. Passed it over the desk so Kyle could see it. Kyle took her time to look at each shot carefully. She still said nothing.

"Obviously I'm not expert in digital images, but . . ."

Kyle nodded grimly. "Who else has this?"

"No one. You're the first. It looks like all these girls used the same recording studio, or whatever this place is. Then they up-loaded these recordings onto YouTube, presumably hoping to get picked up by a scout, A. & R. That's the connection, that's how they must've met the killer." Cat paused to let the implications sink in. "If I wanted to make some cash, then these are the money shots."

Kyle considered, then nodded. "Fine. Good work." There was no apology forthcoming, nor would there be. Kyle didn't work like that. But there was no aftertaste either. The past was past.

Except maybe where it involved dead foster-daughters and Griff Morgan.

"There's more." Cat started playing one of the reels, then another, then the third, stopping them at the points where the performances were similar. Kyle watched carefully.

"OK, they've all been trained by the same person. These tapes — you think he made them as some kind of trophy."

"Maybe. But it could be that the interpretation someone else puts on the performances is dooming the girls."

Kyle's expression was as uninviting as ever, yet Cat felt determined to pursue her line of thought to its final destination. "There could be a drug angle here. One of the girls — Katie Tana — was handling Mandrax, small quantities. There were traces on the two dead Tregaron girls, too, and at the scene there."

Kyle waved her hand dismissively. "They could have got that anywhere."

Cat cleared her throat, ignored Kyle's contemptuous gesture.

"Maybe they sourced it at this mystery studio. Their supplier is someone high up the supply chain. Tana's pills were wholes, not halves, which are how they're usually dealt. And there's evidence to suggest that all these pills trace back to your marina bust. The canoes that got away. Then there's Morgan's name all over this — the accusation."

"Except Morgan has been in a high-security prison until a couple of days ago. It's difficult to see how he could be the direct source for the pills."

"I know."

"So what's your theory?"

"Forget Morgan for the time being, go back to the drugs. Let's say these girls use the same studio. Get their drugs from the same guy. Someone high up the supply chain. At least one of them was busted with those drugs on them. No charges, because it was counted as personal possession, but our Mr Big is worried. He's scared that that girl, or maybe one of the others, is going to grass him out. So he cleans up. Nastily."

Kyle put her palms flat on the desk, pushed her chair back. "Class dismissed," Cat muttered under her breath. Kyle locked eyes with her as though she had heard, or at least sensed the note of dissent.

"No. These girls were tortured. A clean-up would not have involved that. The torture was professional, not recreational."

"I know. We're missing something. We don't have a full picture yet."

"Or we're not looking at it all the right way up."

Cat nodded. "Exactly. But what we do know is someone likely watched all of these YouTube videos of the girls. Probably watched and rewatched. Can we get IP addresses on all the watchers over the last two years, say?"

Kyle nodded, eager. That medieval warrior look again: the zealot.

Cat said, "I'm imagining this time a warrant should be easy enough."

"I'll action it."

Cat was sure she didn't want to work from an office. Not Cathays, not Camarthen, not Tregaron. Someone, not her, had leaked highly sensitive information to Della Davies. Riley had claimed he hadn't been trying to kill her and she'd taken him at his word, but bad things were happening. Women had been tortured to death for a truth towards which, Cat felt, she was inching ever closer. It was better to fly solo awhile. No offices. Stay moving. Watch her back.

She could see Kyle coming to the same conclusion herself. There was no reason why Kyle should even know where she was.

"If you could email it through," Cat murmured.

Kyle stood up, nodded, brisk. She was about to leave the room, but as she did, she made an odd gesture, putting her hand out to touch Cat's shoulder, then withdrawing it at the last second.

"Take care," she said, in an unnatural voice. She left too fast for Cat to respond.

CHAPTER
NINETEEN

It was raining more heavily, tepid dirty summer rain, when Cat got near Victoria station. She begged a phone directory from the information desk and found a local car hire firm. Not one of the chains, a backstreet affair that wouldn't ask too many questions. She got there, found an old Ford Fiesta with filler over the wheel arches, and paid for a week upfront, using cash.

They asked to see her driving licence, but Cat said she didn't have it. Just showed her warrant card instead. She gave her name as Katherine Pryce, just about close enough to her own name for the hire place to accept.

It was a relief having a car. She drove for forty minutes, watching her tail, threading back on herself. Better safe than sorry — her granny's way of putting it. Better paranoid than dead — her way.

When she was sure she wasn't being followed, she took herself south of the river. Found an internet café. She reckoned she could be the Egon Ronay of internet cafés the amount she used. Plywood cubicles were distributed around three walls, each containing a screen and keyboard. The towers were stowed on the floor beneath the desks.

About half of the cubicles were occupied. A waiter dressed in chinos and black polo shirt stood behind a stand of sandwiches and pots of tea. A serving hatch gave a limited view of a steam-filled kitchen. Cat got her time-coded slip and chose one of the cubicles on the back wall.

She called Thomas, who picked up on the second ring.

"Price," he said. "What can I do for you?" His voice was normal. He sounded busy, said he couldn't talk.

"Just had one fuck of a bollocking from Kyle."

"Naughty — bet Della underpaid you, though." It was hard to tell if he was joking. It was always hard to tell with him. From the noise in the background it seemed he was back at the operations room in Camarthen.

They spoke about the case a bit. It seemed to Cat, Thomas was doing a lot, achieving not much. A big wind of work and no results to show for it.

Riley, apparently, had no more to give. The missing girls were being intensively investigated now, but useful correlations were few and far between; they showed no sign of having known each other.

"What about you?" said Thomas

"Don't know. Kyle's gone all disciplinary on me. Not suspended exactly, but I'm not Ms Popular either."

"Nothing new there, then."

She hung up.

Cat felt like she'd cut herself off from the world. Like she was sinking.

She checked her email account: nothing yet from Kyle.

She clicked back into the PNC and the records of the two young males Rhiannon Powell had been with. Paul Fuller and Marcus Roberts. Neither felt that interesting to her. Neither looked like useful members of society, but there were no connections she could see to any of the other girls, or to the case in general. Fuller had been busted a couple of times on tip-offs from his electricity supplier for small grows of cannabis. Roberts's idea of a night out seemed to be going into A&E and trying to blag some prescription painkillers. Neither exactly major league.

Cat smiled. In the last entry on file, Roberts had got a caution for getting on a drug trial under false pretences. Under sedation Roberts had admitted only being along for the buzz, and the police had been called. Later it had emerged he'd been attracted by reports the trialled drug produced a number of weird side-effects, including out-of-body experiences.

She knew how he felt. She noted their address was given as the same as the old address Rhiannon had given. She called up the videos of the missing girls and printed A4 stills of them. As she went to collect the last of the printouts, she got the dual-tone that signalled an incoming message.

It was the email from Kyle, only not from her normal office address, but what looked like a hotmail address set up specially for the purpose. If there was paranoia here, at least it was shared.

Cat clicked through to the attachment, shocked at the number of megabytes in the file. It took half a minute to load. It was one huge spreadsheet containing thousands of entries. Cat groaned inwardly; she felt like she used to before taking a school exam. Still her police training meant she was handy at crunching data, and besides, she had no other route forward.

Best bite the bullet. And quickly.

After all, there were ways to refine this list. Any casual browser might stumble onto a YouTube clip and watch it. A single view didn't mean anything. On the other hand, a user who had watched multiple versions of the same song might be a different beast entirely. That might mean they had a thing about "Street Spirit". She started there. It took two coffees and one cigarette break just to sort a set of addresses that had watched all the performances. Good. Closer, but far from close enough. Because this still left hundreds of addresses. The song seemed like a magnet for nerds, like some OCD Mecca. And besides, many of the addresses would surely be obsolete by now. She tried a different angle, started with the IP addresses of the site users who had left comments on the girls' reels. But none of these had watched the reels more than a few times each. And while she couldn't be sure, those comments *felt* normal. There was neither the slightly crazy air of the true obsessive nor the over-careful approach of the wannabe stalker. Some stalkers might not even risk leaving messages.

She ditched that angle, went outside to smoke another roll-up.

Then she went back into the internet café, collected her things, paid and left. She deleted her own email account from her email program. She didn't know enough about her enemy to know how much they knew, how much they could trace. But if you're going to disappear, you don't even want your nose above water.

She took the battery out of her phone and threw both parts into her bag. Went to an ATM, took out £400, then shoved her bank card into her bag, a zipped inside pocket, where she couldn't reach it inadvertently.

She drove around, watching her tail, then took herself to another part of South London. She bought a pay-as-you-go phone, without registering it. Bought it for cash.

In another café, more or less identical to the one before, she set up a new hotmail account, creating a username that held no clues to her name or initials. Hesitating only briefly, she called Kyle's mobile. Going through to voicemail, she left her new email address and phone number. As she hung up she felt strange, like a diver, fifty metres below the surface, looking back at the air-line that snaked upwards to safety. Cat was the diver. Kyle was the air-line. But who was the shark?

Time to find out.

Cat ordered more coffee although she already felt jittery, had a think. Back at the computer, she sliced up the data a different way. Scrolling down through the information, she confined her search to double and triple matches from *multiple* accounts. Because if you really liked the song but had nothing to hide, why not just watch performances from the same account? Or why not even download the clips, then you can watch them without going online? Multiple accounts and not downloading didn't necessarily mean anything in itself, but it could mean somebody didn't want the risk of a clip being pulled from their hard drive one day. Chopping things this way brought the number right down. But still there were far too many to research. So she repeated the process, looking for multiples that had accessed all five reels. This took longer, but after half an hour more she had sliced the numbers down to just thirty IP addresses. She could work with that. There was no guarantee that *the* address was contained in those thirty, but the probabilities seemed more favourable.

Cat went outside, stood smoking in a patch of sunshine, cracked her knuckles.

Remaining disciplined, she went back to the café, gathered her things, paid up, adding a sandwich for the road. She found herself a third location to work from, humming with impatience now.

Her next step was linking her IP addresses to bricks-and-mortar addresses — a big ask. A simple online IP address locator revealed that a dozen of Cat's thirty addresses were overseas, some as far afield as South Africa and New Zealand. There was one viewer apparently based in Russia. She removed all these addresses from her list. The Russian address bothered her a little. To hide your online activities, you need to operate via a proxy server, which acts as a cloak for your own location. Many proxy servers used by the criminal classes were based in Russia, because there's such a low probability of Western law enforcement reaching that far. But when she looked closely she saw the origin accounts were Russian-language only, and the dates did not quite tally.

She discounted it, ploughed on.

Most of the UK addresses were dynamically assigned. That meant that the internet service provider assigned a new address each time a given user logged on; it was a way for the ISP to minimise costs, maximise efficiency. But there were four static addresses on her list. Three of them didn't yield anything significant. The fourth did. There had been over five watches per day of some reels from this address. That was pretty intense, more than from any others. The geo-locator placed it within three miles of Deptford, the location of Tana's first address, and within shouting distance of both Rhiannon's addresses. Geo-location was an uncertain business, accurate only to a few miles. In which case, the true location could be even closer than that.

Cat went to one of the phone boxes provided, and called Kyle, gave her the IP address and the name of the related internet service provider. Kyle didn't need to worry about geo-location technologies, she could just go straight to the ISP with a warrant.

"I'll call you back," said Kyle and hung up.

Out on the street. Another roll-up. The day had been alternating sunshine and showers, but now a steady drizzle made for miserable streets. Cat smoked in a doorway, like an office refugee.

The call back took thirty minutes. Kyle gave a name and address, then added, "It's in Deptford. An internet café. Half a mile from the girl's flat."

"Thanks." Deptford it was then. Kyle seemed uncharacteristically lost for words. They shared a moment's awkward silence, then cut the call.

Cat got her things and drove to Deptford.

It was early rush hour now. Windscreen wipers and slow-moving traffic. Lights.

She arrived outside. The sign above the shop was crude, cheap, old. Black lettering on a yellow background. Unpainted plywood partitions inside. A basic service at a basic price. A sign outside the café also offered low-price calls to "all your favourite locations". Poland, Russia, Somalia, Iraq, Iran.

She didn't go inside.

A couple of dozen yards down the road, there was a Currys standing next to an independent mobile phone shop. The two premises were surveyed by an external CCTV camera, mounted on a lamppost. The CCTV was focusing on the electronics shops, but would catch the café in its field of view. A swirling green logo on the side of the camera identified its owner as Secura-Lock. A local outfit, not a national one.

She called Directory Enquiries to get a number for Secura-Lock, then got an address. It was so close by, she didn't even need to drive.

A girl with a high-pitched voice, a Middle Eastern accent and lots of make-up was behind the reception desk. Cat slapped her police credentials down on the counter. She didn't use the words "immigration check", but she didn't have to. She had the girl's attention.

She explained what she needed. The file with the IP addresses gave dates and times of log-on and log-off. Cat requested video footage for an hour on either side of the most recent of those periods. If she had to go further back, she would.

The girl was jumpy — a good sign. Once, she accidentally called Cat "sir". She confirmed that Secura-Lock retained footage from all their CCTV cameras for at least six weeks, promised to have the footage made ready for her as soon as possible.

"I need it *now*," said Cat.

"It will take time to download. But we can email it through?"

Yes. Even better. Cat said as much, gave her details. The girl promised to call as soon as the email was sent.

The internet café of interest was open till ten that evening. Cat prepared by getting herself a take-out cappuccino from a nearby coffee shop and drinking it outside, while smoking in a doorway. Feeling better from the coffee and the nicotine, she browsed the biker mags in a newsagent, till she got the call from the girl at Secura-Lock.

Back to work. She went into the café now, set up, found twelve Secura-Lock emails in her inbox. Twelve, because even zipped, the files were so large as to need chopping down into sub-segments.

Cat unzipped the videos, opened up a player to view them. She opened the first email to set the time, noted that it covered the earliest period she had requested, moved to the sixth, which, she estimated, was the most likely to include the moment that she was looking for.

Right at the beginning of the footage two teenage boys exited the café, one still pocketing change. They disappeared into Currys, nudging each other and laughing. Cat let the wmv. file run on. It hadn't been a busy day. Even the traffic and passing trade seemed sparse. She went through it again but as far as she could see the café was empty, start to finish. If her man had been at the back of the shop all the time, she wouldn't catch him. Otherwise, she guessed, she'd pick him up, even if only as a smudge of movement.

She checked all the other files she had. Nothing. Her optimism was fading. It's not that the café had been completely empty. It wasn't. An elderly Afro-Caribbean man entered the shop, looking stately and dignified. A couple of teenage girls. Two women, possibly Poles or Russians, making a cheap long-distance call. No one was what she was looking for or stayed enough time.

So perhaps this whole thing was wrong — perhaps those teenage girls, for example, were hooked on "Street Spirit"; perhaps the Deptford thing was pure coincidence. Or something else.

Cat was betting on something else.

She checked the back of the café. There was no yard, not really. You could just about jam a car in, but it would have been obvious and intrusive to the café owner. There was no side street, which left the front, or maybe an upstairs room of a neighbouring property.

Cat went outside to check the buildings on either side, but there was nothing vacant. Nothing boarded up, or easily accessed by a fire-escape.

She went back to the CCTV footage and checked the cars immediately outside. None of those parked had any occupants. Another car was parked opposite Currys. A white estate, nondescript. Running across the top of the windscreen a strip of green plastic doubled as a sunshield and advertising banner. Cat halted the video, leaned in to the screen, squinted. Just managed to make out some of the lettering: the word Pegasus, it looked like. There was a yellow and black rectangle on the side of the car advertising something.

She let the footage run on for a few seconds, focused on the car's interior, stopped it again when she saw the outline of a man appearing, sitting in the back on the opposite side to the driver, hunched over something resting on his thighs. It was not clear but from that range she thought it would still be possible to piggyback the café's wi-fi.

She went outside with her own laptop to check how far she could go before the connection broke. Two yards, five, ten, twenty-five. She was beyond the relevant parking bay now, and her signal was one-bar but still working.

Back to the café. The owner glared at her, like she was a weirdo, but without much malice. If you want to avoid weirdos, don't set up an internet café.

The white car's registration number wasn't visible. She viewed the fifth video, then the fourth, hoping that she could catch the moment when it arrived, getting a different angle on the plates to read them. It was in the middle of the third section of footage that the car arrived. She stopped the film there. The plate was blurred, needing sharpening and contrast enhancement in Photoshop, not the whole of it visible, but the yellow-and-black advertising section resolved as the details of a minicab firm: Pegasus Cabs.

She exhaled slowly, feeling the cold rush of adrenalin prick through every capillary in her body. Benzos? Screw them. Her current intoxicant of choice was altogether sweeter.

She used Google to get the company location and drove there fast, feeling pumped. The cab firm was positioned four blocks west of Deptford Bridge station. She noted how close it was to Rhiannon's first address, only two streets away.

She was moving in ever diminishing circles.

The area was a mixture of social housing and small, down-at-heel businesses. The mini-cab company stood next door to a take-away kebab shop, little more than a kiosk. The two businesses occupied a property that had once been single usage, but someone along the way had put in a crude dividing wall.

She parked, climbed out, walked straight in the front door. The cab office had little to it beyond being a place where clients' calls could be taken and drivers directed via a two-way radio system. In one corner of the room sat three casually dressed men in their mid-twenties — cabbies, waiting for a fare to call. They were occupying chipped chairs while conducting a desultory conversation about the Premier League in heavily accented English.

Most of the back of the office was occupied by a counter topped with a built-in shutter that had been left open. Behind this sat a squat individual with sleek, black hair. He wore a garish open-necked seersucker shirt in pink and yellow. Tendrils of chest hair were clearly visible above the top buttons. On his wrist sat a heavy gold Rolex watch. Cat pulled her warrant card out of her pocket, waved it in front of him.

"I'd like to see your fare book from June."

Rolex was almost too quick for her, but she managed to stick her fist under the shutter to prevent its closure.

"You want a charge of ABH against an officer, do you?" she shouted into the gap between shutter and desk, refusing to retract her arm.

He seemed to understand the situation. Gradually the shutter was raised, the fare book pushed begrudgingly across the counter. The records had been entered in a leatherbound ledger with a stained cover. Inside, there were greasy smears hinting at a more than casual link with the kebab house next door. Cat turned the pages quickly, searching first for the correct date, then the time that she had seen the cab parked opposite the cybercafé. About halfway down the page she found a reference to a drop-off.

"So which driver is seventeen then?"

Out of the corner of her eye she caught a sudden movement. A rustling noise as a newspaper was put down. One of the three waiting drivers was leaving by a doorway to the right of the counter. The shutter slammed down loudly as she ran after the driver into the building's back yard.

The yard measured no more than twenty feet from one end to the other; most of it taken up by overflowing bins. There was a door that would have given access to the street but had rusted shut. The wall was less than seven feet high and the cabbie was halfway over it. Cat grabbed the man's legs as he scaled it, used all her weight to bring him back down. She wasn't taking any chances. As he dropped, she wound her right arm around his neck, squeezed it back towards her shoulder so that it obstructed his windpipe, tensed her arm a little so that her hard bicep bit into his soft throat.

"All right! Fuck's sake."

His face was contorted, his arms up in a gesture of surrender.

She kept her arm where it was, but loosened her hold slightly. He smelled of inexpensive aftershave with an overlay of sweat. She could feel his fear.

"I'm not immigration, I'm not interested in your papers. OK?"

He nodded slowly. Half-turned and threw a longing glance at the wall, freedom.

"Who was the man in your cab with a laptop?"

He shook his head. "I don't remember."

Cat wasn't too bothered; he'd have to resist at least one question for his self-esteem.

"I am becoming a little more interested in your papers now."

She saw him glance to the right, followed his gaze. She saw the office owner with the Rolex and the two other drivers now moving across the yard towards her. Rolex came in close, sneering. He must be as stupid as all hell to threaten a police officer, but if people weren't stupid, policing would be a quiet job.

Cat gave driver 17 a last, hard squeeze on the Adam's apple to leave him choking and temporarily incapacitated. Then in one flowing move stepped forward and kicked Rolex in the groin. It wasn't a precise martial arts kick, Walter would be tutting disapproval, but she was Welsh and liked to allow herself a robust rugby punt, now and again. Rolex sagged to the ground.

"Back off!"

The growl that emerged from her throat had the desired effect on the men who cupped their hands in front of their crotches. They hesitated, not wanting to lose face and retreat but looking as if they didn't fancy it either.

Back to driver 17, who was beginning to revive. She pushed his head against a wall to give her back the initiative, then resumed her choke hold and pulled him backwards with her down some steps. She just managed to right herself in time to maintain her hold. The steps led down to a doorway. In the yard, the three men were moving closer, recovering their courage. She backed through the door, dragging driver 17 by the throat after her. They came into another small yard. The smell of spices mixed uneasily with the stench of the bins.

She had some time, but not much.

She moved against the wall, briefly increasing the pressure to remind her prisoner who was boss. He grunted in response, moved his head from side to side in an attempt to gain some freedom. And some air.

"Who is he?" Cat asked again.

"Don't know."

He had a lot to lose by holding out, and she'd been told a lot of lies in her time but there was a tone in his voice that made her believe him. She tried another avenue.

"Where do you pick him up?"

"I can't remember."

"Where?"

He pointed at the passageway out to the street.

"That one, he always comes off the street."

She sensed he was telling the truth. But it was a truth that didn't tell her anything she could use. She increased the pressure on his neck again, was rewarded with a strangled grunt.

"Up close what does he look like?"

"Always he wears glasses, a scarf."

"The drop-off?"

"By that café. He just sits there, uses his laptop."

"He get out there?"

"No, he asks me to drop him on the street, different places each time."

"Accent?"

"English man. I don't know."

She could feel the man relax, the tension in his muscles ebb away. This meant he'd told her everything, he knew he could not be made to give more. He even allowed himself a flourish now. He extended his arm, made a claw with his hand, then made a gentle throwing motion. "He's there, then he's gone."

"Like magic, huh."

Cat slumped, relaxing her hold. She knew how close she had got, which made the dead end that she had hit all the more painful. Feeling Cat's grasp weaken, the man slipped his neck from her hold and half-turned, cautiously backing off towards the white door. Cat closed her eyes. The killer had been there in front of her, then disappeared, as a dream evaporates on waking.

"Pick up or drop him on these streets?"

She reeled off the three local addresses, both Tana's and Rhiannon's.

"Last one maybe. Once, I think."

She gave the address again. He shrugged. It was a long street, she knew. She was clutching at straws now.

"Fuck it," she shouted. The frustration was unbearable.

She heard the advance of feet from the adjoining yard as the cabbies gained the confidence to come again. Something told her she'd need to conserve her energy. She turned, jumped and slapped her palms on top of the wall of the yard, hoisted herself up, lifting her legs, she balanced momentarily on top of the wall, before dropping down into the street below.

The fading daylight did little to improve the look of Rhiannon's former lodging. The rain had stopped for a couple of hours but was now returning intermittently, a skein of droplets on the windscreen. In Wales weeks could pass in this state of perpetual dampness. This felt like home.

She pulled into a space on the same side as the property, about thirty yards short. Out of the corner of her eye, by the dim light of a flickering street lamp, she caught a sign hanging in a window. A dirty flag, with a pentangle painted on it.

It was draped like a curtain from an upper window in the grimy brick tenement block. The front garden had a fridge-freezer rusting in the garden. A buddleia was trying to shoot from the old icebox. There was no doorbell, just a couple of wires poking out of a rotting doorframe. No lights on in any downstairs room. She knocked, her knuckles making little impression on the heavy door. She would have peered into the front room just beside her, but a red fake velvet drape hung in the window. A dead pot plant sat between the drape and the window, a little sanctuary for the home's spiders.

She traversed round to the back of the house where the long low extension had a flat roof, sheeted with roofing felt. A couple of dustbins and a teetering drainpipe gave her a way up. She climbed onto the roof. Jumping down the other way would place her in the garden and allow her to try the back door, but there were no lights there either. A window faced out onto the roof. She banged on it a couple of times, just to check there was no one there. She prepared to smash the window with a boot heel.

But the second knock brought a face to the window. A thin man, Asian, wearing a yellow T-shirt, none too new. She banged again, pressing her warrant card up against the glass.

"Police," she snapped. "Open up immediately."

The face disappeared to be replaced by a woman's face. Then the man fiddled with the window lock and threw the window up. Cat climbed in. The room was ten foot by six foot, and housed three people: the immigrant couple and a two-year-old daughter. There was a kettle and a pair of electric rings in the corner. The three of them shared a single, ancient mattress.

Cat was already on her way out and upstairs.

Deeper into the house, a red bulb on an upper landing glowed its seedy invitation. Cat wondered about exit routes. Wondered if it was right to be here. Wondered if she should tell Kyle her whereabouts.

Too late. She was heading up.

The stairs creaked under her. The place stank of an overflowing toilet and uncleaned carpet. She made for the top floor, trying to feel centred. Trying to find her fighting energy.

At the top there was a single door. Music was coming through beneath it. She knocked hard, yelled, "Police."

Nothing. She knocked again and slammed the door with her boot. She was about to make a more serious effort when the door opened. A cadaverous man — maybe early twenties — in skinny black jeans and a Led Zeppelin T-shirt hung in the doorway smirking at her.

"Fuller?" The man hesitated. "Roberts?" He still hesitated, but at the same time scratching his scrawny neck. She reckoned she'd got Roberts.

"Pigs?"

"May I come in?" Cat was polite, because she had to be. She had no legal right of entry. She couldn't step over the threshold without an invitation.

"You got a warrant?" Roberts smirked at her, enjoying his little one-upmanship. Incense and the sweet smell of marijuana hung in the air.

"Buddy, I don't have a warrant, but if you want me to come back here with a van full of cops and a sniffer dog, then I will, I will."

He smirked a bit more, then flung himself aside so the way was clear for Cat to enter. She did so and the moment she did, he swung the door shut and locked it.

"For your comfort and safety," he said.

Cat checked the lock. It wasn't a Yale that could be unlocked from the inside, but a mortice lock and Roberts had pocketed the key.

He swept past a dirty kitchen and an unspeakable bathroom into a surprisingly large living room. Blackout curtains prevented any street light entering from outside. There was no electric light, only twenty or thirty wax candles. Apart from Roberts and Cat herself, there were three people in the room: an unusually tough-looking hippy in combat gear and dreadlocks — Fuller? — two girls, all dramatic eye make-up, black dresses and beads. There was a table covered in black cloth, and at the centre a human skull.

One of the girls was more finely dressed than the other and more alert. Her close-fitting black jacket looked like something a professional horsewoman would wear.

The girl eyed Cat apprehensively, whispered something to her friend. As Cat approached, she saw that she looked about the same age as her friend, but, with her finely cut clothes, she exuded a greater air of authority. A woman trying to look older than her years.

"Do you believe in the devil, pig?" said Roberts.

"Does the name Rhiannon Powell mean anything to you?"

"Look out over London. Tell me, who's winning?"

"I have reason to believe that Rhiannon Powell used this address. She was murdered." And here Cat looked at the two girls. "Murdered recently, in her own garden."

"Or sacrificed." The hippy was standing now. He had the dissociated look that goes with PTSD or a bad drug experience.

"What do you mean?"

"Don't pay any attention. He's out of it." Roberts again.

The guy was tall — six two, six three even — and a strong bastard, gym-muscled. He stood too close, breathing tobacco and garlic breath into Cat's hair.

"Oi," said Roberts, but the hippy wasn't listening.

"She was frightened as shit that's what." The hippy stared at her. "Aren't you?"

"I think you should leave." It was one of the two girls speaking, urgently but quietly.

"Frightened of what?" asked Cat, but she got no answer.

"Fucking pig." The hippy had his hand on Cat's chest and was pushing her back against the wall. She didn't know the room layout and the place was so untidy she had no idea what might be lying on the floor to trip her.

"She wouldn't tell us." One of the girls looked more frightened than the others. She went over to Roberts.

The hippy was still closing. Cat was pinned against the wall. The girl took the key from Roberts, was opening the door. Then it slammed and she was gone.

The hippy had his bearded face up close to Cat's. "I don't remember inviting you in here."

"Steady," Cat said, "steady," as though talking to a horse.

He pulled his head back. Cat wasn't sure why. He was going to either spit or headbutt her, and if it was the latter she wasn't sure she'd win any fight that followed.

She stamped on his instep, and brought her knee up as his face folded down with the pain. She made good contact — felt blood soaking into her trouser leg — and flung the guy to the side.

"Fuck's sake, man." That, from Roberts.

She needed to move fast to reach the girl. She edged towards him and the door, hoping that he'd be only too happy to let her out.

He was. She ran forwards. Roberts first forgot he had a key, then remembered, then fumbled the lock, then undid it. The hippy was at the end of the short corridor, with a Gothic-looking hunting knife in his hand. Cat fled. She pounded down the stairs, to the back room with the immigrant family in it, didn't trust that the front door could be opened from the inside.

Without a word of explanation, she flung open the window and bundled herself out onto the roof, from there to the pavement.

She leaned panting against a graffitied wall. She had to laugh at herself, really.

Reaching the street Cat saw the retreating back of the girl. Keeping a steady pace she kept her close, waited until she was out of sight of the house. Further down, the street branched off into separate roads containing large Edwardian houses. The girl crossed over to the other side.

The clatter of retreating heels was not the syncopated click-clack of the self-possessed: their rhythm was quicker, more urgent, brisker than a purposeful stride. The footfalls had upset in them. Cat turned, looked again, saw now that the girl was running.

She crossed the street again. Cat made her move. "Wait!"

The girl spun around, looked startled. Cat could see the marks of tears on her cheeks. She clutched a balled tissue in her right hand, sniffed.

"You were a friend of Rhiannon's, weren't you?"

Cat moved closer, put a hand on her left arm, squeezed gently. The girl did not nod, but she did not move away either. Shock kept her still.

"I'm police, but not what your friends thought." She gestured back behind them. "Can we talk?"

The girl did not stop, and Cat walked fast beside her. "I never really knew her. I mean, she answered an ad for the room, paid the rent, but she was hardly there."

The girl hoped this was enough but Cat stayed on her.

"All her stuff — she didn't have much — she took to the other flat."

"Two places she had?"

"Maybe more, dunno."

"OK, I believe you," Cat said gently. "Did she see an older man ever?"

"No. I don't know. She never mentioned anything like that, but she kept going away." The girl bowed her head. "It just feels so wrong that she —"

The girl started to cry. Cat asked for a name — Jen — and gave her own. Cat patted her pockets, pretending to look for a tissue but knowing she didn't have one.

"She was a singer, wasn't she?"

Jen nodded.

"Listen, can I ask if any of these pictures mean anything to you? Do you know where they might have been taken?"

Cat showed the printouts she'd made of the missing girls. All singing the same song. "These ring any bells?"

Cat kept her eyes fixed on the girl's face for any sign of recognition. She showed close-ups of the victims' faces, then focused on features of the stage. The peeling paint on the proscenium, the corner of the flat at the back with the painted battlements. Nothing produced so much as a flicker.

"No, I've never seen anything like that before."

The girl removed her hand from Cat's, put the tissue to her nose as she shook her head. She pulled away, moved across the street to a hatchback. Its scratched paintwork had faded to an unattractive pinky-orange. The back bumper was dented in several places. The girl removed a bunch of keys from her pocket, opened the door, slid in quickly behind the wheel. The engine coughed briefly, then caught.

Something clicked in Cat's mind. "Wait?" She screamed, belted forward, reached the car just as the girl was pulling out into the road. She banged an open palm on the windscreen, her rings clattering on the glass. Cat mimed winding down the window, held her hands together in a plea, caught the girl's eye with her imploring own. A small chink appeared at the top of the driver's window. Cat moved round, breathless.

"Rhiannon, she didn't have a driving licence, did she? You gave her lifts."

Jen nodded. "Sometimes, yeah. I mean, she had a bike too, but . . ."

She gestured quickly upwards, by way of explanation, at the rain. But something in her mood had changed. Her hands were tensed on the steering wheel, her leg moving as she pumped the clutch, inching to get away. Cat knew she would have to act fast. "Ever drop her off in the Deptford area?"

There was an almost imperceptible twitch in the girl's cheek. "Yes."

"Where? Where did you take her?"

The girl took a deep breath, cleared her throat. "It was funny. She never told me where she was going. Just asked me to drop her by the river."

"Jen, this is really important. Really, really important. Can you take me there? Take me there now?"

Jen reached over to move a patterned straw shopping bag from the passenger seat. "Be my guest," she said.

CHAPTER
TWENTY

Jen dropped Cat at an unlit spot near the river. She told Cat her friend always went off past the yards by the water, and that the place gave her the creeps. Cat could just make out the yards, a building site and a taller structure beyond them.

"Listen, wait here for me. If you see anything that scares you, just call the police straight away. Say you're calling in relation to Operation *Bedd Arthur*." The Welsh name was Thomas's invention, his little Welsh welcome present to any interference from London.

Cat made Jen repeat the name, made her check she had a phone signal, got her to lock her doors and turn the car so it was pointing out of the complex and ready for a quick get-away. Jen sounded compliant, but Cat expected her to disappear as soon as her back was turned.

Nearing darkness, the river was just a wasteland of rubbish and industrial flotsam, some moving upstream on the tide. Cat hugged herself for warmth, and peered around. There was a strip of empty lots and a couple of builder's supply yards, with wide turning areas for incoming trucks. Wire-mesh fences and cameras; security lights starting to blink on. Not exactly a place to coax a fine performance from a wannabe singer. Across from the waste ground and the builder's yards, there was what looked like a deserted chapel. Any view it had once enjoyed had been taken by a warehouse to the front, currently undergoing conversion to flats. As a working place of worship, the chapel must have been impressive in its glory days, but now it was just a fume-blackened shell, ripe for restoration or, more likely, demolition.

The sky above turned an unearthly mauve, the chapel lit by a corona of light coming from a small break in the clouds. She shivered and approached through an evening that was now as cold as it was wet.

A path threaded off the pavement, round the back of a yard. She took it. The chapel was set back behind a box hedge which had been left to go wild. A no-trespassing sign was sealed in polythene against the elements. Incongruously, some borders had been planted with roses, perhaps to lighten the air of dereliction. The brightness of the roses seemed feeble against the ruin. Rubbish was strewn in the borders and gang tags covered the wall behind. The gate was stopped with wire and secured with a padlock, but gaps had been worn in the hedge to the side.

She glanced up at the chapel. It seemed familiar somehow.

Inside the grounds, the paving was broken and moss-covered. A big pile of weeds and hedge clippings sat in a wide, woven polythene builder's bag, awaiting removal. To the side of the chapel entrance, a glass-fronted board lay shattered on the ground and covered in graffiti. It's been deconsecrated, she thought. Desecrated as well, perhaps.

Just then, her phone rang. She jumped — literally jumped. The panic was momentary — only Kyle had her number — but her reaction revealed her own state to her. She palmed the phone from her pocket and answered.

"Price, you OK?"

"Yes. Making progress."

"Anything you want to tell me?"

"Not sure. Maybe not right now. It's not a brilliant time."

"OK. Look, one thing you ought to know. I went by your flat just now. I thought I ought to."

Cat gulped. Fear wasn't an intangible thing. It was real. It gripped you. It could make you choke. She fought out a word. "Yes."

"Someone's gone over the place. I'm standing in it now."

"Fuck."

"It's a shit-hole, but I expect it was before."

"Yes." Cat tried a little ghost of a smile. She thought that was probably Kyle's humour at work. A rare misshapen thing, but delicate and easily bruised.

"There's no computer here," said Kyle, returning.

"There *was* a desktop. A black tower unit —"

"I know. Only the monitor's here and the keyboard. They've just taken the computer itself."

"There was nothing on it. Personal stuff, I mean."

"A fishing trip," said Kyle. "You're safe?"

"Yes."

"Phones, credit cards, email accounts?"

Cat told Kyle what she'd done on all those fronts.

"Good," said Kyle.

"Is the flat in a real mess?"

"Yes." There was a moment's hesitation, then Kyle chose to opt for honesty. "They've knifed most of your clothes, your bedding, your mattress. Not looking for anything, I don't think, more just sending a warning."

"They could have tried a card": Cat's own feeble attempt at humour.

"Yeah, look, you can come in. We can bring in the Met. Throw resources at it. Make this whole damn thing so big, so public, so out there, you won't be a target any more."

"Unless I want to be."

"Yes, there's that."

"And going big might just make our man bolt for the hills."

"It's your call, Price. My advice would be to call it a day."

"Thanks." Cat fell silent for a moment. Gulls cawed overhead in the purple sky. Ahead stood the smoke-blackened facade of the chapel. "Look, I'll call you back."

Cat pocketed the phone. She had no headache. She was fighting her way clear. This is what being clean would feel like one day. Clarity you could taste.

She approached the main door to the church and twisted the iron handle. It moved to the right, but when she leaned against it there was no give. She made her way round the side of the building. The path was narrow, slippery with lichen in places. At the back there was another door. This looked in worse repair. The varnish had peeled and the wood was exposed to the elements, had cracked in places. She bent down, placed a wide eye to a crack, looked inside but could make out nothing. She pulled her hand back into her jacket, pushed her arm at the rotten section of the door, felt it give. The panels made no noise as they crumbled. Reaching in through the gap, she moved her arm upwards until she felt the door handle on the inside. Down an inch or so. She changed her position slightly, worked it until it turned.

Inside it was damp. She felt the atmosphere collecting in her throat. She coughed, rebuked herself for the noise, listened. Nothing. If the killer was in here he was silent as the grave. Had he already heard her? Cat stepped forward, cracked her shin on something, heard a scraping. If she carried on in the dark, inevitably she'd make more sound as she moved forwards. She decided to chance a light, pulled her phone out, flicked the beam level down by touch. She was in the vestry. There was an old open-fronted cupboard where once surplices and cassocks had hung. A door gave onto a narrow cubicle containing a toilet without a seat, rust stains in the bowl.

She opened the door, moved slowly through the gap between the pews into the nave. At first she wondered at the strange quality of the light, then the flapping wings of a pigeon alerted her to the cause. She looked up, saw that a hole in the roof diluted the coloured patterns created by the fading daylight filtering through

350

the stained glass. Briefly she wondered whether the place was structurally sound.

Ahead there was no chancel or altar. Instead, in a central area which should have contained more pews, a curtain sheltered a covered space. She listened. Again, nothing. She moved the velvet drapes apart, nose wrinkling at the displaced dust.

Inside it looked like some sort of stage, a small performance space. The rostra had been fastened together, stood no more than six inches off the floor. On each side a couple of wooden uprights had been painted eau de Nil, decorated with Baroque gilt scrolls. There was the illusion of a grand old theatre, although one that had seen better days.

Above, instead of a formal arch, a steel pole acting as a batten on which theatrical spotlights had been hung. Laid on its side, supported by a row of old chairs, a threadbare theatrical flat depicted a fairy-tale scene: a Mad Ludwig castle topped with jagged battlements. There were patterns on the battlements, some moss painted in between the faux-boulders of the castle walls and in an area on the right-hand side, superimposed over the rest, was what looked like an advertising poster. She studied it — a vintage ad for a Scotch whisky — and wondered why the scene painter had bothered to put it in. It diminished the illusion of the castle and the colours didn't harmonise with those of the wall.

In the centre was a microphone on a stand, an instrument which had likely captured the voices of five girls who were now dead. On the ground, in front of the stage, three low tables and plush chairs formed a child's vision of nightclub sophistication. A painted vaudeville-style sign advertised the Café Moon.

Cat stood, drapes still clutched in her hands, listening carefully for any sound. She heard only the flap of the pigeons flying in and out through the roof. Strange to be here at last, knowing that her flat had been trashed, believing that someone would dearly love to kill her. Not properly understanding why.

She stepped inside the drapes, picked her way warily around the stage, walked behind it. There was a bed there, a fairy-tale-style half-tester, satin sheets, white eiderdown. A vase on a table, empty of flowers. A silk carpet on the floor.

Silk carpets and pigeon-droppings.

She reached for her phone, took a picture of the bed. She moved round to the front, listened carefully again, opened the drapes wide, took more of the stage area, the tables and chairs at the foot of the stage. She checked through each shot to make sure the camera's night setting had worked.

The door to the vestry was still as she had left it — pulled to, but not closed. She winced as it scraped against the floor. She'd damaged the door somewhat when she forced it. But not much, it had been in bad shape before.

She stopped with her back against the door, listening. The gulls were still there, but there was something else besides. A scraping, shuffling sound outside on the street. Heart in mouth, she eased round the building, trying to get a clear view. The gates, previously padlocked, were open. A white Berlingo van was parked just beyond, its rear backed up to the entrance.

A man crouched by the gate, dropping weeds into a bin bag. He tugged the bag full of weeds to the open doors of his van. And turned to his side. He was average build, early or mid sixties maybe, with a boozer's veiny nose. He walked with a slight limp.

Cat held back, watching him. He seemed an improbable Mr Big, but Cat didn't feel like testing the limits of chance, not right now.

She heard the van's back doors closing, then the gate being shut. Waited until she heard the sound of the van starting, then ran through the gap into the hedge, to find Jen still waiting bravely.

Cat leaped into the car, grinned at Jen, and told her to follow the van.

"Really?" Jen tried starting the car with the handbrake on, stalled, tried again and Cat needed to release the handbrake herself before they got going. "Sorry," said Jen. "Nerves."

A high-speed chase it wasn't. The van cruised slowly, never breaking the speed limit. It took backroads, past scrapyards, rows of lock-ups, a closed-up garage specialising in the repair of freezer lorries. The road ran downhill, underneath a railway embankment, through red-brick arches black with years of pollution. After about ten minutes, the van pulled into a small yard framed by two open steel doors. At the back of the cobbled yard there was a low warehouse.

Jen drove, on Cat's orders, just beyond the steel doors and parked up. Cat got out and hurried back.

She stood under the yard's wall, bobbed her head out, got a look through the open gates. The place was small. In front of the warehouse, a jumble of items littered the ground. There were extending ladders, stacks of buckets, squeegees on extendable poles, stacks of roof tiles, wheelbarrows that looked too rusted to be of any practical use, rolls of electrical cable, sacks of compost. The gardener had stepped out of his van and was unlocking the back doors to tug out his bag of weeds.

Cat surveyed the yard. The awkward way the man was moving suggested he had bad arthritis.

She approached through the open gates, moved quietly over the cobbles towards him. She could see him clearly now. Apart from the booze-wrecked nose, his other features were moleish: small mouth, deepset eyes. She was practically within touching distance before he realised that she was there. As he heard her he whirled round. He flinched, reached for his heart, put an open palm across it, steadied himself.

"What? You made me jump."

She'd go in softly at first. "Sorry, I did shout," she lied. "You didn't hear."

"Right." He nodded. "Lugholes not what they were."

He looked at her, lowered his lids, seemed puzzled. She could see his wits gathering as the surprise began to wear off. He was about to ask her what the hell she was doing in his yard. She nodded back up the road in the direction of the chapel. "That your place back there? The chapel?"

He frowned, realised she'd followed him down, as she had intended he would. He seemed to take a moment to gather himself, took a greasy rag out of his pocket, reached into the back of the van, pulled out the hedge cutters. He wiped them with the rag, ran his finger along the opened blade. Was he trying to menace her?

"Who are you?" He was angry now.

She reached in her pocket and took out her police ID. His face wrinkled as if she was handing him something rancid. He didn't look at it. From the first time she saw him close up he had reminded her of someone she knew. Or was that just her nerves and the failing light? She didn't know.

"I'm the landlord," he said. Standing up straight with the box in his arms, he paused, turned to her. "I've a few units around here, bedsits and one-beds mostly, nothing fancy. Bought the whole portfolio from a foreclosure sale. A buy-to-let thing that went bad. That dump came with it."

"It's tenanted?"

He looked to the side, as if seeking some reason to excuse himself. Cat noted his reaction. "Well?"

"In a manner of speaking."

"Are you being paid rent for it?"

"Punctually."

"So, who's paying?"

He dumped his box on the ground, puffing with the exertion. "I've never met him, and he doesn't seem to use the place."

"Someone does."

He rested the hoe against the van, picked up the box, carried it towards the doors of the warehouse. Cat followed him, moved in front so he wasn't able to open the door. "There's sound equipment there, lights. It's like a film set for a nightclub."

He flapped his hand dismissively, reached in his pocket for the keys. Cat put her hand on his arm. "So this is a sitting tenant you inherited?"

He pulled his hand out of his pocket, the keys hanging from his middle finger. "He just leaves cash in an envelope every six months."

Cash, no receipt. The way you paid if you wanted to stay out of the system. The way she was using now. "So what name's he given you?"

"Never has. His predecessor was called Archibald Leach."

Cat thought that she saw a flicker of a smile on that otherwise morose face. She knew the cause of his amusement. "Archibald Leach, huh?" It was one of the more famous pseudonyms in show business.

"That's right. I've got Cary Grant for a tenant. And him well over a hundred by now." He gently moved Cat aside as he locked his van. "Look, I don't ask questions. I'm paid above market rate. I've never seen anyone in there. A big place like that, no heating, no roof, just an empty shell, it would be impossible to rent otherwise."

So near and yet so far. The front of Cat's brain felt like she was chasing shadows again. No sooner did she catch up with one, than it melted away under her grip.

That wasn't what the back part of her mind thought, however. That part felt the light bulbs stringing together again, blinking on, illuminating the darkness. She didn't feel defeated. She felt whatever it is you feel one stop before triumphant.

CHAPTER
TWENTY-ONE

Crouch Hill, the following morning.

Cat had spent the night in another anonymous hotel. She scrubbed her clothes with a bar of soap when she undressed for the night, hung them out to dry, and put them on again, still slightly damp, in the morning. She'd had three cups of coffee, three roll-ups, not much by way of food. She'd done some good work on the internet and phone, checked in with Kyle, chatted with Thomas.

The house she was after was a two-storey detached affair made from pale stone, and topped by a loft conversion. It had to be worth a fair bit, maybe as much as three-quarters of a million now that Crouch End had become one of the fashionable suburbs.

She paused before she pressed Farrell's doorbell, felt the confusion of the case temporarily bulge in her mind: the certainty that he had done it, the certainty that he could not have done it. She felt herself spinning into the unthinkable. Light bulbs flickering on and off in the dark. But more on now than off.

She concentrated on the doorbell. It looked like an original fixture but when she rang it, the buzzer played the first bars of "Summertime". After only a few seconds there was a click as the door opened a crack. She put her hand against it, pushed. There was nobody on the other side.

"In here. Close the door behind you." The speaker had a rough voice, a smoker's voice with too much phlegm. Frogspawn sliding over gravel. She followed the sound along a short passageway. The light faded as she moved away from the front door. On her left a door was ajar, the wheezing audible from within, a flickering emerging from the room.

She stepped inside. The place was a shrine.

Every surface had been covered in photographs, some in sharp minimalist frames, others in elaborate antique versions. The curtains were closed, the lights off. Each frame was lit by its own candle. The photographs all featured the same woman. Farrell, a gaunt, bent figure in a tracksuit, was sitting in an armchair in the corner, a dark outline beyond the reach of the light. On the wall opposite hung a large flat-screen TV, a home cinema system resting on a table beneath it.

Farrell looked at Cat, almost smiled when he saw her gawping at the photos. His expression said, *Go ahead, take your time*. Cat moved in closer, took a good look. One in particular made her think of the girls in the "Street Spirit" videos. A woman in a long, flowing white robe moving through an immaculately manicured garden, arms outstretched, a beatific expression on her face, as if in the throes of some religious — or erotic — trance. Her mouth was parted, her face hinted that she was looking at the world for the first time and liked what she saw.

"This is her?" Cat asked, but it was a stupid question.

"Yes. That's her."

Hetty Moon, a singer. At the chapel, the stage set was intended to evoke — or more precisely, to replicate — a nightclub, a smoky jazz singer's dive. The poster on the castle wall had been the tell. If you want to evoke a castle, paint a castle. If you want to evoke a set *pretending* to be a castle, then insert something, in this case an advertising poster, that makes the pretence clear.

The lead Cat had worked with initially was that "Café Moon" sign. She'd searched for nightclubs of that name. First in London, then nationwide, then internationally. When that search had become too frustrating, she switched tack and started searching for female singers, with the surname Moon. Five minutes and she had her: a minor club singer from the Nineties. Her stage name, Hetty Moon. Jimmy Farrell had once been her manager, was still her brother.

Cat's eyes became more accustomed to the light. She noticed the three paintings on the wall. Two were traditional head-and-shoulders portraits. The third was a version of the garden scene in oils. In between the portraits Farrell had hung half a dozen prints of medieval paintings, all pietas.

Farrell coughed, the sudden noise startling Cat. It was his signal that her gazing was now over, that the visitor needed to talk.

"Beautiful girl, your sister," Cat said.

He looked up at her, his fist clenched in front of his face as though suppressing another cough. He was weak, but his eyes looked canny and stubborn. She sensed a wounded awkwardness. She'd got this interview pretending to be a journalist for an obscure jazz magazine. She'd probably have to continue with that charade now.

For a few minutes she asked conventional questions about Moon's singing career. She adopted a reverential tone, as if she were talking about someone whose importance the world had yet to see. Throughout Farrell murmured approvingly.

Cat sensed she'd done enough. "I heard she took up with a rich bloke," she said.

Farrell made another noise. Not a cough this time. A sudden cry of pain. He hunched over in his seat, bent down towards his lap. Revealed a bald patch on the top of his head, haloed by badly cut, greying hair. Cat moved over to him, put a hand on his shoulder. Her hand vibrated as his body shook. She waited for him to regain control.

"He used to come and watch her every time she was on. Never missed a show, wherever she was singing."

She leaned forward, squeezed his shoulder gently. "So who was he?"

He made a choking noise. "A big player, a high roller. She thought he was the love of her life. He took her all over the world. The Far East, South America."

"Very nice."

"Not so nice in the end. There was a yacht fire off Uruguay, Punta del Este, and her body came back in a box." Farrell pulled a crumpled handkerchief out of his pocket, used it to mop his eyes. "The man disappeared into thin air."

"Maybe not as thin as all that."

She crouched on the floor next to Farrell's chair, studied his face. Close up she saw traces of the same gene pool that had made his sister beautiful, but in her older brother these features looked distorted, as if drawn by a vicious cartoonist. He was too thin and his face was deeply wrinkled, tears still tracking down the runnels.

"There must have been an investigation?"

"The boat went down in disputed waters. Argies, Uruguyans, Brazilians, they all think they have a claim there. No one wanted to know. You've seen her sing, I assume? That's why you're here?"

"No. Recordings, but not —"

The man groped around beneath his chair for a remote, aimed it at the TV.

Almost immediately the screen was filled with a close-up of Hetty Moon. Her face was so pale in the spotlight that it glowed, her eyes wide as she emitted a luminous smile. The camera pulled back to reveal a stage framed with black velvet curtains. At the front gaslights flared. Hetty Moon was dressed in a white dress that flowed down to the stage. In the background there were the battlements of the fairy-tale castle, the poster on top of the boulders that made the castle's walls. It was the stage set she had seen in the chapel, only this was the original version, the real fake-castle not the reconstruction.

Hetty's eyes closed. She moved to the mic, started to sing "Help Me Make It Through the Night", her voice clear and true as a choirgirl's. There was no sign of any jazz intonation, nor any accompaniment. At first she stood still, hands down at her sides. Then, at the beginning of the second verse, she raised them almost to shoulder height, made a series of fluttering movements.

Cat kept her eyes on the singer's face, noticed how its mood was gradually changing. The transition from the joyous, ecstatic expression at the beginning of the song to her sombre demeanour at the end was subtle, perfectly timed. By the time she had finished her hands were back at her sides, her head bowed. Then there was silence for a few seconds.

The spotlight cropped her more closely.

Then slowly it started, the Devil's Song: the version of it — Hetty's version — which had bewitched the killer, made him find and coach girls to copy it. Hetty lifted her head, took a breath, moved into "Street Spirit". She barely made it through the first ten bars before her tears started. She sang gently, the brutal words transformed into a dark, sad lullaby. Beautiful enough for angels; dark enough for Riley's devil.

Cat listened intently, felt herself going too, felt the strain, the dark thoughts, the isolation, felt moved by Hetty Moon's version of the song in a way that she had not with the other girls. For the first time she understood what Rhys had meant all those years ago when he'd said the song could have been written by God about the devil. She understood how Riley could have got transfixed by the song far beyond the point of ordinary journalistic professionalism. It was unremittingly hopeless, but intoxicatingly so.

Cat felt it too. Felt it here in the presence of Hetty's version. She heard the same strange vocal tic in the mid-section of the song, the one she had first heard with Esyllt and the other girls. Hetty kept her hands by her sides. They had gradually clenched into fists by the end of the performance. Had he been there in the crowd, the killer, watching this very performance, cannibalising the experience into his own dark mythology? Moon held the last note, long enough for the spotlight to fade to black. The gaslights flickered to extinction.

Cat found she was rubbing her eye sockets with her fingers, her throat and eyes burning with unreleased tears. She looked round at Farrell. He was sitting on the edge of his chair, his expression rapt like a religious convert receiving his first communion.

"Go now," he said, unable to bring himself to look at her. "Just go."

He seemed too moved, too locked into the pains of his past to be with anybody. She wanted to comfort him, but she saw it was useless. She left the house and drove over to Hampstead Heath.

CHAPTER
TWENTY-TWO

When Cat arrived, Thomas was stood by his unmarked car, cigarette in mouth, door open, listening to "Satisfaction" on the car stereo. He was trying his best to look unflustered, but he must have started early to get here from Camarthen, must be itching to know why Cat had brought him here.

She parked, climbed out, walked towards him. Cat was rattled and knew they had to move fast, but she couldn't resist a tussle with Thomas. "Cock rock, is it?" she said, nodding towards the stereo.

"It's class, that's what that is." He paused, wanting to needle her. Wanting to pour cold water on her theories, but also too intrigued to see what Cat was intending.

She smiled. "You don't believe me now, Thomas, but you bloody well will."

They chose to drive the short distance to Morgan's house. The mood changed. Neither of them spoke.

Nearing the house, Cat noticed that there were fewer journalists. She saw only a couple sitting on the pub terrace, smoking. She glanced at the windows of the hostel where no lenses glinted. It seemed that most of the media vultures had waited too long for their

Morgan death shot and moved on, to circle a different imminent corpse perhaps.

"Drive right up to the door," Cat told Thomas.

"We going to do a ram raid, are we?"

"Something like that. Trust me."

They neared the house. Off to the side, the gate to Morgan's private parking area was closed as before. The house still had an air of mourning. Nothing stirred. The blackness of the shutters and the paintwork glinted faintly, as if sheltering something ancient and implacable.

She didn't have time to mess about. She was going straight in the front.

"Stay in the car."

Cat got out, walked quickly towards the house, swung the low black gate open, entered the small front garden and looked at the imposing front door. It was strange, just to be able to do that, walk right up and stand at Morgan's door. But she knew it would no longer be that easy.

Cat pushed the polished brass bell. It gave a slow bass ring, but there was no response to the sound from within. She pushed again, could feel the eyes of the two remaining journalists behind her boring into her. Asking themselves why they hadn't thought of that, just knocking on the door: maybe Morgan would open it in his dressing gown, give them an exclusive, make them a bacon sarnie. But that didn't happen. No answer; the sound of the bell intoning in the cavernous silence of Morgan's house made Cat feel lonely. She stepped away, tried the gate which led to the private parking area. It was locked, but there was an intercom on the gate post. She put her face to the intercom and buzzed. First there was nothing, then the line opened, although no sound came out. "It's Hetty Moon," said Cat. "Back from the dead."

There was a long pause then a rumbling. The big gate was slowly rolling open.

Cat turned, faced the car, registered the look of disbelief on Thomas's face, tried to keep a look of triumph from her own. She nodded Thomas to drive in, and he edged the car through the now fully open gate into Morgan's private parking area. Cat walked through. She stood now in a yard, lined with tidy bay trees. There was no one about. Thomas parked beside the row of three black BMW seven series, climbed out, walked over to Cat.

"How the fuck?" Thomas asked.

"Friends in low places."

To the side, French windows were closed and curtained. Ahead, an old trellis rose grew behind creepers which looked untended and dying. Cat nudged Thomas and pointed at the rose. Through its elaborate, maze-like shapes was just visible the livery of a Parcelforce Yamaha laying on its side. They looked at each other in silence, stepped towards it. As it came into view, they saw that someone had ploughed the bike straight through the window. Shards of glass and splinters of broken timber lay all about.

Cat felt the engine. "Still hot." There were keys in the ignition. She raised her eyebrows at Thomas. "We could bring in the locals?"

He hesitated, half-cautious, half-mischievous. Then said softly, "*Cachau bant*, Price. The locals can kiss my hairy Welsh arse." *Cachau bant*: fuck off.

Cat smiled her agreement, but they were both nervous. Even knowing what Cat knew, the bike wasn't meant to be here. It was a rogue factor, dangerous.

Thomas stepped cautiously through the broken window, glass crunching underfoot. Cat followed. Inside, they waited until her eyes adjusted to the curtained half-light.

The ground-floor space was larger than it appeared from outside. It was decorated as a formal eighteenth-century drawing room. A rocaille mirror hung over an imposing fireplace, and at the other end what looked like a Canaletto took pride of place. The room smelt musty, as if it had not been aired for many years. Every surface she touched was thick with dust.

They moved towards the staircase. Her heart was thrashing inside her, but she felt calm, had felt no withdrawal symptoms for several hours. She felt like a robot of justice; but whether that justice complied with the laws of the land or not remained to be seen. From above there were no sounds. They came up into another large room. Between the curtains thin bars of light fell. What looked like a pool table lay under dust cloths. The leaves of a long dining table that could have seated several dozen were stacked against the wall. All this unused opulence waiting on the whim of a dying drug lord.

Cat continued upwards, aware of Thomas beside her. On the floor above, the gaps between the three curtains gave a clearer view of things. The internal walls had been removed to create a large study. At the far end of the room, a man was sitting in a swivel chair with his back to them in front of a television. The TV's sound was off and the walls swam with its whirring light. To the right a small stairway led to the next floor. Cat listened but there were no sounds from above them.

"Morgan," Thomas whispered, his expression unreadable.

He approached the figure. Cat sidled round laterally, keeping an eye on the door they'd come through. There was something about the silence of the room and the stillness of the figure that peopled the room with ghosts.

Nia Hopkins: tortured to death.

Delyth Moses: the same.

Esyllt Tilkian: missing and now, surely, to be presumed dead.

Katie Tana: dead, also tortured. A Croat girl who ended her life dumped in an Essex landfill.

Katie Marr and Sara Armitage: both missing. Both known to have been alive for some time after their first disappearance. But now? What, really, were their chances now?

And Rhiannon Powell: found dead and fox-bitten in her Blackheath garden.

"Morgan," said Thomas again, this time louder, to the back of the man's head. He didn't move, didn't reply.

"It's not Morgan," Cat said softly.

The door was clear, the room empty, the house silent. Cat felt secure enough to step right up to the chair, knowing that this moment would teach her about herself. Slowly, deliberately, she spun the chair round.

The seated figure was naked, bound to the chair. His head was slumped down on his chest. This was the man known to the world as Griff Morgan: the man who'd been released from prison, who'd come home to die. But he'd never intended to die like this. Cat stepped back, taking in more clearly what her eyes had seen with their first glimpse. Every part of the man's body was bruised. Around the genitals she could see deep serrations and burn marks. He had been tortured, just like the girls. Same technique. Same pitiless violence.

Cat checked his pulse. Nothing. But when she touched his neck there was still a faint warmth there.

"Same MO as the girls," Thomas said, sounding composed. Cat pulled the curtains to and turned on a lamp. Thomas gestured towards the scorch marks and missing nails. The damage was almost identical to that visited on the girls. The body had the look of a baroque painting of a martyred saint.

"Same routine," Thomas said. "Tortured until his heart gave out." He sounded almost too calm, too professional. Cat wondered about her demeanour: how she looked to an outsider.

Thomas straightened, looked at Cat.

"What did you mean it's not Morgan? That's fucking Morgan, all right. Or was."

Cat opened her mouth to answer, but the answer came from elsewhere.

"Two stupid coppers. One more stupid than the other."

Cat span around. She'd been too busy with the corpse to keep her eyes and ears open. A man was walking towards them from the foot of the stairway that ran to the upper floor. He was moving quickly, wearing the Parcelforce livery, and in the visor of his bike helmet she could see her wide eyes reflected. He lunged at her but she backed away, raising herself on to the balls of her feet, her fighting stance, ready for him now.

But the helmeted man had turned his attention to Thomas. He had a firearm in his hand and pulled the trigger. Across the room there was a flashing like miniature lightning. Thomas dropped to the floor racked in agony.

She did not have time to react, to check if Thomas was alive, because now the man was coming back at her, aiming the thing at her face. It was a taser, she saw. She moved back to the window, grabbed a curtain, ripped it down and pulled it across her in one movement. The lightning pulsed towards her, was dissipated by the swish of material. Groggily, she threw the curtain to the floor, heard Thomas groaning a few feet away. In the recharge lag she ran at the man, but glimpsed the flicker of a blade.

She grasped his wrist and kicked his legs from under him. The blade spun away. He fell, legs splayed on the floor. She kicked him in the balls, bent down and pushed the lower edge of his helmet onto his windpipe. The man lurched forward. Thomas was up now and staggering over to hold him. Thomas took the taser off the man and brought it down on the man's chest in a crunching blow.

Cat roughly pulled his helmet off. It was Hywel Small, the mid-range wholesaler who'd led them to Morgan's house. She looked in his eyes. Although he was wounded and vulnerable, he was still defiant. He winked and spat in Thomas's face. Thomas punched him a couple of times until Small settled down.

Cat cuffed his hands behind his back. Thomas used his own cuffs to link the man's bound wrists to the radiator behind.

"There," he said, "this is nice, isn't it?"

Small remained expressionless. Thomas seemed to consider his options briefly, then gave his prisoner another punch and a kick for good measure. "That's for tasering me, you prick." Small just smiled back, said nothing.

"Now," said Thomas, "can someone tell me what the fuck is going on?"

Cat thumbed at Morgan's chair. "Detective Inspector Thomas, meet Diamond Evans. Diamond Evans, DI Thomas."

Small grinned his evil assent.

"Here's the way I see it," Cat continued. "At the Penarth Marina bust, Evans already knew he was ill. Maybe he knew he was dying. So he took the fall for Morgan. Neither men had previous, no prints or DNA on the system. The switch had been safe as long as no one talked. So Morgan got away and the whole world thought he was behind bars. All the time, it's been business as usual for him. And all the time, there were those mandies. A nice business line that just needed a little care and attention. Small here was charged with managing the roll-out. The marketing guy, if you like. The drug drop in that back garden was set up so that Evans could watch over it as he lay dying here. Maybe a kind of drug dealer's *homage*. A goodbye and thank-you for everything. That plan would have worked once the press melted away. It was our intervention that spoiled it, made the whole thing too dangerous. I guess our friend here," she kicked Small only somewhat gently in the shin, "came by to find out what went wrong."

Thomas caught up slowly. "Fuck," he said.

Cat nodded. And she hadn't even said the important bit. Drugs were only drugs. Murder was murder.

"Meanwhile, Morgan had a — uh — rather specialised hobby. He was crazily in love with this singer, Hetty Moon. I've seen a video of her. She's magnetic, something really special, or was. He was obsessed, but — she died. Morgan killed her. Inadvertently, no doubt. A total accident, but it was his yacht, his drugs — his responsibility. He went a bit crazy with it all. He kept trying to bring her back. Retrieve the memory, relive the experience. Make other girls play her role. That's what the hotel worker saw."

But there was still a gap in her explanation here. A hole. Why create all these fake Hettys, these substitutes, and then kill them? Torture them to death, no less? It made no sense. Cat had a hunch as to the real truth, but the pieces were shadowy and the darkness was frightening.

"Well," said Thomas, "shall we hand our killer here over to our not very enterprising London colleagues?"

He got his phone out to make a call.

"Yes," said Cat, "only he's a drug dealer, not a killer." On Thomas's questioning look, she added, "The body's cold. The motorbike was warm. Small here came to find out what was going on. He wasn't going to kill anyone. I guess he had a key to the outside gate, but found the front door locked on him. The lad showed enterprise."

Thomas made his call. His accent was always fairly strong, but he added a little juice to it, Welshing it up as much as he could, to cause maximum offence. "That's right, DI Thomas, from Tregaron in Ceredigion. Got another corpse for you. And a drugs dealer you didn't quite manage to catch. But I'm sure you'll be fine from here. Just shout for help, if you need anything."

Thomas winked at Cat as he made the call. Cat herself was on the phone to Kyle, giving her brief details, keeping her updated.

As Cat spoke, she kept her eyes out onto the yard outside. If Morgan was Evans, then where the fuck was Morgan?

She heard a sound, looked down into the yard. The gate giving access to the private parking was slowly rolling across. The nearest BMW seven series was gliding out and the gate was closing. *Fuck.*

She grabbed Small's helmet and his taser, then charged down the stairs. She punched the manual over-ride, trying to stop the gate from closing so they could chase in Thomas's car. But the gate stayed shut.

She felt a sudden, impotent rage. It looked like Morgan had just slipped them another dummy. The house had all the latest in security equipment, cameras trained on the front door and the gate. But the BMW's tinted windows would conceal any view of Morgan leaving. She still had no usable visual of her quarry. She'd been in the same building as him and still had no idea what he looked like. She crunched up her fist in frustration, until it hurt.

She ran for the yard, where Small's Yamaha still lay on the ground. She put on the helmet, wrestled the bike up onto two wheels, started it, bumped it up through the broken window and into the house. She rode across the drawing room, leaving a black track across the wooden floor. Cat made the entrance hall, paused, then opened the bike up and cracked it hard into one of the reinforced windows. The glass cracked, the wood struts crunched and split, but not enough. Cat herself was thrown half off the bike, against the wall. She repeated the manoeuvre, twice, faster each time. She forced it all the way open and bounced down through the front entrance and down the steps. She was out and onto the road. As she revved away she caught a glimpse of the two journalists still holding their drinks, eyes wide with disbelief.

There was no sign of the BMW. It had had too much head-start and, in any case, Morgan was too cautious. He knew there were intruders in the house. Perhaps he even knew they were police. The BMW would be used as a getaway, then discarded. He'd be in a taxi now, or a car registered to some clean alias.

It didn't matter. When people leave a burning house, they take the one thing — photo, ring, diary — that matters to them more than anything. When Morgan was fleeing a failed operation, he'd do the same thing.

Cat rode steadily, not fast, around the Hampstead ponds, then doubled back towards town. The traffic thinned as she ran down the hill, then she drifted with other traffic south towards Marylebone, then on towards Park Lane. She didn't accelerate hard from the lights, didn't make use of the bike's power. In London traffic, a Yamaha would always outrun a car. She didn't need to push it. She headed down towards the river and followed the embankment east. Then over Tower Bridge.

Would her hunch be proved correct? It was impossible to be sure. Perhaps, with Morgan, caution would win over obsession. He'd know that his switch with Evans had been sussed. He would have contacts at airstrips, at marinas. In hours he would be overseas, invisible again. Moving drugs, grooming girls. If that was how he chose to play it, the old story would be repeated again. And again. And she could string herself out for a hundred thousand years, chase cases like this until the sun exploded, and it wouldn't make any difference: the innocent always suffered. The devil always won.

Or maybe not.

It all depended on the next few minutes.

The riches of central London gave way to the rags of Deptford. Blackened railway bridges, halal butchers, second-hand furniture depots. And builder's yards. Ruined chapels.

Cat rode down to the nearer of the building yards and parked there, dumping the helmet. She called Kyle. Told her everything. Gave her the location. Told her about Evans and Morgan. Told her about Small. Told her where she'd left Thomas: doing his best to piss off the entire Metropolitan Police.

Kyle listened, asked questions where she had to, took notes in the background.

"You want support?" she asked.

"Yes," said Cat. "Big time. Road, air, river. The whole fucking cavalry."

"OK. You'll wait for them?"

"Maybe."

"I can make that an order."

"Sorry, ma'am, I think I'm losing signal."

Cat cut the phone, looked over at the chapel.

It was now or never.

She breathed in. The air smelt of the river. She had no headache. Her blood ran clear.

It would be now.

She walked towards the chapel, slid in through the gap in the hedge again. She moved to the main door and put her ear to it. There was nothing audible from within but in the stained-glass above she could make out a faint light.

She made her way round to the side door. The gap she had made previously was still there. She put her hand through, eased open the latch and stepped inside, lifting the door to avoid it scraping on the flagstones within. She knew the way now, walked through the dark vestry towards the nave, quietly opened the door. The light she had seen from outside was brighter now. It seemed to be coming from the far wall where the altar had once stood. The curtains that had hung around the stage on Cat's first visit to the chapel were open.

She edged towards the flickering. Projected on the painted backdrop of the stage was an image of one of the girls, super-imposed across the painting of the Mad Ludwig castle. Cat recognised her, it was footage of Delyth Moses. She loomed up and filled the wall. She wore a flowing white dress and her eyes were almost closed, as if in a trance. Her lips moved soundlessly. Cold fury moved into Cat. He was getting off on the girl even after she had been horribly killed, owning her even in her death. Cat moved closer to the stage, listening. A light shuffling sound could be heard from behind the theatrical flats, coming from the space in which Cat had seen the half-tester bed.

Cat withdrew her taser and walked on soft feet towards the noise.

A man stood there. He was opening out two suitcases on the bed. He had his back to Cat. His movements were decisive, but not anxious, not hurried.

She moved to within easy tasering distance and raised her weapon.

"Police," she said, in a quiet voice. "Raise your hands above your head and turn around slowly."

The man didn't turn straight away. He moved his head back with a brief laugh of surprise, the way someone does who receives a new and unexpected

378

piece of information. But then he raised his hands — weaponless — and turned slowly.

His face was the one she'd always known. The face she had half-expected to find.

"Just you, Cat?" said Martin Tilkian. "You shouldn't have come alone."

"I'm not alone."

Tilkian looked around the deserted church. A pigeon flapped somewhere in the roof. "You look alone to me."

"There is an electric cable on the floor four feet to your right," Cat said. "I want you to unplug it from the socket and wind it securely round your ankles." Stupid mistake, coming here to make an arrest with no cuffs. But Cat's taser was level and her aim steady.

Tilkian laughed again, shook his head, then bent to unplug the cable. He made no further move, though, just swinging the flex in his hand.

"You know you can't do this. I saved your life. We made an oath. An oath sealed in blood."

"Five seconds, Tilkian. Four. Three. Two."

He bent down, as though to comply with her instructions, but at the last moment flung the cord at her, hurling his own body towards the shelter of the big speakers behind the stage. Cat had expected the move and was undistracted by the flying flex.

She fired. The taser's darts snaked through the air, hit flesh, passed some unimaginable voltage through his system. He collapsed. Thrashed in pain, as she'd seen Thomas do shortly before. She used her opportunity. Ran forward, and smashed the butt of her weapon down, hard, on his head. He reached for her ankles but the movement was clumsy and oversignalled, weakened by the electric shock and the blows. Cat hit him again, then stepped back and stamped hard on his crossed ankles. She was wearing her motorbike boots. Somewhere, bone crunched. He curled in pain. She stamped once more. Bones would heal and she didn't want him running.

He yelped again and Cat staggered back. Tilkian wasn't out for the count by any means, but he didn't have to be. Kyle would bring a whole damn army to this place in a matter of minutes. It was enough to delay him, to enfeeble him. The man was as good as arrested already.

"Where are they?" she asked.

Tilkian — Martin Tilkian, also known as Griff Morgan — nursed his head and ankles, and didn't answer.

Cat looked back at the bed and the suitcases. He'd been packing them. And he didn't have forever to do it. Whatever he'd been intending to put in the cases lay close at hand.

Maybe very close. Cat approached the bank of speakers and put her hands to the black material that covered the first speaker's front. It took her two goes to get a purchase: her hands were shaking too much. Then Tilkian swung his body upright. He still had too much mobility for her liking. She delivered a fluid roundhouse kick to his head and dropped him. This time he was out cold enough that she could approach close to knot the electric cable round his ankles, pulling them as tight as she knew how. She could hear Rhys's voice in her head, encouraging her on. "Good going, girl. You drop the little bastard."

Tilkian groaned. He was conscious, but not struggling. He knew he was beaten.

Back to the speakers. This time she got the purchase she was looking for. In one long movement, she ripped away the black material that covered the front of the nearest speaker. The casing was packed high with shrink-wrapped banks of pills. The Mandrax. A few million quids' worth of it. The dirty lure at the end of this long and murderous chain.

Cat stared at the pills for a moment.

"Martin," she said, "please tell me . . . the girls, that you didn't . . ."

"No." He shook his head groggily. "I would never do that."

"That cottage in Tregaron and here. They were prisoners?"

"No. Never prisoners. They had freedom to go at any time. I gave them passports, identities, cash. I gave them a base, safe houses really, where they could regroup, get their heads together. When they needed more help or more money, or just a rest, they came back to me. We spent time together."

Cat thought about that a moment. It sounded good, but wasn't really. Tilkian might not be a murderer but his selfishness and obsession had still ruined these girls' lives. Turned them into a succession of Hetty Moon imitations, his one true love. Turned them into targets for those who wanted to find him. So they became fugitives and dependants. He wouldn't have told them any of that when he'd recruited them.

"Moose Hopkins, Nia's brother, wrote graffiti accusing you of murder." Cat repeated the words of the graffiti. "He was too frightened to say he'd written it, but he wanted you caught."

"I know. The Kilroy part I put there. I told Nia that it was my old tag. Nia must have told him so, when the girls went missing, he presumed I was the killer and wrote the words underneath." He gestured into the near darkness. Against one wall over some planks leaning there she could just make out several faint scratches, Kilroys, their eyes peeping back at her. Silent witnesses.

"And the accusation?"

"Look, I loved Nia. I would never hurt her. I was giving her a new passport. I told her I was turning her into somebody else."

"And Esyllt?"

"She's fine." Cat didn't let that answer go and kept her gaze boring into her one-time friend, until he gave a fuller answer. "I gave her three thousand quid and sent her to the Caribbean. After Nia and Del, I was afraid for her safety. I thought I could make her safe and use her absence as a way to get you involved. Maybe track down the people who did *that* to Nia and Del."

"And Katie Tana."

"Find the people who did all the killings."

Even under these strange circumstances, in the gloomy chapel with pigeons flapping in the roof, Cat could feel the ghost of their old friendship present.

382

Even knowing what Tilkian had done, their friendship flickered still. It mattered that he had never killed or used violence. That would have been unforgivable.

But something had shifted in the atmosphere. Tilkian felt it too. Where the fuck was the support Kyle had promised? Was the Met deliberately going slow because Thomas had pissed them off so much already? There was something bad in the air and Cat had a nasty feeling she knew what was coming.

"Martin, are there weapons here?"

He shook his head. "I've never been into that."

They stared at each other with apprehension in their eyes. Someone had, like Cat and Riley, stumbled across the Hetty Moon sound-alikes as a way to track Griff Morgan. Riley had wanted a story. Cat had wanted justice. These others wanted Morgan's drugs and were prepared to kill and torture their way to them.

At the far end of the chapel, there was a dull boom merging with the groan of metal. A second boom told them what was happening. Someone was using a silenced gun to shoot away the lock on the main door.

Tilkian looked frightened but composed. His ankles were tied and his feet were now too damaged to walk on. He nodded at Cat with a half-grin.

"You know the old tethered goat trick?"

She smiled back her assent, moved off between the theatrical flats, out of sight. There was a pile of spare timber, offcuts from the stage set. Cat chose herself a length of two by two. Not the best weapon, but all there was. Her taser had fired two shots. It had no more.

Cat palmed her phone, set it to silent. She couldn't risk calling Kyle but she could text her. "SOS", she wrote. "NOW".

She clicked send. At the end of the church, there were a couple of heavy, dulled blows and the sound of the big door opening. Tilkian glanced across at her, caught her eye. He mouthed something. First she couldn't read it, then she could.

Your turn, he was saying. To honour the oath. To save a life.

She'd do what she could.

There were footsteps coming up the aisle. More than one set. Odds that were maybe manageable, maybe not.

Must be a strange sight for the newcomers. To find Tilkian battered and bound at the foot of his mountain of drugs. A tethered goat indeed.

Cat craned cautiously round her corner. Two men in face masks. Both armed with automatic weapons. One built of muscle, the other older, fatter, but still chunky, still powerful. The sadist and the brains.

The bigger man pointed at Tilkian with his gun, asking something of the other man. Asking permission to kill, Cat guessed. Tilkian heard the same. His eyes, in a moment's giveaway, flashed towards Cat. Only for a moment, but the tell was there.

The smaller man was saying "Fuck's sake, no," but things had already moved on.

The bigger man raised his gun and shifted position. He was planning to fire first at Tilkian, shoot next at whatever it was his eyes had darted to.

Cat didn't plan her move, just made it. She burst from her position, waving her timber. One step, two, three. Walter's words were in her head: "Not rage, Catrin. Not fear." Words that made no sense until you understood that those words held the only sense there was.

There was a shot from somewhere. Fired at Cat, but missing. Her move. She swept her make-shift club down. Simultaneously, Tilkian lashed out with his bound feet. Tilkian's move was understandable, but wrong. It shifted the balance. Instead of catching the bigger man's head, Cat's blow caught the man on the angle of his shoulder and neck. The blow was hard, but the man had built his body from countless gym-hours and protein-powder.

Ox-like, he blinked off the pain and raised his gun a second time. He was too close to miss. Cat dived, looking to roll into shelter behind the speaker, but it was a desperate move and any shelter would be strictly temporary.

Where the fuck was Kyle's cavalry?

She heard the shot, felt her body smash onto the stone floor. She executed her roll badly, but somehow found herself behind the speaker.

She wasn't dead.

She looked for the wound. Patting herself down to find crimson. She found nothing. Muzzily she looked up.

The smaller man was looking down at the big one. The man he'd just shot dead. Above them, Cat could finally hear rotor blades. Out on the road there were sirens, screaming in the distance but closing fast. She could hear nothing from the river flats, but there would be armed police there too. Searchlights. Boats. Assets.

Cat dragged her way out of shelter.

She was exposed to the older man's fire but this brutal endgame was finally coming to a close. He hadn't much use for his weapon now. He held it at his side, but indolently, not poised. She pulled off the big man's mask. Probert. The bastard who'd grabbed her at Kyle's place. Fucking sadist.

The older man looked at her. Humour in his voice. "I thought I'd cancelled that lot," he said, gesturing outside at the sirens, the helicopter. You could see the copter's searchlight beaming down on the chapel now, poking through the holes in the roof, baffling the pigeons.

"I got Kyle to un-bloody-cancel, didn't I?"

The man removed his mask. Thomas. "Well," he said, nodding at Cat, at Tilkian, at the world. "Fair play to you. I was close but no cigar, eh?" To Tilkian, he said, "Nice to meet you at last. Funny the way these things work."

And then in one fluid move, he raised the gun to his head and fired. He hit the floor before his gun.

Briefly, just briefly, the chapel felt silent.

CHAPTER
TWENTY-THREE

It was mid-afternoon and the pier lay in outline against the ribbon of the sun dilating the clouds over the estuary. Cat had her old helmet on, the one with the strap under the chin. The air rushed free over her face so she had to squint. She buzzed along the front. As she worked the throttle, her shoulder ached, but not unpleasantly.

She dismounted at Penarth Marina. Already the chill of autumn was in the air, and there were fewer birds over the water. For a moment she watched them. The gulls flapped slowly back towards the shore. Further out, a large black bird swooped down towards its shadow. It glided at an even height above the glistening foam, hardly moving its wings.

All the time its shadow was there, a few feet behind, like something following under the surface of the water. Finally the bird rose and disappeared. She thought of Thomas. He had shot himself in the head but, the stupid sod, his hand had been shaking. He'd blown off the right-hand parietal part of his skull, driving bone fragments deep into his brain. He'd been in intensive care for two weeks now, in a coma for the first few days, then in a state of very low responsiveness, unable to talk, unable to eat.

He might live, he might die. If he lived, he might make a full recovery. Or he might spend the rest of his life brain-damaged and high-dependency. He deserved death for his crimes, but he had still been Cat's partner. A friend. Could you wish someone gone and yet still grieve for them? Was someone still alive if the essence of who they were had vanished? If they were dependent on an IV drip for nutrients and liquid? Cat was discovering the answers now.

What Thomas had done to the girls was unforgivable, and for what? To find the drugs and sell them for cash. She did not even pity him. He had tortured for cash. She guessed that he had probably got Probert to do the dirty work, egging him on, exploiting his sadistic tendencies. She saw him managing things, stopping Probert now and again, giving the girls a chance to talk. Not that they would have had anything to tell the two men. None of them would have known Morgan's real location.

And so in the end Probert had gone further, until their hearts stopped with shock and pain. Was that why Thomas had shot Probert in the chapel? Because he hated him for the torture, hated Probert even though he, Thomas, had colluded in it? Perhaps that bullet in Probert's head was really aimed by Thomas at himself. A sighting shot for what would follow.

Or was it that he didn't need Probert any more? That he'd decided to take the drugs for himself, alone. Or was it Cat? Was it that, when it came to the crucial moment, he found he couldn't let Probert kill her? All possible answers. Cat would never know. Perhaps Thomas didn't even know himself.

She walked down the ramp to the quays. She could see Kyle already, beckoning her to a small sail boat moored at the end. Cat approached, stepped up and onto the boat. At the back of the deck was a seating area, some wine open on a low table. Kyle wore a long fisherman's jersey, her legs bare and tan.

"Wine?"

Cat refused and Kyle passed her some water from a cooler at her feet. The bottle of wine was almost empty — drunk alone before lunch — and Kyle looked tired and slightly ashamed. Her connection with Probert, though innocent on her part, was not something that would be forgotten in a hurry, and it could always be used against her. There were rumours of an imminent inquiry. Cat felt for Kyle. As far as that was possible.

Kyle half-smiled, looked at her, seemed about to say something friendly then changed tack. "Thomas had an informant who knew Diamond Evans. That's how he heard about the switch on the night of the bust. He knew Morgan was out there with the first half of the stash. He just had to find him."

"That's where Probert came in."

"Right. He'd been mouthing off about Morgan's connection to my Tilly, about Morgan's obsession with Hetty Moon. Thomas must have heard him yammering on about it."

Cat raised her eyebrows. The post-bust clean-up was running full steam, but what the courts would be told wasn't always the whole truth. A portion of that truth sat here in the boat with Kyle.

"My foster-daughter, Tilly. She was his first avatar — his first Hetty Moon. The girl in the hotel-room story. At any rate, that's what he wanted her to be. Pressured her. Used drugs." Kyle's face puckered with emotion. There was grief present in the mixture. Also anger. Also something unreadable beyond both things. "He didn't get what he wanted. But he'd messed with her head. She was fragile anyway and the drugs . . . Don't ever tell me that Morgan didn't kill. He killed all right. And not just Tilly. Those others. He was responsible for them, too."

Cat nodded. She couldn't disagree.

"And that was it. Thomas and Probert. Both knew a piece of the truth, wanted to get rich. They teamed up."

"The brains and the brawn," Cat commented. "I thought Thomas moved out to Tregaron because of burn-out. But it wasn't that. It was the opposite. Your foster-daugher, Tilly, was in Tregaron. Odds were then that Morgan had some link with the place too. It was just too remote for him to have found her otherwise."

"But Tregaron itself didn't give them their breakthrough. They must have found the Croat girl, Tana, online covering Moon's act. When they saw she had form for mandies they knew they were getting close. They found Tana, tortured her, but she could tell them nothing. Morgan had not disclosed his location nor his identity to her."

Cat put down her water.

"But Morgan was an obsessive with a conscience. When Tana got pulled, he gave the rest of his girls access to safe houses. The cottage by the mine for the Tregaron girls, the chapel in London for the others. Passports, identities, cash, just like he said. The girls' presence online was shut down completely. So Thomas and Probert were back where they started. The trail went dead."

Kyle nodded in recognition.

"Then after a year," Cat continued, "the girls got slack. Stupid really. They began posting their reels again in the hope of attracting talent scouts. I imagine Morgan never knew about that; he wouldn't have been so stupid. Thomas and Probert picked up their performances. Used their IP addresses to track them to Tregaron. Then did exactly what you did. No warrant, just a quiet word with the relevant ISP. Got an address. The safe house at the mine. I imagine they arrived when only Delyth Moses was there. Nia Hopkins must have been terrified when she found her friend gone, so she began using the mine itself to hide in. A place she knew, because it had been a teen drinking hole."

Cat didn't say it, because it was too horrible to think about, but she knew she had led Thomas to Rhiannon. She'd asked him for the IP address, given him the identity of his next victim. Had Probert been in the area anyway, ready to make the kill? Quite possible: if they were already investigating Tana's Deptford address, Probert would likely have been in the area. Thomas would have told him to move fast, not to

391

spend time enjoying himself, to get out quick before Cat arrived.

Cat's intervention — intended to save a life — had ended up taking one. Something she'd just have to live with. And that was OK. Her heart was already held together by scars.

"How do you feel about it?" asked Kyle. "About Tilkian, I mean. He'd been a friend."

Cat shrugged. She didn't know. That he had lied to her was nothing: everybody lied all the time, that's how the world managed to work. It was what he had done to the girls that preyed on her mind. Although he had in the end tried to protect them he had sucked them into his dark sex charades, used them to satiate his own haunted needs, projected the face and voice of a dead lover onto them, with no thought for who they were themselves.

Kyle looked at Cat, a rare softness in her eyes. She saw the battle within Cat. There were to be no games today, no rank pulled. "You OK Cat? Off the tranks?"

"The tranks are not an issue. It's Martin — Morgan — he's my wound."

"Seems to me you got lucky, Cat."

"Why lucky?"

"Because you've got it both ways. You saved his life. And you put him in jail where he belongs. Best of both worlds."

Well, yes, there was that way of looking at it. The CPS were preparing their case against Tilkian-Morgan now. They'd be pressing for the longest possible sentence. Ask for it, and almost certainly get it.

392

Cat got out her tobacco, loaded a roll-up with canna, blew the smoke out to sea.

"And Thomas. You knew not to trust him. But how? You haven't told me that."

"Small stuff. Whispers not screams. That's why I called you, not him, that evening."

There had been other things, she had realised, about Thomas. He wasn't a by-the-book copper. He'd been happy to beat a defenceless Riley, but had refused to hand over an IP address, which would have been a far smaller infraction of the rules by which policemen lived. The clincher had been his effort to get Cat chucked off the case by leaking stuff to Della Davies. He'd known she'd be suspected, must have assumed she'd be suspended, pending an inquiry. That had been a low move, really low, and after that, after Rhiannon, Cat had known her life was no longer safe. So she'd dropped out of sight. Out of sight even of a police pursuer with access to every electronic database in existence. She'd trusted Kyle and Kyle alone — and she hadn't been let down.

Kyle had countermanded Thomas when he told the Met to put the cavalry on hold — but more than that, Kyle had believed in her, despite appearances.

The sun was still bright but the temperature cooling. Cat glanced towards the water. The large black bird swung back across the bay.

"Are we going to take the boat out?" said Cat, changing the mood.

"Yes, but . . ."

"But?"

"We've been waiting for someone. Here she comes."

Kyle gestured along the quay. A pony-tailed girl, blue-and-white striped boat top, was walking towards them, searching. She broke into a smile when she saw Kyle. The girl was very tanned.

Kyle waved and Esyllt broke into a jog. She got level with the boat and clambered in with that late-teenage combination of ridiculous grace and clumsy awkwardness.

"Hi." To Kyle first, then to Cat: "Hi, I'm Esyllt? Tilkian?" She also had that rising teenage inflection.

"Hi, Esyllt. I'm Catrin."

"I know." Cat saw the girl eye her warily, resentment maybe mixing with gratitude.

Cat was aware of Kyle casting off the boat, pushing the bows out towards the open water. Kyle was enjoying Cat's confusion; she knew that somehow.

"When Dad sent me to the Caribbean, he told me who he was. I hadn't known before that."

Cat nodded. That was probably true, but even if it wasn't, it wasn't police practice to start whacking family members with conspiracy charges.

"He said there were three possible outcomes to . . . to everything. One, he got killed. Two, he got jailed. Three, he made his escape and would be on the run for the rest of his life." A tear, glassy and brief, slid down her cheek. She continued, her voice less steady. "Don't expect me to thank you for what you did, but . . ." Still tears came. She said nothing more. Esyllt lowered her eyes, and Cat thought she saw a faint smile of something like acceptance there.

Cat rubbed her shoulder, and glanced again towards the water. The large bird still glided low. No doubt it was looking for food near the surface. A couple of feet behind, its shadow followed.

"Come on, Cat, untie that sail," Kyle said.

Cat rose and pulled the sail as Kyle steered the boat out onto the sea.